P9-CCK-002

THE BENEFACTOR

THE BENEFACTOR

A Jack Taggart Mystery

Don Easton

DUNDURN
TORONTO

Copyright © Don Easton, 2014

All rights reserved. No part of this publication may be reproduced, stored in a retrieval system, or transmitted in any form or by any means, electronic, mechanical, photocopying, recording, or otherwise (except for brief passages for purposes of review) without the prior permission of Dundurn Press. Permission to photocopy should be requested from Access Copyright.

All characters in this work are fictitious. Any resemblance to real persons, living or dead, is purely coincidental.

Editor: Shannon Whibbs
Design: Jesse Hooper
Printer: Webcom

Library and Archives Canada Cataloguing in Publication

Easton, Don, author
    The benefactor / Don Easton.

(A Jack Taggart mystery)
Issued in print and electronic formats.
ISBN 978-1-4597-1058-0 (pbk.).--ISBN 978-1-4597-1059-7 (pdf).--ISBN 978-1-4597-1060-3 (epub)

    I. Title. II. Series.

PS8609.A78B46 2013   C813'.6   C2013-905471-5
                                          C2013-905472-3

1   2   3   4   5   18   17   16   15   14

We acknowledge the support of the Canada Council for the Arts and the Ontario Arts Council for our publishing program. We also acknowledge the financial support of the Government of Canada through the Canada Book Fund and Livres Canada Books, and the Government of Ontario through the Ontario Book Publishing Tax Credit and the Ontario Media Development Corporation.

Care has been taken to trace the ownership of copyright material used in this book. The author and the publisher welcome any information enabling them to rectify any references or credits in subsequent editions.

J. Kirk Howard, President

The publisher is not responsible for websites or their content unless they are owned by the publisher.

Printed and bound in Canada.

VISIT US AT

Dundurn.com | @dundurnpress | Facebook.com/dundurnpress | Pinterest.com/dundurnpress

Dundurn	Gazelle Book Services Limited	Dundurn
3 Church Street, Suite 500	White Cross Mills	2250 Military Road
Toronto, Ontario, Canada	High Town, Lancaster, England	Tonawanda, NY
M5E 1M2	L41 4XS	U.S.A. 14150

Dedicated to Mike, Akiyo, Steve, Kelly, and Ava

Chapter One

"Have you had sex yet with Mr. and Mrs. Rolstad? Or either one, for that matter?"

Mia Parker fidgeted with her purse strap on the table beside her and cast her eyes around the hotel room. They were in Richmond, a large city that bordered Vancouver, and the room was a dayroom rented at the last moment to protect them against any electronic surveillance.

Normally their meetings were brief and took place in a parkade or city park, but today was different. The use of the hotel room made her feel that this would be more of an interrogation than a quick exchange of information.

She was not surprised that this was the first question her secret contact — or case officer as he was known in the trade — asked. She had correctly guessed that the meeting was to analyze her lack of success.

She felt the subtle brush of his knee against her knee, prodding her for a response. Mr. Frank, who was an expert at interrogation, sat in a chair drawn up facing her chair. His eyes locked on hers and she consciously steeled herself not to be intimidated by his hard, cold stare.

She knew him as Mr. Frank, but suspected that was not his real name. He was a head taller than her and had an athletic build and a pockmarked face. She guessed he was twenty years older than her, putting his age at forty-eight. Today he wore a pale green suit with a tie that had yellow daffodils imprinted upon it. *Suitable for the first day of spring*, she thought, before realizing her brain was deliberately avoiding the subject matter.

"Your hesitancy to answer tells me you have not," said Mr. Frank, flatly. "Therefore the question remains, why not?"

Mia smiled apologetically. "The right opportunity has not presented itself."

"The right opportunity?" scoffed Mr. Frank. "You've lived in their basement suite for eight months. I would have thought you would have had plenty of opportunity?"

"I need to correlate opportunity with trust. There are other issues. I'm not certain if Mrs. Rolstad could be cajoled into such a relationship."

"You have told me that she is extremely insecure and prone to be a follower, rather than a thinker. I'm guessing you could convince her to experiment in that department."

"I admit she has confided in me that she is perplexed at her husband's lack of desire with her, but that does not mean she is ready to enter into the type of relationship you mention."

"Perhaps her husband is bored with her. He, at least, should be easy to seduce."

"There is no indication that Mr. Rolstad is not loyal to his wife. For an intimate relationship to develop as the benefactor desires, it may take longer than —"

"Please, do not insult my intelligence, or that of the benefactor," said Mr. Frank. "Today, Mr. Rolstad has his fortieth birthday. His wife is eight years younger. They are both attractive people, yet we know from their medical records that they have been having sexual problems for a year. His doctor prescribed Viagra, but a lack of renewed prescriptions indicates that he is not taking it. Going by what his wife has told you, there is something wrong."

"There has to be desire to start with, otherwise Viagra will not work," noted Mia.

"Their therapist believed it was simply stress-related," persisted Mr. Frank.

"He does appear to be under a great deal of stress," Mia agreed. "With his position in Maple Leaf Consulting, he travels constantly back and forth to their office in Ottawa. Combined with his lack of performance in the bedroom with his wife ... it serves to add to his stress, creating a downward spiral."

"Yes, yes, but we both know that sex is also a release for stress." He leaned back and looked down at the open-toed heels that Mia was wearing, before letting his eyes drift up her slim white slacks to her waist. Mia nervously crossed her legs and his eyes lingered over the ample cleavage of her breasts that protruded from her red satin blouse before making eye contact again. He saw that she blushed. "You are an extraordinarily beautiful woman who has poise and charm. Are you telling me that Mr. Rolstad has not cast his eyes upon you with desire?"

Mia paused. She knew she was beautiful. Her father was of English heritage. She was only three years old when he died in a hit-and-run car accident while crossing the street, but her mother had several pictures of him. She knew he was tall, good-looking, and had red hair. She felt anger with the knowledge of what her mother had told her about the accident. The police knew who did it, but never laid a charge due to political influence.

Mia's mother was of Chinese heritage and Mia, who was their only child, had physical qualities from both parents. She was slightly taller than most women and had long black hair that glistened with crimson highlights in the sunlight. Her skin was slightly darker than most Caucasians and a hint of Asian qualities around her eyes gave her an exotic appearance. She was well aware that men stared longingly after her. Mr. Rolstad was no exception.

"I am waiting," prodded Mr. Frank.

"Yes, on a biological level, he desires me," admitted Mia. "However, a quick dalliance may well backfire. It could cause guilt, leading him to reject me from his circle and therefore put our primary objective at risk.

I need to build trust and not come across like some call girl in the night."

Mr. Frank nodded thoughtfully. "They quit going to their therapist two months after you moved in. I take it they appreciate that you received your master's in psychology before switching over to political science?"

"Yes and no." Mia frowned. "Mrs. Rolstad has opened up to me completely, but Mr. Rolstad has been hesitant to confide in me, which is not unusual. To achieve our aim, I need to have his complete confidence as well."

"I would think his concern about his marriage would grow with every passing day. Mrs. Rolstad is younger ... a trophy wife ... he must worry that she will find a lover. She, too, must feel abandoned and frustrated."

"She does. She still works three days a week for her husband's office in Vancouver and the occasional weekend when he is away." Mia's face brightened and she added, "Which reminds me, last Saturday I went to the office with her for an hour before we went out for lunch."

"Did you have time to install the latest software?"

"Yes, I told her I wanted to go online to check my test results from university. It only took a minute."

"Good."

"She has also been spending more time volunteering with different charity organizations."

"A sign that she is unhappy?"

"She isn't happy, but the charity work could simply be a way to bring in new business."

"I thought their frequent house parties were for that."

"That, too, but I think the real reason she is unhappy is because she wants to have children ... something he has now decided he does not want."

Mr. Frank shrugged indifferently. "How many people will be attending the party tonight?"

"Mrs. Rolstad indicated about thirty, but she was not forthcoming with the names."

"You reported that at Christmas the Rolstads indulged in cocaine for the first time."

"Yes, they smoke pot a couple times a month, but cocaine was something new for them. I think using cocaine is a manifestation of the stress they are under."

"Interesting they would do that, when the psychological profile we have indicates they consider themselves intellectuals. He, too, has a degree in psychology, albeit not a master's."

"I think it is part of trying to bring back their youth and regain their vitality. Despite being self-centred, they are both insecure and work hard to maintain an image of being hip, modern, and fun."

Mr. Frank opened an attaché case and handed Mia a small paper bag. "Take what is inside the bag and put it in your purse," he ordered.

Mia pulled a plastic baggie out and saw that it contained numerous small folds of paper. "Cocaine?" she asked.

Mr. Frank nodded. "Twenty-eight grams."

Mia saw that there was a second baggie and glanced at Mr. Frank.

"Take it as well," he ordered.

"That's a lot for me to be carrying!" exclaimed Mia. "Don't you think it is a mistake to —"

"I don't make mistakes," said Mr. Frank, arrogantly.

"But —"

"Relax. Do you think the benefactor would send a fool to look after you?"

"No, of course not. It's just —"

"It's not like we can see each other often. Besides, who knows who else will attend the party. There may be someone worthy of attention."

"What's in it?" asked Mia, reaching for the next baggie.

"Ecstasy," said Mr. Frank.

"They have never used that before," said Mia.

"Maybe they should. For some, I hear it promotes sexual stimulation while removing inhibition."

"I don't know if they will take it, but I'll see," said Mia, putting the drugs in her purse.

"Then don't ask them," said Mr. Frank firmly. "See that they get it. Tonight will be the ideal time. When the guests leave, give Mr. Rolstad the birthday present you know he longs for."

"I still don't feel it is necessary," said Mia. "We have the computers to —"

Mr. Frank gave a loud clap of his hands in front of Mia's face and she jerked back. "We have been over this before!"

Mia swallowed, then nodded quietly.

The anger disappeared from Mr. Frank's face and he patted her knee. "You know they will confide in you more about their client's behaviour if they indulge in similar behaviour with you. Things that are not written in any of their internal reports. Do not tell me it is not a wise move. You may have your master's in psychology, but are you going to sit there and tell me you are more knowledgeable than the benefactor?"

"No, of course not," replied Mia, shaking her head. "But there is the trust issue. Like I said, it could cause guilt and —"

She felt both his knees touch hers as he leaned in close to her face. "Is building trust the real reason for the delay, or could it be something else?" he asked.

"Such as?" questioned Mia, forcing herself to remain erect and not cower back.

"Your own embarrassment of having to play such a role."

Mia stared back, then sighed and looked away. "Yes, I admit that to perform such a role causes me anguish. I know sex or love are important tools, but I've never used either before for such a purpose."

"You have been trained on ways to facilitate such action."

"Being told what I should do and actually doing it are two different things."

Mr. Frank nodded, appearing sympathetic. "When the moment comes, put your mind elsewhere. Close your eyes and pretend you are with your boyfriend."

"I do not have a boyfriend." Mia said with a shrug.

"Oh? What about Pat Harris? The benefactor tells me you've been seeing him regularly."

"Pat Harris! Are you kidding me? He's only a friend I'm helping tutor." Mia stared at Mr. Frank and tried not to let sarcasm enter her voice. "Perhaps you should let the benefactor know he is gay."

"I see."

She felt bitter when she realized the benefactor knew that she had been seeing someone. *Am I being watched at university? They wouldn't waste an asset for that. It could even risk exposing me.* Then it struck her. *I've been contacting Harris with my laptop …*

Mr. Frank interrupted her thoughts. "The point is, you've had boyfriends that you were intimate with. In your mind, pick one of them."

Mia folded her arms across her chest and stared at the bright-red nail polish on her toes.

Mr. Frank shook his head. "You need to learn to relax. I know it is difficult for you." He glanced at his watch and said, "There is plenty of time before the party starts. Sit for a moment."

Mia waited as Mr. Frank went to the washroom. She heard the sound of ice in the sink, and when he returned he had a glass of wine in each hand.

"It's early yet," protested Mia. "I have to be alert for tonight."

"Drink it," ordered Mr. Frank. "One glass will help you relax. As nervous as you appear, they would suspect something is wrong."

Mia nodded and accepted the glass with both hands. She took a deep breath and slowly exhaled. Up until today her role for the benefactor had seemed exciting and glamorous. It was like being in a movie.

What she was being told to do now was different. *Far from glamorous ... it is deceitful and dirty ... but apparently necessary ...*

Mr. Frank smiled as he raised his glass in a toast. *Time to see what effect ecstasy has on you ...*

Chapter Two

Nancy Brighton sat in her overstuffed leather chair looking out the front window of her house while petting her dog on her lap. She paused to massage an ache in her leg that was the result of recent surgery for a knee replacement. Except for her knee, she felt spry and in good shape. Or as good of shape as could be expected for someone who was seventy-five years old.

"Toby! Hush!" ordered Nancy, as her terrier let out a few yips when her phone rang. She leaned over to the end table. The call display told her it was Betty.

"Hey, little sister, where are you?" asked Nancy, as she cradled the phone to her face with her shoulder while adjusting Toby on her lap.

"No room on your street, so I'm parking in the grocery store lot. Be at your place in five minutes. Are you sure you don't need anything? I always feel guilty using their lot if I don't buy something."

"How about two cans of tonic and a lime? I'll pour you a stiff one when you arrive."

"Make me a stiff one? Don't get me started."

Nancy grinned as she hung up. Minutes later, she saw Betty walking up the sidewalk carrying a plastic bag. She eyed Toby and said, "Toby, we have company. Front door, boy! Front door!"

Toby immediately started barking, then leaped from her lap and ran to the front door. Nancy glanced at her cane, then decided against it and hobbled to the front door and opened it. Toby immediately ran out to greet Betty, who had turned up the stone pathway that cut across the front lawn to her house. The pathway was bordered on both sides by rhododendrons and Toby ran circles around one of them as he enjoyed his freedom.

"Toby! Come back here!" demanded Nancy.

After leaving the rhododendrons and doing a couple more circles around Betty, Toby obediently obeyed.

"Hey there, sis, good to see you," said Nancy.

"You, too," replied Betty, giving her sister a hug, before glancing back at the stone path. "More blooms are out on your rhodos. They look beautiful."

"Yes," replied Nancy, wistfully. "Wish Burt were still here to see them."

"Do you ever think of selling? Being hemmed in by all these apartment buildings, not to mention the traffic and having to look after the place by yourself … it must be a lot of work. I bet you could get a really good price."

"Realtors are always knocking on my door, but I'm not ready yet."

Betty stooped to pat Toby as she continued to talk. "How's the new knee working out? Not using your cane, I see."

"I keep it close, but I'm getting better. You won't have to babysit me much longer. I know what the traffic is like in Vancouver this time of day. I should be paying you for gas."

"Forget it. Hell, coming into Richmond is nothing." She stood and glanced at Nancy's leg. "Are you still in pain?"

"Not bad. I've cut back on the pills. Probably should have had both knees done. The worst part is that it makes me feel old."

"You'll be seventy-six next month."

"You're only a year behind me, so don't rub it in. Besides, you're only as old as you feel."

"I thought it was you only feel as old as *who* you feel."

"Betty Donahue! What would mom say if she were alive to hear you talk like that?"

"Probably laugh," replied Betty.

Nancy smiled. "Bet you're right. Come on in. There's some gin in the cupboard to the left of the fridge."

"I know where it is. You sit. I'll make them. Should I walk Toby first? After a few snorts I may not be able to."

"No, do it later. Let's visit first."

"Later? Hell, by then I might be blind drunk and stumbling around looking for a taxi."

"Perfect. It would be a good opportunity to see if Toby will make a good seeing-eye dog before I do get old."

* * *

Mia went to use the washroom and Mr. Frank leaned forward in the chair and took the opportunity to refill her wine, but when she came back she reached for her purse to leave.

Mr. Frank grabbed her arm. "Where are you going? We're not done."

"Aren't we?" she replied, pulling back. "You have more questions ... or instructions?"

"I need to get you to relax. You're still too nervous."

"I'm fine ... actually that is not entirely true," she added glancing at the wine bottle. "I feel strange ... sort of tingly." She turned back to Mr. Frank and said confidently, "Don't worry, I will do what is expected."

"Strange? Tingly?" replied Mr. Frank. "Your nervousness is manifesting itself." He stood up and held her glass of wine towards her. "You're far too uptight. Drink this before you go."

"No, I'll be okay."

"I can see that you're not. We need to roleplay. Close your eyes and pretend that I am Mr. Rolstad. I want your response to appear natural," he said, putting his other hand around her waist and pulling her toward him.

"That will not be necessary," replied Mia, trying to pull away.

Mr. Frank held her tighter. "Have some more wine," he urged.

"No! I've had enough!"

"I need to know how you will react," he replied, squeezing her tight to his body. She tried to push him away but he used his weight to topple her onto the bed. The wine he held spilled onto her blouse as he landed on top of her.

"Get off me!" she demanded.

He intentionally brushed his chest across her breasts as he placed the wineglass on the bedside table.

"Relax," he ordered, before kissing her on the nape of her neck while trying to arouse her by slowly grinding his pelvis against hers. "I need to see how you will perform," he whispered, moving his lips to the top of her breasts.

"I'll perform for the benefactor, not you!" shouted Mia. "Let me go or I will contact the benefactor personally and explain how your actions led me to quit."

Mr. Frank looked at her sharply and pulled away. "Direct contact is forbidden. As far as you are concerned, I am the benefactor. This is your destiny."

"My destiny does not include having sex with you. That I know. Get off me," she hissed.

He reluctantly got up and watched silently as Mia scrambled to her feet and grabbed her purse. Seconds later, she slammed the door shut.

He cursed himself after she left. Mia was one of the most valuable assets they had. For that reason, she was only one of two that he was assigned to handle. He had let his own lust interfere. *Giving her wine spiked with drugs ... the benefactor would never tolerate such action ...*

Chapter Three

Nancy said goodbye to her sister and returned to her chair. Toby expectantly looked up at her and waited until she gave a welcoming pat on her knee before leaping up to lay on her lap.

She smiled, reflecting upon the visit with her sister before nodding off to sleep.

Mia got into her white Lexus and slammed the door shut. After pulling out of the hotel parking lot, she reflected upon how strange she felt for only having had one glass of wine. *The ecstasy ... did he? He wouldn't dare.*

She thought about the stress she was under as she drove. *Is it my nerves reacting over what I must do tonight? The thought of it makes me sick ... yet I must for the common good.* She glanced at her purse containing the two bags of drugs and her thoughts returned to Mr. Frank. *Whatever the reason I feel strange, never again will I accept anything to eat or drink from him. Mom would be so angry if she knew I drank from a bottle that I had not seen opened and poured. She taught me better.*

She examined her face in the rear-view mirror and saw that her mascara was smudged under her eyes and used her fingertips to wipe it. A lurching jolt of her car and the sound of screeching metal brought her hands back to the wheel. She had sideswiped an oncoming car and her hands spun the wheel hard to the right. It resulted in an overcorrection and the right corner of her Lexus hit a parked car and came to an immediate stop.

Nancy immediately sat upright, startled from her sleep by the sound of a car accident in front of her house. The commotion caused Toby to bark excitedly.

"Toby! Hush!" she commanded, reaching for the phone while peering out her window. She hesitated when she saw a woman in a red blouse get out of a white car and run back to a silver car. Seconds later, the woman driver in the silver car also got out and was using her cellphone.

"Looks like they don't need our help, Toby," said Nancy.

Mia scrambled from her car and ran over to the woman driving the silver Nissan. "Are you okay? Are you injured?" she asked.

"I, I think I'm okay," she replied. "You drove right into me."

"I'm sorry. A bee flew into my face and —"

"Looked to me like you were putting on make-up," snapped the woman.

"I'm going to check my car," replied Mia, deciding not to engage the woman. "Then we can exchange driver's licences and car registration. Don't worry, insurance will cover the damages. The important thing is that nobody was hurt."

Mia returned to the Lexus to get her documentation. She knew she would have to call a tow truck as well. The sound of the woman talking on her phone caught her attention.

"Yes, it's an emergency! I was driven into by a woman who is drunk. She has booze slopped down the front of her ... no there are no injuries, but ... thank you. Please hurry. I'm in Richmond at —"

Shit! Breathalyzer? Arrest? Am I stoned? Mia didn't wait to hear the rest. She grabbed her purse from her car and retrieved her own phone. As she pretended to make a call, she walked over to the sidewalk, conscious that the other driver was watching her.

Mia dropped her purse on the ground and turned her back to the woman as she bent over to pick it up. As she did, she quickly grabbed the drugs from her purse and stashed them under a flowering rhododendron.

Two police officers from the Royal Canadian Mounted Police arrived in a patrol car within a matter of minutes. Mia was subsequently given a roadside breathalyzer test. The machine paused on *pass* ... then flickered into the *warning* zone.

The policewoman hesitated. "You smell strongly of alcohol," she said. "Your motor skills and physical appearance are also indicative of drug use. Do you mind if we search your car and belongings?"

Mia sighed. "I had one glass of wine earlier, but the man I was with wanted me to have more and poured another one. I refused and he tried to kiss me. I pushed him away and he ended up dumping wine down the front of my blouse," she said, indicating her blouse. "If I'm acting strange it's because I'm still really angry." She looked at her car and added, "Then to have this happen ... well, I feel stunned."

The officer stared at her a moment. "Okay, relax. I know the type," she said, rolling her eyes for emphasis. "Still, you're lucky that no one was hurt. I'm going to write you up for driving without due care and attention."

"I understand," replied Mia. "Will it take long?"

"Officers!"

Mia saw an older woman standing on the front porch of the house with the rhododendrons. A dog was at her feet. "Can I talk to you?" she called.

Mia swallowed and felt the dread as the other police officer went to speak to the woman. Seconds later, the woman pointed to the rhododendron at the front of her house.

Oh, fuck ...

Chapter Four

For the second time in two days, Mia met with Mr. Frank. This time the meeting was brief and they met in a stairwell of an underground parking garage. Mr. Frank was too cautious to ever speak inside a vehicle or any other place he thought could be subject to electronic surveillance.

"The wine you spilled on my blouse was the reason the police came," said Mia with a scowl on her face. "It's your fault! The police also asked if I had taken drugs."

"Keep your voice down," cautioned Mr. Frank, nervously peering up the stairwell. "There is nothing to worry about. The matter will be looked after." He tried to soothe her by patting her shoulder. She pulled away in anger. Perhaps his gesture would have been more convincing if the tone of his voice had not betrayed his nervousness. He knew he was to blame and feared the fatal consequence it could have for him.

"My first court appearance is next Friday," continued Mia. "That is only a week away. They are charging me with possession. I was told they had even considered charging me with possession for the purpose of trafficking."

"That is one good thing," Mr. Frank remarked.

"Good thing?" She seethed. "If I end up with a criminal record …"

"I would never allow that to happen. It will be dealt with. Everything will be okay."

"How?"

"The police are corrupt. You know that. A payoff will have to be made to the station commander, but that is all. I will look after it."

"So I don't need to show up next week?" asked Mia.

"These things take time," he replied. "Show up and plead not guilty. The matter will be resolved long before any trial takes place. The important thing is that nobody finds out."

"The Rolstads only know that I skipped their party because I was in an accident and was too upset. So don't give me a bad time for not going to the party when I returned —"

"No, I understand. Did you tell your mother what happened?"

Mia sighed. "No. I was too embarrassed to tell her."

"Embarrassed? Because you had an accident?"

Mia studied his face closely as she responded. "No, I was embarrassed that I accepted a drink from you when I didn't watch it being poured. Mom taught me better than that."

"What are you saying?" asked Mr. Frank angrily.

"That I felt too strange for only having one glass of wine," she retorted, suspiciously.

"Do not blame others for your own mistakes," replied Mr. Frank. He shook his head in admonishment. "It was your nerves. I saw that at the time, which was why I wanted you to stay and help prepare you for your assignment."

"Bullshit! I know what you wanted to do with me," snapped Mia. "And don't deny it!"

Mr. Frank shrugged. "I'm not denying it. I'm human. You dressed provocatively ... sending out mixed signals. I thought you wanted me to come on to you."

Mia frowned. "I was dressed for the Rolstads, not for ... well, either way, let's put it behind us. I don't want my mom to know because I don't want her to worry."

"And there is no reason for you to worry, either. Do not give the matter another thought."

Mr. Frank stared after her when she walked back up the stairwell. He knew he had a problem. He was not acquainted with any corrupt police officers. Action would have to be taken, but he could not jeopardize his own position. It was time to ask for a favour.

It was two o'clock Wednesday afternoon the following week when RCMP Corporal Connie Crane of the Integrated Homicide Investigation Team arrived at the scene. She flashed her identification at a uniformed officer to allow her access through the security perimeter tape and walked up the street.

She was the second member of I-HIT to arrive. The first member, Constable Stan Boyle, was new to the team and had asked for Connie's assistance. She saw him talking to another uniformed officer farther down the street. Boyle was a big man whose gut hung over his belt and he forever had bits of sleep in the corners of his eyes. Connie didn't care about his appearance, providing he was capable of doing his job — something she had yet to determine.

Boyle spotted Connie and broke off his conversation and ambled toward her. As he approached, she glanced at the yellow emergency blanket up ahead on the sidewalk. The body — or bodies, as she soon discovered — were still sprawled on the concrete.

Boyle muttered to himself and shook his head as he looked at Connie, somehow expecting her to know what was troubling him.

"What's up?" asked Connie. "I thought it was a simple hit and run?"

"It is," replied Boyle, "but uniform is trying to say otherwise. The guy is being really obstinate. If I hadn't called you, he said he would."

"Who have you been talking to?"

"Some jerk. A Corporal Dave Rankin. Come on, I'll introduce you."

Connie was introduced to Rankin. He was a uniformed policeman assigned to traffic and was the first on the scene when the 911 call came in.

After the initial greeting, Connie asked, "What makes you think this isn't anything more than a hit and run?"

Rankin shook his head. "Because it's not." He pointed down the block. "The broken remains of a cheap bottle of wine are farther down the sidewalk where the car first jumped the curb at the entrance to that apartment building. It then travelled this way at a high rate of speed down the sidewalk, hit the victim, then veered back onto the road at the next apartment entrance."

"Must have been going fast for the victim not to get out of the way," noted Connie.

"The car came from behind her, so she wouldn't have had much time to react ... but it was going fast. She was also walking a dog. I think she panicked and got the leash tangled in her legs and fell before the car hit her. Considering the type of vehicle involved, if she had been standing, she would have gone over the car or into the windshield. She didn't. She was dragged under the car for quite a ways. Her and the dog."

"Witnesses?"

"One. The offending car was a blue Honda Accord. The witness was two blocks farther down the street, driving in the same direction when the Honda passed him at a high rate of speed. He caught a glimpse of two people in the car, both wearing baseball caps and he thinks dark sunglasses. He also thought they were Asian because of their black hair, but he wouldn't swear to it. He never got a plate."

"So what makes you think it wasn't some punks who were out drinking and lost control?"

"Because the driver didn't lose control. Anyone else accidentally hitting a curb and bouncing onto a sidewalk would have tried to veer back. There aren't any signs of that."

"Maybe going too fast," offered Connie. "Once committed, the next available escape route past all these parked cars was the next apartment entrance."

"There is also no sign of braking and they would have had a clear view of the victim prior to hitting her. I don't think they were drunk. We were supposed to think that. Bet there aren't any prints on the broken bottle."

Connie studied the route the car had taken. None of the vehicles parked along the curb appeared to have been hit. There were a few broken branches from a hedge, but other than that, the car had managed to drive down a narrow pathway.

"That's the other thing," said Rankin, after Connie looked at the scene. "To take that route and not hit anything significant isn't the sign of a drunk. It took some skilful driving."

"Or lucky," suggested Boyle.

Rankin shook his head. "As I told you before, I've been doing this work for twenty years. I've been to hundreds of fatalities and thousands of accidents. Believe me, this was no accident."

"Who's the victim?" asked Connie.

"A seventy-four-year-old woman who was walking her sister's dog. The dog was killed too."

"You run the vic's name?"

"Yes. It's Betty Donahue." Rankin frowned. He knew what he had to say didn't fit his theory. "There's nothing on her. Not even a parking ticket.

She lives in West Van and is a retired schoolteacher. So is her husband."

"What's the sister like?" asked Connie.

"Nancy Brighton. She was one of the first ones on the scene. She's still bawling her eyes out. I got someone to take her back home and sit with her." He pointed and said, "She lives in the house halfway down the block between the two apartment buildings. The one with all the flowers."

"Anything on her?" asked Connie.

"Nope. Also retired. Used to be a Crown prosecutor."

"No kidding?"

"Yeah, but it was long before our time. I feel sorry for her. Her husband passed away two years ago from cancer. There are only two entries on the system for her address. One four years ago from her husband complaining of a noisy party from one of the apartments. The other was from Nancy last week. She spotted some woman stashing dope under one of the bushes in her front yard."

"How much dope?" asked Connie, with obvious interest. "Maybe someone got the wrong person?"

"That's just it. The woman was only charged with possession, so it couldn't have been much. She had a non-injury MVA and the other driver called the police. She then panicked and tried to hide the dope before the members got there, but Nancy spotted her doing it and tipped them off when they arrived."

"Straight possession. Hardly worth killing someone over," noted Boyle.

"Who was charged with the drugs?" prodded Connie. "Any gang connections?"

"No gang connections noted on the system. It was a university student by the name of Mia Parker. She also doesn't have any record ... or won't unless she's convicted."

Connie looked at the long streak of blood, skin, and hair on the sidewalk from where the bodies of the woman and the dog were dragged under the car. She gave a nod of her head where the trail ended at the emergency blanket. "You're positive it was intentional?"

"Yup, I'm positive."

"Then how would they have known when to drive down the street at the precise time to run over her?" mused Connie. "They were two blocks away when they passed the witness."

"I don't know," replied Rankin. "Maybe they kept circling the block."

"If they were professional enough to set all this up to make it look like an accident, they would be professional enough not to draw attention to themselves by driving round and round the block," said Connie. "I want the plates of every vehicle on the street."

"Already done," replied Rankin.

"Have any left since you arrived?" asked Connie.

"No. I didn't think I should let anyone leave until you gave the go-ahead, but so far, nobody has even tried to leave."

"Good job."

"So you believe me that it was intentional?" asked Rankin.

"Not yet," replied Connie, "but I won't rule it out, either. I'll treat it as a homicide for now and see where the investigation takes us."

Connie looked at Boyle. "Start canvassing the neighbourhood for other witnesses."

Boyle let out a big sigh and frowned at Rankin to show his disgruntlement.

"I also want to check every apartment security camera within a four-block radius." Connie looked at Rankin and said, "If you're right, the only way they could have known when to strike would be to have a spotter. Maybe we can pick something up from a security —"

Connie quit talking when Rankin raised his hand for her to pause as he answered his portable police radio. A blue Honda Accord had been located minutes ago. It had been reported stolen yesterday, but was found abandoned in an alley after being set on fire.

Connie frowned as she recorded the licence plate from the car in her notebook. *Too coincidental for it not to be the same car. Would a couple of drunks out joyriding in a stolen car think to torch it? Possible.* She looked at the narrow distance that the car had travelled before driving over the woman and the dog. *If Rankin is right, what's the motive? Petty possession of drugs doesn't seem serious enough …*

Two hours later, Connie and Boyle reviewed the security-camera footage from two different apartment buildings at each end of the block. The apartment at the end of the block showed a white delivery van going past on the street moments before the blue Honda

Accord roared into view on the sidewalk and bounced back out onto the street.

Connie zoomed in on the licence plate on the Honda from where it drove out of the apartment entrance. She wasn't surprised that it matched the stolen car. The glare off the Honda's windows made it difficult to see who was inside, only that the passenger was wearing a ball cap.

She reviewed the footage again. The delivery van had passed the first apartment building five hours earlier before passing the apartment at the end of the street. Like the Honda, it was not possible to see who was driving.

"Maybe the van lives in the area," suggested Boyle.

"Maybe," replied Connie.

Neither of the apartment cameras was able to see the licence plates of vehicles passing on the street, but one camera was able to zoom in and give Connie a name on the door of the van. It was for a Vietnamese restaurant in Vancouver called Hanoi House.

Boyle phoned the I-HIT office to check the name of the restaurant and sat with his pen poised over his notebook while Connie continued to review the footage in slow motion.

Connie saw Boyle make a notation in his notebook before hanging up. "I've got nothing further," she said. "What do you have?"

Boyle shrugged. "Nothing, really. There's a report on the Hanoi House, but it's three years old. Back then it was simply listed as a known hangout for Asian drug dealers."

"Was the report put in by Drug Section?" asked Connie.

"No. By the Intelligence Unit."

Connie grimaced. "Do you know who wrote the report?"

"Yeah," replied Boyle, glancing at his notebook. "It was a Corporal J.B. Taggart."

"Fuck," muttered Connie.

Boyle looked at her in surprise. "Why? What's wrong?"

Connie sighed. "I know Jack from several other investigations. On a plus side, he always gets results and is considered one of the best undercover operatives the force has. So is his partner, Laura Secord."

"So? What's the downside?"

Connie bit her lower lip for a moment. "He's not so good at following the rules. There is also another problem. Anytime he gets involved, I end up with more work than I started with."

"Oh?" replied Boyle, unsure what Connie meant. "Well, it's likely only a simple hit and run anyway."

"And if it isn't?" asked Connie. "What about Nancy Brighton? What if she was the intended victim? We can't sit back and wait to see if they get her next time."

"People don't murder someone over a simple possession beef."

"I agree it doesn't make sense," said Connie, "but we can't chance it. It could be some other reason that we don't even know about yet. Maybe they did kill the right person."

"You're talking like it is a murder."

"We have to treat it like it is," replied Connie, gruffly.

"So what do we do about Nancy Brighton? Supply round-the-clock protection for someone when all we might have is a simple case of hit and run?"

"We're going to have to make sure she's safe until we investigate further."

"If it's over the drugs, it could take a year to run it through court ... or longer. It would be ridiculous to protect someone twenty-four-seven over a possession beef. Get someone to pull the charge and be done with it."

"Pulling the charge isn't a precedent we can set. It would open the door to have more witnesses whacked." Connie sighed. "But you're right, it would be a tough thing to try and justify putting her in the Witness Protection Program."

"So what the hell do we do? We need answers fast. All we really have is the opinion of some traffic guy who probably wouldn't know a homicide even if he were the victim. Where do we go from here?"

"We have a report from Jack Taggart," said Connie.

"That's three years old," replied Boyle, with a wave of his hand. "Are you going to call him over that?"

"I don't have any choice," muttered Connie. "If it is a homicide, we can't leave any stones unturned. Besides, like you said, we need answers fast." She reached for her phone and punched in Jack's number.

Listen to what my gut tells me ... Jack Taggart ... oh, yeah, this is a homicide all right. She glanced at Boyle as the phone rang. *Poor sap. He's got no idea of what we might be getting into. Guess I don't, either ... other than to expect more bodies ...*

Chapter Five

It was six o'clock in the evening when Jack and Laura arrived at Connie Crane's office within the Major Crime Unit based out of Surrey. Introductions were made with Stan Boyle and the four sat around Connie's desk as she explained what she knew so far.

Jack noticed that Boyle sat with his arms folded across his chest while making frequent glances at his watch. "You need to be someplace?" he asked.

"No," replied Boyle.

Oh, so what you were really saying is that you feel that inviting us over is a waste of time ...

"I've had someone drive past the Hanoi House, but there was no sign of the van," continued Connie. "The 911 call for the hit and run came in at twelve-forty-eight, so who knows where the van could be by now."

"If it is even relevant," yawned Boyle.

"What have you done with Nancy Brighton?" asked Jack.

"At the moment, we've talked her into staying with friends in Chilliwack, but she isn't happy about it and I doubt she will stay there long."

"Witness Protection?" asked Jack.

Connie shook her head. "I already brought that up with her and there is no way she will accept it. Being as we're not sure it wasn't accidental, or even had anything to do with her, I can't say as I blame her. Not that it would matter. She made it perfectly clear that even if it does involve her, she's not going into the WPP."

"Our office hasn't had anything to do with that restaurant in over three years," said Jack. "It came up as a haunt for a lot of Asian drug dealers. Most of them low-level. We turned it over to Drug Section who made some buys and busted a few of them. I called them after you called me. Everyone they busted has already been through the court system and, for the most part, received probation. They've had no interest in the place since then."

"I was hoping you might have an informant with the Viets to let us know what is going on, or if the van was even involved," replied Connie.

"We don't have any Vietnamese informants at the moment," said Jack. "Even if we did, the odds are remote that the informant would know anything about it. There are dozens of different Vietnamese gangs and they seldom have anything to do with each other. The situation with all the gangs is fluid. Those who are allies today could be enemies tomorrow. At the moment, the Vietnamese look after the majority of the marijuana grow operations and come under the control of Satans Wrath, who use them to insulate themselves from prosecution."

"The bikers' involvement in marijuana crops is a huge concern for us," said Laura.

"Who cares about pot?" snorted Boyle. "It's not exactly a hard drug. Bet more people smoke it than don't these days … or have a least tried it."

"It's the ideal wedge into corruption," explained Jack. "There is huge money to be made from it and many people share your belief that it is not really a bad thing. That makes it an easy tool for criminals to open the door to corrupt officials who might not otherwise be corrupted."

"Once the initial corruption takes place, the corrupt officials are then easy prey when it comes to other organized crime favourites," added Laura. "Like influence-peddling, market manipulation, drug-trafficking, slavery prostitution rings, union corruption … and of course, the murder of rivals or those who are innocent or refuse to be bought."

"Kind of like using good old B.C. bud as the key to opening Pandora's Box," said Connie.

"Exactly," replied Jack. "The same thing happened over alcohol during the Prohibition years in the U.S. It was how organized crime really managed to gain control over a multitude of other criminal activities." Jack gave Boyle a hard stare and said, "Which is why it concerns us that an organized crime family as strong as Satans Wrath is in control of the marijuana situation."

"So you're saying the bikers could be behind it?" asked Boyle. "Maybe Mia Parker is a girlfriend to one of them?"

"In my opinion, the bikers wouldn't contract out a hit for something so trivial," replied Jack. "Especially over a girlfriend. She might not even be convicted."

"Might get Parker's fingerprints on the bags," said Boyle. "Coupled with an eyewitness ... she's done."

Jack glanced at Boyle and said, "I take it you've never worked drugs. Her lawyer will attack the credibility of the witness. An older, retired woman peering through blinds or curtains on a window. Does she wear glasses? Was she sure she had them on? When was the last time her eyes were checked?"

"Yeah, but fingerprints —"

"If fingerprints are found, the lawyer will get the client to take the stand and say she dropped her purse, saw the dope, and touched it before realizing what it was and putting it back. Which he will suggest is what the witness saw. Parker has no previous criminal record. I'd say her chances of being convicted are about fifty-fifty. The bikers know this, so I would be surprised if they had anything to do with it."

"So you're saying it isn't a homicide?" said Boyle, with a nod of his head at Connie to say he had been right all along.

"I didn't say that," replied Jack. "I'm saying I can't think of a probable motive, but it doesn't mean there isn't one. Also, it's not only the bikers who are involved. Although they basically control the Vietnamese over the marijuana crops, the Viets still have a lot of their own action going and are comprised of dozens of different groups who generally operate independently of each other."

"So having one informant, unless by fluke he was with the right gang, wouldn't be able to tell us much," said Connie.

"Yes, although the higher up you go on the corporate ladder, significant decisions become limited to a select few," said Jack. "At the moment, a lot of B.C. bud is heading south of the border. With Satans Wrath's guidance, the Vietnamese are trading a lot of the marijuana for guns, heroin, ecstasy, and cocaine with the Chinese gangs. The Chinese are well established up and down the west coast of North America and have been handling much of the actual smuggling going on back and forth across the border."

"So what the hell does all that have to do with our hit and run?" asked Connie.

"Good question," replied Jack. "If this was a hit, I think we're missing the real motive at the moment. I'm not saying that the Viets aren't involved. Someone else could have hired them, but it doesn't fit in with a normal Asian organized crime hit. They're usually bloody and done with machetes or guns to make a statement."

"To make a statement?" asked Boyle.

"Telling someone not to mess with them," replied Laura.

"Yeah, well, thanks for … all your help," said Boyle, sounding dismissive, as he leaned back in his chair so Jack and Laura wouldn't see him. When Connie looked at him, he gave a sideways glance at Jack and Laura, then rolled his eyes as if to say, *Why did you bother calling these two yokels over …*

Connie chose to ignore him and leaned forward in her chair, clasping her hands on her desk. "Jack … I called the Asian Organized Crime Task Force before giving you a call, but they don't have anything that would help."

"Who did you speak to in AOCTF?" asked Jack.

"One of the secretaries. She was pretty short with me. Said if something came up, they would let me know."

"In future," said Jack, "if you need something from AOCTF, I would suggest you give Sergeant Roger Morris a call."

There was something about Jack's tone of voice and how he looked at Connie that told her there was something he was trying to imply. "Oh?" she asked.

"Roger's a good guy," replied Jack. He gave Connie a hard look, shifted his eyes momentarily to glance at Boyle, then looked back at Connie and said, "I trust Roger."

"Yeah, AOCTF are really busting their asses over there," interjected Boyle. "They've taken a lot of weapons off the street. Equates to saving us a lot of work."

Connie looked at Jack and gave a faint nod that she understood. *AOCTF has a leak … be damned careful who you talk to…* Connie glanced at Boyle. *And Jack doesn't trust him enough to talk about it in front of him…*

Laura glanced at Boyle. "You're right about AOCTF being busy," she said. "They're so tied up with the punks doing the gang shootings that they don't have time to go after the guys higher up."

Connie cleared her throat and looked at Jack. "I know you're busy, but I wouldn't have called asking for help if there were, uh, alternative investigative methods I could do myself. I'm really at a loss. I know you two have a knack for turning informants or getting information."

Jack smiled. "What did you do when you looked up my number," he asked, "look in your phone book under *last resort?*"

Connie would have smiled if someone else had said that ... but Jack was telling the truth. Their eyes locked momentarily. "Something like that," she admitted. "I have a serious time issue. If Nancy Brighton was the real target, we need to know and get a handle on it pretty damned quick. Any ideas?"

"I have some," replied Jack. "Any chance of getting a search warrant for the van?"

"Based on it driving by on the street? Not a chance."

"A witness said it was possible that Asians were driving the Honda," noted Laura. "We've got a Vietnamese delivery van, so there is an Asian connection."

"Are you kidding me?" replied Connie. "Over half of Richmond is Asian. A judge would laugh me out of the office."

"Besides," said Boyle, looking at Jack, "we're talking about a delivery van for a restaurant." He did not keep the sarcasm out of his voice when he added, "What could you hope to find in it, other than about a hundred different sets of fingerprints?"

"I take it you've never spent time on surveillance in the back of a van," replied Jack.

"Not really. I prefer a more active approach to police work," replied Boyle.

"Yes, I can tell by the sleep in your eyes that you must be run off your feet," replied Jack.

Boyle took Jack seriously and nodded, rubbing his eyes.

"I've spent countless hours on surveillance," continued Jack. "You get the munchies. You get thirsty. There could be candy wrappings or —"

"Candy wrappings tossed back by service people in the van," interrupted Boyle. "Means nothing."

"Or perhaps fingerprints on a set of binoculars," added Jack.

Boyle paused. "Oh, uh, yeah, I guess," he replied. "Still, the point is moot. We can't get a warrant. You said you had *some* ideas. What are your others?"

Jack ignored Boyle's question and nodded to Laura, indicating it was time to leave. "I'll call you tomorrow, Connie," said Jack, over his shoulder as he and Laura walked out.

After they left, Boyle looked at Connie and said, "What a jerk. Did you see that? He treated me like I wasn't even here." Boyle glanced in disgust in the direction Jack had left and added, "He doesn't have a clue what to do."

"You were rude, too, when you sat back in your chair a moment ago, rolling your eyes."

"Maybe, but it's not like either of them saw that."

"Jack did. Right after you did it, he looked at me, frowned, then rolled his eyes to mimic you."

"There's no way he could see me. I leaned back —" Boyle then caught his reflection in the window behind Connie. "Oh, maybe he did see me."

"There is no maybe about it," replied Connie, firmly.

"Yeah, well, big deal. It's not like they can help us."

"We don't know that yet. I told you they are both UC operators. They have certain talents that neither of us have."

Boyle chuckled. "Come on, Connie. Don't you think they might have a little difficulty going under-cover as Asians? What are they going to do? Scotch-tape their eyes back?"

Connie thought of Jack and Laura's demeanour as she glared at Boyle. *They accurately read your per-sonality as soon as they met you....* She took a deep breathe to calm her response. "You're new, so let me give you some advice. Show some respect and don't fuck with them. We need their help."

"Why?" replied Boyle, defensively. "What can they do that we can't?"

"What would you do?" replied Connie.

"Well … I know Forensics likely won't come up with anything on the Honda, but they still haven't told us if there are any prints on the broken wine bottle left at the scene. Tomorrow we could canvas the neigh-bourhood where the Honda was stolen from and see if anyone saw something."

"And if both of those avenues turn out to be dead ends, then what?"

"I don't know. What would you suggest?"

"I don't know, either, which is why I called Taggart."

Boyle frowned. "Okay, okay, I'm sorry if I came off sounding like an ass, but I wouldn't get your hopes up on him. He said he had some other ideas, but didn't come up with them when I asked. Bet you don't get any phone call from him tomorrow."

Connie gave a grim smile. She believed Taggart would get results. It was how he would get results ... or the consequences of his results that worried her.

Chapter Six

It was eight o'clock at night when Jack and Laura drove to the Hanoi House restaurant. They found the van parked in the alley behind the restaurant. It was a dented, older model Ford Econoline with curtains across the back window. The licence plate was registered to the restaurant.

Parked next to the van was a new silver Audi. Jack radioed in the plate and discovered it was registered to Tom Nguyen, who was fifty-six years old. Jack then had them cross-check the name through the Canadian Police Information Centre database.

Tom Nguyen was listed as having a long criminal record for drug-related offences, assault and armed robbery, but no criminal convictions within the last fourteen years. There was also a notation on CPIC that Nguyen was of interest to the Asian Organized Crime Task Force with a request that they be notified of the circumstances or reason for the check.

"No criminal convictions of Nguyen for fourteen years," noted Laura. "What do you think?" she said, with a wry smile. "Is AOCTF hassling some poor guy who has long since learned the error of his ways and is trying to be a good, hard-working citizen?" she mocked.

"I'm sure he's no poster boy," replied Jack. "More likely he has clawed his way up the corporate ladder and has others do the dirty work."

"You going to give AOCTF a call?"

"I'll wait until tomorrow and give Roger Morris a call when he comes in."

"Wish they could find the leak," said Laura, frowning. "Bet it's one of the Asian translators they're using on their wiretaps."

"I asked Roger about that six months ago when he first told me he thought they might have a leak. I asked him if it could be one of the monitors who is the leak. I recommended a good friend of mine, Vivian Mah, out of Victoria, but he thinks his monitors are clean. He's not even a hundred percent certain they have a leak. They were getting close to busting the head of one of the triads when things went sideways. From the circumstances, he only suspects they were tipped off."

"Time will tell," replied Laura. "It always does."

"Hopefully, but in the meantime, he warned us to keep it in mind before passing anything on to them."

Jack and Laura parked in the next alley over so they could see if the van left. A call to the restaurant told them it was open until two o'clock in the morning.

They took turns napping in the car and there was no activity until thirty minutes after the restaurant closed. The Audi left first, followed by the van. When the vehicles reached the end of the alley, they went in opposite directions.

Jack and Laura followed the van, which went to an older home in nearby Delta. The van parked in a garage facing the back alley and the driver, a heavy-set Asian man, walked across the yard and into the house.

Jack had barrelled out of the car to watch, then used his portable radio to have Laura pick him up a block away.

"Well?" she asked, when he got back in the car.

"Saw about four or five Asian males watching TV in the living room," said Jack. "Most looked to be in their twenties, except for the guy driving tonight. He looks to be about thirty-five. I also scooped the licence plates to four cars out front."

"How long do you want to give them?" asked Laura, stifling a yawn.

"Either one hour after the lights go out," replied Jack, "or if they don't, then I'll chance it and go in one hour before sunrise. Go ahead and sleep. I'll take the first hour."

"No warrant," sighed Laura. "Nothing will be admissible."

"If we get an informant, he won't know if we had a warrant or not."

"Think Connie knows what we're doing?"

Jack shrugged. "She knows we operate in the grey zone."

"The grey zone? You mean breaking the law."

"I like to call it the grey zone."

"Yeah, that will work really well in front of a judge," Laura said, facetiously. "Gee, your Honour, I thought operating in the grey zone was the same as diplomatic immunity. You mean you're sending us to jail?"

Jack's mouth quirked in response.

Laura sighed. "Well, right now I would like to enter the sleep zone," she said, tilting her seat back and closing her eyes.

At three-thirty the lights went out, and an hour later, Jack picked the lock on the side door leading into the garage as Laura stood beside him, watching the house. Once inside the garage, Laura took up a position where she could see the rear door to the house through a garage window.

The van was unlocked and Jack used his flashlight to search inside. The two seats in the front of the van had a curtain behind them, blocking any view into the rear cargo area. Jack parted the curtain and saw that the floor was littered with candy wrappers and a couple of plastic soda bottles. Unfortunately, so was the front of the van, indicating that the garbage may not have been left by anyone doing surveillance.

Jack opened the glove box. It held nothing of significance, so he went to the rear of the van for a more detailed search. He collected a few of the candy wrappers and one part full plastic bottle of cola. With the amount of garbage still in the van, he figured it would not be missed.

It was when his flashlight scanned over a part-full bottle of grape Gatorade that he knew the hit and run wasn't accidental. The fluid in the bottle was yellow.

I-HIT has a murder on their hands …

Chapter Seven

It was nine-thirty in the morning when Jack returned to his office after dropping the Gatorade bottle and candy wrappers off with Forensics.

Laura blinked and sat up from where she had been sleeping with her head on her desk and raised her eyebrows.

"I told them the bottle was a priority," said Jack. "Keep your fingers crossed. We should hear by noon, but if you want to go home and get some sleep, go for it."

"I'll hang in," replied Laura. "I won't be able to sleep until I find out if they can identify bottle-boy."

"Forensics is pretty busy. They said it would take longer for the candy wrappers."

"Yeah, but with the bottle, I'm betting it was a one-man surveillance."

"Possibly."

"You guys are so lucky that way. You've got better equipment."

"You could pack a funnel," suggested Jack.

"I've thought of it, but the idea grosses me out."

"I also swung past the Hanoi House on the way back from Forensics," said Jack. "The van was already back. One of the other guys at that house must be working the day shift at the restaurant."

"Sounds like it." Laura yawned and gestured to the paperwork on her desk. "I ran the four plates you scooped from the cars parked out front. One was a neighbour who lives across the street, so count it out. The other three are all Vietnamese males and all have criminal records related to drug trafficking. One of 'em is still on probation. Here's the info on all of them," she added, handing Jack their photos and criminal records.

Jack scanned the photos and recognized the heavy-set driver of the van. "This is who drove the van last night," he said, tossing the picture back onto Laura's desk.

"Louie Nguyen," said Laura. "He's the one on probation. The owner of the Audi parked out back of the restaurant was named Tom Nguyen. Maybe they're related."

"Nguyen is the most popular surname in Vietnam. It is used by thirty-nine percent of the population. Next is the name Tran, used by eleven percent. It doesn't necessarily mean that they are related —" Jack paused to answer his phone.

"It's Gerry down at Forensics," responded a happy voice. "Got some good news for you."

"That was quick," said Jack.

"Yeah, well, I didn't think you would be standing at my door first thing in the morning with a bottle of piss in your hand if it wasn't important. I got some prints. I'm sure it was him who refilled the bottle because the thumb-print was near the base, pointing down."

Jack gave Laura the thumbs-up sign, then wrote down the details. When Gerry was done, Jack said, "Gerry, I have a favour to ask. My investigation could involve an unidentified member who is leaking information."

"Son of a bitch."

"Could you keep the work you did for me to yourself? If anyone asks, deny I was ever there this morning and let me know who does the asking."

"You got it," replied Gerry.

"Thanks. I owe you one."

"Maybe next time bring me a full bottle of amber rum instead of piss."

"Will do," Jack chuckled.

"We did it?" asked Laura.

"You bet," replied Jack, bluntly. "We've got our man." He glanced at the notes he made and said, "He doesn't match any of the plates we ran. His name is Harry Ho … and no, it is not spelled *H-a-i-r-y*."

Laura grinned and said, "Someone has a warped sense of humour. Bet he is a hell of a fighter or a fast runner."

"I doubt his parents knew enough English to realize 'ho' is slang for whore and put the two names together. Anyway, he's twenty-three years old and on probation for his third conviction of trafficking in drugs."

"Perfect." Laura smiled. "We've got our surveillance man. Makes pulling the all-nighter worthwhile."

"Peaks and valleys. Right now we're on a peak," said Jack.

"What's this asking Forensics to tell you if anyone calls about it? Do you really think Boyle is that stupid?"

"You must be tired. Do I need to answer that?"

Laura grinned and shook her head.

"Besides, AOCTF think they have a leak," added Jack. "Who knows where this will end up. If anyone starts nosing around, I want to know."

While Laura went to obtain a photo of Harry Ho, Jack ran his name through the Motor Vehicle Branch and discovered that he owned a newer-model Mazda RX7 registered to an address in Richmond.

When Laura returned with his photo, Jack examined it carefully. "Young punk," he muttered. "He's even smiling in the mug shot."

"Not like he had anything to be afraid of," replied Laura. "His record shows he was sentenced to another term of probation, even though he was still on probation for his previous conviction when he got caught that time."

"He won't be smiling when I grab him by the throat," said Jack, bitterly.

"Want me to risk checking with his probation officer?" asked Laura.

"Go for it," replied Jack, "but keep it general in case it gets back to him. Say that we were running licence plates in regard to a drug investigation and

Ho's car happened to be parked in the vicinity. While you're doing that, I'll call I-HIT and let Connie know she has a murder to investigate."

Connie Crane hung up her phone and walked over to where Boyle was sitting at his desk and said, "Jack called me. Says he is confident that yesterday's hit and run was a targeted hit by the Vietnamese. He won't confirm a motive yet, but suggested we discreetly find out everything we can about Mia Parker, along with anyone she associates with."

"Why is he confident it was intentional?" asked Boyle.

"He wouldn't say, except that he expected to meet with a confidential informant in person tomorrow to get more details."

"Yeah, right," said Boyle, sarcastically. "He's blowing smoke up our asses."

"Why do you say that?"

"The victim was killed yesterday at twelve-forty-eight p.m." Boyle uttered the time of death as though he were mimicking giving evidence in court, then continued, "As of last night Taggart said he didn't have any Vietnamese informants."

"I know when she was killed. If you are trying to impress me with your memory, you're going to have to do better than that."

Boyle glared. "I'm simply saying he wouldn't have had time to get an informant this soon. He's bullshitting ... trying to make himself look good."

Connie eyed Boyle for a moment. "Jack doesn't need to make himself look good when it comes to getting results. He is very good at what he does. Sometimes he needs to make himself look innocent, maybe, but not good."

"What do you mean by that?"

"I mean that we better do what he suggests and see what tomorrow brings."

"So you think we should take him seriously?" Boyle frowned.

"From what I know about Jack, it would be a fatal mistake not to," replied Connie, gravely.

"Well … it would have been nice if he had offered us some evidence before we go to all this work," griped Boyle.

"Oh, I'm sure the evidence will come soon." Connie sighed. *We'll probably be putting it in body bags …*

Chapter Eight

After speaking with Connie, Jack remembered that AOCTF were interested in the owner of the Audi parked at the Hanoi House Restaurant next to the van and called Sergeant Roger Morris.

After a friendly greeting, Roger said, "I got the computer kick-back this morning, saying you ran Tom Nguyen's name last night. I was wondering if you would call."

"No idea on who your leak is yet?" asked Jack.

"Not a clue," sighed Roger. "Like the old shell game. Keeping track of who you tell or what misinformation you spread. I feel shitty about the whole situation. I think we've got a great group. Bugs the hell out of me to think someone might be dirty. Only a few of us in the office know what I suspect and I want to keep it that way. Our secretary is one person I trust because she came on board two months after the initial leak."

"You told me you weren't a hundred percent certain you had a leak," said Jack, nodding at Laura who gave him an exaggerated smile after hanging up from speaking to a probation officer about Ho.

"I know, but I think when I called you, I didn't want to believe it," lamented Roger. "Since then, we have had a couple of other things go sideways. Always with the Chinese. We've nailed a lot of the Viets without much problem."

"I hate it when someone on our side goes dirty," said Jack, bitterly. "Hope you nail 'em soon."

"Yeah, well … sooner or later I'll figure it out." He paused, then asked, "So why are you interested in Tom Nguyen?"

"His Audi was parked behind a restaurant I'm interested in. The Hanoi House."

"That figures," replied Roger. "We heard through a source that he was the silent partner of a restaurant, but didn't know the name and haven't had time to work on him." Roger paused, then noted, "So this is connected to a possible homicide."

"How do you know that?" said Jack, before remembering that Connie had called AOCTF yesterday to ask them about the Hanoi House. Having worked for the last twenty-six hours straight, yesterday seemed more like a week ago. "Never mind, I know," he added. "And for your info, it's no longer a *possible* homicide."

"Involving Tommy boy?" asked Roger.

"Don't know yet. Laura and I expect to be meeting an informant tomorrow." Jack saw Laura raise her eyebrows at his comment and added, "At least, with any luck we will. What can you tell me about Tom Nguyen or the Hanoi House?"

"The Hanoi House not much, except they have a bunch of low-level dealers running a dial-a-dope business out of there. We work a level above those punks. Drug Section isn't interested either. Too low on the food chain."

"And Tom Nguyen?"

"He's a VC-3. He would be a good guy to work on, but we're too busy chasing the shooters who are below him."

"A VC-3? What's that stand for? Viet Cong?"

Roger snickered and said, "In his case, it probably could, but doesn't. We've had to come up with our own system to keep track of these guys in our minds. There are so many common names with the Chinese and the Vietnamese, that it's next to impossible to keep track of who is who."

"Tell me about it," replied Jack, sympathetically. "I've only had a few investigations that touched a bit on Asians. Between the Trans, Nguyens, Wongs … it's hard to keep straight."

"Yeah, not to mention that some of them really do seem to look alike," replied Roger. "So for the Asian criminals in British Columbia we devised a system. VC-3 stands for Vietnamese Criminal, third rank from the top. Sometimes we add a name to it and say Tom Nguyen VC-3 to help keep it straight, but the important thing is to know their position in the group so you know what degree of importance to put on whoever or whatever it is you're talking about."

"So he's the third guy down. Pretty important," noted Jack.

"One of many third guys down. Let me give you an outline. The VC-1, who currently is friendly with Satans Wrath —"

"That would be Dong Tran?" said Jack. "Sixty-two years old and heads an importing company?"

"Yup. Figured you would know him," replied Roger.

"I'm up on Satans Wrath, but haven't had time to take a good look at the Asians yet."

"You know that Dong Tran VC-1 is the connection Satans Wrath uses as a go-between for the Chinese?"

"Yes, but I also know Dong Tran likes to run his own show as well," replied Jack. "I've been leaving him for you guys, although I realize you're busy with the shooters."

"That we are, so any help you can give us is much appreciated. Anything you want, let me know. I'll send you over some reports and photos of these guys as soon as we're done talking."

"Thanks, I really appreciate that," replied Jack.

"Basically the head Chinese mobster in Vancouver, or CC-1 as we call him, is Benny Wong. He's sixty-seven years old and for the Chinese, he's like the guy that Marlon Brando played in the old *Godfather* movies."

"Do they have to kiss his hand?" asked Jack, jokingly.

"Naw, just his ass. Wong owns a shipping company, deals in commercial real estate and several other ventures. The Chinese triads are a really complicated bunch to figure out because they've been around forever. They victimize a lot of the new immigrants who are straight citizens, but have a tendency to fear the police."

"Things like extortion, gambling, loan-sharking and protection rackets," Jack remarked.

"Exactly. Fortunately, your interest is in the Vietnamese, who aren't as well established or organized. They operate their grow-ops like independent farming operations, but funnel their product through whomever Satans Wrath tells them to. At the moment, Dong Tran VC-1 looks after that end of the business. He is who Satans Wrath use as their go-between for Benny Wong CC-1."

"I suspect Satans Wrath want to keep the Vietnamese as independent farmers. Easier to control than if they were to unite under one banner."

"Definitely. So going back to Dong Tran VC-1, there are five bosses directly below him that we know of."

"What you would call VC-2s?"

"You got it. Then each VC-2 has about four or five VC-3s working for them."

"Who is Tom Nguyen VC-3's boss?"

"Bien Duc VC-2. But if you're investigating a murder, then you should know that most run-of-the-mill drug-related murders, such as defaulting on debt, do not need approval from the VC-2s. The VC-3s hold the power to do that. It would only be if a murder could have serious ramifications, like an all-out war … or trying to kill a cop or a judge or something, that a VC-3 would need permission from higher up."

"Do the VC-3s get their hands dirty?"

"Not personally. They select the shooters to do the murders. The status of being picked as a shooter puts you one step up from the street criminals."

"Not much of a promotion, but I don't imagine they're picked for their brain power. More likely it's their lack of brain power that promotes using them."

"That's for sure," replied Roger. "Most are punks. You can tell the ones who have done a hit by watching them swagger around after. Of course, the VC-3s pretend to respect them and give them a pat on the back with promises of great things to come."

"You guys have your work cut out for you."

"We don't have the manpower to go after who we would like. To try and stop the current bloodletting, we are forced to concentrate on the shooters."

"Informants? Wiretap?"

"We run a lot of wiretap, but these guys are experienced enough not to let much slip. As far as informants go, it is next to impossible to get any of the shooters to inform. They know that if they cooperate and are found out, they're dead. If they go into Witness Protection, then a loved one or a relative will be killed."

"And you think you have someone leaking info' to the Chinese in your office." Jack sighed.

"It seems to be Chinese-oriented, but regardless, if you're meeting a Vietnamese informant tomorrow, be damned careful what you put down on paper or who you tell. CC-1 and VC-1 meet regularly. If it is serious enough, I could see the information being passed on."

Jack thanked Roger and after he hung up, he passed on what he had been told to Laura who copied the information down in her own notebook.

When Jack was finished, Laura perused her notes and said, "If AOCTF is right, it looks like Tom Nguyen VC-3 would have told the two punks in the car and Harry Ho in the van to do the hit ... but why?"

"Which is what we need to find out. Speaking of Harry Ho, what did you learn from his P.O.?"

"Ho is currently serving probation on top of a previous probation period for his third conviction of trafficking in cocaine."

"Bet that teaches him a lesson," said Jack sarcastically. "No, wait, yesterday he sat in a van and picked out someone to be murdered. Could it possibly be that our criminal justice system has a flaw in it?"

"Actually his P.O. has great hopes for him," replied Laura.

"Wonderful," said Jack, lamely. "I take it the P.O. doesn't know why we're interested?"

"No. I gave him the bogus bit about his car being one of dozens that we were checking and said he might not be involved in our investigation."

"Third dope trafficking conviction with no penalty," Jack muttered. "Why would the P.O. think he would change?"

"Says he is holding down a job as a take-out delivery driver at a restaurant and —"

"Let me guess. The Hanoi House?"

"My God, Sherlock? How did you figure that one out?" replied Laura, with mock surprise.

"And he is obviously making good money on tips to be able to afford a new car," added Jack.

"Obviously. I don't think the P.O. realizes that besides delivering egg rolls, they also deliver dope. The fact is, Ho must be making really good money. The P.O. said Ho has no parents and is living with his grandmother and helping her pay the mortgage. On top of that, he is supporting a younger sister living in the home who is still going to school."

"Perfect," said Jack. His face hardened and he looked at Laura and said, "We've got a rat in a trap. Time to go home and get some sleep. We'll start our next shift at three in the morning."

"What will we be doing at three a.m. on a Friday morning?" asked Laura.

"First I'll get a cheap transistor radio."

"Then what?"

"Smash it with a hammer." Jack grinned at Laura's puzzled expression. "You'll see. It'll be fun. Another one of those grey areas."

Chapter Nine

It was eleven-thirty on Friday morning, when Harry Ho pushed a shopping cart across the parking lot of a bulk grocery store. He loaded the order of chicken and pork for the restaurant into the back of the van and was about to close the rear door when he heard a woman's voice behind him.

"Excuse me, are you done with the cart?" she asked.

Ho turned around and saw a man and a woman. Before he could reply, the man grabbed him by the throat with one hand and shoved him backward onto the van floor. Ho opened his mouth and gasped in fear. Fear that gave rise to absolute terror when the man stuck the business end of a Smith & Wesson 9mm semi-automatic pistol into his mouth.

"You're under arrest," growled Jack, noting the relief flash across Ho's face when he realized he wasn't about to be murdered.

Ho remained silent as Jack searched him. The only item found of significance was his cellphone, which Jack handed to Laura.

Seconds later, Harry Ho was sitting with his hands handcuffed behind his back and propped up against the inside wall of the van. Jack parted the curtains leading to the front to allow light in as Laura left, closing the rear door behind her.

Jack then sat, resting his back against the van wall while staring quietly at Ho who was across from him.

"What's this all about?" sneered Ho, putting on a false bravado. "You got nothing on me. What am I being charged with? Dope?"

"Dope? Why would you jump to that conclusion?" asked Jack.

Ho stared sullenly at Jack, then blurted, "Give me my phone back. I want to call my lawyer."

"You may be interested in what we have on you," replied Jack, "and the consequences of your actions."

"What consequences?" snickered Ho.

"That will be for you to decide. I'll explain all about it when my partner returns. In the meantime, relax." Jack smiled. "Tell me, how is your grandmother doing?"

Ho frowned. "She's fine. Why? What does this have to do with her?"

"And your little sister?"

"She's fine too. Why are you asking? They don't have anything to do with anything."

"You're not entirely a bad guy," said Jack. "Helping out with the mortgage. Making sure your little sister goes to school. Although, someday, I suppose you think the house will be yours."

"That is not why I am doing it," said Ho, defensively. "My grandmother raised us since we were little. She will live a long time yet. I'll have my own house by the time she dies."

"Really?" Jack smiled as though he were hiding something.

Ho scowled at Jack and said, "I'm not talking to you anymore until I speak with my lawyer."

Jack nodded. "Actually, I wouldn't mind if you were quiet. I've become quite sick of listening to your voice this past while."

Ho looked startled. "What do you mean by that?"

"You'll see."

Eventually Laura returned and opened the rear door and motioned for Jack to step out so she could talk to him in private.

Jack eased himself out of the van, but left the door open to keep an eye on Ho as he and Laura stepped back out of earshot.

"He made a call to another cellphone," whispered Laura, "starting six minutes before Betty Donahue was run over and ending about the time of her death."

"Do we know who owns the other cellphone?" asked Jack.

"Nope. Likely disposable. This idiot should have disposed of his."

"Wouldn't make much difference if he had, as long as this works," replied Jack.

"You really don't think he knows the difference

between a bug and a radio circuit board?"

Jack half-smiled. "I doubt it."

"If this goes sideways, at least we can't be charged with an illegal wiretap," noted Laura, optimistically.

"You worry too much about the grey areas."

"Yeah, well, I've been getting them in my hair from working with you."

Jack eyed Ho in the van and whispered, "Let's do it. I also don't want to tip him off that they got the wrong person ... if in fact they did."

Ho stared nervously as Jack and Laura climbed back into the van and closed the door behind them.

"It's time to let you in on something," said Jack, glaring at Ho. "We've got you for murder."

"Murder?" Ho did his best to look surprised. "You've got to be kidding? You're joking ... right?"

"It's no joke to drive over and kill a woman out walking her dog," snarled Jack.

"I never did that!" replied Ho, looking shocked. He quickly regained his composure and added, "I have no idea what you're talking about."

"Your part was to sit in this van and watch when she left her house, then call to have her run over," said Jack.

"I said I don't know what you're talking about," said Ho, defiantly. "I want my lawyer right now!"

Jack shrugged. "No problem, but you may want to know what we have on you, so you can tell him. Are you interested to hear what that is?"

"Go ahead. Tell me what you think you have, but I'm not answering any questions," replied Ho.

"It wouldn't matter if you did," said Jack. "We haven't read you your rights yet, so anything you do say to us would be inadmissible." He glanced at Laura and said, "Go ahead."

Laura thumbed through her notebook and said, "Here it is ... Wednesday ... two days ago, we have photos of you in this van arriving to watch her house at seven-forty-five that morning. You saw her come out of her house at twelve-forty-two and notified your buddies." Laura looked up at Ho, smiled and waved his cellphone in her hand before continuing. "You stayed on the line for six minutes until they drove over her and left."

"That don't mean squat," replied Ho. "So I made a call. You trying to say my phone was bugged?" he laughed. "Go ahead and bullshit, but I bought that phone this week. I know it's still cool."

"Oh, we're not talking about having your phone bugged," said Jack. "You see, we were working on you for drug trafficking out of the van. Imagine our surprise when our monitors got around to reading what you had to say."

"What ... what are you talking about?" asked Ho.

"Guess the investigation is over," said Jack, looking at Laura. "I may as well take the transmitter out."

Ho watched intently as Jack reached up and pulled off the plastic cap over the interior light in the back of the van to expose a small slit in the roof lining. He then reached in with his fingertips and pulled out an electrical wire connected to a small circuit board and put the item in his pocket.

Ho's face went white. "You had the van bugged," he gasped.

"You really picked the wrong van to watch her house," noted Laura.

"Thought you were a dope dealer," said Jack. "Didn't know you were a murderer too."

Ho started to hyperventilate, then squeezed his eyes shut to try and calm himself while shaking his head in sorrow for being caught.

"Maybe we have some good news for you," said Jack. "As an alternative to spending the next twenty-five years in jail as somebody's bitch, you could work for us and not be charged."

Ho glowered at Jack and said, "You mean to rat. I ain't nobody's rat!"

"You're only twenty-three years old," said Laura. "Think how old you would be when you got out."

"We would never burn you," said Jack. "Although we can't guarantee you immunity from any other officers, anything you tell us will be kept confidential and not used against you. We are after who orchestrated the murder. We know you were just a flunky."

"I'd rather go to jail than be murdered for being a rat," replied Ho, stubbornly.

"No arrests would ever be made if it would mean having you identified," said Jack. "With your help, we would figure out a way to do it so you were safe."

"Forget it!" Ho sneered at Laura. "You're right. I am only twenty-three," he said smugly. "Basically an innocent kid. If I ever was convicted of doing what you said I did, I would be out in about seven years at the most."

"There is one more thing," added Jack. "Have you thought about what will happen to your grandmother and your sister while you're in the joint?"

"They'll manage," replied Ho.

"You should know that we will be seizing your grandmother's house," said Jack.

"You can't do that! My grandma's got nothing to do with it!"

"We have you for dealing dope," said Jack, sounding matter-of-fact. "You have been helping pay the mortgage. The house is therefore considered the proceeds of crime and I will see that it is seized ... unless you co-operate!"

Ho looked wild-eyed back and forth at Jack and Laura's stony faces. Soon tears welled up and he whimpered, "Are you sure nobody will find out?"

Chapter Ten

After thirty minutes of intense questioning, Jack and Laura let Ho return to the Hanoi House so he wouldn't be missed. They then returned to their office and Jack listened to a phone message from Connie Crane.

Connie said that discreet inquiries on Mia Parker did not reveal any criminal connections. Mia had graduated top in her class when she obtained her master's in psychology and was currently taking political science. She was single and living in a basement suite a short distance from the University of British Columbia. The owners of the house, Maxwell and Julia Rolstad, were also checked and had no record of any criminal involvement.

Connie noted that Parker's mother, Jia-li Parker, was a Chinese Canadian and a freelance journalist without any known criminal ties. The only record on file for Jia-li was due to her husband being killed in a hit-and-run accident twenty-five years ago. It happened when he was in a crosswalk at dusk on a rainy day. Although the hit and run was unsolved, Jia-li was definitely ruled out as having any complicity in the crime and Mia was only three years old at the time. Inclement weather and speed were listed as the likely cause.

Jack passed the information on to Laura and they reflected on the similarity of Mia's father dying in a hit-and-run accident, but considering her age at the time, decided it was not relevant.

What Jack did decide might be important was the Chinese ancestry. He reviewed his notes as to what they had been told by their new informant. As usual, he had worded his notes to protect who had actually given him the information.

- *One day prior to murder — Tom Nguyen (VC-3) ordered Anh Dang to kill an elderly woman who lived alone. Anh Dang lives in a house in Delta with others who work with him at the Hanoi House Restaurant.*

- *Anh Dang was ordered to pick two others to help him. He picked Paul Cong and Harry Ho. Cong lives at the same house in Delta and Ho lives in Richmond with his grandmother.*

- *Tom Nguyen never gave the reason behind the murder. He simply supplied the address and described the victim as an older woman who lived alone and had a dog.*

- *It was imperative to make it look like an accident and Tom Nguyen told Anh Dang to steal a car and drive over her.*

- *Anh Dang stole a car and was the driver. He told Paul Cong to be his passenger and Harry Ho to watch the woman's house from the van and call him when she left.*

Jack then flipped the page of his notebook to what he thought was the most important detail.

- *The hit was of extreme importance — Tom Nguyen VC-3 told Anh Dang that the orders came down from the top (Dong Tran VC-1 to Bien Duc VC-2 to Tom Nguyen VC-3 and then to Anh Dang).*

"So what do you think?" asked Laura, when Jack looked up.

"It still doesn't make sense to me," replied Jack. "Why would the top Viet order such a hit?"

"He is under Satans Wrath control," noted Laura. "Maybe it has something to do with them."

"I don't think so. They would have made sure it was done right. The real target, Nancy Brighton, is still alive." Jack shook his head as he tried to think of a motive, then added, "Dong Tran is still a crime lord onto himself. I don't think Satans Wrath were involved."

Laura grimaced as she thought about it. "If it was over Nancy Brighton fingering someone for a possession beef ... that seems ludicrous."

"Coincidental, though," replied Jack. "It was only the week before that Nancy saw Mia Parker stash the drugs."

"Yes ... but for possession? What would she get? A small fine or probation?"

"You know what I think of coincidences," muttered Jack. "I don't think we can rule anything out. We're going to have to keep digging. Maybe get a wiretap and do something to get the bad guys talking. I better give I-HIT a call."

Connie Crane glanced at her watch as she spoke to Jack on the phone. *Forty-eight hours since the murder ...*

"Laura and I have a well-placed source who is in a *delicate* position in regards to the murder," said Jack.

"By delicate ... you mean involved?" asked Connie.

Jack let his moment of silence answer the question, then said, "Before I disclose anything to you, would you be happy enough to get the driver of the car and the person who ordered him to do it, without charging anyone else in the event you ever did find out who else was involved?"

Connie paused. "Do I have a choice?"

"Sure, you can continue to investigate on your own without our assistance."

Yeah, like our unit could come up with anything ... we're already at a dead end ... Connie sighed and said, "Can you clarify what you mean when you said one of the people who ordered him to do it?"

"Orders were passed along like a military command. The driver was the grunt assigned to complete the task."

"And you are willing to give me the driver and his boss?"

"Exactly. Maybe other bosses, too. My idea is for you to get a wiretap and catch the driver and his boss talking to each other about it. Maybe do a media release or something to spark conversation. Any action you take in regards to anyone else would have to be done with my approval."

"Under the circumstances and what we have so far, or I should say, what we don't have, your proposal sounds great to me."

"Good."

"Hold on before you say anything. First I'll want to run it past a prosecutor as a formality to ensure someone doesn't try to change our agreement later on."

"I was about to request that. Glad we're on the same page. I also want a prosecutor to commit the decision to paper. If someone does screw around and try to charge the informant, I'll be handing the agreement over to the defence lawyer to get the case squashed."

"They'll hate doing that. It infers that we don't trust them."

"I don't. You shouldn't trust anyone these days. Besides, they're lawyers. Tell them I said a verbal agreement is only as good as the paper it is written on. That, they should understand."

"Yeah, okay," replied Connie. "What you are offering is probably the best deal we could ever come up with.

I'm sure they'll go along with it, but once I get something on paper from them, I'll need something from you in writing as well if I am going to apply for a wiretap."

"I'll do a report. You'll get a copy as soon as we get the green light, but treat it on a need-to-know basis only."

"Gotcha." Connie hung up and immediately called a prosecutor who agreed to meet her later that afternoon. She then updated Boyle on what had transpired.

"You said Taggart was good," replied Boyle, "but nobody is that good. Today is Friday. Only two days since it happened. To come up with a source that quick ... something is fishy. What did he do? Torture somebody?" he added, jokingly.

Connie stared blandly at Boyle and didn't reply.

Boyle dropped his smile and said, "No seriously, how did he do it?"

"I didn't ask and neither should you. The important thing is he knows who is responsible. It's a fantastic deal when you think about it. He'll give us the driver and who ordered him to do it. What more could we ask for? Once the prosecutor gives us the go-ahead, Jack will send us a report. We are to treat it strictly on a need-to-know basis."

"But there were others involved," noted Boyle. He leaned back in his chair, folded his arms across his chest, and abruptly said, "His source has to be one of them. I don't cut deals with scum. Everyone involved should be charged."

"Yeah, in an ideal world ... but we don't work in and ideal world. He is willing to hand us what the courts would consider to be the key players. Any others wouldn't receive much anyway."

"Well … I don't like it," grumbled Boyle.

"Like he said, we're free to investigate it on our own without their assistance," replied Connie, somewhat sarcastically.

Later that afternoon, Jack was typing his report when he received a call from Gerry in Forensics.

"You asked me to call you if anyone made any inquiries about you coming in on Wednesday with that bottle of piss," said Gerry.

"Let me guess," replied Jack, dryly. "You got a call from Boyle at I-HIT?"

"Yup, about a minute ago. I told him we never did any work for you. I take it he is the dirty member?"

"I think more stupid than dirty, but thanks for letting me know. I won't forget the amber rum."

Jack hung up and told Laura about Boyle nosing around.

"What an idiot," she replied. "He's trying to figure out how we came up with the info."

"At best, or wants to identify our source and scoop in and interrogate him in the hopes of charging everyone involved."

"Defence would love that. Talk about opening Pandora's Box. Illegal search of a van … let alone try to convince them the bug was a fake …"

"And our word to Ho that we would protect him," said Jack, tersely. "We'll have to keep quiet about Boyle asking around or the idiot might figure it out."

"So you're going to let him get away with it?"

Jack looked surprised and then frowned. "You know me better than that. What is it I say?"

Laura paused. "You play with the bull you get the horns?"

"Exactly. Time to send I-HIT a report to use as a basis for the wiretap application."

"If Boyle was stupid enough to call Forensics, you know he won't respect the contents of our report. Maybe we should let Connie know and only give her a copy."

Jack smiled. "No. I'll do a report that will put Boyle and anyone else off track of who our source really is."

"Sounds good."

Jack leaned closer. "Also, the bad guys are Vietnamese, but Parker's mother is Chinese."

"What are you getting at?"

"A possible connection. We know that Benny Wong CC-1 meets regularly with Dong Tran VC-1. The only common denominator so far is Asian ancestry. Parker's mother is Chinese. Could she somehow be connected to Wong? It's a remote possibility, but one I think we should explore."

"If it was the Chinese, I would think they would do their own hit and not bother asking the Vietnamese," replied Laura.

"Perhaps, or it could be a favour or in lieu of a payment for a drug debt or something. Maybe they did it to insulate themselves from any suspicion." Jack paused, then lowered his voice. "Let's find out."

"How?" asked Laura, feeling uneasy as Jack got up and closed the door before returning to his desk.

"AOCTF thinks they have someone leaking information to the Chinese. If that's true, I'm sure that Benny Wong would be privy to it. I have no doubt that some ... idiot ... will pass our report on to AOCTF to check our credibility, if nothing else."

"You mean the informant's credibility," said Laura.

"No, knowing what Boyle thinks of us, I would say our credibility. If he is caught, then he will say it was to check out the informant."

"Sad, but I bet you're right," said Laura.

"So ... if the Chinese are responsible, why waste time working on the Vietnamese?"

"Okay ... but how do we find out if they're behind it?" asked Laura.

"I'll word the report to see if there are any consequences," said Jack.

"Consequences?"

Jack used his finger to simulate slashing his throat.

Oh, those consequences. Laura grimaced. *Oh, man ...*

Chapter Eleven

Jack took his report to his boss, Staff-Sergeant Rose Wood, to add her signature below his, before forwarding a copy to I-HIT.

Rose quickly scanned the report. The first section identified the criminals mentioned in the report, along with their dates of birth and Fingerprint Section numbers associated with their criminal records. Jack also explained and used the identification method used by the Asian Organized Crime Task Force to make it easier to understand the importance of some of the players.

The gist of the report was brief, but one word caught Rose's attention. She glanced at Jack and said, "I know you are usually articulate when it comes to any reports containing informant information, but did you proofread this?"

"I did," replied Jack.

Rose's eyebrows furled. "On first read, it seems okay, but under close scrutiny there is something the bothers me."

Jack nodded, indicating he knew, but Rose took it as a sign to continue and said, "Let me read this part aloud. 'Dong Tran VC-1 gave Bien Duc VC-2 an order to murder a woman living at the aforementioned address with instructions to make it look like an accident. Bien Duc VC-2 *had* to pass the order on to Tom Nguyen VC-3, who ordered Anh Dang to complete the task. Anh Dang drove over the intended victim's sister in a stolen car. To date, it does not appear that the murderers realize they killed the wrong person. Investigation further indicates that Anh Dang was assisted by others. It is not known if the informant will be able to identify who these others are without arousing suspicion.'"

"Sounds right to me," replied Jack.

"*Had* to pass the order on?" said Rose. "It could be construed that you are subconsciously protecting your source for taking part in a criminal act … making it sound like he was forced to pass the order along. The wording could cause someone to think that Bien Duc VC-2 is the informant. Would you care to change it?

"No, I do not wish to change it."

Rose eyed Jack for a moment. "Does the wording of your report have something to do with the leak that the Asian Organized Crime Task Force thinks they have?"

"That has crossed my mind, although this report is for I-HIT, not AOCTF. Unfortunately, one of the investigators at I-HIT is somewhat overzealous."

Rose raised her eyebrows. "Overzealous?"

"I suspect he would like to identify the informant and have him charged. He has already made inquiries in that regard to try and identify our source."

"He what? I'll have his ass! Who is this —"

"His name is Constable Stan Boyle. A newcomer to I-HIT. Unfortunately, if he were to be confronted about his actions it could ... uh, disclose a sensitive procedure used to obtain the informant, let alone cause another investigation that would ultimately identify the informant."

"Sensitive procedure?" replied Rose staring at Jack.

"Grey area," he replied.

"Grey area? I'm your boss. What did you do?"

Jack recalled what Rose had once said to him concerning an incident that resulted in her receiving disciplinary action precipitating a transfer prior to her arrival in the Intelligence Unit. He gave a half-smile. "My grounds for a search that identified the person turned into an informant may not have met the judicial criteria needed to conduct the search."

Rose frowned as she recalled her own words, before taking a deep breath and slowly exhaling. "I see," she said abruptly.

"Thought you might," chided Jack. "However, concerning Boyle, I believe he will pass the report on to the AOCTF. How the report is worded will provide added protection for the informant."

"And if you are right in your assumption that AOCTF will receive the report and it is leaked ... close scrutiny of the wording may direct suspicion toward Bien Duc VC-2."

Jack nodded. "Instead of the real informant."

Rose gave Jack a hard look. "I-HIT could potentially be looking at you for conspiracy to murder."

"Goodness, no," mocked Jack, throwing his arms up from his sides, as a fake gesture of innocence. "Should that happen, I'll explain that the triads operate like a paramilitary structure. My wording reflected that, when I said orders at the top *had* to be passed along."

Rose raised one eyebrow and stared at Jack as she thought about it, then nodded and glanced at the report and continued, "You conclude the report by saying that the investigation is still in the preliminary stages and any obvious reason for trying to murder Nancy Brighton has not yet been positively identified. Further investigation will examine all associates of Dong Tran VC-1 in an effort to identify a connection or motive to the murder."

"The top VC-1 would not normally be involved in a murder. I think there must be something personal that we don't know about yet. Maybe he is doing a close friend a favour or something, but we need to dig deeper to find out."

"You mentioned when we spoke earlier that Nancy Brighton had witnessed Mia Parker hiding some drugs and was responsible for having her arrested."

"Yes, but it only resulted in a charge of possession. I've known a lot of Vietnamese in the past who have been charged with trafficking, yet did not resort to murdering witnesses. I think the whole situation needs to be investigated more thoroughly. If I suggested that as a motive and it later turned out to be wrong, defence lawyers would use it to tell a jury that someone else had reason to commit the murder. Nancy Brighton used to be a prosecutor, who knows, maybe it stems from someone she put in jail years ago."

Rose stared silently at Jack, then said, "I think you are the reason I drink." She then signed off the report.

When Jack returned to his own desk, he winked at Laura.

"She didn't see it?" asked Laura.

"Oh, she saw it all right, but she still signed it off."

"What if Boyle doesn't pass it along?" asked Laura.

"It would make us look more innocent if he does, but if he doesn't, then I'll have a word with Roger and see if he will do it to see what transpires. The important thing is to protect our informant."

"I still hate protecting guys like that," muttered Laura. "Our informant should go to jail for what he did."

"Think how stressed he already is. Believe me, we'll make him pay his dues over a lifetime, far longer than the couple of years he would ever get in jail ... not that there is evidence to charge him to start with."

"So you don't plan on cutting him lose after this investigation?"

"Hell, no. Not for what he did. I have long range plans for him. We'll coach him in what is needed for his own advancement in the gang while targeting others who might be promoted over him. In a couple of years he'll become a VC3, then later maybe a VC2. See how stressful he finds working for us then."

"He'll wish he had gone to jail," said Laura, wrinkling her nose and sounding vengeful.

*   *   *

Later that Friday afternoon, Jack received confirmation from Connie that his offer had been agreed upon in writing by the prosecutor. Jack immediately provided Connie with a copy of his report so she could start working on the application for the wiretap over the weekend.

It was Monday morning when Roger Morris arrived at AOCTF and read Jack's report. It was a photocopy and did not include the usual signatures at the bottom. He walked over to the secretary and waved the report in front of her. "Where did this come from? Has it been lying on top of my basket all weekend?"

"I first saw it this morning," replied the secretary. "I was told that a Constable Boyle from I-HIT came over late Friday afternoon after we left. He said he had some intel on a murder and wanted to know if we knew anything about the guys in the report or if we thought the information was credible. It floated around the office all weekend and ended up in my basket this morning. I then put it in your basket as you arrived."

"Something stinks," replied Roger. "The last page looks like it had been cut in half before being photocopied. How come it's not signed?"

The secretary shrugged. "I presumed he cut something off that he didn't want distributed to other sections. Maybe to protect his source."

Roger shook his head. "Do you notice the initials behind the paragraphs?"

The secretary glanced at the report and saw either *B/R*, *C/R* or *C/R/C* behind each of the paragraphs in the report.

"Yes, I wondered what that meant. Is it a code for who supplied the information?"

Roger shook his head. "Nope. I've seen it before. It's used by the Intelligence Unit for informant debriefing reports. Stands for 'believed reliable,' 'completely reliable,' or 'completely reliable and can be used in court.' They also use *UR* for unknown reliability or sometimes *DR* for doubtful reliability. This report didn't originate from I-HIT. My money is that it was written by Jack Taggart."

"So this goof on Friday was trying to make people think it came from him," replied the secretary. "What an ass."

Mr. Frank downloaded a report provided to him by the benefactor and waited a moment as the cryptographic program on his laptop revealed the contents. The report originated from the Asian Organized Crime Task Force and his face paled as he read it, his heart beating rapidly. When he finished reading, he silently cursed himself once more for trying to seduce Mia Parker. *Fortunately her name was not mentioned in the report …*

He tried to calm himself further by noting that in an addendum to the report, the benefactor was not concerned about the attention the police would be giving Dong Tran VC-1 as AOCTF called him, but knew Tran was closely associated to Benny Wong CC-1.

The benefactor noted that Wong was sometimes used by Mr. Frank and therefore suggested that Wong be warned as a courtesy to promote his continued co-operation.

Mr. Frank knew that Wong's standing with the benefactor had recently gained new significance. A scientist specializing in the field of agriculture biotechnology was frequenting one of the massage parlours that Wong controlled in Vancouver. Hidden audio and video cameras had recently been installed. New technology that cost the Canadian government years of research and a truckload of money to invent could soon be in the hands of the benefactor.

Mr. Frank recalled how he first turned Benny Wong, whose contacts as a shipping magnate were valuable. Wong had fled from China ten years previously due to corruption charges. Mr. Frank assured him that the benefactor would see that the charges against him would not go ahead as long as he co-operated. They would only remain pending because the benefactor was in a position to squash any deportation request.

Wong was well aware that his life would end abruptly if anyone was told of the benefactor or was to identify Mr. Frank as anyone other than a trusted friend. A friend who was not to be spoken about.

Mr. Frank went over his decision to have the witness murdered. He had not believed that the police investigation would progress this far and rehashed the decision he had made.

Did I really have a choice? If Mia Parker was convicted, the benefactor would have discovered that it was over my stupidity ... the spilled wine ... the drugs ... trying to seduce her.

He swallowed nervously as he considered the consequences. *I would be terminated ... perhaps executed. Yet if I had admitted my mistake in advance, the benefactor would not have given permission to kill the witness. The fear of a police investigation identifying the benefactor's hand in such a matter would be catastrophic. The benefactor's presence to the Canadian authorities would become a high priority and could jeopardize other interests. I had no choice ... my whole career would be over. Years of faithful service ...*

He pondered what to do next. Wong hadn't dared question his request to have the woman murdered. In fact it was his suggestion to use the Vietnamese to insulate any possible contamination of the benefactor. Wong said he would appease Tran by arranging for his people to receive a kilo of cocaine as payment. An amount which for Wong meant absolutely nothing. Mr. Frank agreed with the plan and Wong subsequently made the request to Tran. Wong would not know who Tran would have passed the orders on to.

Will Tran be angry with Wong for getting his people into trouble? It is not Wong's fault the Vietnamese screwed up. On the contrary, passing on the contents of this report will make it clear that Wong's source of information is accurate and help place him in the trusted confidence of Tran ... something that could be valuable in the future.

Mr. Frank took a deep breath and slowly exhaled as he thought of another consequence. *The police know it was murder ... will they connect it to Mia?* He clenched his fists tightly, then slowly opened his hands as a means to ease the tension. *Relax ... she has been trained to handle interrogation. Not knowing anything about it makes it even easier for the interrogators to spot her innocence. Later, when she comes to me, I will simply deny any involvement ...*

Mr. Frank subconsciously nodded as he reached a decision. *I need to bring the police investigation to a dead end. The benefactor will not care if the Vietnamese murder each other ... as long as I'm not implicated.*

Mr. Frank knew he would have to meet with Benny Wong again.

Chapter Twelve

"You're kidding," said Jack, trying to sound disgusted as he spoke with Roger Morris over the phone, while at the same time giving Laura a thumbs-up sign. "Yes, I wrote it. Also had it signed by my boss. As far as I-HIT was concerned, it was for their eyes only. I was going to tell you about it, but didn't want it to go through your whole office for obvious reasons."

"I'm sorry, but I thought you should know." Roger sighed. "You may want to put Boyle's head on a chopping block."

"Boyle can always bullshit and say he was leaving no stone unturned, but he still should have checked with me first," said Jack, sounding angry,

"Let alone try to take credit for it," noted Roger.

"I'll take the matter up with Connie Crane. She's his supervisor," replied Jack.

"Your report is a real attention-getter. Very high-level stuff naming Dong Tran VC-1 as personally ordering a hit. We've never had grounds to get wire on Tom Nguyen VC-3 or Bien Duc VC-2, let alone Tran. I have to tell you, I have a real concern that it could be leaked."

"If it happens, between you and me, don't worry about it," said Jack.

"Really?"

"Really. More people than my informant knew about this. Several bad guys were in on it. In the meantime, I'm hoping the report will give I-HIT the grounds they need to apply for a wiretap."

"Doubt that will work with VC-1 and two."

"I agree, but they might have better luck with VC-3 and the driver, Anh Dang."

"I'm sure it will take them a couple of weeks to get the paperwork done for a wiretap, but keep me appraised, will ya?"

"Will do." Jack hung up the phone and reflected on the situation. *A lot can happen in a couple of weeks ...*

"Didn't take Boyle long to pass it along," noted Laura. "I thought he would do it this week."

"Likewise," said Jack. "He must have hustled over to AOCTF as soon as he got it."

"That jerk. He is still hoping to arrest everyone and take credit for it all."

Jack ignored the comment as his brain evaluated the situation. "We probably should have been watching Bien Duc VC-2 this weekend. We better get out there, but first I'll call Connie and give her a bad time."

"If your theory is right and someone decides to kill Duc, it didn't occur to me that you would want to save him," said Laura.

"I don't plan to. Whoever is sent to do it will be following someone else's orders. It would be nice to turn whoever that is so we can work our way up the ladder."

"So we need to watch Bien Duc to find out who kills him," sighed Laura. "Another grey area."

"If anyone does try," replied Jack. "This is only a theory. A long shot, really."

Laura eyed Jack warily. *Probably a long shot with a sniper rifle ...*

"Boyle ... you overstuffed stupid asshole!" yelled Connie as she strode towards Boyle's desk.

Silence descended over the office as numerous investigators stopped what they were doing.

"What?" asked Boyle, scowling as he looked up at Connie.

"We barely get Taggart's report on Friday and you hustle it over to AOCTF! I explicitly told you it was on a need-to-know basis!"

"Well," said Boyle, haughtily, "if we are to believe Taggart, we are investigating a murder committed by Vietnamese gangsters. All avenues need to be pursued. For your information, AOCTF investigates Vietnamese gangsters."

"His report contains sensitive information. Didn't it occur to you to check with him first before doing that?"

"Why? We're all police officers. We should be able to trust each other."

"Then you cut Jack's name off the bottom and tried to take credit for the information!"

"I wasn't trying to take credit. I did that to protect the informant so nobody would know who the informant worked for."

"That's ludicrous! Bad guys don't care what cop an informant works for, they only want to know who the informant is."

Boyle saw that all eyes in the office were upon him. "I thought I was doing the right thing," he mumbled.

"I warned you not to fuck with them," seethed Connie. "Then first chance you get you try to scoop the file out from under them," she added contemptuously.

"I was not!" protested Boyle. "I was just doing my job!"

"Bullshit! You know it and I know it. So does Jack. I got off the phone with him and I can tell you he is some pissed off."

"Yeah, well, so what if he's pissed off? We've got the info now. We don't need him anymore."

"Great attitude. I'll be sure to reflect your comment on your next assessment."

"What? For doing my job and exploring all avenues in a murder investigation?"

"Let me give you a word of advice. You have no idea what the future will bring or who we will need to help us. All I can say is that your reputation has gone down the toilet." She glanced around the office and added, "Nobody will ever want to work with you."

Boyle avoided eye contact with his colleagues and stared at his desk as Connie walked away.

Over the next several days, Connie worked feverishly on her application to apply for a wiretap order. Unless Jack and Laura received further information from their informant regarding the case, which they said they didn't expect to, Connie believed that for all intents and purposes, Jack and Laura were finished with the investigation.

At nine o'clock Thursday night, Jack and Laura were parked, watching Bien Duc VC-2's house through binoculars, when they saw Roger Morris from AOCTF drive past the house. Jack radioed him and he pulled up alongside their car to speak.

"Glad I ran into you," said Roger. "I was dialling your number when you radioed me."

"What's up?" asked Jack, then added with mock surprise, "I didn't think sergeants ever worked past four o'clock ... or is it three o'clock during golf season?"

"If I could trust everyone in my office, I wouldn't be," grumbled Roger. "I still can't sleep at nights trying to figure out who the leak is. Tonight we've got something strange going on. Coupled with your report being tossed around our office all weekend I'm really worried."

"What's up?" asked Jack.

"We heard one of our shooters over the wire bragging about being able to eat good food at a restaurant while doing bodyguard work last night in a meeting between Benny Wong CC-1 and Dong Tran VC-1."

"Do you know which restaurant?" asked Jack.

"The Phnom Penh in Chinatown. It serves Vietnamese, Cambodian, and Chinese food. It's a good place and there's nothing unusual about that because Wong and Tran usually meet once a month at different restaurants. The thing is, I know they met about two weeks ago, so last night's meeting doesn't fit their normal schedule."

Laura exchanged a glance with Jack and she raised one eyebrow, but didn't voice what she was thinking. *Yup, there's going to be consequences ...*

"I take it there is something else to bring you out?" asked Jack, turning back to Roger.

"Yeah. Three hours ago we heard there was a meeting tonight between Tran and his VC-2s. This is a little unusual. He often meets with them one on one, but not normally all together, other than for something like Tet."

"Their new year's celebration," noted Jack. "Wrong time of year for that."

Roger nodded. "Obviously something is up, so my team tried to follow Tran, but lost him when he got out on foot in Chinatown. They did see two other VC-2s walking past in the same area, so we know the meeting is on, but there was no way us round-eyes could follow them without being burned."

"Thought you had some Asians on your team?" replied Jack.

"None that these bad guys don't already know. Anyway, the guys called me at home to update me and

I got to thinking about your report. I came to see if Bien Duc VC-2 was at the meeting. Looks like he is the only VC-2 still home. I have to tell ya, that makes me feel pretty uneasy, considering the report you did last week."

"I told you not to worry about it," said Jack.

"You seem so calm about it. Me, I'm worried."

"I presume you have lots of Asian translators in your office to monitor the lines," noted Laura. "Any of them come on board in the last six months since you think you've had a leak?"

"A couple, but personally I think they are all good people. Really dedicated. There is nobody I suspect."

"As I said, I wouldn't worry too much," said Jack. "Especially about Bien Duc. There is a possibility that we heated him up on surveillance. Got a little close to him earlier, so maybe he thought it best to skip the meeting."

"Hope so." Roger paused a moment, then gestured with his thumb toward Duc's house. "I'm not trying to be nosy, but I hope he isn't your informant. If that report was leaked and he wasn't invited to the meeting …" His words trailed off as he stared intently at Jack, waiting for a response.

"He's not our informant," said Jack, firmly.

Roger nodded thoughtfully, then gave Jack a sideways glance. "So if he's not your informant, then I presume you're out trying to identify more of his associates to help Connie get her wire?"

"Exactly. Watching him intermittently, along with VC-3 and the driver," replied Jack, nonchalantly.

"Yeah … right," replied Roger, not sounding sincere. He locked eyes with Jack and said, "You know I've been at this game a long time."

"I realize that," replied Jack, "and I respect your abilities."

Roger nodded. "Guess it's time I acted like a sergeant and went home. Happy hunting."

As Roger drove away, Jack looked at Laura and said, "That is a guy you could trust to have your back."

"I kind of got that feeling, too," replied Laura. She then gestured to Duc's house. "A high-level meeting without him being invited … sounds to me like your theory may become more than a theory."

"Time will tell," replied Jack.

After working long hours of surveillance over the weekend and on Monday without seeing anything of significance, Jack and Laura saw a taxi arrive at eleven-thirty Tuesday morning and watched Bien Duc come out of his house with a small suitcase. They followed him to the Vancouver International Airport and watched as he met up with Tom Nguyen VC-3.

At three o'clock that afternoon, Duc and Nguyen boarded a plane for a thirteen-hour flight to Hong Kong. With the time difference, it would be seven o'clock Wednesday night in Hong Kong when the flight arrived.

Jack was still at the airport when he received a call from their informant.

"I just found out from Anh Dang that Tom Nguyen and Bien Duc are going to Hong Kong for a couple of days," said Ho, excitedly. "Supposed to be an important meeting. They're leaving sometime today and coming back Friday morning."

"What's the meeting about?" asked Jack, not letting on that he already knew.

"They might be arranging to smuggle some women into Canada to work as whores. Tom is really excited. This is the first time he has been sent to look after something like this."

"Thanks for letting me know," replied Jack. "Do lots of your friends know about the meeting in Hong Kong?"

"I doubt it. Why?"

"Just curious. Any other meetings you know about?"

"No. It's been a really quiet week."

"If anything unusual happens, or if there are any other meetings taking place, let me know."

After Jack hung up and told Laura, she said, "Doesn't sound like Nguyen is getting whacked if they are sending him on an assignment like that." She yawned and pushed back in her seat to stretch her legs and added, "Maybe our report wasn't leaked after all."

"Which puts us back on the Vietnamese again," replied Jack. "We're going to have to get a much higher-level informant than our current friend. I better call Connie and update her a little," he added, reaching for his phone and dialling. "Hey, CC, how are you making out on the wire?" he asked as soon as Connie answered.

"Good. Been working sixteen hours a day since Friday, trying to put in all that crap why other means of investigation wouldn't work before seeking permission to trample on their civil rights."

"Which means describing all past investigations and summarizing reports."

"Yeah, you got it, but at the rate I'm going, I hope to have it before a judge next Monday."

"Who are you naming?"

"The ones you gave me. Dong Tran VC-1, Bien Duc VC-2, Tom Nguyen VC-3, and the driver, Anh Dang."

"Got some news for you. A few minutes ago, Bien Duc and Tom Nguyen boarded a flight to Hong Kong."

"Aw shit! Really?"

"The good news is they are scheduled to return Friday morning."

"Do you know why they are going? Anything illegal that I could add to my affidavit?"

"Illegal, but I won't disclose it to protect my source. Not enough people know about it."

"Understood. I'll want to confirm their return on Friday. I've only got sixty days on the order. I don't want to start it if they're delayed and not around."

"No problem, go ahead. Laura and I watched them check in. Both had small suitcases. They don't plan on being gone long."

After Jack hung up, Laura looked at him and said, "So what do we do? Any ideas?"

"I've got one idea. We've worked nonstop for the last eight days. Let's take the next two days off. Give us a chance to rest and figure out a new strategy."

"You're the boss. You don't have to convince me on that idea. Maybe after a real night's sleep I can get my hubby to shave off his beard tomorrow."

"He grew a beard?" asked Jack.

"Yes. I've been away so much that he said he would refuse to shave until we had time for sex. Must be down to his chest by now."

Jack chuckled. "Okay, point taken. We have been working long hours."

"Don't mind if we get results," sighed Laura.

"Peaks and valleys," said Jack. "Guess we're in a valley."

Neither Jack nor Laura would be getting the next day off ... and Laura's husband would forgo shaving his beard.

Chapter Thirteen

It was eight o'clock Wednesday morning when Anh Dang arrived at the Hanoi House to start his shift. He was surprised to be met by Vien Ngo who was temporarily in charge while Tom Nguyen was in Hong Kong, but pleased to discover that he was immediately being sent on another mission.

Anh Dang knew his reputation was becoming known. It had been exactly two weeks since he had driven over the woman with the dog. He prided himself as he recalled how calm he remained while the woman screamed as she was dragged under the car down the sidewalk. His passenger, Paul Cong, whose only job was to drop the empty wine bottle, squealed in panic when the woman was stuck under the car.

Anh knew when the car's back tires finally bounced and spit her out the back that she was dead and had turned to Cong and told him to calm down. He said it was no big deal.

Anh was pleased that the comment was not lost on Cong, who later chatted excitedly to Tom Nguyen as he described every detail, including Anh's prowess as a driver. Anh purposely added little to the conversation and pretended to brush it off as being hardly worthy of discussion.

Tom Nguyen had praised him on a job well done. It was his first murder, but Anh hid the excitement he felt and hoped his reputation for being cool would soon reach the ears of the truly big bosses.

Today he did his best not to appear excited again when Vien Ngo gave him a .38-calibre Smith & Wesson revolver, along with a rolled-up bundle of cloth that held a plastic bag containing crack cocaine. The details of the murder were simple but deadly. The victim, belonging to a rival gang, was going to be murdered near the border of the territory of yet a third gang. The drugs found in his car would make it look like he was there to sell drugs and subsequently murdered by the third gang.

Anh understood the potential consequences of such an action. The two gangs — living under a tentative peace agreement — might decide to go to war with each other. *Will my own gang then step in to pluck what is left when the other two gangs have been weakened?*

He glanced at Vien Ngo and solemnly realized the great position of trust in which he had been placed. If word of what really happened ever leaked out, both gangs might decide to unite against his gang. Secrecy was of the utmost importance.

Anh was told to go to an alley behind a strip mall where he would be met by someone who would give him further instructions and supply a stolen car to go to transport him to the victim. The hit, he was told, would be easy. The victim rented a parking stall on a monthly basis and parked his car every day at the same time to start work at noon. He would not be expecting anything and could be shot in the head at close range.

"Who will I be meeting behind the strip mall to get the stolen car?" Anh asked.

"I'm not sure." Vien frowned. "I was told that for security reasons, it is best I do not know or that you ever say. I only know that it is someone you will know and who knows your car. I must warn you. Be absolutely certain that you are not being followed. The police may have you on their radar. You are supposed to be at the strip mall by nine-thirty, but if there is any suspicion that you are being followed, cancel the plan and return here."

Anh drove in a manner to detect surveillance. His destination was out in Surrey, but most of the traffic was going into Vancouver at this time of the morning. After speeding down a few alleys and driving through quiet neighbourhoods, he was confident that his assignment would not need to be cancelled.

At nine-thirty, he pulled into an alley behind a small strip mall and parked. Minutes later, he gasped when he recognized the man who walked up to his car. Despite the ball cap and glasses he was wearing, Anh recognized him. It was Hieu, who was one of the personal bodyguards for Dong Tran, the godfather of Vietnamese criminals in Vancouver.

Anh already knew his mission was crucial, but the sight of Hieu made it difficult to remain calm. *Dong Tran himself must know I have been selected for this mission ...*

Anh reached for the door handle, but a gesture from Hieu told him to stay where he was and wind his window down.

"You brought the drugs?" asked Hieu, tersely.

Anh nodded.

"Show me."

Anh reached under his seat and pulled out the bundle of cloth, which Hieu took from him, cautiously glancing around before unrolling it.

"Good," Hieu grunted. "And the gun?"

"Also here," said Anh, reaching under the seat. As he started to pull the gun out, he heard Hieu curse to himself as the plastic bag of rock cocaine fell from the cloth, bouncing off the dash and landing on the floor by Anh's feet.

"It is okay, it did not spill," noted Anh. He gave a sideways glance at Hieu as he leaned down to pick it up with his other hand.

In a fraction of a second, Anh realized who the murder victim was to be and his mouth gaped open as the muzzle flashed on the 9mm semi-automatic Glock pistol held by Hieu. It was at point-blank range. The bullet entered Anh's skull above his left eye and spewed blood, brain matter, and pieces of skull out of the right side of his head.

Chapter Fourteen

Connie walked into the office of her immediate superior, Staff-Sergeant Randy Hundt. She knew by the grim look on his face that the news was not good.

"Think you may want to take this one," said Randy. "A guy shot to death in his car behind a strip mall here in Surrey about half an hour ago. The car is registered to one of the guys you're naming in your wiretap."

"Anh Dang!" exclaimed Connie.

"Yes. How did you know?"

"Son of a bitch," growled Connie. "The only other guy I had a glimmer of hope catching in the wiretap order was his boss, Tom Nguyen VC-3. I was counting on getting the two of them talking together. Nguyen flew to Hong Kong yesterday, along with his boss, Bien Duc VC-2. I don't think I have a hope in hell of getting those two to talk on a wire. Duc has been around too long to pull a blunder like that."

"I'm sorry," said Randy, shaking his head in sympathy. "I know you've been burning the midnight oil trying to get it done."

"Yeah, I don't know why I even bothered to try and get wire with Jack involved," grumbled Connie.

"What's he got to do with it? He's the guy that busted this case wide open for you and gave you the names of those responsible."

Connie frowned. "I've worked on a lot of cases with him in the past. Every case ended up with more murders than I started with."

"Just a coincidence, I'm sure." Randy said, shrugging.

"Coincidence?" stammered Connie. "Don't even get me started on that."

"Whatever, but you better get going. Forensics is already on their way."

After telling Boyle what happened, Connie called Roger Morris at AOCTF, requesting he meet her at the scene.

"You going to call Jack Taggart, too," grumbled Boyle, as he stood cracking his knuckles while Connie spoke with Roger.

"Not yet," replied Connie, when she hung up. "Besides, I wouldn't be surprised if he already knows about it."

"I doubt he knows anything," replied Boyle. "He would have called us if his so-called informant knew anything."

Connie gave Boyle a disgusted look and said, "You really don't know Jack, do you?"

"What's there to know about the guy?"

"It wasn't Taggart I was referring to."

It was eleven-thirty in the morning when Jack hauled some wieners out of the fridge to barbecue for lunch. He glanced at Natasha, who was taking the condiments out, and said, "How about we feed the boys first tonight, then have a romantic dinner later in the dining room?"

"Hoping to make up for all the hours you've been working?" asked Natasha.

"Something like that," admitted Jack.

Natasha gave a pert smile. "You're lucky I can't grow a beard ... but maybe I should quit shaving my legs."

Jack chuckled, but his mood changed when the conversation was interrupted by a call from his informant, Harry Ho.

"Me and some of the guys were called in for a meeting with Vien Ngo a few minutes ago," said Ho, speaking rapidly in a shrill voice. "He said that he was to be our new boss!"

"Interesting," said Jack. "Why are you so keyed up?"

"There's more to it! I asked what was happening with Tom, thinking maybe he got promoted. I was told that neither Tom nor Bien Duc would be coming back from Hong Kong."

"Neither one is coming back?" asked Jack, in surprise.

"No ... and we were told never to talk about either one of them again," he added, pausing to take a couple of breaths before continuing. "I don't know what the reason is, if they screwed up ... or if it has something to do with me telling you about them ordering the hit on that woman?"

"Relax, I know you're okay," said Jack.

"How can you be so sure?"

"Do you think you would be alive if you weren't?" asked Jack.

"That's not exactly comforting," replied Ho, sounding angry.

"Laura and I promised we would look after you. Trust us, we've been doing this for a while."

"But what about Tom and Bien Duc? Something is going on."

"We didn't make them any promises," replied Jack, tersely. "You have an agreement with us. They didn't. I hope you're not thinking of breaking our agreement?"

"No! Never! Like, I'll always be straight —"

"Do you know where Anh Dang is right now?" interrupted Jack.

"Uh ... he wasn't at the meeting, but Vien mentioned he sent him to deliver a parcel this morning."

"Dope?"

"Yeah, that's what Vien meant, but he didn't say the word. When I left the Hanoi House, Anh hadn't returned yet. Why are you interested in him?"

"Leave the questions for me. Call me again if you see him," added Jack, before hanging up.

Natasha looked at Jack and sighed. "No romantic dinner?"

"Sorry, Nat, gotta go."

"Me, too … and throw out my razor."

Jack gave an apologetic smile as he dialled Laura's number.

"Knowing it was you, I almost didn't pick up," said Laura, as soon as she answered.

"Have you made plans for today?" asked Jack.

"Yes … and you're not invited. My guy just opened a present I bought for him."

"New razor blades?" asked Jack.

"Yes. Were you stalking me?" joked Laura.

"No," sighed Jack. "Our friend called. Vien Ngo is his new VC-3. He was told that neither Tom Nguyen nor Bien Duc would be coming back from Hong Kong."

"Neither one? They whacked Nguyen as well?"

"Sounds like it. The way my report was, I could see Bien Duc taking some heat, but I never expected anyone else to. We're missing something. What the hell is so important? First of all, the Chinese want to appear to have had nothing to do with killing Betty Donahue. Then they knock off not only the one guy they may have thought was an informant, but two guys below him as well."

"And all without a logical reason for killing Betty Donahue to start with," added Laura.

"They thought they were killing her sister," noted Jack. "The only reason I can come up with is to stop Mia Parker from getting a criminal record."

"That seems like a pretty lame motive for murder."

"I agree, which is why I think we're missing something. If she is connected, she has to be more than some girlfriend."

"I feel like we're farther behind than we were when we started."

"One thing we've learned is we need to be targeting the Chinese instead of the Vietnamese."

"Mia Parker aside, what about Duc and Nguyen being murdered in Hong Kong?" questioned Laura. "If this is over your report being leaked, we have another problem besides murder. The leak has to be identified."

"Last week Benny Wong CC-1 meets with Dong Tran VC-1, who then has a meeting with all his VC-2s except the one I name in my report. That VC-2 is then murdered, along with who he gave the orders to. Pretty obvious that the report was leaked to Wong and he passed it on. I don't think there is any *if* about it."

"I could see from the wording that someone might suspect the VC-2 you named in your report as being the informant, but why kill the VC-3 below him?" Laura asked.

"The only thing I can think of is they know we were on to him and decided to make sure he wasn't caught and turned or given a plea bargain deal by testifying."

"Anh Dang was also named in your report."

"Exactly, which is why I'm calling."

"We better get out there and watch him," sighed Laura.

"If we're not already too late," replied Jack.

* * *

Connie and Boyle watched as Roger Morris peered inside Anh's car.

"Don't touch anything," cautioned Boyle. "We're waiting for Forensics."

"Yeah, which is why my hands are in my pockets," noted Roger. "I don't need some jackass like you to tell me that."

Boyle took a breath and was about to protest, but a glare from Connie caused him to change his mind, so he scowled and looked away.

"So what do you think, Roger?" asked Connie.

Roger stepped back and stroked his chin with his fingers for a moment. "A bag of dope and a gun. If it was a rip, why didn't they grab the dope?"

"It's down by his feet," noted Connie. "Also looks like he was going for a gun. Maybe whoever capped him panicked and took off. Might not have wanted to take the time to open the door and grab it. Or maybe —"

"Or maybe Anh grabbed the dope and tried to do a rip," interrupted Boyle. "The perp may have shot him and then panicked and ran."

"Which was what I was going to say before you interrupted me," added Connie.

Roger looked around and said, "Anh is way out of his territory."

"What are you getting at?" prodded Connie.

"We're standing on the border between two other gangs," noted Roger. "It's like no-man's land. The Indos basically control the drug dealing on this side," he said, with a wave of his hand, "and a gang comprised of Caucasians control the other side. If Anh was doing a dope deal, he could have been whacked by someone from either gang."

"Maybe explains why he was packing a piece," replied Connie. She glanced at Boyle. "Go check with uniform. See if they've come up with any witnesses yet."

Once Boyle was out of earshot, Connie looked at Roger and said, "Sorry about Boyle. I'll deal with him as soon as I can."

Roger shrugged. "I'm not pissed at you, so don't worry about it."

"Thanks." Connie gestured to the car. "So this looks like a simple gang hit? Anh got caught poaching in someone else's territory?"

"Looks that way. Makes me feel relieved," said Roger.

"Relieved?" asked Connie.

Roger glanced around to ensure nobody was close enough to hear. "I've been concerned about a leak in my office," he said, quietly. He gave a nod toward Boyle. "Last Friday that dumb-ass brought Jack's report over. It was left lying around the office all weekend."

Connie shook her head. "That pecker-head was told that the report wasn't to go anywhere without Jack's permission. I reamed him out about it."

"Jack and Laura were watching Bien Duc VC-2's house last Thursday. I'm sure the potential for a leak was on their minds as well."

"I didn't realize they were watching him," replied Connie. "Guess that figures. They did tell me they saw

Duc and Nguyen fly to Hong Kong on Tuesday."

"Which adds credence that Anh's murder had nothing to do with Jack's report," replied Roger. "If those two are okay, then I think Anh was caught poaching and paid the price."

Connie nodded in response. "Guess I better call Jack." She glanced at Anh's body and added, "Glad this wasn't a result of what Boyle did ... or Jack either, for that matter."

"Don't blame Jack. Even if it was over his report being leaked, if anyone is to blame it's me, for not finding the leak yet."

Connie glanced at Roger as she punched Jack's numbers into her phone. *Yeah? Well you don't know Jack Taggart ...*

Jack had barely hung up from talking to Laura when his phone rang. The call display told him it was Connie. He knew then that it was too late to watch Anh.

Chapter Fifteen

Jack gave a grim smile as Connie talked to him on the phone, telling him that Anh Dang had been murdered. *Too bad I wasn't there to watch it ... Connie will be some upset if she knows I expected there to be consequences ... sorry, Connie. Time to do a number on you ...*

"Are you alone to talk?" said Jack, abruptly.

"Can be," she replied. "Roger just left. Forensics is arriving ... let me walk away from the scene a bit ... go ahead."

"Seconds before you called me ... Jesus," seethed Jack.

"What is it? What happened?"

"I'll tell you what happened! I got a call from my informant telling me that Bien Duc VC-2 and Tom Nguyen VC-3 have likely been murdered in Hong Kong."

"Oh my God!"

"My report had to have been leaked," said Jack, vehemently. "Nine-thirty this morning Anh Dang gets whacked. Duc and Nguyen would have cleared customs in Hong Kong at about six-thirty this morning our time ... and a few minutes ago my informant tells me they're both toast. Do you have any doubt that it was because of my report?"

"No ... it, it would be too coincidental."

"The same report I told you not to release without my permission!" yelled Jack. "As a result, practically everyone I named in the report has been murdered!"

"Jack ... I'm sorry," she spluttered.

"Jesus Christ, Connie! You're always blaming me for people dying! Maybe you better take a look at your own backyard before you start slinging shit!"

"Jack, I'm sorry. I don't know what to say."

"This is sickening," griped Jack.

"I, I know," she mumbled. She felt the tears well up in her eyes and didn't know whether it was from how bad she felt or at the frustration over the realization of the disastrous consequence of Boyle's actions.

"So what do you plan on doing?" snapped Jack. "So much for your wiretap. The only guy still alive that you were naming is Dong Tran VC-1. You know he won't be talking."

"I know. I ... God, I don't know what to do. I never thought Boyle would do something like that. I'll see if I can get him taken off the street. Maybe I can get him transferred."

"Yeah, right," said Jack, sarcastically. "He'll say he was seeking information to see what they knew about the people I named. I never did tell him that Roger suspects a leak over there because we don't want whoever is leaking stuff to know the heat is on."

"Damn it ... maybe there isn't much hope of a transfer, but I guarantee I won't be letting this slip under the rug," said Connie, tearfully. "It will be well documented on his file."

"I don't want you to say anything to him yet," said Jack.

"Why not?"

Jack paused. He knew Connie felt terrible and was feeling remorse for deceiving her. *Maybe I overdid it....* He sighed audibly and said, "I'm angry, but I'm not blaming you for what Boyle did. I should have figured out what he was all about before I sent you the report."

"You had no reason to know he was that much of an asshole."

"No, I guess not, but maybe I should have worded it differently or something."

"I appreciate what you're saying," sighed Connie, "but ultimately he works for me. I'm responsible for his actions."

Jack lowered his voice for effect. "What I am about to tell you is for your ears only and because I trust you."

"I'm listening," replied Connie in a hushed voice.

"My informant is still alive, but I'll want everyone else to think he is dead. Keep a lid on it until Friday. When Duc and Nguyen don't return from Hong Kong, tell everyone you suspect they are dead. I'll also let it slip that one of them was our informant. It will add further credence that they were murdered and give the real informant more protection."

Connie glanced in Boyle's direction. He was talking to a uniformed member in the alley. "It'll be hard not saying anything."

"I told you I trust you. Don't take that away."

"I won't."

"Come Friday morning when they don't return, let's have a meeting in the afternoon and include Roger Morris. Maybe we can come up with a new game plan."

"I hope so," replied Connie. "'Cause I'm all out of ideas. Come to think of it, that's why I called you into this mess in the first place. Then to have my office screw things up ... I'm really sorry."

After hanging up, Connie walked over to join Boyle. *I'll have to literally bite my tongue not to say anything.... One thing is for certain, come Friday, I'll be all over him like a hungry weasel on a chicken.*

Chapter Sixteen

Natasha looked at Jack when he hung up from speaking with Connie. "Is everything okay?"

Jack smiled. "Everything is fine. Bad guys killing bad guys, but you know how Connie feels about that."

"I see. A good offence is a good defence."

"Bad guys killing each other is one thing, but do you know what the best thing is?"

Natasha shook her head.

"Our romantic dinner is back on. I don't have to go to work."

"You sure?" questioned Natasha.

"Well, as sure as I can ever be. I need to call Laura back and let her know. Why don't you go shave your legs while I do." He grinned.

Jack's call to Laura was brief.

"Looks like Boyle won the most valuable player award," replied Laura.

"Yeah, he scored a hat trick."

"With an assist from you," added Laura.

"Me?" replied Jack, with mock surprise.

"Yeah, act surprised, show concern, deny, deny, deny. Do you think Connie will ever figure it out?"

"She has her suspicions," admitted Jack.

"She'll be ticked off if she ever finds out," said Laura.

"At least we know we need to concentrate on Benny Wong CC-1. Boyle saved us a lot of time. We could have spent months working the Vietnamese without ever learning that Wong was somehow connected."

"You don't think Wong was simply doing the Vietnamese a favour? Maybe letting them know the heat was on?"

"According to Roger Morris, any leak in the past was in favour of the Chinese. I don't think Wong would risk burning his source at AOCTF by helping out the Vietnamese if it didn't affect him. I'm sure it was for his own benefit."

"Makes sense. Too bad we didn't see who whacked Anh."

"That would have been nice."

"Also, makes me wonder why they wasted airfare on Duc and Nguyen. Why not shoot them like they did Anh?"

"I think it was because Duc and Nguyen had more prominent roles in society and they figured it would attract unwanted police attention locally. How much attention would two guys disappearing in Hong Kong bring?"

"Good point."

"As far as Anh goes, he was a low-level hood. His murder was set up to make it look like another gang hit. Something the police would be expected to believe."

"So where to from here?"

"Let's take the rest of the day and tomorrow off. Come Friday afternoon, we'll sit down with Connie and Roger and go over a few things."

"Like whether or not we should be charged with conspiracy to murder?"

"It wasn't us who passed the report on to AOCTF. I explicitly told Connie that it was to be treated on a need-to-know basis. How were we to know that Boyle would try to back-stab us and use the report to try and figure out who our informant was?"

"Other than we knew he called Forensics to see if they had fingerprinted anything for us and that he is stupid and egotistical ... gee ... how could we have known he would do that," said Laura, sarcastically.

"Exactly. To give Connie credit, she wants to transfer him, but isn't sure if she will be able to do it."

"Too bad."

"No worries. Come Friday I'll have a private conversation with him. I have a feeling he will be asking for an immediate transfer."

You play with the bull you get the horns, thought Laura.

Later, back at her office, Connie sat at her desk and glowered through her open door at Boyle who was out in the main office. *Jack read that asshole right the first*

*time he met him. I'm surprised he let him get a copy of
his report ... especially when he was concerned about
a leak in AOCTF.*

Connie re-read Jack's report again. One phrase
caught her eye: "Bien Duc VC-2 had to pass the order
on to Tom Nguyen VC-3 ..." *Had to pass the order on?
Goddamn him ... did he word it that way on purpose?*

Connie took the offensive immediately when Jack
answered his phone. "Okay, Jack, what the hell were
you doing when you put in your report that Bien Duc
VC-2 *had* to pass the order on?"

"I meant it in the context of a paramilitary structure, where subordinates have to follow the orders given
by their superiors."

"Oh," replied Connie.

"What the heck do you think it meant?"

"Uh ..."

"Wait a minute Connie! What are you implying?"
yelled Jack.

"Nothing! Uh, sorry. Just ... you know, trying
to foresee any questions the prosecutor might have.
I needed to clarify that nobody had a gun to his head
or anything. Gotta go."

After hanging up, Connie reflected on Jack's
response and how upset he sounded. *Was it all an act?
Everything with that guy is smoke and mirrors ...*

She felt a twinge of nervousness. *If he did plan
this ... what the hell does he have planned next?*

Her next task was to send a memo to all mainland
law-enforcement agencies requesting that for the next
six months, she be notified of any homicides involving

Asians. She proofread her memo, then added a request to notify her of deaths that appeared to be accidental as well.

Okay, Jack, I'll be watching ...

Chapter Seventeen

Shortly before three o'clock on Friday afternoon, Jack and Laura arrived at the I-HIT office. As they walked past Boyle's desk toward Connie's office, they caught the scowl on his face as he glared at them.

"Looks like Connie had a chat with him already," whispered Laura when they were out of earshot. "You would think he would be embarrassed at what he did and be apologizing."

"He's too egotistical to admit to himself that he made a mistake," replied Jack. "Let's talk with Connie and then I'll have a chat with him."

"By chat, do you mean toss him headfirst out a window?" asked Laura.

"Too many witnesses to make it look like a suicide," said Jack, sounding serious. He saw a look of concern cross Laura's face and gave a lopsided grin.

She realized he was joking and gave him a jab in the ribs with her elbow. "No, really," she said. "How are you going to handle him without him clueing in that we broke into the van to get an informant? If you mention you know he called Forensics, he'll figure it out."

"By the look he gave us, I don't think being confrontational will work. Connie has already taken that route. I'll come across as more sympathetic."

"That'll be a doozy to pull off," said Laura. "Can I listen?"

"Sure, providing you keep a straight face," said Jack, as they walked into Connie's office.

"What do you mean, keep a straight face," frowned Connie as she stared up at them from her desk. "What are you two up to?"

"Plotting to convince Boyle to ask for a transfer," replied Jack.

Connie rolled her eyes. "Good luck. I called him in and reamed him out an hour ago. I told him that neither Duc nor Nguyen returned from Hong Kong this morning. I also checked and found their tickets weren't refundable. With Anh Dang being murdered, I told Boyle that I believed Duc and Nguyen had likely been murdered as well. All as a result of him leaking your report."

"How did he take it?" asked Laura.

"Like a dork. Said he was being diligent by going to AOCTF. When I said he should have checked with you guys first, he said he doesn't seek approval from outside units to tell him how to run a homicide investigation."

"Think you can get him transferred?" asked Jack.

Connie lowered her voice and said, "For this one-time incident, I doubt it. I'll be putting in a shitty assessment on him, but he is pretty proud that he is a homicide investigator. I don't see him leaving without a fight."

"We'll go have a chat with him," said Jack. "Clear the air before the meeting."

Connie shook her head. "I went up one side of him and down the other. He only became more defensive and cocky. Give him shit if you want, but with him it's like water off a duck's back. I told him that I would leave it up to you if he should be excluded from our meeting."

"We'll see how it goes," replied Jack.

"Hey! You guys starting the meeting without me?" asked Roger Morris with a smile as he entered Connie's office.

"Not yet," replied Jack. "Laura and I are going to have a word with Boyle. We'll start the meeting right after."

"Yeah, come on, Roger," said Connie. "Drop your briefcase on my desk and we'll go grab a coffee and bring it back." She glanced at Jack and Laura and said, "Good luck. I mean it."

When Jack left Connie's office, he gave Boyle a sympathetic smile as he and Laura walked over to talk to him.

"Meeting starting?" asked Boyle, sliding his chair back.

"Not yet," replied Jack. "Connie and Roger are grabbing a coffee, but stay seated, there's something we need to talk to you about in private."

"Yeah, I know you're pissed at me," said Boyle defensively, crossing his arms across his chest as Jack and Laura slid two more chairs up next him.

"Pissed? I'm not pissed," said Jack. "That's what I want to talk to you about. I feel awful for getting you into trouble."

"You do?" asked Boyle, subconsciously becoming a mouth breather as he tried to understand what Jack meant.

"How were you to know AOCTF and the Anti-Corruption Unit were investigating a leak over there?" explained Jack.

"I didn't know any of that," replied Boyle, gesturing with his hands as a show of innocence.

"Exactly," said Jack, nodding. "And as far as not contacting me first to get permission, well, we all make mistakes. What with everything you have to do and the importance of the time factor on investigating a homicide when it is fresh ... I fully understand."

"Am I glad to hear you say that," replied Boyle with a sigh of relief. "Have you told Connie that? She was all over me an hour ago. She was so upset her face was purple. I thought she was gonna have a heart attack."

"I'll talk to Connie," said Jack, "but it's the Anti-Corruption Unit that I'm worried about. I don't know what I should say to them."

"They're involved?" asked Boyle.

Jack lowered his voice. "Yup. Over trying to identify the leak. What you did placed you in their sights."

"I'm sure as hell not the leak," said Boyle, his voice tinged with anger at the suggestion.

"I don't think you are either," replied Jack, patting him on the shoulder, "which is why I'm not sure what to do. I know the stigma over false allegations can have a devastating effect on your career."

"What do you mean, you're not sure what to do?" asked Boyle. "Other than it was your report ... which by now, I'm sure everyone knows about, what is there to do?"

"It's this other thing," said Jack, shaking his head.

"Other thing?" asked Boyle.

"I'm confused about it," said Jack. "On Wednesday, when I heard that Anh was murdered, I wondered if someone had been staking out his house like they did with the woman in the hit and run ... then followed him to the strip mall and killed him. I checked around the neighbourhood where he lived and found a candy wrapper out on the street near his house. I brought it into Forensics to check for prints. Do you know what I found out?"

"Prints belonging to a criminal?" asked Boyle. "They do live in a slummy neighbourhood. It might be coincidental if —"

"No, they didn't find any prints," said Jack. "But they mentioned you had called their office a couple of days after that woman had been run over, asking if I had brought something in to be fingerprinted."

The tips of Boyle's ears turned crimson and his mouth hung open. "Uh, uh," he uttered.

"Naturally I was surprised," said Jack. "I was thinking you were trying to speculate on how we obtained our informant. A curiosity type of thing."

"I, uh, no, I was —"

"That's okay," said Jack, not wanting to give Boyle the opportunity to lie to him. "Good cops are naturally nosy. It's how we find out things and learn. I don't care about that, but I think there is something you need to know." Jack glanced at Laura and said, "Too late to protect our guy, we may as well tell him."

"Tell me what?" asked Boyle, his voice barely a whisper.

"Our informant was one of the guys who disappeared in Hong Kong. He was always really good about calling us. I'm certain he's dead … which means Anti-Corruption … well, you must know what they're like."

"Actually, I've never had anything to do with them," replied Boyle, nervously.

"You're lucky," replied Jack. "Let me tell you, they'll be looking to put somebody's head on a stake."

Boyle momentarily closed his eyes in a subconscious desire to block out what he heard. "Oh, Jesus, I'm sorry."

"The thing is, I know I'll be really grilled by Anti-Corruption. If I tell them you were trying to find out who our informant was one week, then the next week you hand our report to AOCTF … well, you know how that looks."

"What do you mean? Obvious AOCTF does have a leak."

Jack shook his head. "AOCTF doesn't think so anymore. They figure they've been looking at the wrong people. I'm already hearing rumours that you sent the report over to AOCTF to cover your tracks and send them on a wild goose chase."

"It wasn't me," spluttered Boyle. "I had no idea your informant would get killed."

"That's my dilemma," said Jack. "I don't feel that you're a bad guy, but simply a bit naive. I would feel bad if you ended up getting charged criminally."

"Oh my God! You think that could happen? They couldn't do that! What —"

"The news media would have a field day with it," noted Jack. "Of course, it would only be circumstantial evidence, but Anti-Corruption would consider it a feather in their cap. Needless to say, your career would be toast regardless of conviction."

"But I'm innocent," pleaded Boyle.

"Of course you would say that," replied Jack. "But I have to think, you were spying on me with Forensics … well, the thing is, what if I'm wrong about you? If you are dirty and I don't say anything and you are left in I-HIT, it could be like putting the rat in charge of the cheese factory. You could conceivably be investigating murders that you are responsible for." Jack shook his head sympathetically. "I hope you understand, but I don't know how I could sleep at night if I didn't tell Anti-Corruption what I know."

"What, what if I asked for a transfer?" asked Boyle. "Would you still feel that you had to tell Anti-Corruption?"

Jack took a deep breath and slowly exhaled as he sat silently for a moment, pretending to consider it. "I guess not, providing you didn't end up on any section that dealt with sensitive issues." He glanced at Laura and said, "What do you think? You have to be on board with this too. You know what Anti-Corruption is like. We'd have to keep this secret until the day we die, or else they're liable to turn around and charge us with aiding and abetting."

Laura stared at Boyle. "Can I trust you to keep your mouth shut?"

"Christ, yes," replied Boyle. "It would be my ass. I'll tell Staffing I would like a transfer."

"Think you should do more than ask them," said Jack. "People are always whining to them. I don't have much time before I'll be called in. Say something to make it a priority. Tell them you can't handle the stress and are about to flip out and eat your gun."

"That will work," nodded Laura.

"They'll think I'm weak," protested Boyle.

"Naw, are you kidding?" replied Jack. "They'll respect your honesty. That's a big deal for them." He looked at Laura and asked, "What do you think?"

"Oh, for sure," said Laura.

"Trust and honesty is what it is all about," said Jack. "You don't see Staffing working homicides. They'll like and respect you for telling them that. It'll be more like you are one of them."

Boyle bit his lower lip, but didn't respond.

"Now would be a good time to go to them," prodded Jack. "By Monday morning Anti-Corruption will know our informant is dead. They'll be coming to me pretty quick. The faster you can get out of here, the better."

Connie and Roger returned with their coffee in time to see Boyle get up from his desk and shake hands with Jack and Laura.

"Thanks, guys. I owe ya one," said Boyle quietly. He looked at Connie and said, "Can I talk to you for a moment in private?"

Connie glanced suspiciously at Jack before nodding and gesturing with her hand for Boyle to come into her office, where she closed the door behind him.

Moments later, Boyle left Connie's office and disappeared down the hall as Connie waved for them to come in.

"Mind telling me what you said to Boyle?" asked Connie.

"I told him that I thought he was too naive to be in I-HIT," replied Jack.

"Yeah, I bet you did," replied Connie, shaking her head in disbelief. "Whatever you said scared the shit out of him. He told me he can't handle the stress and wants a transfer. I didn't believe him, so he called Staffing right from my desk and told them the same thing, only added that he is having suicidal ideation."

"Where did he go?" asked Roger.

"I could hear Staffing gasp from where I'm sitting," said Connie. "They told him they wanted to see him immediately. I bet he only comes back to clean out his desk."

"Wonder if they'll let him keep his gun," mused Roger.

Connie looked at Jack. "You obviously threatened him with something."

"Me? He told me it was you who tore a strip off him. I wonder if he'll name you for putting all the stress on him?"

"Me?" replied Connie.

"You are pretty blunt sometimes," noted Jack. "I wouldn't be surprised if they send you for sensitivity training."

"Sensitivity training! You bastard," growled Connie. "What the hell did you say to that guy? I saw him shaking your hands out there. Christ, he even thinks you're his friends," she added, shaking her head.

"I said he was naive," Jack said, smiling.

Chapter Eighteen

Roger moved some items aside on Connie's desk and took out large sheets of paper from his briefcase and unfolded them. They were similar in size to what blueprints for a building would be, but in this case, they were blueprints to several interconnecting Chinese criminal organizations headed by Benny Wong CC-1.

In the centre of the first sheet of paper was Wong's name in a circle within overlapping rectangular boxes containing the names of companies and businesses he owned. Lines went out from there like spokes on a wheel, connecting to circles containing people's names or boxes that identified companies who were associated either directly or indirectly to Wong. It included associate Chinese criminal organizations as well as non-Asian criminal groups. Jack observed one line that went to the Vietnamese, identifying Dong Tran VC-1, which then had a line going from him to a circle labelled Satans Wrath. Jack knew that each of the individual groups would have their own link-charts.

The Chinese criminal link-chart expanded exponentially by aligning other sheets of paper up with each other like a huge map, with an increasing web of lines showing more criminal connections to the people who were under Wong, as well as those who were indirectly connected to him through others. Analytical Services usually prepared these link-charts so that investigators could see at a glance what would be next to impossible to remember if it were simply detailed in writing.

Jack stabbed his finger at Wong's name. "I think we can agree that with three murders happening within five days of my report being released, that he is either responsible or knows who is responsible for ordering the hit-and-run murder of Betty Donahue."

"With the latter three murders being the result of a report that I am certain was leaked out of my office," Roger added, glumly.

"We need to identify the traitor," said Jack, tersely. "Whoever you used from Analytical Services did a fantastic job, however, could it be someone from there that is leaking the information?"

"I didn't use Analytical Services," replied Roger.

"You're kidding?" said Jack in surprise. "These are the best link-charts I've ever seen."

"We've got a member who has a problem with a disintegrating disc in her lower back," confided Roger. "We are trying to keep her on the payroll for as long as possible. For the last year and a half we've been letting her work from home by correlating all our reports and making link-charts."

"Year and a half," noted Jack, "and you think the leak started —"

"Roughly six months ago," said Roger. "Mind you, that is when we thought we had an opportunity to target Wong and the fellows directly under him. Still ... I'm sure it's not Jo."

"Joe?" questioned Connie. "I thought you said it was a her?"

"Her name is Josephine Bagley. I see her often. She lives alone with two cats."

"What about —" Laura started to ask.

"No boyfriends or anyone coming and going," said Roger, beating her to her question. "Even if there were, most of the reports are computerized and she doesn't print them out. The only paper is her charts, which show the links, but doesn't give the actual details of the association."

"What about janitorial services in your office?" asked Jack. "Any changes there?"

"Same people we have had for years," replied Roger. "They are only allowed in when we are there, so it's not like they could go snooping."

Jack's eyes drifted back to the link-chart. "We need a source close to Wong. Then you could feed false info to a few select people and see what we hear back."

"We've tried to get a source for years," sighed Roger. "We have very few Chinese informants at all, other than low-level punks and a few straight citizens who tell us stuff. Even they tend to use Crime Stoppers to protect their identity."

"So why would someone like Wong, basically the godfather of Chinese crime in Vancouver, have Betty Donahue murdered, plus contract it out to the Vietnamese?" asked Connie. "If that is what happened," she added, leaning back and folding her arms across her chest. "Especially if it was over Mia Parker being stuck with a simple possession beef."

"That has been driving me nuts, too," replied Roger.

"You've checked out her mother?" asked Jack.

"Yes," replied Connie. "She is Chinese. Her Canadian name is Jia-li Parker, but her maiden name is Chao. Her husband, Brent Parker, worked for a computer company in Beijing. They married there and moved to Vancouver about thirty years ago. Brent was killed in a hit-and-run accident when Mia was only three years old."

"Another hit and run," mused Jack. "I recall you mentioning it before. The case wasn't solved?"

Connie shook her head. "No, it is still an open file. It happened twenty-five years ago. He was killed in a crosswalk. I hauled out the file to look at it. They had a partial photograph from a gas-station camera. It showed someone speeding past in the car, but the picture was blurry and only showed a profile of the driver. It was also dusk and raining. An investigator was able to enhance the photograph about five years ago using new technology. It was then put through the computer to see if we could do a facial recognition with driver's-licence photographs, but nothing came up."

"Out of curiosity, could you tell if the suspect was Asian?" asked Jack.

"Could have been. Had dark hair, but it was only a profile and you couldn't see the eyes. The only thing that stood out were what looked like three small moles in a line along his lower left jaw."

"I've also checked out Jia-li with the information Connie gave me," said Roger. "There are no connections with her or Mia to any of the gangs, Chinese or Vietnamese. Jia-li is a freelance journalist and has done articles on a wide range of subjects, but generally avoids the crime beat and has no known association with any of the bad boys we work on. Certainly nothing that would raise any flags."

"Maybe Mia doesn't have anything to do with this," said Connie.

"If she is convicted she will receive a criminal record," noted Jack.

"Yeah, but for possession?" questioned Connie.

"It would be enough to have her barred from entering the U.S.," replied Jack. "Didn't you tell me that she had a degree in psychology and is currently taking political science?"

Connie nodded.

"A criminal record wouldn't be a good thing to have if she was wanting to run for office," said Jack, "let alone trying to enter the States."

"Say you're right," interjected Roger. "And I could see that being a good theory if she was Wong's mistress or something … but we would know if she was. There has never been any connection between her and any criminal that we can find."

"And living in a basement suite doesn't give the

impression she could hire someone to do the hit," added Connie. "At least not at Wong's calibre or have this many players involved."

"Someone supplied her with cocaine and ecstasy," noted Jack.

"Yeah, but how hard is it to obtain that stuff at university?" noted Roger. "Lots of so-called straight kids do dope once in awhile."

"And they don't have people murdered over it," added Connie.

"That's another thing," said Roger, looking at Jack. "If your premise is correct, why would Wong contract it out to the Vietnamese? The Chinese have no qualms about murdering people themselves. You work organized crime … answer me that."

"I don't know," replied Jack. "It could have been done to hide their involvement if the police did find out who actually drove over Betty Donahue. That would also explain murdering the three I named in my report to sever any connection."

"But like I said, they have no qualms about murdering people themselves," said Roger. "If we can't prove it, they don't really give a damn if we know. Whatever they are trying to hide would have to be something more sinister than murder."

"Maybe it is to them," said Jack.

"What could be worse than murder?" noted Connie. "That's tops on my list."

"Money," replied Jack. "It's what bad guys murder people for. Maybe they're trying to protect some financial scam that involves Mia Parker."

"Maybe, but she sure hasn't come up on our radar," said Roger.

"In a nutshell, what can you tell us about Wong?" asked Jack. "All I really know is he is sixty-seven years old and owns a shipping company and deals in a lot of commercial property."

"Yeah, hang on." Roger dug into his briefcase and tossed some surveillance photographs on the desk. "You can have these. The first one is Wong, along with his wife. They have been married forever. They have one son who is forty years old and lives in Beijing, where the head office for his shipping company is. Wong appears to have left the day-to-day operation of that for his son to look after and spends most of his time socializing in the community or checking out his commercial properties. It should be noted that a lot of the massage parlours in town owned by the triads are located in rental property owned by Wong."

Jack looked at the photograph and saw that Wong had a round face and little hair. His skin was mottled with liver spots.

"He's not smiling in that photo, but he has a few gold teeth in his mouth," noted Roger. He is also tiny by stature, so he got to where he is by using his brains and not brawn. Comes across as polite ... well-mannered with the police, but make no mistake, he is dangerous and could have you killed with a snap of his fingers."

"Dangerous fingers. I'll keep that in mind," replied Jack.

Roger paused, looked at Jack and said, "The Chinese fear him for good reason, so don't ever say I didn't warn you."

Jack nodded. "What about the people close to him? Any that might be disgruntled or want to do a coup and take over?"

"Not that I'm aware of. His henchmen are loyal. No doubt he has enemies because he walks around with at least two bodyguards. There is nobody close to him that we know who would be willing to talk. He is also generous with charities and community fundraisers, so many citizens think he is a nice guy." Roger dug out two more photographs and put them on the table. They were of Chinese men who were in their early thirties with short black hair and both were heavyset and muscular. "These are two bodyguards who live with him," said Roger.

Jack turned the pictures over and saw the names on the back were Zhang Wei and Shen Xiao.

"Zhang Wei appears to have had proper VIP security training," said Roger. "He knows what he is doing and runs the show in that department."

"Where does Benny Wong live?" asked Laura.

"In Point Grey, about a block and a half from the Royal Vancouver Yacht Club."

"Expensive neighbourhood," Jack remarked.

"You might say that. His house is worth over six mil.' It's on the waterfront facing English Bay. I think the only people living there are he and his wife, two bodyguards, and a couple of older woman who do the housekeeping and cooking."

"Cars?" asked Jack.

"He has a couple of vehicles, but I've only seen him being driven around in a silver Lexus LS 460. He also owns a black SUV, but I think his bodyguards use it when they need to."

"Six-million-dollar home," mused Jack. "Not bad. Guess renting property to the massage parlours is the way to go. I'm sure he gets a kick-back from the prostitution."

"He never works out of an office or anything," said Roger. "I've had the taxman take a run at him several times, but nothing ever comes out of it. Most of his money comes out of, or goes through China and on paper is either connected to his rental property or connected with the shipping industry."

"At least one set of books would say that," replied Jack. "Would love to see what the other set would say. The shipping industry will be his most profitable. Explains how the Chinese are bringing dope and guns into Vancouver."

"Oh, I'm sure," said Roger. "In exchange for B.C. bud. Likely smuggling people as well, but knowing, finding, and proving are a different matter. Six months ago we were set to bust a container of coke scheduled to arrive on one of Wong's ships out of San Francisco, but at the last moment, the container was never placed on the ship."

"Was the DEA involved?"

"No, we kept it to ourselves. That was when I first suspected someone was tipping them off."

"So what do we do?" asked Connie.

Jack glanced at his watch. "It's Friday and I suspect the end of the day for you two. How about Laura and I take a look at Wong over the weekend and see what we come up with, then meet again Monday? That'll give us time to check him out and read everything available on him before planning a course of action."

"Sounds good to me," said Roger. "You can keep all the stuff I brought with me. Also got a bunch of reports for you," he added, passing Jack a computer memory stick.

Connie nodded in agreement, but stared quietly at Jack. *Brought you in to assist on one murder less than three weeks ago and now we have four murders. What the hell are you really going to do this weekend? ... I should probably tell the coroner to pack extra bags ...*

Chapter Nineteen

"What now?" asked Laura, as they walked out of Connie's office.

"Drop what Roger gave us at our office, then let's see what a Chinese godfather does to entertain himself on a Friday night," replied Jack.

At five o'clock, Jack and Laura sat in different vehicles on opposite sides of Wong's house on side streets facing Point Grey Road. Jack was to the east and Laura to the west. To park any closer could draw suspicion, but if Wong were to leave his house, his route would take him past one of them. The side streets they were on were also busy enough that Jack was confident they could blend in to their locations without being noticed.

It was seven o'clock when Laura thumbed her police radio. "Heads up. Got a silver Lexus coming off Point Grey southbound on Alma Street. Two figures in the front and someone in the back. Too dark to see if it is our main guy. Stand by ... will be going right past me ... okay, got a visual on the bodyguard, Shen Xiao, in the front passenger seat."

"Copy that," replied Jack. "Zhang is likely driving, which means T-1 should be in the back. I'll head south and parallel on Collingwood."

Moments later, Laura radioed again. "Okay, I've picked up two cars for cover. He has his left indicator on. Going to be heading east on West 4th Avenue."

"Copy. They should be coming straight at me."

"Visual contact broken," radioed Laura. "Stuck in traffic. Might take a sec' to catch up."

"Don't worry," replied Jack. "We're no longer VCB. I've got the eye and we're continuing eastbound on 4th."

Fourth Avenue was a main artery and the traffic was heavy. Despite this, once Laura caught up, Jack still ensured that they took turns moving up or falling back in traffic so that the same vehicle would not be behind Wong for too long.

"He's committed to the Granville Street Bridge," reported Laura. "Looks like we're going downtown."

Minutes later, Jack reported, "Okay, they're looking for a place to park. Around one-fifty East Pender. Practically in the heart of Chinatown. Suggest we do the same."

Laura checked her watch as she parked. It had been less than fifteen minutes since Wong had left his house. She used her radio again. "Want to get together and look like a couple? It's crowded. Bet we could tag along close enough to listen."

"Not a bad idea, except we don't speak Chinese," replied Jack. "Nix that idea in case we need to split up.

I don't want to take a chance on heating them up. I'm more curious to identify who he meets and who his friends are."

"Copy that. I'm out on foot."

"Likewise," said Jack, sticking a wireless earpiece into his ear. He thumbed a small microphone hidden in his hand and said, "Radio check. Copy?"

"Copy," replied Laura.

"Likewise," said Jack. "They're out of the vehicle. T-1 has his wife with him."

"Guess she was too short for me to see," replied Laura.

"They're both short," replied Jack. "Especially with the two panda bears they have protecting them."

"I thought Chinese people were short."

"Someone forgot to tell Zhang and Shen that," replied Jack. "Those two make me look small. Okay, they're all walking eastbound down the north side of the street. You cover them from behind and I'll take the opposite side."

The entourage they were following took their time and Jack watched as Wong used an ATM machine while Wei and Xiao dutifully watched people passing by. Jack and Laura also browsed, looking in store windows. A few minutes later the entourage continued to stroll down the street.

Eventually the group turned into an alley on the north side of the street and Jack knew he had to cross over. "Time to be a couple," radioed Jack.

Although the street was busy, Jack and Laura still made a short pretext of meeting each other and giving a quick hug before walking hand-in-hand toward the alley. When they entered, they saw that it was a short alley and only caught a glimpse of Shen, Wong, and his wife turning a corner at the far end.

Jack and Laura quickened their pace to catch up as Jack reflected upon what he had seen. *Where is Zhang? Perhaps a few steps ahead of Wong and had already turned the corner?*

They hurried past a parked delivery truck and were nearing the end of the alley when two Asian men appeared from around the corner, coming toward them. Both men were in their thirties and maintained direct eye contact with Jack and Laura, before stopping abruptly in front of them.

One man, who sported a ponytail, held a newspaper over his hand, which he raised and pointed at Jack. The other man, who had sideburns down to his lower jaw line, did likewise with Laura. The newspapers hid what they were holding, but there was little doubt in Jack's minds as to what was being pointed at them. He only didn't know the calibre or if they contained silencers.

Before Jack could respond, someone grabbed his arm from behind. His question of where Zhang was had been answered.

Chapter Twenty

Mia Parker excused herself from the man who was trying to impress her with stories of his athletic prowess on the football field and got off the sofa and went to the kitchen to pour herself another glass of Chardonnay.

The party at the Rolstads was only getting started, with about a dozen people in attendance and another dozen expected to arrive. Mia stared at the wine swilling into her glass as she poured and thought about her targets. Julia Rolstad had been smoking B.C. bud most of the afternoon. Coupled with the wine she was drinking, Mia knew Julia was feeling the effects before the party began. *Tonight will be the night.*

By the curious and lingering look that Max Rolstad had given her from across the room moments before, she knew that Julia had said something to him. *What an idiot. You would think he would be a little suspicious ...*

Mia placed the bottle down and turned with the glass in her hand and saw Max approach. He had a goofy grin on his face to hide his embarrassment and she gave him a friendly smile.

"Hey you," he said, lowering his voice while wrapping an arm around her waist and pulling her close to his side. "What's this you were telling Julia about giving us some hands-on tips to rekindle our love life."

"Oh, simply a few things I learned when I worked at a psychologist's office while taking my master's," Mia said with a shrug.

"But 'hands-on,' you said? A little ménage à trois?"

Mia giggled and playfully pushed Max back. "Not exactly, but I consider you both my friends, which is why I am willing to bend the rules. The physical and sensual stimulation techniques I would employ would be far more therapeutic than simply talking about them. I am willing to assist each of you to rekindle the fire, but leave before things get too hot." Mia paused, then gripped Max's hand and earnestly added, "Believe me, even that would have to stay between the three of us. I'd be mortified if anyone found out."

"I see," replied Max. His face blushed and he dropped the charade of making fun of the offer and pulled his hand away. "Actually, uh, I appreciate that you are trying to help us, but I find it a rather personal issue. I'm embarrassed that Julia told you about our, uh, problems. I think it is simply stress-related. We need some time to relax, but that has been hard to do lately, what with flying back and forth to Ottawa."

"Oh, please," said Mia, reaching out as if she was not conscious that she was using her fingertips to gently stroke up and down his index finger. "I really like ... and trust the both of you. Don't be upset with Julia. She feels abandoned and needed someone to turn to. I let her know that I am available and have worked in couples' therapy. I think she was afraid you wouldn't go along with it."

"She's willing? I wasn't sure when she told me. I thought she had some doubts."

"She loves you and will say whatever she thinks will please you. Personally I don't see what it would hurt to try. It would only be a one-time session." Mia studied Max's face for a response. She had used the same lines on Julia, but there was no indication that he knew.

"I'll need to think about it," said Max.

Mia let go of his hand. "By all means. Rome wasn't built in a night. You both need to be comfortable. It is intended as a fun, erotic adventure. You have to be in the right mindset."

Max nodded. "You know, maybe it wouldn't hurt to try. Guess if I feel uncomfortable, we could always stop."

"Exactly," replied Mia, giving a fake smile. *Believe me, once I get started, you won't stop until that little brain between your legs is totally spent ...*

The doorbell rang and the conversation came to an end when Max went to answer.

Mia caught a glimpse of the taxi limousine driving away, but it was the passenger who had been dropped off that caught her attention. From photographs she had studied, she recognized him as an important client of Max's company.

Mia searched her memory for what she knew of him. *Sterling Wolfenden. Married ... one ... no, two children ... once suspected of having an affair with a young woman on staff who abruptly left the company later....*

Mia judged him to be in his late forties. His hair was black with contrasting grey over the ears. Portly, with chubby fingers, one of which was adorned with a gold wedding ring. She sucked in her breath at the thought that one of the benefactor's most valued targets was standing in front of her.

She heard Wolfenden tell Max that he could only stay for a couple of hours. She knew she would have to work fast.

Mia smiled and walked over for an introduction.

"Hi, Mia," said Max. "We have an important guest. Seeing as you are taking political science, you may be interested to know that this —"

"Is Mr. Sterling Wolfenden," said Mia, extending her hand. "Member of Parliament and someone I have been personally admiring for a long time," she added, pursing her lips and glancing down as though blushing.

Chapter Twenty-One

Jack saw Laura's eyes flash at him for an indication of what action to take. He gave a subtle shake of his head, telling her not to reach for her gun. *There is no reason for these guys to be doing a hit on us ... and by Zhang grabbing my arm, he is potentially putting himself in the line of fire ...*

"I strongly suggest you take your hand off my arm," said Jack menacingly, staring straight into Zhang's face.

"If you are police officers, do not be alarmed," replied Zhang politely, while maintaining his grip. "If you are not police officers, I have some questions as to why you are following Mr. and Mrs. Wong."

"We are both RCMP officers," replied Jack. "My identification is in my back pants pocket, below my sidearm."

"Would you mind if I removed it to take a look?" asked Zhang. His face was blank, hiding any emotion or indication of his thoughts.

"You may remove my identification," replied Jack, "but if you touch my weapon, there will be a problem."

"As I would expect," replied Zhang. With his other hand he retrieved the leather wallet containing Jack's badge and identification card and flipped it open. He nodded, but appeared to study the identification card carefully before handing it back and letting go of Jack's arm.

Jack cast a glance behind him as he shoved his identification back in his pocket and realized the delay was to allow the two men who had been holding the newspapers to disappear.

"My apologies," said Zhang. "You must be new to AOCTF. I don't recognize your faces."

"You may want to remember us," replied Jack, "because if you grab me like that again, my response won't be so congenial."

Zhang gave an exaggerated smile, indicating he would look forward to such an altercation. He then dropped the smile and said, "Would you care to search me?"

"Not now," replied Jack. "I'll wait until the time is right."

Zhang frowned in response, then said, "Mr. Wong would like to speak to you on the phone. Would you mind?"

Jack shrugged. "Give me his number, I'll call him."

"Oh, I'm sure you already have his number," replied Zhang, taking out his own cellphone. "But I have him on speed dial." Zhang spoke rapidly on the phone in Chinese before handing it to Jack.

Jack looked at Wong's face on the iPhone and saw that he was being regarded with disdain as Wong spoke. "Hello, Detective Taggart. This is Mr. Wong. My apologies for the intrusion."

"For your information, I'm with the RCMP," replied Jack. "We don't have a detective rank. We simply refer to it as being on plain clothes. I'm a corporal, but if we are going to be civilized, please, call me Jack. Is that okay with you, Benny?"

The delay in response told Jack that Wong wasn't happy with being called by his first name. Eventually he responded, "You must appreciate that one must be careful these days during these hard economic times. There are many desperate people who would not hesitate to rob or kill someone for a few dollars."

"Benny, Benny, Benny," replied Jack in admonishment. "If we are going to get to know each other … and believe me, we will, let's not start off our relationship by lying to each other. Would you have me believe that you thought we were common criminals out to mug you? You and I both know that isn't true."

Another moment of silence followed before Wong replied, "So what is your reason for following me? Do you really expect to catch me running down an alley with a suitcase full of opium and a hookah pipe?"

"I was simply bored and became curious to see what rich people do on a Friday night," replied Jack.

"Tsk, tsk, Corporal Jack," replied Wong. "What were you saying about being truthful?"

Jack paused, hesitant as to what to say. He was angry with himself at being spotted doing surveillance, but more upset that Wong might clue in that they knew someone was leaking information from AOCTF and had linked him to Betty Donahue's murder. He needed to convince him that there was another reason. Something Wong would believe. Jack glanced at Zhang. *Why the bodyguards if he isn't afraid of something ...*

"Cat got your tongue?" asked Benny.

"No," replied Jack. "Actually I never see any cats in Chinatown ... odd."

"Your humour is outdated and politically incorrect," said Wong, abruptly.

"Sorry. To the matter at hand, I do not wish to alarm you needlessly, but we have received information concerning your safety. It is not confirmed, but —"

"Someone wishes me dead?" blurted Benny.

"Possibly. All I can say is your name was passed on to us recently as a potential target. There is nothing concrete and it may simply be talk. I see no reason for you to be alarmed at the moment."

"There must be something, or you wouldn't be following me," replied Wong, sounding anxious. "Your information, did it come from China?"

Jack hid his smile and decided to play along. "So you already know that the threat originates from there?"

Wong's sigh was audible. "No, but I have enemies there who are jealous of my success."

"Or perhaps upset with you over past, uh, business dealings," suggested Jack.

"Possibly," admitted Wong. "So why follow me if there is no reason for alarm?"

"It has been my experience that when dealing at, uh, this corporate level, that such an attack may originate from someone you trust. I was hoping to identify who you associate with and perhaps see if I can find a link to the person we know who might be doing the hit."

"I see," replied Wong in a monotone voice that did not indicate if he believed Jack or not.

"Perhaps I should have simply approached you, but was hesitant that you would supply me with such a list. Are you willing to do so?"

"I'll give it some thought," replied Wong. "Perhaps if you were to tell me the name of the person you know, it would simplify the matter."

"So you could murder him? Sorry, Benny. No way."

"I see," replied Wong, with a tinge of anger. "Of course your fears that I would do such a thing are totally unfounded. I am a legitimate businessman and would never stoop to such criminal behaviour." He paused and when Jack remained silent, he continued. "I admit it is possible I may have some associates acquainted with the kind of people you are talking about. I will conduct my own inquiries before deciding whether or not to use your services."

"That is your own prerogative," replied Jack. "The only thing is, inquiries you make could alert them to the fact that we know about it and jeopardize our source of information. They may seek out another hit-man whom we don't know."

"I see," replied Wong, his tone of voice indicating he believed Jack. "Let me think about it for a few days. As you can see from your own experience, my men are skilled at spotting anyone who is watching or following me."

"That they are," admitted Jack, with a glance at Zhang. "Which brings me back to who can you really trust? Who, persuaded by a larger salary, may decide to switch sides?"

"I trust my men. I do, however, thank you for your concern. I will ensure that extra precautions are extended to other people, such as parcel delivery ... or perhaps even policemen ... such as yourself ... to ensure my safety."

"Policemen such as myself?" reiterated Jack.

"You questioned the loyalty of the people who work for me. I can assure you they are well paid. Hardly the same can be said for people in your profession. Who knows what such underpaid people would do for an extra dollar or two."

This was not where Jack had wanted the conversation to go as he envisioned some poor postal worker being manhandled by Zhang or his fellow thugs. "I can assure you there is no immediate danger," he replied. "I will be in a position to know if there is and would warn you immediately should that be necessary."

"Of course you would. Isn't it obvious I have lots of faith in the police?" said Wong, contemptuously. "Do you plan on watching me all night?"

"At the moment, I don't know where you are," replied Jack.

"My wife and I are going to a restaurant for dinner and then home. If you care to watch us, I will talk to the maître d' and arrange a nearby table."

"That won't be necessary," replied Jack, feeling irritated at the game being played. "Perhaps some other time."

Chapter Twenty-Two

Mia smiled as she brought Wolfenden another beer. His eyes lingered on her cleavage as she leaned over to refill his glass. She was glad she had chosen not to wear a brassiere under the blue satin blouse she was wearing. When she sat on the sofa beside him, she adjusted her short white skirt as she crossed her long legs. A move that brought another furtive glance from Wolfenden.

"Thanks," he replied, picking up his glass. "As a gentlemen, I should have brought you a drink."

Mia shook her head and lowered her voice. "As you can probably tell by the smell from the back of the house, that is where the people go who want a taste of something a little stronger than alcohol. I didn't think it would be prudent for you to get too close, given your position."

"Ah, good old B.C bud," replied Wolfenden. "I do appreciate you looking after me in that regard."

He grinned and added, "Not that I have ever really inhaled."

"Ah, yes, the popular quote of Bill Clinton," snickered Mia. "The one of his I like is, 'Being president is like running a cemetery: you've got a lot of people under you and nobody's listening.'"

"I like that one too," replied Wolfenden. "Sounds like you know your politics."

"Is that how you find things in politics?" asked Mia. Before Wolfenden could reply she said, "Naw, I bet people really do listen to you."

"I'm not the P.M." chuckled Wolfenden.

"Yet," replied Mia, giving a friendly pat on his thigh while raising her glass in a toast.

So far, their conversation had been relatively mundane, with him talking about his family and his children playing hockey, while Mia portrayed herself as an ambitious student who decided that psychology was boring and had opted for a future career in politics.

She smiled as he clinked glasses with her and they each took a sip, then he put his glass down and asked, "How do you know the Rolstads?"

"I rent their suite downstairs," replied Mia. She saw the surprised look on Wolfenden's face, followed by a glance toward Max who was talking with a cluster of people on the far side of the room. "Oh, don't get it wrong," continued Mia. "They don't need the money."

"Oh, I, uh, wasn't thinking that," lied Wolfenden.

"My mom is a freelance journalist and last year interviewed Max in his role as a political spin doctor," explained Mia.

"Ouch! I wouldn't want the things we tell Max's company to ever go to the media," said Wolfenden, looking concerned.

"Oh, God, no." Mia smiled. "His company is locked up tighter than the Canadian Mint for things like that. It was more of a personal interview relating to how people climb the corporate ladder to success. I don't think what Max actually does had much to do with it."

"I see."

"Anyway, Max mentioned how much he was flying back and forth to Ottawa and Mom noted how lonely it must be for Julia staying in this big house all by herself. She told Max about me and said I was looking for a place closer to the university. One thing led to another and here I am. They barely charge me any rent. I'm more for companionship for Julia than anything."

"That's nice it all worked out. Your mom's a journalist, so what does your dad do?"

"My dad died in a car accident when I was three."

"I'm sorry."

"Thanks. I was an only child, but it was tough on my mom, having to make ends meet. Once I was older, she went to university and took journalism."

"I deal with journalists quite a bit. Is she friendly to any particular political party?" asked Wolenden, with a mischievous grin. "Maybe I could get her to do a favourable piece on me."

"Well, her profession demands that she not show any bias, but I could talk to her," said Mia, seriously. "She has told me that she likes your party, but she would never admit it openly to anyone else."

"How was her piece on Max? He never mentioned it to me."

"I'm afraid it never made it to print. Perhaps someday down the road it will."

"Oh, that's too bad." Wolfenden glanced at his watch as he stifled a yawn.

Mia knew there wasn't much time. She had already plotted her strategy and was counting on Wolfenden's choice of drinking beer to assist her in that regard. "Do you enjoy living in Ottawa?" she asked. "I plan to look for a job there next year when I graduate."

"It's a beautiful city," he replied. "I love it there."

"I'm definitely interested," replied Mia. "Maybe you could give me your number and email address as a contact when I get there?"

"Well ... it might be better if I give you a number for our Human Resources, although Max could help you out in that regard when the time is right." He drained the last of his beer and said, "I'm sorry, but I need to leave. I have an early start tomorrow."

"So soon? I feel like I'm just getting to know you," pouted Mia, while reaching out and giving his hand a squeeze.

"Believe me, I would like to stay, but I have to be at the Boeing plant near Seattle in the morning. I have an entourage to meet at the airport at five o'clock in the morning. There'll be a gaggle of mucky-muck military types all standing around in outdated sports jackets waiting for me. They'll throw a tantrum if I'm late."

"Boeing? You're not the defence minister. Do you plan on buying a private fighter jet for yourself?" teased Mia.

"No, I think I'll hang on to my BMW," chuckled Wolfenden. "I'm the point man assigned to check on the progress of something."

"Something?"

"I can't say what I am really going to see. Secrets you know," he said, grinning and putting his finger to his lips.

"Gotcha," replied Mia. "Still, it's early. Where are you staying?"

"The Fairmont at the airport."

Mia glanced at her own watch. She knew she would be meeting Mr. Frank tonight. He in turn would have to reach out to his contact. Photos would be taken at the airport. Players would need to be identified. She gazed at Wolfenden briefly. *Even if nothing else happens tonight, Mr. Frank and our dear benefactor should be pleased ...*

"I should really go," said Wolfenden, leaning forward on the sofa to get up. "I need to say goodbye to Max and Julia, but first, can you point me in the direction of the bathroom?"

"Yes," replied Mia, while gesturing for Wolfenden to lean closer, "but I don't suggest you use it. I was in earlier and someone had left a couple of lines of coke on the top of the toilet tank cover."

"That's all I need is to be linked to that stuff," replied Wolfenden, giving a frown toward Max on the opposite side of the room.

"I'm certain the Rolstads don't know about it yet," replied Mia. "No worries. Follow me and I'll let you use mine."

Moments later, Wolfenden followed Mia downstairs, past her bedroom door and to her bathroom.

"Thanks," replied Wolfenden, but before he could shut the door, Mia walked in with him and he looked at her questionably.

"Two rules in my bathroom," smiled Mia. "The important one is you sit! I don't want to walk in here in my bare feet in the morning on a sticky floor."

"I think I can do that," grinned Wolfenden. "What's the second rule?"

Mia picked up a pen lying on top of a newspaper crossword puzzle on the vanity counter. "Complete one of the words that I haven't got yet," she said, clicking the pen before putting it down.

"I promise I'll try," he replied with a chuckle.

"Promises, promises. Typical politician," teased Mia as she walked out and closed the door behind her.

Wolfenden had no idea that the pen not only worked, but concealed a wireless video recorder capable of recording up to seventeen hours. Far more time than Mia needed.

Mia listened at the door as she slipped off her panties and tossed them in her bedroom, before undoing another button on her blouse. Wolfenden had not bothered to lock the door, but even if he had, the manufactured pinhole on the outside doorknob would have allowed easy access.

"I'm not done yet!" said Wolfenden, clamping his knees together when Mia re-entered the bathroom.

Mia closed the door behind her and stared at the floor. "Don't move!" she said. "Don't move your feet!"

"What? What —"

"One of my contacts fell out," she said, wiping her eye for effect. "It's in here somewhere," she added, bending over and placing one hand on the top of Wolfenden's bare thigh while pretending to look on the floor.

"But I'm not done," stuttered Wolfenden. "Maybe … let me pull my pants —"

"Oh, God, I wonder if it fell down the front of my blouse," said Mia. "Can you see it?" she asked, leaning over his face while placing one hand behind his head, urging him to take a closer look.

"I, uh, I…" Wolfenden stopped talking when one of Mia's breasts fell from her blouse.

"Maybe it went straight through," said Mia softly. "I'll see if I can feel it down here," she whispered, reaching down and first cupping, then gently squeezing his scrotum while staring at his face.

"Oh, Jesus," muttered Wolfenden, leaning back against the toilet seat and briefly closing his eyes while arching his pelvis upward and spreading his thighs as his erection grew.

Mia appeared to use the vanity for support as she got down on her knees, but in doing so, she moved the pen to catch the day's newspaper headline before sliding it farther back on the vanity for a fuller image.

Wolfenden subconsciously held his breath, then breathed in shallow gasps as he felt the excruciating slow progress of her tongue lick and probe up his shaft, to be followed by her mouthing and slowly twirling her tongue around the head of his penis. She repeated the process several times, all the while using her other hand to cup and gently squeeze his scrotum while urging him on.

He was on the verge of climax when she stood and used her hand to guide his penis inside her as she slowly lowered herself onto him.

"Protection," he gasped.

"I haven't made love in over a year," whispered Mia. "Plus I've got a morning-after pill."

His reply was only a grunt as he braced his feet and thrust upwards.

"No, stay still," she whispered. "I'll do the work."

Wolfenden soon relented to the pleasure of allowing her to control the movements as she slowly eased her body up and down while she undid the remaining buttons on her blouse.

He eagerly fondled her breasts and kissed her nipples before she pressed the side of his head tight to her chest, facing the counter. Eventually he could contain himself no longer and wrapped his arms around her as his body jerked and shuddered, lifting her feet entirely off the floor as they each released primal moans.

Chapter Twenty-Three

It was after Wolfenden pulled up his pants and flushed the toilet that he heard Mia sob and saw her put her hand over her face from where she stood in front of the vanity mirror buttoning up her blouse.

"What is it? What's wrong?" he asked, putting an arm around her so she faced him.

"I, I can't believe this happened," she replied. "Cocaine and marijuana upstairs … the two of us coming down here and having sex. I really like you … but, my God, I can't believe I let it happen. You must look at me like I'm a prostitute or something."

"No, not at all," replied Wolfenden. "I have to say, this was totally —"

"I don't know how we got to this point," mumbled Mia. "I feel so strange … like I want to keep rubbing myself," she said, placing a hand between her legs. "It feels all tingly."

Wolfenden gave a half grin and said, "Well I'd be

glad to help you with —"

"I think someone must have put ecstasy in my drink."

"Ecstasy!"

"I had it once before. Years ago. I felt the same way then as I do now. Except then, nothing happened."

"You think someone would do that?" said Wolfenden in surprise.

"I don't know. When I left my drink with you to go to the kitchen, did you see anyone fiddle with it?"

"No ... and I certainly didn't or wouldn't!"

"Oh, my God," replied Mia, looking concerned. "Don't think for a moment that I thought you would. You're a man I really look up to. I always thought you were handsome, too, but ... now I feel so ashamed. I beg you, please never tell anyone about it."

Wolfenden hugged her and said, "I assure you, it will be our little secret."

"Oh ... and Max," she cried.

"What about him?"

"He's the guy ... where he works ... that's who you guys tell all your personal secrets to, so they're prepared in advance for damage control in case some scandal erupts. Max thinks of me like a daughter, please, don't ever —"

"Like a daughter?" said Wolfenden, sounding concerned.

"Yes. It would be devastating if anyone found out that —"

"Believe me, nobody but us two will ever know," said Wolfenden, firmly.

"Thank you," replied Mia, holding him tight before kissing him on the cheek. When she pulled back she looked at him and said, "I bet you never want to see me again."

"No! Are you kidding? I'm flattered. I'll give you my email and private number at work. I'll be flying out west again soon. Maybe we could go for dinner?"

Mia paused to wipe a tear from her eye. "I'd really like that," she said quietly, "although in your position ... I would never want to jeopardize that ... we would have to be discreet."

"Uh," Wolfenden was about to suggest meeting at his hotel when he returned, but hesitated.

"I'd be willing to meet you anywhere," replied Mia, "as long as it is not in a bathroom! I still feel disgusted over what we did here."

Wolfenden grinned. "It's a deal ... no bathrooms," he said, before kissing her passionately on her lips.

It was eleven-thirty at night when Mia crossed the Lion's Gate Bridge. A few minutes later she pulled into the north end of Klahanie Park. She felt mixed emotions. On one hand she was excited. It was the first time she had ever used her computer to request a high-priority meeting. Up until now, the cryptographic messages she had sent were either mundane or simply training exercises. This time it was the real thing.

Something else tonight was also the real thing ... this is the first time I have ever seduced someone for the benefactor. She stared at herself in the rear-view mirror. *I feel so dirty and disgusted. Is it what I did, or who I did? An overweight, middle-aged man whose inflated ego makes him think I am actually attracted to him.* She shook her head in disbelief. *God, he even believed it when I faked my orgasm. What a chump …*

Normally Mia would not have brought her car so close to the meeting spot, but there was no other traffic in the park this time of night and she knew she was not being followed.

She had barely stepped out of her car when a low whistle from Mr. Frank directed her to a wooded area. She glanced around and saw that her car was the only one present. As usual, Mr. Frank had opted to park farther away and walk the final distance to ensure he was not being followed.

Mia handed Mr. Frank the covert pen and quickly relayed the events of the evening.

"Absolutely fantastic," replied Mr. Frank, beaming with delight. "Your conversation about the drugs following … uh, what happened, will clearly implicate him in what was going on. Few people will believe he didn't partake. He may even be suspected of slipping you the ecstasy. Well done!"

Mia nodded in response. Her stomach was acting up and she wondered if it was from the mouthwash she had used.

"And he let it slip that he is heading off to the Boeing plant in the morning," said Mr. Frank, shaking his head in amazement. "His naïveté is astounding."

"Him and some military types who will be wearing civilian clothes," added Mia, sounding distracted.

"What's wrong? You should be pleased with the work you accomplished tonight."

Mia looked at him and shook her head. "I feel dirty ... like a whore. Doing that on a toilet."

"We are in a war," replied Mr. Frank. "Sometimes you need to sacrifice your emotions."

"A war?"

"Not one that has been officially declared ... although that could easily change," he added. "Still, make no mistake. We are in a war to defend ourselves against a corrupt regime that is trying to take over our country and destroy our culture. We need to level the playing field to maintain status quo. Much like the Russians and the Americans, each one afraid to attack the other because of their balance in technological and military might. Your work could conceivably save thousands of lives by preventing a military war. You have no reason to feel ashamed. In fact, it is the opposite. You have become a true heroine."

Mia was silent for a moment. "Guess I hadn't really thought of it that way. Until tonight, I looked at it like an adventure or a game."

"This is no game," said Mr. Frank, coldly.

"Tonight, I realize that," she replied, then gave a nod toward the covert pen in his jacket pocket. "What do you think the benefactor will do with it?"

"I doubt anything at the moment. You are much too valuable to risk by disclosing your involvement at the present time."

"Because if an attempt is made to blackmail him and he goes to the police ... my cover would be blown," said Mia.

"Exactly. Still, there are many possibilities. Perhaps tidbits will be released to the media at a critical time indicating he is using drugs. It could sway an entire election."

Mia nodded and said, "I thought as much, which is why I worded the drug conversation with him as I did."

"Journalists protect their sources in Canada," said Frank. "All they need is to hear the conversation and confirm it is Wolfenden's voice to support the authenticity of the allegation. Then they would be on him like crocodiles attacking a calf in the river. Once that starts, I am sure they would dig up other, uh, dalliances he has had as well."

"Wolfenden would not know who was behind it," replied Mia, feeling relieved that she would remain anonymous in the matter.

"It may depend on his future success in government," continued Mr. Frank. "Psychological analysis may tell us if such a man, ambitious for power and having a loving wife and family ... would be willing to throw it all away. He may be susceptible to blackmail, but that is a decision for the benefactor. Much of it depends upon your future success with him as well."

"Mine?"

"Your continued relationship with him. Future access to his hotel rooms. Does he travel with a laptop? If the laptop could not be corrupted, could a hidden camera pick up his password? What influence might you have on him to benefit us on a commercial level? If you relocate to work for some firm in China for a year, would he want to come and see you and use investment in Chinese industry as his excuse? These are things the benefactor needs to weigh. It is evident he has access to technological and military secrets ... so in my mind, that would take priority."

"It is difficult to believe that such an individual can be so stupid," said Mia. "The only thing larger than his stupidity is his ego."

"In my experience, given time, he may come to realize that he is being used without a need for any overt action on our part. By then he may simply decide not to rock the boat and give us what we want rather than risk the penalty he would receive if his actions became known." Mr. Frank shrugged and added, "Who knows, he may fall in love with you."

"And love is blind," said Mia. "Or in his case, it could be wilfully so."

"Exactly. Hopefully he will follow through with his promise to meet you again."

Mia held up her hand for Mr. Frank to stop talking as she received a text message on her BlackBerry. She smiled. "It's a message from Wolfenden. He is on his way back to the hotel and is asking how my mother is, as well as saying he is looking forward to seeing me again soon."

"Perfect," chuckled Mr. Frank. He paused, then asked, "Your mother?"

"I wanted to meet with you immediately, so when we rejoined the party I said I had received a call from my mother, telling me she had fallen and hurt herself. I said she didn't think she needed to go to Emergency, but that I was going over to check on her."

"And you alerted your mother in case someone calls her?"

"I did."

"Good. Jia-li is one of the best agents we have. She will be so proud of you."

"Thanks. I'm heading over there to see her now." Mia looked at her watch, then hesitated, looking at Mr. Frank.

"What is it? There is something more?" he asked.

"The Rolstads. They will still be up. I have laid the groundwork that tonight could be the night ... but...?"

"No, you are right. Wolfenden is a far more valuable target. Do not do anything that would jeopardize that. Tell the Rolstads that you have changed your mind about any, uh, hands-on therapy."

Mia nodded and Mr. Frank watched as she turned and walked toward her car. He allowed his eyes to wander up the back of her legs and linger at her hips. He thought of her performance tonight and briefly felt jealous of Wolfenden. *I must put such thoughts out of my mind. Never again will I make that mistake ...*

He thought of the years spent on her development. Years of waiting for Mia to blossom had come to fruition. She was extremely gifted on an intellectual level, as well as being beautiful. Coupled with a mother who had coached her since childhood, she was a rare and valuable asset. *Perhaps the most valued asset in all of North America ... and it is I who the benefactor has entrusted to look after her.*

He smiled. It was the proudest moment of his life. He reflected that in China, the narcissus plant was a symbol representing the blossoming of hidden talents. *The presence of a narcissus in one's life is said to enhance the effort you put into your work and bring added reward. It can bring luck and promote one's career to a higher level.*

Mia, you are my narcissus ...

Chapter Twenty-Four

It was one-thirty in the morning when Jia-li Parker paused from strolling down the sidewalk and turned and hugged her daughter. "What you did is a great thing," she whispered.

"Thanks, Mom." Mia squeezed her mother tight, savouring the security of her mother's love for a moment before reluctantly breaking free.

"How old do you think Wolfenden is?" asked Jia-li as they turned to head back to her apartment building.

"I think he is about five years younger than you," replied Mia.

"So about forty-eight then," sighed Jia-li.

"I'm sorry, Mom. I've done the math. It has been twenty-five years since Dad was run over. Wolfenden would have only been about twenty-three then."

Jia-li nodded. "And the handler I had then indicated it was an older person."

"Indicated?" asked Mia. "Can you remember his exact words? Could it have been someone younger? Maybe a son of a politician or —"

"No." Jia-li frowned. "I was in too much shock and anger to remember his exact words, but basically he said that the police knew who did it, but wouldn't lay charges because whoever did it was high up in politics. Wolfenden would have been too young to be high up. He was likely still in university back then."

"I hate them all," said Mia, bitterly. "The police, the politicians ... they are all corrupt. Canadians are stupid and selfish."

"You are Canadian," chided Jia-li, giving Mia a friendly dig with her elbow.

"Where I was born does not imprison my heart ... and in my heart, I am Chinese."

Jia-li smiled and patted her on the back.

After walking in silence for a few minutes, Mia said, "Perhaps I should return to the Rolstads'. I feel so dirty having been with that man. I need to have a long shower. I don't know if I'll ever be able to use a toilet again without thinking about what I had to do. The whole experience makes me wonder if I could ever force myself to be with him again."

"You must learn to block it out," advised Jia-li. "Being with him is simply a bodily function like going to the toilet. It means nothing ... except that he is stupid."

"Blocking it out is easier said than done," replied Mia, then wrinkled her nose to show her disgust.

"You have a great life. The benefactor has provided you with an education. Me, too, for that matter.

Be thankful we didn't end up working in one of Benny Wong's brothels. Imagine what that would be like."

"Benny Wong? *The* Benny Wong? What does he have to do with anything?"

"What does he have to do with anything?" Jia-li shook her head in admonishment. "Come on, Mia, think about it. In China most of the brothels, massage parlours, and even the karaoke bars are owned by triads who co-operate with the benefactor. Those places, including most of the hotels that any Westerners use, are bugged and have hidden cameras."

"Yes, of course. I knew that, but I didn't realize it was happening outside of China."

Jia-li shrugged. "I know that the benefactor sometimes uses Benny Wong to bring people in and out of Canada. It is logical they would use his brothels to gather intelligence, too, although I have no personal knowledge of that."

"I hadn't thought about it before, but I bet you're right," said Mia. "The CIA once asked the Mafia to kill Castro so it would appear they weren't involved. Maybe the benefactor uses Benny Wong as a front man to protect themselves also."

"It would be logical," Jia-li said. "And as far as the massage parlours in Canada go, it could even be more rewarding because people would not expect it. I would think only the exceptionally stupid or naive would avail themselves of sexual opportunities while in China."

"Sexpionage," sighed Mia. "I feel so dirty. How did you do it ... or I guess how do you do it? You have told me that sometimes it is necessary, but you've never talked about actually doing it yourself or how you felt after."

"I admit I know how you feel," said Jia-li, momentarily biting her lip. *This secret I have carried for so long ... becomes heavier with every day. The guilt I feel ...* She eyed her daughter. *Will she understand? Perhaps ... and for her not to make the mistake I did ... it is time to tell her.*

"What is it, Mom?" asked Mia. "You look upset?"

Jia-li sighed and said, "Not upset ... perhaps a little worried."

"Worried?"

"You are lucky that Wolfenden is an older man ... or at least to you he is."

"How does that make me lucky?"

Jia-li stopped and turned to face Mia. Her voice was solemn. "I was twenty-one when I became involved in my first honey-pot operation. For me, it was a disaster."

"You felt shame?"

"Initially ... but the real disaster was when it turned out that he was the man I fell in love with."

It took Mia a moment to understand what her mother was really telling her. "My God, no, Mom," she mumbled. "That's how old you were when you met Dad." Mia's eyes were pleading as she looked at her mom, hoping she was wrong.

"Yes, it was your father."

Mia's mouth flopped open a moment. "He was a target? You are saying he was a stupid man who —"

"No, he wasn't stupid," said Jia-li, as her eyes brimmed with tears. "At first I thought he was. He was involved in high-tech computer software. He was only five years older than I was. He was the first man I ever slept with."

"You're talking about my Dad," cried Mia. "Someone you taught me to look up to! How could you have done that?"

"I fell in love with him," replied Jia-li. "It was a terrible mistake. I did not let the benefactor know. When your dad was transferred back to his head office in Vancouver, the benefactor was pleased that I was willing to accept his proposal for marriage and go with him. The benefactor believed it was dedication and not love that made me willing to marry him."

"So you were spying on the man you were married to! How could you do that?" Mia asked, grabbing her mother by both arms and shaking her.

"I didn't once we were married," cried Jia-li, pulling away. "I was too ashamed. I told my handler that he wasn't bringing anything of importance home. That pillow talk did not work."

"You didn't corrupt his computers?"

"Back then our spyware wasn't as sophisticated as it is now. What we had then was easily detected or prohibited through the company's firewalls. In the end, I didn't supply any information of value. I was hoping that the benefactor would forget about me."

"But you are active! I know you are. You always make sure you look beautiful … and you're still dating that electrical engineer. I know you're not retired."

"Yes, I am still working," replied Jia-li firmly, "but after tonight, we must never talk of who I am dating again."

Mia nodded silently in compliance while her stomach churned and contracted into a cramp, as if trying to digest what she had been told.

"I was inactive for a while," continued Jia-li, "but when your dad was killed I was stuck with bills to pay. There was a little insurance money, but it didn't last. Then the benefactor stepped in to help. After I got over my initial grief, I was angry. I loved your dad very much. Working for the benefactor eased my anger." She wiped her eyes with her fingertips and added, "Please, don't you be angry with me."

"Why didn't you tell me sooner?" asked Mia.

"We both work intelligence," replied Jia-li. "You shouldn't have to ask that question. I have taught you better than that."

"Yes, everything is on a need-to-know basis," said Mia bitterly. "But you're my mother. You should have told me," she said, placing her hands on her hips as she faced Jia-li.

"Which is why I am telling you," replied Jia-li. "I want to protect you from the shame I felt. After your dad died, I was lonely. In time I ended up having an affair with my case officer."

Bet he didn't try to drug you first, thought Mia.

"I knew he was only using me, but the loneliness I felt was worse. In time, he encouraged me to go back to work for the benefactor. I obliged ... perhaps out of fear that without him, I would have no one in my life."

"You had me," said Mia.

Jia-li smiled. "Yes, I had you and I am grateful for that. I also had financial responsibilities. I went back to work and felt pride in my accomplishments. Since that time there have been six men that I've had to give myself to, including this electrical engineer. It becomes like a game ... but it is no game if you're in love with someone ... like I was with your dad."

Mia stared down at her feet. Her brain felt numb at what she had been told and she folded her arms across her chest to protect herself from the cool night air.

Jia-li used her index finger to lift Mia's head so they could look eye to eye. "Someday you will fall in love and I pray it is not with a person of interest. When you do meet someone you have feelings for, you must deny any further requests from the benefactor."

"So I can quit?" asked Mia, gesturing with her hands in the air. "You told me before that we have an enormous debt to pay ... plus you have hinted that to refuse would mean our relatives who are still in China might have problems. My grandma or —"

Jia-li frowned. "Yes, yes, that is true, but only if you behave unpatriotically by accepting favours and not giving anything in return. The benefactor is fair. Yes, we have been provided with a lot of money over the years, but there will be an end to what we owe."

"Are you sure?" asked Mia.

"Of course, I'm sure. My previous case officer retired in Vancouver. I still visit him once a year or so. His wife died last year, but he is content."

"You still have, uh, a relationship with him?"

"Nothing romantic anymore, if that's what you mean. The point is, he has told me he is happily retired."

"Would he be able to tell you if he wasn't retired?" countered Mia.

Jia-li smiled. "I have taught you well ... that is a good point. However, my past relationship with him makes me believe he is telling the truth."

"But no doubt he would remain on some list, if something urgent arose where he was needed."

"I am sure we all would be," replied Jia-li. "I know the benefactor has tried to gather information from many of our countrymen who are living here. Unfortunately, most have been seduced by the propaganda and promises of wealth Canada offers and refuse to co-operate."

"Same goes for most Canadians, even those who have lived here for generations," said Mia. "Not intentionally bad, but blinded by the propaganda of a corrupt system with no idea of how a correct society should function."

"Yes, but as far as quitting goes, in time of desperate need, of course we would be called upon, but I see that as being less likely. I think the benefactor is moving more toward economic control verses military intervention."

"That should be easy in these tough economic times," noted Mia. "The government is so corrupt that one only needs to dangle a carrot in front of their noses for them to co-operate. It's all about the money."

"So work hard for the next ten years or so. Be thankful and respectful of how much the benefactor has helped us. Until then, put your emotions on hold."

"I don't see myself falling in love for a long time," said Mia. "Thinking about what I did tonight … well, if there was someone I loved, I would respect him too much to want to be with him."

"You sound like a spoiled child who is pouting. I should be angry with you … but I am not," said Jia-li, sympathetically squeezing her arm. "This is your first honey-pot operation. It will take time for you to adjust. You need to be strong. Believe in yourself and respect what you are doing." She paused to stare into Mia's eyes, then hugged her. "I am so proud of you and I love you so much."

Mia hugged her back. "Thanks, Mom. I'm glad we talked. I feel better."

"Good … and in the future, we should not share stories about our assignments."

"Yeah, right. When could I ever keep anything from you? You've always been able to tell when I was keeping something from you. Even a tiny lie … I could always tell how you looked at me that you knew."

"Perhaps, but you have entered a whole new arena. It is not wise to talk to anyone who does not absolutely need to know … and even then, they should be told only what they absolutely need to know to fulfil the task."

"That you have told me many times before, but you're my mother. It is different."

"Different perhaps, but not wise. Even out here on the street … every time you talk you are taking a risk. Your relationship with Wolfenden could bring unwanted attention. You will need to be vigilant and strong. Continue to make me proud."

"I will, Mom," replied Mia with determination. "I will."

Chapter Twenty-Five

It was ten o'clock Monday morning when Jack and Laura met with Roger Morris and Connie Crane in the I-HIT office and went over their failed attempt to follow Benny Wong. As Jack and Laura talked, they viewed past surveillance photographs that Roger had copied to his laptop in the hope of identifying the two men who used newspapers to hide the guns they had pointed at Jack and Laura in the alley.

"You two are like chameleons when it comes to fitting in," said Connie. "How did they spot you so quickly?"

"I suspect the bodyguards had a secondary vehicle checking to see if anyone was following," replied Jack. "By the time we arrived in Chinatown, it was probably obvious."

"You think he swallowed your story as to why you were following him?" asked Roger.

"I think so," replied Jack. "He must be worried about some potential threat on his life to have the security he does."

"Hopefully he doesn't know we've connected him to Donahue's murder," said Roger.

"He sounded uptight when I told him I had received information that someone was considering having him killed," said Jack.

"I think that would catch most people's attention," replied Connie, looking bemused. "However, Wong sounds like he would be one tough nut to crack."

"I agree with you there," said Jack. He pointed to a photograph on the computer and said, "Bingo. That's the two of them together." He looked at Laura, who nodded.

Roger leaned over to look. "I know them. They're the Dongfang brothers. The one with the ponytail is Dai and his brother's name is Rong. They both have records for drug-trafficking and extortion."

"Nice guys," commented Jack. "I'll make a point of meeting them again sometime."

"So where do we go from here?" asked Connie.

"It's your case," replied Jack. "Any suggestions?"

"Christ, don't I wish I had some," grumbled Connie. "We think the godfather of the Chinese Mafia is responsible for trying to have a witness killed and the goofs sent to do the job killed the wrong person. That's if our theory is right. Maybe we're totally off base about —"

"I think the theory is sound," interjected Roger. "Jack's report arrives in our office on a Friday afternoon. The following Wednesday, Wong meets unexpectedly with the top Viet who has a meeting the next night with all his top people except for Bien Duc VC-2, who was named in Jack's report. By the next week, Bien Duc, along with two others named in the report, are murdered." Roger glanced at Jack. "Or are believed to have been murdered."

"I went through our liaison officer in Hong Kong and started an investigation there," said Connie. "Bien Duc and Tom Nguyen cleared customs in Hong Kong and caught a taxi. Security cameras identified the taxi they took. The police interviewed the driver who said he remembered them because they wanted to be dropped off with their luggage at a busy street corner instead of a hotel. They told the driver that a friend would be meeting them. From there, the trail went cold."

Yup, consequences, thought Laura. *You can bet their bodies are cold, too …*

"Anyway," added Connie, "getting back to whether or not I have any suggestions on how to proceed … I don't. I know the murders of Betty Donahue and Anh Dang are my responsibility, but what can I do?" She looked at Jack and Laura and said, "We're dealing with organized crime, that's your speciality. Any ideas?"

"At the moment, I think we should focus on Mia Parker," said Jack. "What is her connection to Wong? If Parker did arrange the murder so she wouldn't get a criminal record, what power or influence does she have on Wong to get him to do it? Or is she of some value to Wong that he thought it was necessary?"

"And you're only talking about Betty Donahue's murder," said Connie. "There have been three more since hers ... so far," she added, staring at Jack for a response, but he simply nodded.

"To my knowledge, she has never had any connection with Wong," said Roger.

"There has to be something," replied Jack. "What if we scared her a bit to see who she would run to?"

Connie's face hardened. "What are you going to do? Put a bullet through her window at night? There's no way I'll let you —"

"Not what I had in mind." Jack chuckled, putting up his hand for Connie to be quiet. "How safe is Betty Donahue's sister?"

"Nancy Brighton?" replied Connie, shaking her head. "Safe enough for someone who refuses any thought of entering the Witness Protection Program. She's still staying with friends in Chilliwack. I've been picking up her mail once a week and running it out to her. She's safe, but not in good shape emotionally. On one hand she wishes she had kept her mouth shut and not told the police about the drugs, but on the other hand ... well she used to be a Crown prosecutor back in the seventies ... she has a strong sense of justice."

"Justice?" said Jack. "Is that how it was back then? Talk about the good old days."

"Yes, I imagine things have changed since then," replied Laura.

"They call it progress," said Jack. "Rehabilitation programs verses punishment. Treat criminals like they are wayward toddlers instead of adults who should be responsible for their actions."

"Some people like the program," said Laura.

"Really? Who?" asked Connie, although her mind was still thinking about what Jack had said. *A lot of the criminals you worked on were murdered. Is that your idea of punishment?*

"The criminals," replied Laura. "They must. They keep getting arrested over and over again."

Connie stared blankly at Laura for a moment, then decided it was time to get back to the case at hand. "Nancy isn't happy about hiding out," she said, abruptly. "She said she has faced down enough criminals in her life to be scared off by some punks. She is becoming more frustrated and angry over the whole situation."

"Can't say as I blame her," replied Jack, "but I do have an idea," he added, leaning back in his chair and clasping his hands behind his head. "The bad guys don't really know they killed the wrong person."

"Not yet," replied Connie, "but they soon will. We have to make full disclosure of our evidence to defence, which should be soon."

"Where does Mia Parker stand with her possession charge?" asked Jack.

"She entered a not guilty plea. It has been set over until next week to pick a trial date."

"Which she believes will never go ahead because she thinks our witness is dead," noted Jack. "How about we let her know the witness is still alive and see if she panics and goes to someone? It isn't the type of thing she would want to discuss over a phone or e-mail. If we have a good surveillance on her, she might lead us to Wong or give us someone else that ties in."

Connie reflected on it for a moment, then nodded. "I like that idea, except with your report being leaked, the bad guys know we know the hit and run was no accident. Your report didn't suggest a motive for the murder. Will it tip our hand to go to Parker and tell her the witness is still alive?"

Jack shook his head. "Wong is no dummy. I'm sure he will expect the police to consider the possibility that the murder could have had something to do with her drug charge, but with the way he insulated himself, he may think we don't know that he is connected."

"So you wouldn't object to hauling Parker in for interrogation?" asked Connie.

"I don't mind, but if she doesn't talk, then what? It would be nice to know for sure how she is connected to Wong, or through whom."

"I agree with you there," replied Connie.

Roger leaned forward in his chair. "Wait a moment, you can't go to her and say, hey, by the way, you killed the wrong person. She'd become paranoid as hell. Good luck on finding who she goes to then."

"I wouldn't do it that way," replied Jack. "The amount of dope she was caught with was enough that she could have been charged with possession for the purpose of trafficking."

"I spoke to uniform about that," said Connie. "They called the narcs on it because they would need them to give expert opinion evidence in court to support a trafficking charge. The narcs were hesitant because they thought it was borderline."

"Or tied up with bigger cases and didn't want to take the time," suggested Laura.

Connie grimaced. "Yeah, that is always a possibility."

"How about sending uniform to her house and telling her the possession charge is being dropped, then tell her a new charge is being laid in regard to trafficking?" asked Jack.

"With a marked police car showing up, she may not be thinking we would be watching her," agreed Laura. "Her defences would be down."

Connie leaned back in her chair and smiled. "I like it."

"So do I," said Roger.

"I'll give Corporal Dave Rankin a call," said Connie. "He's the traffic guy who first clued in that the hit and run wasn't accidental."

Laura reflected on the run-in with Wong's bodyguards in the alley and said, "If she goes to Chinatown we'll need a lot of people for surveillance if we're not going to get burned."

Connie looked at Jack. "Nothing personal about your abilities over getting burned in the alley, but this is a homicide. We can't afford to get burned again. I think it justifies a request for Special 'O.' Maybe I could even get approval for satellite-tracking on her car."

Jack wasn't offended. Special "O" was the designation for an elite team of surveillance specialists whose training and responsibilities in the RCMP was specifically for surveillance duties only. Their function was to watch and report back to the unit who had requested them, although someone who was familiar with the investigation generally travelled with them as well. Special "O" was always in high demand, but a murder investigation would be a top priority. "I'm all for that," replied Jack. "If we're going to do it, let's do it right."

"Will you access her car for satellite-tracking when she is at university?" asked Laura.

Connie nodded. "Might take a few days to get everything set up. I'll aim for Friday. Maybe first thing in the morning before she leaves the house. I'll ride along with 'O,' but I would sure appreciate it if the three of you were around in case I need to consult with you."

"I've booked the rest of the week off," said Roger. "My in-laws are arriving tomorrow from back east. I'll be available on my cell, though." He winked and added, "I might even appreciate a call to get me out of the house if you know what I mean."

"Gotcha." Connie smiled. "I won't hesitate to call if we need you."

"Laura and I will be available," said Jack. "If you want, we can hop in with you as extra ride-alongs with Special 'O.'"

"I don't expect you'll have any problems," added Roger. "She's a university student without any criminal record, so I'm sure she'll be clueless when it comes to checking her rear-view. If you do get Special 'O' and a satellite tracker, it should be a piece of cake to follow her around."

Everyone nodded in agreement.
Everyone was wrong.

Chapter Twenty-Six

On Friday morning, Julia Rolstad was enjoying her breakfast when she heard a car in her driveway. She shot a puzzled glance at Mia and asked, "I wonder if Max forgot something?" Upon standing up and looking out the window she said, "It's a police car!"

Mia quickly stood and saw the RCMP patrol car come to a stop. She recognized Dave Rankin when he stepped from the car as the officer who had charged her. "Oh, I bet he's here for me," quipped Mia. "I witnessed an accident the other day and left my name."

"Oh, you hadn't mentioned it," replied Julia. She watched as Mia opened the front door and gave a friendly wave to the officer before approaching him and getting in his car.

"Have my charges been dropped?" asked Mia, bluntly, once the doors to the patrol car were closed.

"Why would you say that?" asked Rankin.

"Because it was bogus to start with. Wasn't my dope," replied Mia, haughtily. She then stared smugly at Rankin and added, "There, is that what I was supposed to say?"

"I'm not sure what you mean," replied Rankin, "but your charge of possession of drugs is being withdrawn."

"Good," said Mia, reaching for the door handle. "Hope you have a good holiday."

"A good holiday?" repeated Rankin. "I'm sorry, I don't ... anyway, hold on. The reason that charge is being withdrawn is because a new charge is being laid."

"A new charge?" replied Mia spinning around in her seat as her mouth gaped open. "What are you talking about?"

"The evidence was reviewed by Drug Section and they feel there is enough to have you charged with possession for the purpose of trafficking."

Mia's eyes flashed in anger. "Are you shitting me?"

"No, not at all. I have a summons for you that you may want to pass on to your lawyer."

"Oh, I see what you're doing," she snapped. "This is another shakedown. You really are a bunch of greedy pigs."

"I don't know what you're talking about," replied Rankin.

"Yeah, I bet you don't," replied Mia, sarcastically.

Rankin drove three blocks away from the Rolstad home before parking and getting in the back of an SUV with

Jack and Laura. Connie sat in the front seat and Dwight, the Special "O" team supervisor, was behind the wheel.

Rankin relayed in exact detail his encounter with Mia and concluded it by saying, "She was like Jekyll and Hyde. When she came out of the house she was all smiles and waved like we were friends. As soon as she was in the car she acted like she wanted to kill me."

Jack stared at Connie in surprise. "She doesn't know."

"Know what?" replied Connie.

"That anyone was murdered. She thinks someone was bought off."

"That's for sure," said Rankin. "She acted like she presumed everyone was corrupt."

"Not what you would expect the average Canadian to think," noted Jack. "This isn't Mexico."

"Okay, everyone," interrupted Dwight as he looked at an open laptop. "We've got movement. Her car is out and westbound on Belmont."

Jack listened as Dwight alerted the team.

"Time for me to split," said Rankin, getting out of the SUV. "I'll head back to the office and make notes on everything said."

As Connie said goodbye and thanked Rankin for his assistance, a female voice came over Dwight's police radio. "I have a visual. T-1 is alone in the car and southbound on Blanca Street approaching West Fourth Avenue."

"We've got a tracker, so don't heat her up," ordered Dwight.

"Copy that."

Minutes later, Mia parked at the University of British Columbia and Dwight thumbed the radio. "Cheryl, you still taking night classes at UBC?"

"Ten-four. You're gonna be working for me some day, Dwight."

Dwight smiled and said, "Get in there and do inside coverage. Take young William with you."

Connie sighed. "Guess she isn't in a hurry to run to anyone." She glanced back at Jack. "How long do you think we should sit on her?"

"I would give her at least thirty-six hours straight," replied Jack. "Whoever she meets might be busy or there could be a communication procedure she has to go through."

"*If* she is meeting someone," said Connie.

"I don't see her discussing it over the phone or on email. If she was that stupid, AOCTF would have had some record of her."

"Yeah, I guess," replied Connie, looking at her watch.

"Patience, Connie, patience." Jack smiled, before looking at Dwight and asking, "How about your teams? Can you do an all-nighter?"

"Not a problem," replied Dwight. "I'm on until three this afternoon, then the next team will take over. If you want thirty-six hours, we'll give it to you."

Jack nodded and everyone slouched back in their seats to make themselves comfortable. Minutes slowly ticked past into hours with an occasional report that Mia was taking classes, but did not appear to be meeting anyone other than casual acquaintances.

It was three o'clock in the afternoon and the new team from Special "O" was on the verge of switching over when it was reported that Mia was returning to her car.

Dwight thumbed the radio again and called the other supervisor. "T-1 is on the move. You guys in position?"

"Not quite," replied a man's voice. "You take her and we'll catch up."

It was soon evident that Mia was not returning home as she was followed into the heart of downtown Vancouver. Jack smiled to himself. Normally surveillance could be difficult in the downtown area, especially with a light rain affecting visibility and the start of rush hour traffic. Today was different. The two teams from Special "O" had united to work in unison with one another until such time as it could be established what Mia was doing or to identify who she met. That, coupled with satellite-tracking on her car, was more surveillance than Jack had ever had the luxury of having.

Dwight eyed the tracking equipment and reported, "Okay, T-1 is stopping on Dunsmuir, half a block west of the Burrard Street Skytrain station. Somebody get an eye."

"Copy that. I've got a visual," reported a male voice. "She's parking on the north side of Discovery Square. I'm out on foot."

Moments later, numerous Special "O" members were walking and reporting Mia's movements.

"She's walking toward the Skytrain," reported a female voice. "Wearing a magenta-coloured windbreaker over dark slacks and carrying a Louis Vuitton handbag. I think her shoes are —"

"Magenta?" asked Jack.

"Bluish-red," replied Laura and Connie in unison.

Dwight smiled and made eye contact in the rearview mirror with Jack and said, "Strange, if I want a physical description right down to her weight, how she walks, or her probable bra size, I ask my guys. If I want to know exactly what she is wearing, I ask the gals."

Jack grinned and sat back in the seat. He was not in a position to see Mia himself, but the sidewalks were packed with people and blending in for the surveillance people on foot was not a problem.

"Okay, looks like we're taking the Skytrain," reported a male voice.

"We've got lots of people," said Dwight. "Four of you go with her. The rest back to your wheels."

Minutes later another report changed the tactics. "Four of us waited until the last moment to get on, but she jumped back out as the doors were closing. We'll be out of it for a bit until we can turn around at the next stop."

"No problem," came another voice. "Have a good trip. Still plenty of us to handle her until you get back."

Jack quietly glanced at Laura. They each thought the same thing. *Mia may not be the naive university student she appears to be ...*

The surveillance teams continued to report her movement. After leaving the Skytrain station, Mia crossed the street.

"Okay, T-1 is entering the Cactus Club restaurant. Do you want inside coverage?"

"Wait two minutes," ordered Dwight, "then two of you go in."

Three minutes ticked by before the radio crackled again. "We're inside. No sign of her ... wait, she was in the washroom ... she's heading back out the front door. Somebody got the eye? She had a good look at us. We'll be cooked if we leave now."

"Copy, we see her coming out. Got a visual. Crossing the street back again."

Jack looked at Connie and said, "At least we know she's not out buying shoes. She's meeting someone important."

Minutes later it was reported that Mia had entered the Hyatt Regency Hotel. Dwight glanced back at Jack. "Good thing we have two teams."

"Okay, she's taking an elevator ... I can get in with her," came a hushed voice. Seconds later the voice was no longer hushed. "This lady knows her stuff. She asked me what floor I was on, so I said the top and she pushed the button. She got off on the second. I'm out of it. Somebody got her?"

"I'm heading up the stairwell ... damn it, met her coming down," came another hushed voice. "I'm out of it. Someone get in the lobby quick."

Several minutes ticked by before another team member reported, "Okay, picked her up again. She crossed the walkway from the Hyatt and is going down into the food court in Royal Centre. Christ, scratch that, she's doubling back and eyeballing everyone around. I'm out of it. Is someone around to take her?"

"Negative," came a chorus of voices.

Stress could be heard in various surveillance team members as they tried to cover off exits while other team members went inside the complex to look for her. Ten minutes passed without result as public areas and washrooms were checked.

"Damn it, we've lost her," complained Connie. "The Royal Centre is what, forty-storeys high counting the underground? The Hyatt's got over six hundred rooms. We're screwed."

Jack momentarily closed his eyes while massaging his forehead with the tips of his fingers. *Think … I need to think …*

Chapter Twenty-Seven

Mia heard a door open in the stairwell and peeked over the railing. She saw Mr. Frank glance up at her and nodded, but waited for him as he climbed the stairs, taking them two at time.

He beamed broadly when they met. "Last week you sent me your first top-priority meeting request. Now your first medium-urgency request. I take it dear Mr. Wolfenden has contacted you and will be returning to Vancouver?"

"It has nothing to do with him," replied Mia harshly. "They want more money!"

"Who? What are you talking about?"

"The police! Take a look," she said, showing him her summons. "I was given it this morning. The jerk who charged me showed up at the house and said my case has been reviewed and they're charging me with possession for the purpose of trafficking."

Mr. Frank's mouth partially dropped open as his brain tried to figure out this new development. He swallowed and replied, "I don't understand."

"Obviously the cops want more money," said Mia.

"There is something wrong," said Mr. Frank, nervously looking over the railing at the stair casing.

"Of course there is something wrong. He came right to the house."

"Do the Rolstads know?" His dark eyes stared intently at Mia's face.

"No. Only Julia was home. I covered it by saying I had witnessed an accident and that he came to take a statement."

"But you can't be charged," said Mr. Frank, sounding adamant. He looked over the railing again, both up and down. "Are you sure you weren't being followed? That this wasn't a ruse to see who you would meet?"

"I don't think I was followed," replied Mia. "I never saw anyone suspicious and took all the necessary precautions for a daytime meet."

"Good," muttered Mr. Frank.

"Why would you even think that?" persisted Mia. "Isn't it obvious they simply want more money?"

"Yes, yes, but this was totally unexpected."

"Unexpected? No shit!"

"It will be looked after," he hastened to say. "There is no reason for you to worry."

"There is if people find out I was charged. It's not only the record; I'd be discarded like a broken chopstick by Wolfenden and maybe the Rolstads, too. Max wouldn't want me in the company if word leaked out."

"As I said, it will be dealt with. Perhaps the problem is that it only has to appear that the charge is going ahead. These things take time. Your trial would be —"

"My trial!"

Mr. Frank smiled like he was placating a child and said, "It will not come to that. What I wanted to say is that when you appear and plead not guilty on this new charge, your trial wouldn't be scheduled to take place for months or perhaps a year or more. The matter will be dealt with long before then."

"It would be better if it was dealt with before I had to go back to the courthouse," replied Mia.

"Of course it would. I will look into the matter immediately and get back to you. Now go. You have done really well. The benefactor will be pleased with how you have progressed."

Mr. Frank stared at the top of Mia's head as she descended the stairs. *The police ... are they bluffing? Hoping, perhaps, to strike a plea bargain? If they don't have a witness, how could they even hope to succeed ... or do they have a witness?*

One other thing plagued his brain. Last weekend Wong met him and was nervous, saying he caught two plainclothes police officers following him and that they told him it was because someone might be trying to kill him. Wong wanted to know if he had heard of any such plan. He assured him he hadn't, but noted Wong had many enemies and it was possible. *Now this ... have the police connected the dots? Or is it a coincidence?* He shook his head. *First things first. The witness ... is she still alive? I need to find out ... and find out fast.*

* * *

In the Special "O" SUV, Dwight continued to listen to the negative results that came in over the radio in the search for Mia while directing his people to search other nearby locations.

Laura looked at Dwight and asked, "Do you think anyone on your team heated her up?"

Dwight spoke into the radio. "Anybody feel they could have been burned? Speak up if you do."

Silence indicated that none felt they had been detected.

"Mia Parker has been trained," replied Jack. "I've never worked on someone who was this good at counter-surveillance." He glanced at Laura and added, "We haven't trained our own informants this well."

Another ten minutes passed. "Sorry guys," sighed Dwight. "I'll put everyone in there on foot if you like, but they're pretty big places."

"Let's try looking elsewhere," said Jack, thoughtfully. "We might be too late, but it is worth a shot."

"Elsewhere?" asked Dwight.

"With the precautions she's taken, I think if she was heated up, she would have called it off and headed back to her car. She's had long enough to do that."

"Guess that is good news," replied Connie.

Jack nodded. "However, she's used the Skytrain, the restaurant, the Hyatt, and the Royal Centre to cleanse herself. All these places have people around and unless she slipped into a private room, she could never be too sure someone wasn't watching."

"So what are you suggesting?" asked Dwight.

"Laura and I deal with a lot of informants," explained Jack. He looked at Laura and said, "When we meet our informants, where do we usually meet them?"

"For a long meeting, maybe a hotel room."

"She already left the Hyatt. "Where do we meet our friends for a short meeting?"

Laura shrugged and said, "Parks, graveyards, parking garages ... maybe the back of a van."

Jack nodded and looked at Dwight and said, "There's your answer. Split everyone up and cover off any of those possibilities within the area. There aren't any cemeteries nearby, but there are parks and parkades. Same for any vans parked someplace, like an alley."

"There are only a couple of parks close by," said Dwight, "but hang on while I Google parkades." Seconds later he said, "At least nine or ten parkades." Seconds later, he delegated the various surveillance specialists to look in different locations.

During the next twenty minutes, team members scrambled to cover off their assigned locations, but everything came to a halt when it was reported that Mia had returned to her car.

"Forty minutes from the time we lost her," muttered Jack, looking at his watch. "Plenty of time for her to have met someone."

Disappointment was evident in everyone's voices as Mia was followed back to the Rolstads' house.

"So much for it being a piece of cake," grumbled Connie. "We blew it."

"Sorry about that," said Dwight.

"It happens," said Jack. He looked at Connie and said, "I think we can terminate surveillance, but let's take my car and go back downtown and see what we can find in the way of security cameras. The Hyatt will have some. Maybe parkades, too, or any other security-minded place within the vicinity. If the three of us split up to watch the recordings, we could cover it off quicker."

"You one of these guys that says the glass is always half full?" said Connie, gruffly.

"Naw. I say it simply means there's room for more," replied Jack.

"Yeah, particularly if it's beer," quipped Laura.

It was eight-thirty at night when an excited Connie called Jack on his cellphone. "I've got her! You were right. She entered the parkade that you last left me at. Come and take a look. The camera picks up the plates of the cars as they leave. I'll start writing them all down."

Twenty minutes later, Jack and Laura met with Connie in an office belonging to a security company and reviewed the tape. A woman, partially concealed under an umbrella and wearing a yellow windbreaker, could be seen entering the parkade. She stopped to look in her purse for a couple of minutes before disappearing from sight into a stairwell.

"That was her," said Connie. "Same purse, but she must be wearing a reversible jacket. You'll see a facial of her when she walks back out fifteen minutes later."

"Reversible jacket," mused Jack. "Looking in her purse was an act to wait and see who might follow her in. I can't believe she doesn't have a record. She's acting like a real pro."

"Yeah, I think Special 'O' would agree with you there," replied Connie.

Jack took control of the recording and replayed the images again, starting fifteen minutes before Mia arrived. Numerous people were seen coming and going from the parkade and Jack watched intently.

"I've copied licence plates from vehicles leaving, but it was rush hour, so there are lots," said Connie. "How long past when she left do you think we should check plates?"

"Forget the plates," said Jack, freezing the frame. "This is who she met," he said, pointing to a man on the screen.

"You sure?"

Jack nodded. "Watch ... I'll play it back. He walked in five minutes after Mia, stopped to tie his shoe ... guess he didn't have a purse to pretend he was looking for keys ... no packages and not wearing glasses."

"Glasses? Packages?" asked Connie.

"He walked out two minutes after Mia left. Why would he go to his car and leave again? He wasn't dropping off any packages."

"Or had forgotten his glasses." Connie said with a smile.

"Bet if you check the camera footage that came later, you'll see that he never did come back for any vehicle. He was only using the parkade to meet Mia."

Jack enlarged the image to see the man's face. "And he looks to be Chinese."

"Peaks and valleys." Connie grinned, slapping Jack on the back. "We're on a peak. This guy has gotta be the gofer Wong uses to insulate himself from Parker. Betcha Roger will know who he is. Next, we have to figure out why Wong is keeping her so secret."

The three of them stared at the image of Mr. Frank. None of them would have guessed that in reality, Benny Wong CC1, the head of Chinese organized crime in Vancouver, was a gofer for Mr. Frank.

Chapter Twenty-Eight

An hour after meeting Mia, Mr. Frank slowly drove past Nancy Brighton's address. It had been over three weeks since the hit and run. The yard looked like it was being cared for and there was no sign of any newspapers or flyers on the front step.

He parked a block down the street and walked back to the house and knocked on the door. There was no answer, so he peeked in the mailbox and saw that it was empty.

"Hey!" yelled a woman from her porch across the street. "Are you looking for Nancy?"

"Yes, I'll come over to talk with you," he replied, before walking across the street and stopping at the bottom of her porch. "I have something for her. Is she around?"

"No, she hasn't been living there since her sister was killed," replied the woman.

"Her *sister* was killed?" replied Mr. Frank.

"Yes. It was dreadful. A hit and run right down

the street. She was walking Nancy's dog and ... well, both were killed and the driver took off."

"That's awful," replied Mr. Frank, sounding like he meant it.

"Yes. Nancy was one of the first people on the scene. It was gruesome. I still don't think the police have caught 'em yet."

"Do you know where I can get hold of Nancy?"

"I think she's staying with friends or relatives until she gets over the shock. I've been picking up her mail and my son has been mowing her lawn."

"When does she come to get her mail?"

"She doesn't drive. A policewoman has been picking it up for her once a week."

"A policewoman?" replied Mr. Frank, quickly taking another glance up and down the street.

"Really decent of the police, when you think about it," added the woman. "Nancy is in no shape to be running around."

"I see. Do you know where she is staying?"

"No, I only have a cellphone number for her. If you leave whatever it is that you have with me, I'll see that she gets it. I've got some mail for her already. I bet it will be picked up Monday or Tuesday."

"What I have is something to pass on to her verbally," replied Mr. Frank. "It isn't urgent enough to bother her, but I would like to talk to her in person when it is convenient."

"Oh?" The woman studied him closer, noting that he was wearing a suit and tie. "Let me guess," she said. "You're a realtor, aren't you?"

Mr. Frank grinned. "You're pretty sharp."

"One was knocking on my door last week, saying a developer was interested. We get you people around all the time. I'm certain that Nancy isn't interested in selling."

"I see. Sorry to have bothered you," replied Mr. Frank. "In case she ever changes her mind, do you know by chance when she will be returning home?"

"No, but I think it will be soon. She told me she isn't going to put up with it much longer."

"Put up with it?"

The woman shrugged and said, "I presume with whoever she is staying with. You know the adage, company is like fish. After three days …"

Mr. Frank turned and walked away. He tried to control his anger as he walked back to his car. *Bad enough that the police had a Vietnamese informant to tell them that the death was not accidental … but to kill the wrong person? Sheer incompetence!*

As he started his car, his apprehension grew. *The police must suspect it might have something to do with Mia. If she is convicted … or if AOCTF puts their suspicions on paper it will alert the benefactor. They will suspect I was hiding it from them. She will be interviewed. Wine on her blouse … the drugs she had … feeling drugged herself…. Every word she utters will be another nail in my coffin …*

He caught a glimpse of himself in the rear-view mirror. *Drastic action needs to be taken …*

* * *

It was ten o'clock Monday morning and Jack was sipping a coffee at his desk and chatting with Laura when his cellphone rang. The call display told him it was from the elementary school that both his sons attended and he quickly answered.

"Mr. Taggart? My name is Rosemarie. I'm calling —"

"Is everything alright with Mike and Steve?" asked Jack, ignoring Laura's startled glance.

"Yes, yes, they're fine," replied Rosemarie.

"They're fine," said Jack, looking at Laura, who smiled to show her relief.

"Yes, they're both fine," repeated Rosemarie. "I work in administration and, uh, well I wanted to check something out with you."

Jack could tell by the tone of her voice that she was hedging around what she really wanted to ask. She was suspicious of something. "I'm listening," said Jack.

"Well, uh, occasionally we have the children fill out forms in case of an emergency. We ask what their parents do for a living and for a phone number we could use to contact them if need be."

"I understand," replied Jack. "So what is the problem?"

"Well, uh, no real problem. I was only curious about your occupation."

"Oh?"

"Both your sons wrote down 'entrepreneur' as

your occupation. Pretty big word for kids who are only in grades two and three."

Jack smiled to himself. "Entrepreneur" was also a word that drug-traffickers and other criminals sometimes used to explain their business. Rosemarie was astute enough to be suspicious. Her interest was the well-being of his children and he decided to have a little fun with her. "It is a big word," replied Jack. "They shouldn't be using it if they don't know what it means."

"Oh, they know what it means, all right. I had their teachers ask them. Michael politely informed his teacher that entrepreneur was a noun and referred to someone who runs a business at his own financial risk. Your son, Steven, in grade two, said it was a middleman in business who invested in things to make money."

"I see, so what is the problem then? Did they spell the word wrong?"

"Uh, well …"

Jack heard a shuffling of paper before she continued. "Actually, no. They both spelled it correctly. You have really bright children," she murmured.

"Thanks. They take after their mother."

"I see. Well, uh, when they were asked what kind of things you invested in, they were more noncommittal and didn't really know. I was, uh, curious to see if the phone number they gave for you actually worked or was one I could always reach you at."

Jack decided he had toyed with Rosemarie enough and told her his real occupation and explained to her that his work was secret and he had taught his children not to divulge what he did. He also thanked her for her concern and told her to look up the general RCMP phone number and have the switchboard transfer her call to him for verification.

After hanging up, Jack told a bemused Laura about the call.

Laura snickered and shook her head. "Your two little guys are incredible. Remember when we used them in the undercover operation with Sue McCormick in the Sexual Offence Unit to catch that serial rapist?"

Jack nodded, smiling.

"Your little guys played their roles like a couple of pros," said Laura with a chuckle. "Did you know that we left them alone in a car for a few minutes and had another seasoned undercover operator question them to see if they knew their stuff before using them?"

"They told me they had been questioned."

"They had the car doors locked and would only wind down the window a crack to talk. He couldn't get them to break their cover story. They were better than most of the UC operators trained by the force."

Jack gave a half-grin. "I am really proud of them, but when you think about it, it's pretty sad that a seasoned investigator couldn't get them to crack."

"Yeah, but come on. Your kids have been trained since birth."

"Pretty close," admitted Jack.

"It shows," said Laura, matter-of-factly. "Anyway, what do you think us two entrepreneurs should do now?"

Jack looked over as Connie walked in. By the grim look on her face he knew the answer to Laura's question was about to be revealed.

Chapter Twenty-Nine

"We're screwed," said Connie, pulling up a chair and plunking herself down in front of Jack and Laura's desks. "I was at AOCTF. Roger doesn't have a clue who the guy was in the parkade on Friday. We sat in his office and went through a ton of photographs he had on his computer. No match."

"What about facial recognition through driver's licences?" asked Jack.

"Negative on that, too," replied Connie. "Maybe he doesn't have a driver's licence, although the image we got is a little grainy, so that could be the problem also."

"Is it really that big of a deal?" asked Jack. "We know that Benny Wong ordered the hit with instructions to make it look like a hit-and-run accident. With how professional Mia Parker was on Friday in regards to counter-surveillance, it confirms our theory that she is ultimately the reason for Betty Donahue's murder. Mr. X, as we can call him, has to be the go-between. Maybe he's somebody who's been too insignificant in Wong's organization to hit the spotlight yet, which would be a good reason for Wong to use him. Forget Mr. X, I think Wong is who we need to concentrate on."

"All well said and done," replied Connie, "but how?"

"What would you usually do?" asked Laura.

"I was trying to get a wiretap on the Vietnamese," replied Connie. "But that was when I thought we were dealing with low-level punks on the bottom." She looked at Jack and said, "Do you really think we would catch Wong on a wiretap?"

"Possible, but not likely," replied Jack.

"Yeah, that's what I thought," replied Connie, bitterly. "He's been around for years and by the way Parker was, you know she's been trained too well to blab much. Also, if she isn't meeting Wong in person, it's not like she would be talking about it with him regardless ... and that's the guy I want to nail."

"I agree," replied Jack, "not to mention, from what she said to Rankin on Friday, she thinks the police were bribed and doesn't know about the murder."

"That is strange," replied Connie. "After her performance on Friday, I'm confident she's part of their organization, so why wouldn't they tell her they were going to kill the witness?"

"Maybe they don't think she has the stomach for it," said Laura.

"From what I've heard of Benny Wong, if you work for him you better have a stomach for it," said Jack, grimly.

"There's another problem," said Connie, sounding exasperated. "Nancy Broughton is ticked off and wants to return home. I can't convince her to stay in Chilliwack much longer. I've been picking up her mail once a week and delivering it to her, more to keep in touch than anything, but she is becoming more upset every time I see her." Connie looked at Jack and said, "She's expecting me this morning, actually." She paused and added, "Doesn't your sister live out near Chilliwack? When's the last time you visited her?"

Jack stared briefly at Connie, then smiled. "Okay, I'll do it."

"Good, I appreciate it," replied Connie, letting out a sigh of relief. "A neighbour has been looking after her place and picking it up. I'll make the calls so they'll know to expect you. Maybe when you give the mail to Nancy you can use your charm to convince her to stay where she is. She won't listen to me."

"Maybe my charm will be to show her pictures of a bunch of the thugs who work for Wong," replied Jack. "If she's not suicidal, she should listen." He stared at Connie a moment and asked, "Have you thought of what any other motive could be? Other than Parker simply trying to avoid getting a criminal record?"

"That's a puzzler, too," replied Connie. "Roger said the same thing, that Parker has to be a high-valued asset for Wong to do what he did. She's not his mistress, so what is it?"

"Wong is behind major drug, gun, and people-smuggling activities," noted Laura.

"You think Parker is connected to one of those?" asked Connie.

Jack shook his head. "Guess it's possible, but if she is, we should have heard about her. Particularly with her connection to Wong. So with that in mind, maybe she's involved in his more legitimate enterprises."

"Which is the shipping industry, commercial real-estate ventures, and property rental," noted Laura. "Property rental that includes a lot of massage parlours."

"Parker doesn't strike me as being involved in prostitution," said Jack.

"So where do we go from here?" asked Connie. "Considering that Parker didn't even know about the murder, it puts my sights directly on Wong ... but how do we go about it?"

"I have an idea," replied Jack. "A little hazy at the moment ..."

Hazy at the moment? thought Laura. *Oh man ... the words Jack uses when he doesn't want someone to know what he's up to.*

"However," continued Jack, "there is something I would like you to check out. Parker came out of the house on Friday all smiles and waving."

"Yeah, Rankin said she was like Jekyll and Hyde," said Connie, "becoming a real B when she got in the patrol car."

"Her performance outside the car had to be an act so someone in the house wouldn't know about her drug charge," said Jack. "I'd suggest you dig into the owners a bit more and see what they're all about."

"That would be the Rolstads," replied Connie. "They own the house. I checked them out previously. No criminal records on either and both appear to be model citizens."

"What do they do for a living?" asked Jack.

"Some kind of PR company," replied Connie.

"Check into it a little further," suggested Jack. "Give Commercial Crime a call. See if we can find out who their clients are."

"Will do. And you two?" asked Connie.

"We need a source," said Jack. "Someone to tell us what's going on."

"Sounds a bit like déjà vu," replied Connie. "I was stuck and needed your help when I thought we were going after the Vietnamese. Took you less than a day to come up with something. Think you can pull a rabbit out of the hat again?"

"Possibly," replied Jack. "I'm toying with the idea of doing an undercover operation on Wong."

"He already knows what you and Laura look like," said Connie, "from the night you tried to follow him."

"I know."

"I take it you're thinking of a long-term operation using Chinese members?"

Jack shook his head. "That type of UC on Wong would be next to impossible. We have a couple of Chinese operators, but when it comes to someone as high up as Wong, the bad guys would want to know all their family connections. They might even expect to know what cities or villages in China their families were originally from. Our operators would never pass the screening process that Wong would have in place."

"So then you're looking at turning someone who is willing to testify," said Connie. "That's going to be difficult. Even if you do, it would mean turning a criminal, which gives defence a huge opportunity to question the credibility in front of a jury."

"Getting a source is part of my idea," said Jack. "Like I said, the other part is still a little hazy."

"Would your idea result in another three bodies turning up?" chided Connie.

"Wasn't me who passed the report on to AOCTF," replied Jack coldly.

Connie stared silently back at Jack. *It wasn't ... but why do I sense that the hazy part of your idea involves something you don't want me to know about ...*

Chapter Thirty

Jack glanced across the street at Nancy Brighton's house as he knocked on the neighbour's door. He was greeted by a smiling, middle-aged woman with a handful of mail.

"Jack Taggart, I presume?" she said.

"You presume correctly," replied Jack with a smile, "but let me show you my badge as well."

"Officer Crane told me to expect you," she replied, briefly glancing at his badge before handing him the mail. "Please say hi to Nancy for me and tell her not to worry about her house. I'm keeping an eye on it."

"It looks like it is being well cared for," replied Jack.

"Thanks. Tell Nancy that I had a realtor peering at it the other day, but I told him I knew she wasn't interested in selling."

"Did he drop off his card?" asked Jack.

"No."

Jack felt his stomach muscles tighten. "Interesting that he didn't do that. Can you remember what he looked like or any other details?"

"Well … yes. It was Friday around suppertime. He was a well-dressed man in a suit and tie. That's what clued me in that he was probably a realtor. His English was perfect."

"English?" asked Jack.

"Oh, I didn't tell you. He was Asian."

Moments later, Jack showed the woman the picture of the man who met Mia Parker in the parkade.

"Yes, that was him," replied the woman, looking bewildered.

Jack felt nauseous. *I screwed up. I should have had surveillance here …*

An hour later, after making certain he wasn't being followed, Jack arrived at the house in Chilliwack where Nancy was staying. He knew he wouldn't be taking the time to visit his sister today. He had already called Laura to help Connie check whatever security-camera footage was available in the vicinity of Nancy's house to see if they could identify a vehicle connected to the phony realtor.

It took some time after Jack pushed the buzzer before Nancy Brighton was able to hobble over to the door with the help of her cane. She was a petite woman with a thick crop of short white hair. After initial greetings, Jack said, "I'd like to update you a little on the investigation."

Nancy gestured to her knee and said, "The damn thing started acting up again last week, but I can still make you a cup of coffee if you like. Come on in. My friends are out shopping at the moment so it will be only the two of us."

Jack accepted her invitation and followed her into the kitchen and took a seat at the table while Nancy prepared coffee.

At seventy-five, Nancy's face had the usual number of wrinkles and despite an array of laugh-lines spreading out from the corners of her eyes, she looked depressed and her face was drawn.

"So? Do you have some good news for me?" she asked, while sitting down to wait for the coffee to percolate. "Can you tell me how the investigation is progressing?"

Jack sighed. *Good news? Hell no. I screwed up. I should have realized someone might go to her house later ...*

"By the look of your face, I take it there is no good news," added Nancy.

Jack eyed her for a moment. "Guess I shouldn't play poker with you," he replied, then told her what had transpired on Friday, starting with Mia Parker meeting with the unknown man in a parkade. "The same man who then went to your house after meeting with her," noted Jack.

"I see," replied Nancy.

"It was my fault. I should have thought to cover your house as well."

"What time did you identify him through the

security cameras as being the man Miss Parker met?" asked Nancy.

"About eight o'clock Friday night."

Nancy shrugged. "Didn't you say the man was looking for me around suppertime? By eight o'clock he had already come and gone."

Jack frowned. "Yes, but we still would have identified him had we been there."

"Beating yourself up won't help," continued Nancy. "Believe me, I know. It only causes burnout ... which I am personally familiar with."

Jack silently stared back at her. *She's pretty sharp. Dealt with a lot of criminals in her time ... and cops.*

"Besides," continued Nancy, "perhaps he was only wanting to verify that I was still alive and that the police were not simply hoping for a quick plea bargain."

"I'm sure that was part of it," agreed Jack, "but knowing that you're alive means they may try again."

"You really think so?" asked Nancy. "Connie Crane told me you identified the driver who killed Betty and my dog, Toby. She said the man was killed in a gang slaying two weeks ago."

"I think he was killed by his own people to hinder our investigation," replied Jack.

"Really?" said Nancy in surprise. "So who is Miss Parker that she can order a witness killed?"

Jack shook his head. "That's not what we think is going on. Parker doesn't know about your sister being murdered. It was evident from conversation when she was being served with a summons on Friday morning that she thinks the police were bought off to have her charge withdrawn."

"Bought off!" said Nancy. "Where does she think she is? Some third-world country?"

"Maybe China," replied Jack.

"China? I understood from Corporal Crane that Vietnamese hoodlums were responsible for murdering Betty."

"Uh, listen, if it wasn't for your previous occupation, I don't think I would tell you what I am about to tell you," said Jack.

"I know enough to keep a secret, if that is what you are trying to say," replied Nancy. "Tell me what?"

"We think the Vietnamese were hired by a top Chinese gangster as a way to insulate himself. When they discovered we were on to the Vietnamese, they killed them to stop us from finding out who was behind it."

"I see. So it wasn't only the driver who was killed?"

Jack shook his head. "Three Vietnamese were killed. The driver was murdered in Surrey and two men who were involved in arranging it were murdered in Hong Kong, although their bodies have not been found."

"Hong Kong? Sounds like more than your local talent is involved. This gangster must be well connected."

Jack nodded.

"I have to say, knowing that the three of them who were involved are dead makes me feel a little better, but it still won't bring Betty back, will it?"

Jack sighed. "No … and I am sorry for your loss."

"Who is this gangster? Can you tell me?"

"I could tell you, but I think it's best I don't."

Nancy nodded. "I understand." A small smile appeared at the corner of her mouth and she added, "You're probably afraid I'll whack him."

"Stranger things have happened," replied Jack. "I'm sure you know."

"Well, can't say as I wouldn't be happy to read that guy's name in the obits, but I do believe in judicial process. I would like to see him behind bars for the rest of his life."

Jack gave a grim smile. *Is that what used to happen when you worked in the system forty years ago?*

"That being said, I've still decided I'm going to move back to my own house," said Nancy. "After breakfast tomorrow morning, actually."

"What?" replied Jack, astounded. "After what I told you?"

"I never believed in letting criminals push me around. Their lawyers, either, for that matter. As far as your gangster goes, he's obviously been in place for years to be in that position. Well insulated ... protected. How long did you expect me to hide out?"

"Until we run Mia Parker through a trial," pleaded Jack.

"Don't give me that crap, Officer. I may have retired years ago, but I still have a pretty good idea how long that would take."

"We don't have the manpower to protect you," argued Jack. "It would take a lot of people to cover you day and night. Even more to travel with you when you went out. You can't return home yet. We need more time. You'll have to stay here."

"You are not in a position to tell me what I can or cannot do," replied Nancy.

"Our only choice then would be to withdraw the charge against Parker."

Nancy slammed the palm of her hand on the table. "Don't even consider that option! My sister died because of these people! That would be allowing them to win and set precedence that murdering witnesses works!" She leaned back in her chair, folding her arms across her chest before adding, "Do that and I will go to the media. Think your bosses will like being asked on camera why they can't protect a seventy-five-year-old pensioner?"

Jack was quiet for a moment. He knew he was in a losing battle. He returned her stare and said, "I only met you a few moments ago, but I really like you. In fact I feel like giving you a hug, but believe me when —"

"Give me a hug, eh? I know what that leads to. Sorry to dash your hopes, but keep your pants on. I don't hug guys the first time I have coffee with them."

Jack saw a brief sparkle in her eye and gave a lopsided smile. "Let me finish. I wanted to impress upon you that things have changed since you were prosecuting. It's far more dangerous now."

Nancy's expression became serious. "I read the news. I know what's going on out there. It's time somebody stood up to them." She reached across the table and patted Jack on the hand. "Don't worry about me. You've done your bit ... no matter what happens. Don't put any blame on yourself. I can see the compassion in your eyes. It tells me you're a good cop."

Jack sighed. "I do my best, but a lot of the time the bad guys still win. I don't want you to become another statistic."

"I don't plan to." Nancy looked at Jack and her voice became solemn. "There are still a few areas where the law hasn't changed much. I have a right to protect my own home ... or myself, for that matter, if I feel my life is threatened."

"What are you getting at?" Jack asked.

Nancy looked at him and shook her head. "God, you kids are so naive. Is it because you think I am old and feeble? I said I believed in judicial process, but I'm not stupid. I still have an item that used to belong to my husband before he died."

"An item?"

"He used to hunt ducks," explained Nancy. "I've got a pump-action twelve-gauge." She furrowed her eyebrows and added, "I hope the bastards do come for me."

Chapter Thirty-One

Jack walked into Connie's office as she was hanging up the phone.

Laura, sitting across the desk from Connie, glanced at her watch and looked at Jack. "Hey, that must have been a fast lunch you had with your sister. I wasn't expecting you back for another hour or two."

"I decided we didn't have the time," replied Jack. "I cancelled on her."

"We've got bad news," said Connie, whose blotchy red face revealed her anger.

"*You've* got bad news?" replied Jack.

"The security cameras were all turned off," explained Laura. "We couldn't see what vehicle our phony realtor was driving. Any cameras from the apartment building that were catching images of the public areas outside were all turned off. They are only allowed for inside footage."

"What are you talking about?" asked Jack. "I watched them myself only last month. It's how we found the van from the restaurant."

"A new development since then," replied Connie. "Someone caught on camera successfully sued because it was ruled as an invasion of privacy. Security cameras have been shut down all over."

"Yeah, you have the right not to be seen by anyone if you go out in public," replied Laura, bitterly.

Jack sighed and shook his head, before taking a seat. "Well, I also have some bad news. Nancy is moving back home tomorrow morning."

Connie and Laura's disbelief turned to shock as Jack relayed his conversation with Nancy.

"What the hell do we do?" asked Connie. "There is no way we can come up with the manpower to protect her."

"She teased you about hugging her," said Laura. "What you should have done was hug her long enough to put her in a straightjacket."

Jack shook his head in frustration. "When I was leaving, she told me I could come back and hug her if I got to the Chinese gangster before she did."

"You mean Benny Wong," said Connie.

"That's who she meant, but I never told her his name," replied Jack.

"Good thing," said Connie. "By the sounds of it, she is liable to go after him with her twelve-gauge."

"She is a gutsy lady," replied Jack. "I have to say, crazy or not, I do respect her."

"So what do we do next?" prodded Connie. "I'll

notify uniform and have them patrol her street as much as possible, but they won't keep that up for ever. We need to do something."

"I think we should do what Nancy suggested," replied Jack, "and put Benny Wong behind bars."

"Gee, why didn't someone think of that earlier," said Connie. "Do you have your cuffs with you? I'll run out and do that."

"Sarcasm won't help," said Laura.

"I didn't mean it as sarcasm," replied Connie. "I was trying to be funny, but maybe you're right, nothing about this is funny." She looked at Jack. "Oh, I got a call back from Commercial Crime about Rolstad's public relation's company a few minutes ago. Maple Leaf Consulting has an office here and one in Ottawa. Most of their clients out west are large firms, like oil companies or corporate entities who need a little PR when it comes to the environment or purchasing land in areas the public might object to."

"Bingo," said Jack.

"That means something to you?" asked Connie.

"Wong deals in commercial real estate. Knowing what pieces of land are being sought after by large companies would be a huge asset. We could be talking theft of company secrets, stock market insider information ..."

"And you think little Miss Parker is getting her talons into the Rolstads to find that out," mused Connie. "Good possibility. It gets even better. Their Ottawa office specializes in our elected representatives. They're spin doctors for our politicians. Maple Leaf Consulting prepares the best possible response in advance for all the personal stuff that the politicians don't want us to know about, but are ready with an action plan if something is revealed."

Jack let out a low whistle. "So Wong could be getting his tentacles into government, as well. Maybe blackmail or trying to influence government expenditures or even legislative changes."

"Jesus ... this is big," replied Connie.

"Organized crime at its fullest," agreed Laura.

"And Parker has her master's degree in psychology and is currently taking political science," noted Jack. "A perfect candidate to work at Maple Leaf Consulting."

"And her job would likely entail a lot of travel," noted Laura. "Places like the U.S. Having a criminal record would put a stop to that and jeopardize her chances of being hired."

The three paused to look at each other. Connie tapped her fingers on her desk and said, "Finally ... we have a plausible motive." She stopped tapping and looked at Jack and Laura. "Next step, how do we gather evidence to prove the murders?"

"Realistically, who would you hope to catch?" asked Jack.

"Benny Wong, of course," replied Connie.

Laura grimaced. "Benny Wong?" She looked at Connie and added, "Jack said 'realistically.'"

"Well, who else would I want instead?" replied Connie. "Parker doesn't even know there was a murder and as far as Mr. X, our phony realtor, goes, he is simply a go-between who Wong uses so we don't connect him with Parker. Unless of course Mr. X or some of Wong's other flunkies kill Nancy. That would change everything."

"You've got that right," said Jack, tersely. He had only met Nancy once, but the idea of someone murdering her made it feel personal. He looked at Connie and said, "So you're not after whoever killed the Vietnamese driver or his two buddies in Hong Kong?"

"Yeah, I'd ask for them, too, if you were Santa Claus, but I am trying to be realistic," said Connie, frowning. "Whatever minions Wong uses to do his dirty deeds are nothing in the scheme of things. I want Wong. That's who's pulling the strings."

Jack gave a grim smile.

"What's so funny?" asked Connie, suspiciously.

"Sounds to me like you're starting to understand the big picture," replied Jack. "You're starting to think like me."

"Never!" blurted Connie.

Jack knew she wasn't joking, but decided not to pursue the matter. "The important thing is I agree with you about Wong. He is officially our number-one target."

"And we will catch him … how?" asked Laura.

Jack looked at Connie and said, "Any problem with me taking a run at Parker?"

"By run, do you mean in a car?" asked Connie, jokingly, or at least she hoped she was.

"Actually, not a bad idea," Jack said. "We really are starting to think alike …" He put his hand up and smiled to silence Connie's response. "I mean to scare her, but by using the pretext of interrogating her over the murder of Betty Donahue."

Connie shrugged. "I don't have a problem with that. She doesn't even know about the murder, so it's not like I could charge her anyway. The thing is, going by how well she was trained in counter-surveillance, I'm damned positive the only words out of her mouth will be to demand a lawyer. She's no dummy."

"Being as we know she can't give us a confession for something she doesn't even know about, it opens the door to use some methods that the court wouldn't allow," replied Jack. He saw Connie raise an eyebrow and quickly added, "Strictly psychological pressure. I'll use your interview room and you can watch on camera."

"But for what purpose?" asked Laura. "Are you hoping to follow her again after?"

"No, I think we know that won't work," replied Jack. "My real objective is to go undercover. Try and get her to arrange a face to face meeting between me and Wong."

"We can't do that," protested Laura. "Even if you were to scare Parker into co-operating, Wong already knows who you are from the night his bodyguards cornered us in the alley. You talked to him on Zhang's iPhone, remember?"

"I remember," replied Jack. "Relax. To start with, it won't be *us* going after him in an undercover role. I'll be flying solo ... by pretending to be a dirty cop."

Laura felt her heart sink. *Oh, man ...*

"What I would suggest," continued Jack, looking at Connie, "is that you grab Parker at university and bring her in for questioning. Being as you work I-HIT and are investigating a murder, it would make sense that it is your investigation. We would then arrange a scenario when you returned with her to the office that I was butting in and taking over. Make it sound like my investigation from Intelligence somehow trumped yours."

"Butting in, as memory serves me, is something you have a habit of doing," muttered Connie.

Jack ignored the comment and continued, "I would then interrogate her. If she actually does crack, which I don't expect, so much the better. If she doesn't, when I drive her back to her car I'll come across as a dirty cop who can be bought. If I scare her enough in the interrogation by connecting her to Benny Wong and laying murder charges, she should jump at the chance to arrange for me to meet him."

"Why not skip Parker altogether and go straight to Wong?" asked Connie.

Jack shook his head. "Wong has been around too long. He'd be really paranoid. It would carry far more weight if I scared the hell out of Parker first and had her present when I met him. If she's scared, on a psychological level it will put pressure on him, thinking I might be their saviour."

Connie reflected on the idea for a moment before nodding. "That's not a bad idea. Parker already thinks the police are being bought off. She might fall for it. Then if you meet Wong and somehow get an admission about the murders ... maybe even find out who he had do the murders, hell, we could nail him."

Laura stared blankly at Connie. *Yeah, Parker might fall for it ... but Wong has spent years in the bloody trenches to get where he is. There is no way he would agree to meet anywhere other than one of his lairs in Chinatown. Jack wouldn't be able to have any backup ... it could be like the two guys who went to Hong Kong. Never to be seen again.*

"You okay, Laura?" asked Jack quietly. "You understand why I have to do it alone? Wong would have more difficulty believing that both of us were corrupt. Plus at his level, his organization is male-dominated. He wouldn't be as willing to open up to —"

"I understand," snapped Laura. "Doesn't mean I have to like it."

"I don't like it either," said Jack, softly, "but it is the best plan I can come up with. If you can think of a better idea, let's hear it."

Isn't staying alive a better idea? Laura told herself that logically she didn't believe in premonitions, but something told her this was a bad idea. Really bad. She felt her stomach knot and her eyes water in frustration as she blinked and shook her head.

Chapter Thirty-Two

It was eleven o'clock Tuesday morning when Jack walked up the sidewalk between a row of rhododendrons and knocked on Nancy Brighton's door. He heard her shout from the living room, asking who it was.

"Jack Taggart," he replied.

A few seconds passed and she responded, "Come on in, the door isn't locked."

Isn't locked? Right ... Jack entered the foyer and saw Nancy sitting on the sofa with her cane beside her. "Could I bum a coffee?" he asked. "There are some things we need to discuss."

"I'm not leaving my home, if that's what you want. You're wasting your time."

"It has nothing to do with that," replied Jack. "I've brought you something. I also came to ask a favour."

"A favour?"

Jack nodded. "A very difficult one. Can I come in?"

Nancy nodded and Jack slipped off his shoes and entered the living room as Nancy stood up and steadied herself with her cane. "Perhaps it would be better to go to the kitchen," she said, "while I brew the coffee."

"No problem, but first, let's take care of this," he said, bending over and feeling under the sofa. Seconds later, he hauled out a Remington twelve-gauge shotgun and examined it briefly. "You've got a load in the chamber," observed Jack. "Illegal storage and —"

"Let me see your search warrant," said Nancy, evenly.

Jack ignored her as he unloaded the shotgun and examined the cartridge. "As I was afraid of ... bird shot. Great for killing birds ... not so good for people." With that comment he reached inside his jacket pocket and removed a handful of shotgun cartridges. As he started to reload the shotgun with the new cartridges, he commented, "These are what we use. Double-ought buck. Made for killing people." He glanced at her and asked, "Have you ever fired a shotgun? Or any gun for that matter?"

"No," admitted Nancy.

"Then I won't be lending you my wife's little .32 Beretta pistol. Handguns are too easy to miss with and I can't take a chance on you shooting some citizen if you're out shopping. As far as this thing goes ... well, I'll give you some tips. Then I would like you to do something for me in a couple of hours."

Nancy looked startled as Jack reloaded the shotgun with the police ammunition. "Couldn't you get in trouble for doing this?" she asked.

"Probably." Jack shrugged. "Do you know any good defence lawyers?"

"Is there such at thing? Maybe you could settle for competent?"

Jack returned her smile and chuckled, but his humour disappeared when she spoke next.

"So what favour do you want?" she asked.

It was two-thirty in the afternoon when Mia Parker left her class at university and walked toward the parking lot. Minutes before she had ignored the second incoming call she had received on her phone that day, each time with the same Ottawa prefix. This time it was a text message. It was what she had been wanting to get.

> Hey, Mia! I've tried calling you
> but you didn't pick up. I haven't
> been able to stop thinking
> about you and am hoping we
> can get together soon. I'll be
> back in Vancouver Sunday
> night, but then on to Seattle
> on Monday and have to take a
> direct flight home on Tuesday.
> How about dinner? Or better
> yet, maybe I could convince
> you to come to Seattle to visit?
> Great shopping there ;-)
>
> The Wolf Man

As Mia saved the text she thought, *Yeah, I'm sure you can't stop thinking about me … every time you sit on the toilet …* She would send a cryptic message to the benefactor when she got home. The information she had was brief enough that a face to face with Mr. Frank wouldn't be necessary, but she knew he would be meeting her once a decision had been made with how to proceed.

She thought about Wolfenden's message. *There is no doubt the benefactor will want me to go to Seattle with him …* She felt repulsed at the idea of having sex with such an older man again and briefly wondered if she should tell Mr. Frank that she had a test on Monday at university. *Bad idea … he would probably check …*

She continued walking, but when she arrived at her car, she felt a tap on her shoulder and turned around.

"Mia Parker, my name is Corporal Connie Crane, and this is Constable Zachery."

Mia's mouth briefly dropped open as she looked at a woman in a green pantsuit holding a badge for her to see, along with a young man in a navy-blue suit who could have passed for a Mormon missionary.

"We're with the Integrated Homicide Investigation Team," continued Crane. "I want you to accompany us back to my office. There are some questions that you could help us with."

Chapter Thirty-Three

Jack stood in front of the interview room with his arms folded across his chest as Constable Zachery returned to his desk while Connie picked up a file box and walked over with Parker.

Connie looked at Jack sharply and snapped, "What are you doing here?"

"You told me yesterday that you were bringing her in for questioning," replied Jack.

"Yeah, so?" Before Jack could respond, Connie glanced at Parker and gestured for her to go inside the interview room. "Take a seat, I'll be right in."

Once Parker sat down, Connie partially closed the door, but left it open enough on the pretext of keeping an eye on her. She then turned to Jack and said, "Okay, Jack, what gives?"

"Did she say anything on the way in?" asked Jack.

"No. I told her I would explain it all when we got here."

"Good. I'll be conducting the interview, not you."

"You what? Like hell you are! This is my case! I work homicide ... you're on the Intelligence Unit, so back off!"

Intelligence Unit? Mia felt her lungs swallow a gasp of air. She had thought that it was all a mis-understanding. Maybe she had witnessed something without realizing it or her car had somehow been seen in an area where there had been a murder. Mention of the Intelligence Unit changed all that. *What do they know about me?*

"Here's your boss," said Jack, gesturing for Connie to turn around. "He can explain it to you."

Parker saw another man approach. "Sorry, Connie," he said. "I just got off the phone with the brass. I only found out myself."

"Found what out?" asked Connie. "Randy, what is going on?"

"Corporal Taggart will be conducting the inter-view," replied Randy. "You're to give him your file and co-operate with anything he wants."

Connie turned and gawked at Jack, while shaking her head.

"Don't take it personal, Connie," said Jack. "Guess I should have given you a little more notice, but if the brass didn't back me, I knew there was no point argu-ing with you. You are working on one murder. I deal with organized crime ... and who I'm after is respon-sible for dozens of murders, from Canada down to Mexico. It's all about understanding the big picture."

Mia breathed a sigh of relief and felt giddy. She didn't know what it was about, but knowing Jack

Taggart worked on organized crime was better than finding out he worked in her intelligence field. *Who do I know in organized crime? Nobody directly ... at least not that I know of.* Mia paused to reflect. *It has to be someone who attended one of the Rolstads' parties. They want to know how well I really know the person. I wonder who it was ...*

She watched as Crane shoved the file box into Taggart's hands and turned and stomped away. Taggart came in, closing the door behind him, and setting the box on the table. She hid her smile when he pulled up a chair and sat facing her on the same side of the desk as she was. *Textbook ... exactly like I was taught ...*

After introducing himself, his initial questions and his demeanour were as she expected. *Would I like a coffee or glass of water? He's being friendly ... trying to build some rapport.* Mia declined and smiled politely as she sized him up. *He is actually kind of cute ... this could be fun. You think you can manipulate me? Well try this on for size ...*

She squirmed and leaned back in the chair while slowly running her hand up the inside of her thigh on her skin-tight blue jeans while gently massaging her leg. Her lips formed a pout and she half-closed her eyes as if seeking comfort from a pulled a groin muscle while lifting her pelvis slightly. She ended her act by leaning forward to offer a view of her cleavage as she pretended to get comfortable by tugging on the sides of her jeans.

During her performance she watched Jack out of the corner of her eye. *Most men would have stared at my body and swallowed to keep from drooling ... this bastard has the gall to yawn and look away! Okay, jerk. Round one for you. Let's get down to business ...*

As expected, he dismissed her questions about what it was all about, saying he would get to it in due time, but first needed some background information, much of which, she knew, he likely already possessed.

She played the game and recounted a little of her childhood, returning his fake smiles with smiles of her own when the conversation would briefly focus on mundane subjects like what she did for entertainment or what restaurants she liked. *Okay guy, you're beginning to make me laugh. Time to drop the rapport bit. Say something designed to shake my confidence ... and be there to offer support. On a subconscious psychological level make me feel like I'm talking to a priest and prompt me to confess. Well, guess what ... I'm an atheist!*

"So it must have been hard on you and your mom after your dad died," continued Jack.

"It was hard, but we managed," replied Mia.

"You managed quite well," noted Jack. "You are taking another major at university and I understand your mother also went to university and took journalism, is that right?"

"Yes," Mia said, shrugging.

"So when your mom went to university, were you left with a babysitter or —"

"No, I was a teenager then," said Mia.

"Must have been expensive," Jack remarked. "I never bothered to review any records of employment yet, so tell me, how did she make ends meet before then?"

Records of employment? Mia felt her stomach tighten. *This is too detailed to be about someone I might know … it's about me or Mom!* She maintained eye contact with Jack, smiling and shrugging in response, before replying, "There may not be any records. My mother was an entrepreneur. Dabbled in different things. I was too young to understand exactly what it was."

An entrepreneur, mused Jack, reflecting on his recent call from his sons' school.

"I'm afraid I can't waste much more time," said Mia, interrupting his thoughts. "I do have an exam to study for. Can you please tell me what this is all about?"

Jack's face hardened and he glared briefly at Mia who stared unblinkingly back at him.

Mia hid her contempt. *Don't tell me you want to play both good cop and bad cop yourself? Gimme a break …*

"It's about two things," said Jack, tersely. "The first is what Corporal Crane wants you for as a result of your drug charge."

"My drug charge?" Mia felt like laughing with relief. "Good God, is that what this is about?" She gestured with open palms and proclaimed, "I was in an accident and some old bag thought she saw me hiding dope under a bush. In reality, the dope was there all along."

Jack took a deep breath and slowly exhaled. "Okay, first of all, I want you to know that I am not upset with you for lying to me. Under the same circumstances I would, too, but please don't refer to the woman as an old bag. She's a really nice lady and for your information, is very much alive."

"Yeah, well ... alive? What are you getting at?"

Jack stared at her a moment, then got up and opened the door and gave a nod of his head. Mia's jaw dropped open when Nancy Brighton entered the room, clasping a manila envelope to her chest.

"You two obviously know each other," said Jack.

"Uh, of course," replied Mia. "This, uh, lady thought she saw me hiding some drugs in her bushes outside her house." She looked at Nancy and added, "Actually they were already there and I saw them when I dropped my purse."

"I know perfectly well what I saw," said Nancy, "but that is not why I came. I want to show you something," she said, taking a photograph out of the manila envelope and placing it on the table.

Mia glanced at the picture of Nancy and another woman standing in front of a Christmas tree.

"She's my sister," said Nancy, swallowing as she tapped on the photo with her finger.

"I don't understand," replied Mia. "If she was there, too, and thinks she saw something, well, she is also mistaken"

Nancy was trembling as she plunked another photo down on the desk. It was of two tots, both posing for the camera on either side of an older man. "These are her two grandchildren," continued Nancy. "The man was Betty's husband."

Was? reflected Mia.

Nancy started sobbing and spluttered, "Go ahead, Jack! Show her what my sister looked like after her friends got done with her! Show her!" she yelled, before reaching for the investigative file box on the desk.

Jack grabbed her in a hug and held her for a moment as she sobbed. "Not while you're here," he whispered.

"Why not?" she wailed, struggling to break free from Jack's hold. "I was the first one there when she died. You think a moment goes by when I don't think about it! I know what she looks like in your pictures. I want this little bitch to see!"

"Please, Nancy," replied Jack. "It's time for you to go," he said softly, guiding her out the door where Mia caught a glimpse of another woman leading her away before Jack closed the door.

Jack solemnly walked over to the table and reached for the file box. One by one, he plucked out five close-up coloured photographs of Betty's mangled body and dropped them on the table. "It was suppose to look like a hit and run, but as it turned out, it was a well-planned murder," he said as he pushed the photos closer to Mia.

Mia looked up at him in confusion.

"Look!" he seethed. "Look at them!"

Mia glanced at the face in the picture. It looked distorted like a rubber mask and she realized it was from having a broken skull. The bloody body was on a sidewalk next to a mangled ball of fur that she realized was a dog. She allowed her eyes to flicker back to the picture of the two women in front of the Christmas tree.

"I ... I don't understand," said Mia. "What does it have to do with me?"

"It has everything to do with you!" yelled Jack. He gestured to the photographs and said, "Betty Donahue was murdered by mistake because they thought it was the witness who saw you stash the dope! All so you wouldn't have a criminal record for an offence that would have seen you get probation or a small fine," he added, contemptuously.

"They ... who ... they?" responded Mia, with her voice quavering.

Jack took another picture out and placed it in front of her. It was of an older Chinese man and she shrugged her shoulders to show she didn't understand.

"Benny Wong," said Jack. "Are you telling me you've never met the boss man in person?"

The boss man? The words only brought more confusion to her brain and she shook her head.

"Are you going to tell me you don't know this guy either?" continued Jack, as he placed another photo on the table.

Mia looked at the photo of Mr. Frank and her face went ashen.

Chapter Thirty-Four

"How is Nancy?" asked Jack, as he stepped into a monitoring room with Connie and Laura.

"I got someone to drive her home," replied Connie. "She was still crying when she left." She frowned at Jack. "That was a rotten thing to make her do. I thought you were only going to let Parker get a glimpse of her to know she was still alive. You never told me about having her bring the pictures."

Jack sighed and nodded. "You're right. It was a rotten thing for me to ask her to do, but Parker isn't any ordinary student going to school. You saw how she handled herself with Special 'O' ... and that was with two teams trying to follow her. I needed to shake her up."

"Well, I don't know about Parker, but Nancy was sure shook up."

"I know. I feel awful. I was hoping she was still here so I could talk to her."

"She wanted out of here right away."

"I'll swing past her place later," replied Jack.

"Well, with the stunt you pulled in there, forget about ever trying to enter anything Parker says into court," said Connie.

"I'm not interviewing her for court," replied Jack. "This is all a build-up to scare her before I get her to think I can be bought. She needs to be convinced we have something on all of them if Wong is going to take me seriously."

"Her face is totally without expression," noted Laura, indicating the camera monitor. "She's staring at the photos with about as much interest as watching paint dry."

"Probably in shock," suggested Connie.

"She knows she is being monitored," said Jack. "I don't think she's in that much shock. There's something about her that bothers me. To start with, she acted like it was all a game. Anybody else would have been more nervous."

"What are you getting at?" asked Laura.

"Didn't you see at the beginning how she tried to use her gender to manipulate or influence me?"

"Yeah, I loved it when you yawned," replied Connie. "She is one attractive lady. Bet that took her down a rung or two."

"We know she has been schooled on counter-surveillance," continued Jack. "I'm betting that Wong has had a lawyer or someone school her about inter-rogation techniques, as well. She's educated in that department beyond what she would have received with her psychology degree."

"She's obviously intelligent," said Laura.

"Yes, but I sense there is more to her than that," replied Jack.

"Like what?" asked Laura.

"I don't know. I can't put my finger on it yet. She looked upset when I showed her the picture of Mr. X. I don't think she figured we knew who her connection to Wong was." He glanced at Connie and said, "You read her as being in shock as she stares at the pictures. I see her as still being in control of her emotions."

The three of them stared at the monitor for a moment. Jack sighed and said, "I don't know, maybe you're right. I better get back in there. I doubt she will say anything, but hopefully I can shake her enough to convince Wong that he needs me."

Mia brooded over the photo of Mr. Frank. *How much do they know? They know he's connected with me ... and I know Mr. Frank uses Benny Wong ... but they think Wong is the boss. I need them to keep thinking that ...*

Conscious that she was being watched, she brushed the photo of Mr. Frank to one side like he was a fly and picked up the photo of Benny Wong and stared at it while she thought. *Mr. Frank, why didn't you tell me that the benefactor was going to kill the witness? I could have been better prepared ... or is that the reason? My lack of knowledge and innocence would be apparent to the police ...*

She put the photo down when Jack returned, sliding his chair closer to her.

"I spoke briefly with Corporal Crane," said Jack, with a nod of his head toward the camera mounted high in the corner of the room. "She can't wait to get her claws into you. Guess she's not the type to see the big picture."

Mia decided to play along. "The big picture?"

Jack gave a wave of his hand toward the camera like he was dismissing it as being inconsequential. "I'm not sure of everything she has on you because I haven't had time to review the entire file," he said, looking at the box on the table.

Mia nodded solemnly. *Bet you have the whole thing memorized ...*

"However, she only plans to charge you and Wong for one murder," continued Jack. "I'm looking at him for a lot more than that. As I said, I'm not sure of all the evidence she has. She did mention to me that she was pleased by your inept attempts at counter-surveillance."

"Counter-surveillance? I don't —"

"Please, I would rather you simply be quiet than to lie to me," interrupted Jack. "The point is, Corporal Crane looks at your behaviour as another nail in your coffin." Jack paused, then mused, "Maybe she has a point. A judge would be curious. It certainly shows guilt."

"This is your big picture?" asked Mia. "That I may have a bad memory and back-tracked a few times or something when going about my daily life or out shopping?"

"Naw, that's not the big picture," replied Jack. "Murder is the big picture."

"I really didn't know about any murder," retorted Mia, "let alone understand why you think I would be involved in such a thing."

"There is a certain verisimilitude to what you say," admitted Jack. "I spoke with a uniformed policeman who talked to you a few days ago about your drug charge. He had the distinct feeling that you thought someone had been bought off ... rather than murdered."

Mia stared a moment, then said, "If your theory is that the murder involves me, then why didn't I know about it? As far as suspecting bribery goes, it is common knowledge how corrupt your system is. I had presumed that my lawyer had looked after things."

Jack reflected on her choice of words. *How corrupt your system is ... doesn't she mean the system?* He shrugged it off as her meaning the justice system, of which he was a part of and not her. It was a mistake he would later realize, albeit much too late.

"It really doesn't matter as far as Corporal Crane goes," continued Jack. "Even if you didn't realize your colleagues were going to commit murder, it still involves you. If four people go in and rob a bank and one robber shoots someone, all four robbers pay the price. And as far as saying you thought someone had been bought off ... a judge will certainly take note of that as well."

"When I said I thought my lawyer had looked after things, I was referring to paying a fine or something for me," replied Mia. She gave a nod toward the photographs. "How was she killed? With a bat?"

"No, it was a hit and run."

"A hit and run?" replied Mia, sharply. The stress she had been feeling over the interrogation manifested itself into anger when the unfairness of the situation raged through her brain. "You are so eager to connect me to an alleged murder involving a hit and run?" she yelled, jumping to her feet. "Where were you when my father was killed in a hit and run?" she asked, clenching her fist in front of Jack's face. "You certainly didn't charge that person! How much did that guy have to pay you? Or by being a politician, didn't he have to pay anything?"

Jack was taken back. "I don't know what you're talking about," he said. "That simply isn't true. Who told you that?"

"Bullshit!" she yelled. "You're corrupt! You're all corrupt! What is it you want from me? You know I didn't know anything about it!"

Chapter Thirty-Five

Jack hurried in to see Connie. "The wheels fell off my plan," he said, with astonishment. "Did you see her?"

"I thought she was going to punch you," said Laura, looking shocked.

"Bribery ... corruption?" exclaimed Connie. "I personally looked at the file involving her dad. Remember? I told you that someone in our office pulled it out five years ago and enhanced a photo of the suspect and tried to run it through face recognition, but wasn't successful. Too much of a profile shot rather than face-on."

"She thinks a politician did it and we are protecting the person," said Jack.

"Who would tell her such a thing?" asked Laura.

"She didn't say, but people say stupid things and make flippant comments," replied Jack. "Maybe by a friend or neighbour who had been prejudiced by some unrelated news article or something, or perhaps came from another country where such things are common. The sad thing is, Mia believed it as gospel."

"Her mother came from China," noted Connie. "Corruption there is rampant."

"She is sure angry with you," noted Laura, shaking her head in sympathy toward Jack. "So much for getting her to open up to you now."

"After a death in the family, there is a desire to funnel anger toward someone or some organization," noted Jack, then added, "such as the justice system."

Connie and Laura did not respond. They knew he had personal experience in that regard.

Jack looked at Connie and asked, "How fast can you retrieve that file? I want to show her that we have been doing everything we can to find out who killed her father."

"Not long at all," replied Connie. "I've still got it in my office. I hadn't got around to returning it yet."

"Check the monitor," said Laura. "You better hurry. She's pacing the room and looks really angry … now she's looking at the camera … giving us the finger."

Jack left Laura to monitor Mia and went down the hall with Connie to retrieve the file.

"You said the wheels fell off your plan?" asked Connie as she handed Jack the file box.

"After her response, I'm not sure if I should hint that I'm a dirty cop," replied Jack. "She's liable to try and rip my face off."

"So how will you play it?"

"At this point I don't know. I'll be flying by the seat of my pants."

* * *

Jack entered the interview room holding another file box with both hands. Mia stood squarely in front of him with her hands on her hips, before pointing a finger at his chest and saying, "I'm done. Either return me to my car or let me call a lawyer immediately!"

"I'll drive you back to your car if you like," said Jack, "but this box I'm holding contains all the information we have surrounding your father's death. Corporal Crane pulled it out to review when she first started working on you. Would you like to see it?"

Mia was taken back and her mouth briefly flopped open. She saw the name *Parker* scrawled on the side of the box in a black felt pen, along with a file number. She felt excitement at the prospect, then hesitated and said, "Sure, I want to see it. Although more importantly, I would like to see whatever part you took out of it that you don't want me to see."

"Except for exhibits, which are locked in a vault, everything else is right here," replied Jack.

Yeah, like I believe that ...

"Even the actual exhibits will be described in the documentation on file," continued Jack. "It will take a while. Sit and we'll start reading reports from the beginning."

Mia, with Jack sitting beside her, started reading the reports, beginning at the initial emergency call to when the police arrived at the scene. Jack took a manila envelope from the box, peeked inside it, then quietly placed it back in the box before retrieving the reports that followed.

"What's that?" demanded Mia, suspiciously. "What aren't you showing me?"

"Photos of the scene," replied Jack, "similar to those ones," he added, gesturing to the photos still on the table of Betty Donahue's murder. "You are welcome to look at them, but they are extremely grisly. If you decide you want to see them, I would prefer you wait until you have read all the reports."

"Why?" she snapped. "Show them to me."

"Try and cool it with the attitude, will you? You've got a real chip on your shoulder."

Mia glared in response.

"The reason I would prefer you to wait," continued Jack, "is because I want your brain to be as focused and sharp as possible while you are reading the reports. Seeing the photos may cause your brain to lose its clarity and logic while analyzing the investigative steps that were taken."

Mia felt surprise. Surprise that what Jack said made sense … and was to her advantage. "Oh … I see," she replied. "Then I'll wait." She cast a glance at Jack. *Is he being honest? Doesn't he realize that there was a cover-up?*

Two hours ticked past as Mia read countless reports from numerous people who were interviewed, including pedestrians, other drivers, and shoppers in nearby stores. Most of the actual witness statements were similar. It was a bleak winter rainy day in Richmond and her father was walking across the street after work when he was killed.

A man driving a blue car sped up the left turn lane before veering in front of the cars stopped at the red light and struck her father in the crosswalk, sending him flying head-first into the car's windshield and up and over the back of the car. The car continued on without stopping, but was found twenty minutes later. It had been reported stolen.

"Yeah, I'm sure it was reported stolen," said Mia, "right after he killed my dad. Who owned it?"

"I don't blame you for thinking that," replied Jack. "It happens all too often, but I am positive that would have been looked into. Let's keep reading."

The next page reported that the car had been reported stolen shortly before the hit and run. The statement from the woman who owned the car said she left it running outside a nearby daycare as she went in to get her young son. It was a habit she admitted to doing in wintertime, but said she would never do again.

Mia clenched her jaw as her frustration grew. Her excitement returned when a report noted a profile of the man driving the car had been obtained from a security camera at a nearby gas station. She looked anxiously at Jack, who nodded and pulled out another manila envelope.

They both looked at the pictures. One photo was taken farther back, showing a blue car in amongst city traffic. Other photos showed close-ups of the blue car and a profile of a man could be seen, but not enough to identify him.

"It's the same car," said Jack, quietly.

Mia looked at the picture closer and saw the big spider-webbed break in the front windshield and felt sickened when she imagined the impact her dad's head would have made.

"I was told there is more about the pictures later," said Jack, "but let's keep reading to see what was done to solve this."

Mia continued to read. The stolen car was located a short time later in an alley, but Forensics were unable to come up with any evidence. Potential delivery vans who frequented the alley were contacted with negative results. Numerous people were interviewed from the area of where the car was stolen, but it was raining and nobody took the time to notice anything suspicious or anyone loitering in the area. Eventually the file went dormant.

"What does *S-U-I* mean at the bottom of the report?" asked Mia.

"It means it is still under investigation. The file was never closed," said Jack. "There is one more bit of information left to look at," he said, reaching into the box again. "It was reviewed five years ago. An investigator felt with new technology that the photo could be enhanced some more ... but don't get your hopes up. I was told that the enhanced photo was run through the driver's licence database for facial recognition without result.

"Can I see the enhanced photo?" asked Mia.

Jack nodded and hauled several photos out of an envelope and briefly looked at them. Mia could see that something in the photos caught Jack's attention and he glanced at her, before examining the photos further.

"They are of the same picture taken twenty-five years ago, but of different ranges of close-up," he said. "They appear to be of a man of about forty years old. Short black hair and a magnified image notes that he had three small moles on his lower left jaw."

Mia nodded. "Can I see?"

Jack handed her the photographs and she gasped. *This cannot be!* She looked at Jack for clarification. "He's Chinese!"

Chapter Thirty-Six

Once Mia got over her initial shock, she studied the enhanced photos carefully while matching them with the other photos taken twenty-five years previous. *The pictures seem genuine ... the same car ... a far-off picture of the original car shows other vehicles ... of similar vintage. Even the price of gas on the sign is really cheap.* She stared at Jack in bewilderment and repeated, "He's Chinese."

Jack nodded. "Not unusual, though. It happened in Richmond, which has an ethnic Chinese population base of over forty-five percent."

Mia shook her head as she stared at the picture. *All my life we thought ... this can't be true ...*

"Are you okay?" asked Jack, sympathetically patting her on the back.

"Could I have a copy of one of these pictures to show my mom?" she blurted, then quickly added, "No, never mind."

"All these years your mother thought the man responsible for her husband … your father's death … was some mucky-muck the police refused to charge. Isn't that right?"

Mia shrugged in response.

"Helps explain the chip on your shoulder," said Jack. "Regardless of whether or not you co-operate with me, I'll give you a copy," he said, putting the photo into an envelope and holding it out to her.

"Why?" replied Mia, sullenly, folding her arms across her chest in refusal.

"Because it's the right thing to do," replied Jack. "Think how angry you've been all these years … for your mother, I am sure it was far worse. She has a right to know that everything was done to solve the case. Maybe when you tell her what you have seen and show her the picture, it will bring her some peace of mind."

"It would bring more peace of mind if he was caught and charged," said Mia, bitterly.

"I agree, but maybe this will help," he said, holding the photo closer. When she shook her head he added, "From a police perspective, there is not a problem, any more than there would be putting out a wanted poster."

"Yeah, okay, I'll show her later," said Mia, accepting the envelope.

"You have no intention of showing it to her, do you?" stated Jack abruptly.

"What do you mean?" she asked defiantly.

"Let me guess," said Jack, "you haven't told her about your drug charge, have you?"

Mia took time to take a deep breath. She realized her anger was really at herself, more than at Jack for figuring that out. *Okay ... get a grip ...* She stared blankly at Jack for a moment, then grimaced and shook her head. "I don't want her to worry."

"She's your mom. Don't you think you owe it to her to tell the truth about the police investigation into your dad's death?"

"That was a long time ago. My drug charge is current. Even though I'm innocent, it would still cause her to worry."

"Does she know you were in a car accident?"

"Yes ... and that I was charged with driving without due care."

"Tell her you expressed anger when you were being charged that whoever killed your father was allowed to go free. Tell her you were brought in and shown the file. She would not need to know anything else."

"But what if she checked or had questions of her own and called?"

"I could look after that. The file is still in the domain of Corporal Crane." Jack stared up at the monitor and added, "I'm sure she wouldn't deny doing something that was morally the right thing to do."

Connie stared back at the camera monitor. *Sure Jack ... if it doesn't involve someone being murdered ...*

Mia sighed and momentarily fiddled with the envelope holding the picture.

"Are you going to show her?" asked Jack.

"Yes ... thank you." Her thoughts were distracted when she heard her iPhone buzz in her jacket pocket.

"Go ahead and answer, if you like," said Jack.

Mia remembered she hadn't returned Wolfenden's call. "No, I'll get it later," she said. The thought of being with him enhanced how sick she currently felt.

"So ask yourself," said Jack, with a nod toward the file box, "you've spent hours reading the file. You're a smart person. Did you see any gaps in the investigation or any reason to believe something was covered up? Would so many people have been interviewed and would the file still be looked at periodically if that were the case?"

Mia swallowed and didn't respond.

"Who told you it was a political cover-up?" asked Jack.

Mia shrugged. "I don't know. It was something somebody said to my mother. She believed it and told me."

"People say stupid things," said Jack. "However, I'm sure we could compare the photo to the politicians of the time. There are bound to be photos of them on the Internet somewhere. Can't be too many Asians in government back then."

"Don't bother," replied Mia. "I'm taking political science. I know my history and I'm familiar with their faces, both past and present. The photo doesn't match anyone."

"I'm sure it doesn't," replied Jack. "I do know of cases where there was political influence in the justice system, but that usually took place in court where politically appointed judges do a favour for someone. In my experience, the police file contains the truth. Between you and me, most Mounties outside of Ottawa don't see eye to eye with too many politicians."

Mia took a deep breath and slowly exhaled. She felt conflicted and tried to refocus on the real reason she had been hauled in. *My dad's death has nothing to do with that.*

"Didn't your mother ever voice her concern to the police?" asked Jack.

Mia scowled. "She believed they were corrupt … so why bother," she replied defensively.

"This isn't China," muttered Jack. By the glare he got from Mia he knew his utterance was a tactical error. "We seem to have gone off track" he said. "As far as you and Benny Wong go, I would strongly suggest you start to co-operate with me before Corporal Crane decides it's time to charge you with complicity in Betty Donahue's murder."

Mia unconsciously bit her lower lip as she thought. *Okay … the games are back on again. First of all, I didn't know about the murder … the police are desperate … they can't convict me … but what do they know about Mr. Frank? Do they think he is some peon who is working for Wong?*

"I don't see you as being a really bad person," said Jack. "You're a university student … tuition fees are always going up … someone offered you a chance to make some easy money and you probably never realized what you were getting yourself into. Now that you're in this mess, help me so I can help you get out of it."

"And how do you think I am connected to Benny Wong?" asked Mia.

It was a fair question, but one Jack had hoped he wouldn't be asked. He had to speculate. If he was right, his knowledge might scare her into co-operating. If he was wrong, it would reinforce her belief that the police had nothing. "I should tell you that I'm not the main investigator on the Intelligence Unit who has been working on Wong," he replied. "My facts might be a little off, but from what I understand, you have been passing on information to help Wong with his commercial and business investments."

Mia felt uneasy. *He's close ... but Wong has nothing to do with it ...*

"And, perhaps, hoping to give Wong an insider advantage with our federal government," added Jack.

Oh, fuck ... Mia tried to look puzzled, but had the feeling that Jack wasn't buying it. "This all seems really preposterous," she said. "How on earth would I get any information about those things, let alone have contacts in political office? Do you really think my profs who are teaching me political science are introducing me to politicians? That's absurd!"

"I'm fully aware of who lives in the house with you," said Jack. "The Rolstads both work for Maple Leaf Consulting, with offices in Vancouver and Ottawa. Let's face it. They're spin doctors. How much of their work do they bring home and talk about? With your majors at university, I bet you even volunteer to help them, perhaps on the pretext of being hired when you're done university."

Mia's thoughts tumbled wildly in her brain.

"I haven't approached the Rolstads yet to let them

know what you're up to," continued Jack. "I want to give you the opportunity to co-operate first."

Mia gave a pert grin to hide her fear. "Go ahead, but if you approach the Rolstads with false accusations about me, I'll sue you and the RCMP for so much money that you'll all be back riding horses."

Jack acted like he didn't hear her. "There is another reason you may wish to co-operate. Somehow Wong discovered we identified three of the people connected to killing Betty Donahue. His response was to have them all killed. What do you think he will do to you when he finds out what we know? He'll look at you as another link to him. Another person who could decide to make themselves look good by testifying against him."

Jack expected to see some alarm on her face ... but he didn't. *She's got nerves of steel ...*

Mia knew she had nothing to fear from Wong. *He wouldn't dare to cross paths with the benefactor ... but what should I do? I will be finished as an agent ... and so will Mom if they continue to probe deeper.*

Jack had used up all his cards but one. "I'll give you a moment to think about it," he said, getting to his feet and reaching into the file box to retrieve the manila envelope containing the photos of her father taken at the scene of the hit and run. "These are the pictures of your father after he was killed. Take your time and look at them, but realize they are only photos taken of a man who to you is barely a memory."

"A memory? He was still my father!" said Mia, hotly.

"Yes, but try to imagine how Nancy Brighton ... that 'old bag' as you described her ... felt when she was there in person to see her sister splattered along the sidewalk. Fortunately for you and your mother, you didn't have to go through that experience." Jack paused, then quietly added, "Actually, me saying going through that experience is wrong. I don't think you ever do get through it."

Mia stared at Jack, then quietly accepted the envelope.

"I'll give you a moment alone to think about this, but if there is any shred of decency in you, I know that you will co-operate because in your heart, you know it is the right thing to do."

Chapter Thirty-Seven

"Any thoughts on something I should have done differently?" asked Jack, as he stepped back into the monitoring room.

Connie sighed and shook her head. "Psychologically, you played it far tougher than I would ever have been allowed." She pointed to the monitor and said, "Look ... she's looking at all her dad's pictures, but not displaying anything more than curiosity. No trembling, no tears."

"She was only three," noted Jack. "I doubt she has much in the way of memories, other than equating it with how tough it was on her mom as a single parent."

"What are you going to do?" asked Laura.

Jack shook his head. "I feel stumped."

"Me, too," said Connie. "I don't think she believes we have enough evidence to charge anyone for murder."

"I agree," replied Jack, "although she must be worried a little about what the future will bring if she doesn't co-operate. I told her about the guys under Wong being murdered once we found out they were involved. Even though her hands are clean from murder, she still has to worry what Wong's response will be."

"She didn't seem worried about it from what I saw," noted Laura. "Maybe she is hoping he doesn't find out."

"She has nerves of steel," replied Jack. "She has to be scared of how Wong will react. Still, with the attitude she is displaying, I don't see her being willing to co-operate."

"I agree with you there," said Laura.

They glanced at the monitor and saw that Mia was finished looking at the pictures. "Time for me to take her home," said Jack. "On the way, I'll come across as being a dirty cop. It will put her in a position where she'll have to go to Wong and tell him everything about today out of fear that it would be better for him to hear it from her than from me. Who knows, even without her co-operation, Wong might be worried enough to take the bait."

Mia brooded as she stared at her father's pictures. *They think looking at these will cause me to break down ... good opportunity to clear my head and figure out what I should do ...*

She heard her iPhone buzz and this time it gave her some relief. *Up yours, Wolfenden ... I doubt I'll be seeing you again. Mr. Frank will be called back to Beijing. Mom and I will be dropped as agents ...*

at least for years to come. She gave a pert smile. *I'll be free to do whatever ... and whomever I please ... not some middle-aged pig. All I have to do is ride this down the middle. Pretend to help the police and my worries are over.*

She put the photos back in the manila envelope and tossed them down on the desk. *There, Taggart, I rang your bell. Get in here.*

Seconds later, Jack opened the door.

Mia turned in her chair to face Jack. "I've decided to co-operate," she said bluntly. "Whatever you want me to do, I will."

Jack didn't let the surprise show on his face, but simply nodded like it was the intelligent thing for her to say, before closing the door and sitting down.

"My only fear," said Mia, glancing up at the camera, "is who will know and what will happen to me if Benny Wong finds out."

"The only two people watching us are Corporal Crane, who works in I-HIT, and my partner, Laura Secord, who works with me in Intelligence. Neither will say anything about what you tell me, providing you are being honest."

"Laura Secord ... Canada's heroine in the War of 1812," commented Mia, as she subconsciously rehashed the steps she was about to take. "Most people associate the name with the chocolate company, which was actually named in her honour."

Jack stared briefly into her eyes in response. "You're making the right decision," he said softy. "There is no need to procrastinate."

It bothered Mia that he had read her so well, but she gave a half smile, acknowledging he was right and nodded to give the impression she was about to come clean.

"There are different ways we can approach it," continued Jack. "Wong doesn't need to know you talked. We are going to have to trust each other. I will protect you as long as you're being straight with me."

"And what about me being charged with accessory to murder or whatever it is because of Betty Donahue being killed?"

"Over the years, Wong has ultimately been responsible for more than a dozen murders. If you help us catch him, I would say you have fulfilled your obligation. You wouldn't be charged."

As if you could charge me, anyway.

"And my drug charge?" persisted Mia. *That one does bother me …*

"If I catch Wong with your help, that charge will be withdrawn," said Jack.

If you catch Wong … Mia sighed, then nodded. "Okay, you were right. Some guy approached me a year ago and said I could make extra money if I passed on whatever tidbits I knew about the Rolstads' clients. I was asked to listen to what they talk about over dinner or read whatever reports they might leave lying around if they bring their work home with them. The Rolstads also host a lot of parties, so I was told to mingle, as well."

"Some guy approached you?" asked Jack. "You mean him, don't you?" he said, pointing to the picture of Mr. Frank.

"Yes him," replied Mia. *What the hell, Mr. Frank, you'll be recalled anyway ... and it's not like you're using your real name. They have your picture ... maybe they have your alias as well and are testing me.*

"And he is?"

"I only know him as Mr. Frank," said Mia. "I don't know for sure, but I think that name is phony. At the very least, it's not his last name because he is Chinese. I refer to him as Mr. Frank because that is what he told me to call him and I don't know if it's a first name or last."

"I know the Asian culture does that," said Jack. "The surname precedes the given name ... reverse order from Western ways. I have been referred to as Mr. Jack."

"You have Asian friends?" asked Mia, curiously.

"Yes ... many. Back to Mr. Frank ... how do you contact him?"

"Through a computer chatroom. He's super paranoid about triangulation on his cellphone and is always changing it." Mia realized she had blurted the information out and should have considered whether or not such paranoia would be normal criminal behaviour. She glanced at Jack, wondering if he would believe her, although it was the truth.

Jack didn't seem overly surprised by her comment and asked, "Was it Mr. Frank who taught you counter-surveillance techniques?"

I'm not going to tell you it was my mom ... "Yes, it was Mr. Frank. I have to say I'm surprised you have a photo of him without his knowledge. I think sometimes he employs other people to watch meeting spots, as well."

Jack nodded.

"I suppose the photo you got of him was after the fact, otherwise he would have been alerted to your presence if you had been there in person." She looked at Jack for acknowledgement, but he remained stoic, so she continued, "As I said, he is super paranoid and is always changing locations. I never know exactly where the meeting will be until the last minute."

"Has he ever patted you down for a wire or checked your purse?"

"No," replied Mia, allowing enough time to see Jack's face brighten before adding, "He does have some electronic thing he holds in his hand though. Kind of like an airport wand that he checks me with."

"Oh," replied Jack, as his face revealed his disappointment.

Mia hid her grin. It was a small victory, but it still gave her a sense of control and confidence before continuing the deception. "It wasn't until after I had accepted some money from him that he let it slip one day that he worked for Wong. He holds Wong in high regard … probably hopes to get some recognition some day for babysitting me."

"What does Mr. Frank do for a living? He's wearing a suit, so I presume he has some legitimate job."

"I don't know and I've never asked," replied Mia. "He's the kind of guy who asks questions … not answers them."

"How much information have you passed on to him?" asked Jack. "What firms or people were you able to find out about?"

"That's just it; I haven't been able to find out much of anything," said Mia, "although that didn't stop him from slipping me a hundred bucks once in a while."

"A hundred bucks is nothing for these guys," said Jack.

"The Rolstads have big parties occasionally, so Mr. Frank gave me the drugs to take to the party to see if it would loosen anyone up. I tried to talk him out of it, but the guy scares me a bit, so I took them. I don't do drugs ... plus I'm certain the Rolstads wouldn't approve."

"And it was Mr. Frank who said they would deal with your drug charge?" asked Jack.

"Yes ... but I had no idea that anyone would be hurt. He gave me the impression that someone would be bought off."

"He lied."

"I know that now."

"Did Mr. Frank talk to you about where you would work after university?"

"He did," admitted Mia. "He wants me to get a job with the Rolstads' company. I certainly won't be applying there now, even if you don't talk to them. The Roltstads are nice people." Mia paused in self-reflection, gave Jack a nervous smile, and said, "You probably won't believe me, but I'm glad you caught me. I was looking for an excuse to get out of this mess. Putting Wong behind bars will set me free."

Jack nodded. He did believe her. "You wouldn't be the first to feel that way. Lots of people have told me the same thing after they became entangled in situations that they didn't know how to get out of."

"So how do we catch him?" asked Mia. "What could I possibly do to help?"

"Originally I was hoping you would take me to him and vouch for me."

"Like undercover? Pretending to be a drug dealer or something?"

"No. Wong knows what I look like. He caught me following him recently."

"I told you they were paranoid," admonished Mia. "So he knows you're a policeman?"

"Yes, but I was hoping to make you think I was corrupt and have you introduce me to Wong as a dirty cop."

"Then gain his trust and maybe have him spill the beans on some of the murders," noted Mia.

"Exactly."

"So if we did do that and he later confessed when I wasn't there, would he need to know I was helping you? I could still tell him that I thought you were corrupt. I could say I was duped the same as him."

"Yes, but because you know I'm not corrupt, it will be harder to protect you. I can't lie about that in court. The idea would still work, but by admitting I had an informant helping me in the investigation makes it more difficult."

Mia shrugged. "How do I know that you're not corrupt?" She glanced up at the camera and said, "I doubt that you would admit it in here. Maybe you're working for Wong, too."

"I think you know that if I was working for Wong, you would already be dead," Jack stated matter-of-factly.

"Good point," replied Mia. *Or would be if Wong was in control* ... She smiled. "I was simply trying to help you out."

"I will never lie in court. I might refuse to answer a question to protect someone, but I will never lie. Don't worry about that angle. If this works out, he might be charged with some other murder that doesn't involve you. Other players might enter the picture and give evidence against him. Regardless, if this comes to fruition, I'll meet with a prosecutor before trial and figure out how to handle things."

"Would the prosecutor know who I was?"

"No. I won't divulge your name."

"That's good."

"So let's get back to the task at hand. From what you have told me, there is little doubt in my mind that Mr. Frank is one of Wong's more trusted employees and would possess knowledge of Betty Donahue's murder and likely other murders as well."

"Maybe." Mia shrugged. "I don't know much about criminals, other than from television."

"Would you be willing to try and convince Mr. Frank to meet me and take me to Wong on the pretext of my selling them secret information? If you say enough to make Mr. Frank worried, his reaction will help convince Wong."

Mia glanced at Betty's photos, then stared wide-eyed at Jack. "You bet I would. Maybe I could even do more.

If Wong and Mr. Frank were in jail, maybe it would be safe for me to testify if they do say something?"

Jack shook his head. "No, not unless you were permanently entering the Witness Protection Program ... along with all your relatives. Wong's tentacles reach a long way, even from jail. Arranging the introduction would be enough. Tell them you were brought in for questioning and that I approached you and hinted that for enough money, I could make things go away."

"I understand."

"How hard is it to get hold of Mr. Frank through this computer chat room?"

"Not hard." She then muttered, "He tried to force himself on me once. If I told him I was renting a hotel room he would be there in a flash."

"Don't do that," replied Jack.

"Do what?"

"Anything to demean or humiliate yourself. I don't care if it takes a month for you to contact him. Don't put yourself in a situation that, uh, makes you uncomfortable."

Demean myself? Man, are you naive. "I was only joking about the hotel room," snickered Mia, "but thanks for your concern. Do you want to watch when I do go to meet him?"

"I want to know, but I'll let you do it on your own. I don't want to risk him spotting any surveillance because he would think he's being set up."

Mia nodded in agreement. "It will likely be in some stairwell or at a park. He'll freak out when I tell him."

"Should you be concerned for your safety? Maybe I should have back-up available," noted Jack.

"I'll be okay. Your scenario of pretending to be crooked should arouse his interest. He may look at you as a lifeline to help Wong get out of this predicament."

"That's what I'm counting on," replied Jack. "I know they're not going to trust me to start with, but if you arrange the first meeting, I should be able to take it from there. I'll drop a few titillating bits of information to prime the pump. If you and Mr. Frank were at the first meeting, it would help alleviate suspicion. Wong wouldn't feel so much like he was being set up."

"I understand. Kind of like peer pressure. I'll do my best."

"You better," said Jack, firmly. "I'm good at what I do. If you warn Wong what I'm up to, I'll know."

Mia frowned. "That idea never entered my mind."

Chapter Thirty-Eight

Jack introduced Mia to Laura and they drove her back to the university to where Mia's car was parked.

The trip back was relatively quiet, but when Jack turned into the parking lot, Mia was began to worry. *Did I talk too much? What will happen when the benefactor finds out? Will they question my loyalty? If they killed that woman to protect me from getting a criminal record ...*

Fear of survival briefly overpowered her normal pragmatism and she made her first serious mistake with Jack. When he parked alongside her car, she abruptly leaned forward in her seat and asked, "Will you be putting in a report on your computer or laptop that names me?"

Jack turned in the seat to face her. "I will do a report, but you won't be named. You'll be assigned a number and it is that number that goes in the report."

"No, but if people read it, they would figure it out," replied Mia, anxiously.

"Very few people would have access to my report," said Jack. "It isn't something that goes to court or anything."

"Okay, good," replied Mia. *I'm probably screwed. Better tell Mr. Frank everything ...*

Jack studied her face, trying to read her thoughts. He sensed she was holding something back. "I realize you're under stress and I suspect it will only get worse. Even if you didn't know that Wong was going to kill Betty Donahue, you'd have to be a psychopath for it not to bother you."

"It bothers me," muttered Mia.

"Normally I would tell someone in your position not to tell anyone that you are co-operating with us, but I have a feeling that the pressure you are under will cause you to want to confide in someone. Do you have a boyfriend? Someone you trust implicitly?"

"I don't have a boyfriend and I don't feel any need to talk to anyone," replied Mia, adamantly.

"I know you are close to your mom by how excited you were to show her the picture, before deciding you didn't want her to worry. Maybe you should talk to her? Moms are pretty intuitive. She will know something is troubling you. If she is worried, we would be glad to meet with her to try and alleviate her worry."

Mia bit her lower lip as she tried to think what was best.

"I don't care if you do give her the bullshit about it not being your drugs," continued Jack, "but I know this is bothering you and I sense that you will confide in someone sooner or later."

"I'm not a child who needs to run to mommy," replied Mia, defensively.

Jack shrugged. "You might be right, but I am experienced in these matters and my prediction of human nature is usually accurate. You are mature enough that I think Betty's death will eat away at you. In the long run it could affect your emotional health if you try to keep it inside you."

Jack's words and talk about her mother made her feel vulnerable. The urge to regain control came back. "I'll think about it," she said, then looked at Jack and glanced at her car and said, "Can I talk to you in private for a moment?"

Jack exchanged a knowing glance with Laura, but nodded and got out of the car with Mia while Laura remained inside.

"I know she's your partner and everything," said Mia, with a nod of her head toward Laura, "but in the future, I prefer to deal with you alone. There's something about her that makes me feel uncomfortable."

"Not a chance," replied Jack. "Laura and I are a team."

"Big deal. It's not like you're joined at the hip."

"You are deliberately picking me because I am of the opposite sex."

"What the hell? That is not true at all! My God, what a narcissistic and egotistical thing to say."

"On a psychological level you think that if you deal with me alone, it will be easier to manipulate me through flirtation or other sexual overtones. Some people do it on a subconscious level, but for you, it is overt."

"I don't know where you took your psychology 101, but that's silly," scoffed Mia.

"Is it? Do you really think your performance in the interview room of massaging a cramp out of your leg went unnoticed? Give me a break."

Mia stared blandly back at Jack. *The bastard is smart ... if I continue to lie, he won't trust me ...*

"I'll tell you right now that I don't trust you," said Jack, as if reading her thoughts. "If you are straight with me, I'll protect you, but if you're not, I should tell you that I have no qualms about feeding you to the wolves. If you fly with the crows, expect to get shot."

Mia was quiet for a moment, then hung her head and said, "Okay, I'm sorry. I admit I was hoping to control you through sexual innuendo." She turned her face up to Jack, eyes watering, and said, "Do you blame me? I'm scared. I feel like I've lost all control over my life."

"As I said," replied Jack, "if you're straight with me, I'll look after you. You made a mistake taking money from Wong's people, but you're young and have a whole life ahead of you. I won't jeopardize that and will protect you until the day I die ... providing you prove you are worthy of protection. Later, even if it meant dropping Wong's charge, I would do it to protect you."

Mia stared at Jack. *I believe you.* "Good enough," she said, fumbling with her keys as she unlocked her car. "I'll call you when I make contact with Mr. Frank.

Mia watched as Jack returned to his car. *He's a good guy ... and good guys finish last ...*

"Is that what I think it was about?" asked Laura, when Jack got back in the car.

"Yes."

"I wouldn't trust her alone with my cat," said Laura.

"Good thing I'm not your cat." Jack grinned.

"That makes it worse," retorted Laura. "My tom-cat has more scruples than a lot of men I know."

"Only because your cat has been neutered," replied Jack, "which is what Natasha would do to me if I strayed." He glanced at Mia sitting in her car. "Your instincts are right, though. I don't trust her. She's holding something back, but what choice do we have?"

Laura shrugged in response. "I don't know, but you using her to get to Wong makes me feel sick."

"Her holding back could be a trust issue for her, too. Maybe she'll open up more later."

"And in the mean time what do we do?" asked Laura. "Just wait? She said it might take a few days to contact Mr. Frank."

"Were you listening when she was concerned about me putting in a report on my computer or laptop?"

"Yes, I think she is genuinely concerned for her safety. I actually took it as a good sign. If she had no intention of helping us, she wouldn't be so worried."

"Perhaps, but there's something else. Why did she specifically mention computer and laptop? Why not simply ask if I was putting in a report? I think she's holding something back there as well."

"Like what?"

"Like I think I'm going to give Jim Purney a call. He's the best guy I know when it comes to electronics and bugs. I'm going to ask him to check out Roger Morris's office at AOCTF."

"You're thinking Wong could have spyware on their computers?"

Jack shrugged. "Who knows? Stranger things have happened."

"I can't see that happening," said Laura. "If Wong has spyware on the AOCTF computers, he would have it on all our computers. I don't know much about that stuff, but I'm sure our firewall protection is the best there is."

"You're probably right, but it won't hurt to check." Jack glanced at his watch and said, "It's eight o'clock, let's call it a day. I'll phone Jim in the morning."

Mia watched as Jack and Laura drove out of the parking lot. She decided she would call her mother, but not until she returned home and sent a priority message requesting an urgent meeting with Mr. Frank.

Chapter Thirty-Nine

After sending the priority message, Mia stared forlornly at the photo Jack had given her. Eventually she reached a decision and picked up her iPhone.

"Mom … are you at home? I need to talk to you."

"No, I'm in Calgary at the moment," replied Jia-li. "What's wrong?"

"Uh, I'm okay," replied Mia, "Don't worry. I learned something interesting is all. What are you doing in Calgary?"

"There is another proposal to build an oil pipeline from Alberta out to the west coast. If it goes ahead, it would really open up distribution to, uh, Asia and other places."

"How long will you be there?"

"I'm doing an interview with one of the execs tomorrow. It's guaranteed there'll be a public backlash, so I have also lined up interviews with a few people who are unemployed and will put a spin on it about how it would help their families. I've booked a flight home tomorrow, but it will be after midnight before I get home."

"Tomorrow is Wednesday," said Mia, thinking aloud. "I don't have a class Thursday morning. Maybe we could see each other then?"

"What's wrong, honey? I can tell that something has happened. Don't make me wait until Thursday. I won't be able to sleep."

Mia hesitated, then took a deep breath and slowly exhaled. "Remember I told you I was in a car accident last month?"

"Yes, you told me *after* I asked you what happened to your car."

"Okay, okay, but what I didn't tell you, was how angry I was when I got a ticket. I gave the cop a bad time for never charging anyone when Dad died."

Jia-li sighed. "You're going to have to learn to let that go. I wish I had never told you."

"No, you should have!" replied Mia. "As a result of what I said, I was invited to a police station this afternoon and they let me see the file for myself!"

"They showed you the file?" asked Jia-li in surprise.

"Yes. I read the whole thing ... and Mom, I don't think it was done by anyone the police knew. Back when it happened, the police got a blurry picture of the man responsible from a gas station security camera. Five years ago they used modern technology to enhance the picture." Mia paused and when she didn't get a response, added, "It shows the police never gave up trying to solve it."

"Has anyone been arrested?"

"No, but —"

"I didn't think so," replied Jia-li, bitterly.

"But Mom, you can tell the police are trying. They wouldn't have bothered if they were covering something up. They even ran the picture through facial-recognition procedures, but unfortunately it was only the profile and that didn't work."

"Of course they would say that, or make up something to deceive you."

"Mom, no, really … I don't think so. I saw the whole file. They even gave me a copy of the picture. I'll take a picture of it with my phone and send it to you. This guy wasn't any politician."

"I thought you said it was only a profile. How do you know it wasn't someone connected with government if he can't be properly identified?"

"Mom … the picture shows a guy of about forty … and he's Asian. I know every Asian person connected to politics, past and present. It definitely isn't any one of them."

"An Asian?"

Mia's sigh was audible. "Yes, I felt … well, betrayed by it, but it did happen in Richmond. Forty-five percent Chinese. It's a common joke that all the cars in Richmond are BMWs, Mercedes, or loaners from body shops. We don't exactly have a good reputation for safe driving."

Jia-li was silent as her brain tried to digest what she had been told and the memories it brought back from that fateful day.

"You okay, Mom?"

"I'm okay, but I still feel like there is something you're not telling me."

Mia paused. *Should have told her about the drug charge to start with ...*

"Maybe something we should talk about when we're together?" suggested Jia-li.

"Okay, there is something, but don't worry. We should go for a stroll when you get home. I'll come by in the morning at about ten."

Jia-li understood. Some things could not be spoken about over a telephone.

Mia saw a text flash onto her phone, notifying her to go to a certain area of the city. "I have another call ... I gotta go. Love ya, Mom."

Mr. Frank gritted his teeth as he drove and it wasn't from the traffic. *Another priority request to meet Mia. What now?* He swore aloud when another driver cut in front of him. It was a common occurrence and he realized he was tired. *And why shouldn't I be? I've barely slept in four days, ever since Mia dropped the bombshell on me about her new charge, let alone finding out the witness is still alive.*

Since then he had brooded over how to resolve the situation. Murdering Mia was the option that repeatedly came to mind. *But who else knows? Did she tell Jia-li? She said she didn't ... but their mother and daughter relationship is strong. Then there's Wong ... he would not dare tell anyone who I represent, but would the benefactor send someone to interview him if Mia and Jia-li were murdered?*

He slammed the top of the steering wheel with his hand in frustration. *I need to kill all three ... but how could it be done without me being suspect?*

He turned a corner and glanced in the rear-view mirror as he went through his routine counter-surveillance moves, but his mind was still on Mia. *What has the little tart been up to?*

Mr. Frank was about to be handed the solution to his problem ... with a plan that included the murder of Jack Taggart.

Chapter Forty

It was dark when Mia parked her car near the corner of Shaughnessy Street and West Kent Avenue North. It was an industrial area and basically void of traffic at night. She walked along Kent Avenue North. Railway tracks were to her left and less than a block ahead, the Oak Street Bridge loomed high above her.

"This better be good," said Mr. Frank, stepping out of the shadows and into view under a street light. He waited until Mia approached closer, then said, "If Wolfenden has simply changed his schedule, you could have alerted the benefactor online through secure channels."

"It isn't about him," said Mia, tersely. "It's about you."

"Me? What about me?"

"The police were waiting for me at UBC this afternoon and grabbed me on my way to my car after class. They brought me in for questioning about the woman who was murdered in the hit and run."

Mr. Frank felt his guts twist. He suspected she might be routinely questioned as the police tried to come up with a possible motive. He anticipated such preliminary questioning would take place on her doorstep. Her lack of nervousness and actual innocence would be apparent and manifest her lack of culpability in the crime. She might even think it was a coincidence. Being brought in for questioning sounded more ominous. *The police have more than a theory …*

"They are after you for the murder of that woman," continued Mia. "The one you thought was a witness against me."

"Me? What are you talking about?" asked Mr. Frank, sounding flustered.

"Drop the innocent act," said Mia, harshly. "They know … and so do I."

Mr. Frank stared at her, momentarily too dumbfounded to respond.

"Why didn't you tell me what you were doing?" asked Mia. "Was it so I would actually portray genuine innocence if I were questioned? Perhaps even pass a polygraph?"

Do I continue to deny? If Mia knows the truth, she may suspect I acted to save myself and not on instruction from the benefactor. "Yes, that was the reason the benefactor did not want you to know," he responded.

"You told me the police were being bribed … that I had nothing to worry about!"

"The, uh, officer I thought could be bribed has been transferred elsewhere," replied Mr. Frank. "That is why the benefactor had to resort to drastic action to —"

"The officer? I thought they were all corrupt?" replied Mia. "That's what I was always told."

"The benefactor cannot always risk the possibility of identifying his presence by wantonly tossing money about over something that is not of vital importance."

"Am I not of vital importance?"

"Of course you are," assured Mr. Frank. "I was only throwing out possible reasons. You and I play the parts assigned to us, but we are like two grains of rice in a bowl. We have no idea of what action could affect the whole bowl."

"In other words, we don't see the big picture," said Mia, recalling Jack's words from earlier in the day.

"Exactly. It is not up to us to question the benefactor's decision. We are not in a position to know ... and for obvious reasons, we shouldn't be."

Mia briefly closed her eyes. *The big picture ... is what Jack wanted me to see ... the woman crying over the loss of her sister. The pictures of a disfigured and bloody woman lying on a sidewalk next to a dead dog.*

"What are you thinking?" asked Mr. Frank.

Mia opened her eyes. "I didn't know the benefactor resorted to such action in Canada," she replied quietly.

"Which is also why you were not told," replied Mr. Frank. "Such action is extremely rare and not taken without considerable thought." *Rare is likely the wrong word. I doubt it has ever been done ... at least with the benefactor's knowledge ...*

Mia shook her head in shock. "If anyone ever found out ... it would be like when the Japanese bombed Pearl Harbor. Awakening the sleeping giant."

"It is strictly on a need-to-know basis," agreed Mr. Frank. "You were responsible for what needed to happen, but there was no reason for you to know about it."

"I was responsible?" hissed Mia. "It wasn't my idea to stash two bags of drugs in my purse, drink wine, and drive! Not to mention the fact it was you who slopped wine on me before I left."

Mr. Frank stared at her in response.

"I think there was something else you did, as well," persisted Mia. "I felt peculiar for only having one glass of wine. What did you put in it? Ecstasy?"

"I certainly did not!" replied Mr. Frank, vehemently. "It was your own jittery nerves reacting to what you were instructed to do that night. I was trying to calm you."

"That wasn't all you were trying to do," replied Mia, coldly.

"Enough of these foolish thoughts! You said the police know I was involved. You obviously meant that you know I was involved ... not that the police know about me?"

"Oh, they know about you. They showed me your picture."

Mr. Frank gasped. "How? Where was it taken? What did they say to you?"

Mia stared silently for a moment. *For some reason I feel satisfaction in seeing your look of fear ...*

"Don't just stand there!" snarled Mr. Frank. "Talk!" he demanded, raising the back of his hand as though to strike her. "Tell me everything!"

Mia stepped back in fear. "Okay, okay. I'll start from the beginning."

Mr. Frank listened with utmost attention as Mia told how she was picked up at university and brought to an interview room, where a Corporal Jack Taggart of the RCMP Intelligence Unit questioned her about the hit and run and brought in the victim's sister.

"So they hoped to rattle you with the sister and gain a confession," said Mr. Frank, contemptuously.

Mia nodded.

"But of course, you really did not know anything … so as you can see, the benefactor was right in their decision not to tell you. Continue."

"The officer said he knew Wong was behind the woman's murder and made it clear that Wong was who he was after."

Mr. Frank glared at Mia. "Where did I come into it? Get to the part about me! You said they had my picture."

"I think the police followed me last Friday when I went to meet you, but lost me. I think later they pulled security camera footage from the area and discovered you. Perhaps not seeing you drive in or out of the garage or something triggered their —"

"Or you were careless and brought them straight to me," he replied, accusingly, putting his hand up to gesture for her to be silent as his eyes probed the shadows around them. "Okay, continue."

"I did everything I had been taught to do," replied Mia. She then told him about Taggart's plan.

"So Taggart wants to pretend to be a dirty cop in the hope of gaining my trust?" reiterated Mr. Frank.

"Yours, but more importantly for Taggart, he wants Benny Wong's trust. Taggart thinks you are only a two-bit player who works for Wong. It's Wong who he hopes to arrest for the murder. He knows I knew nothing about it."

Mr. Frank was silent as he digested the information.

"Obviously, your position is compromised," prodded Mia, hoping to learn what he was thinking. "Mine, too, for that matter."

"The police have nothing," said Mr. Frank, in a confident voice that he hoped would sound convincing.

"I agree, as far as the murder goes, but there is still my drug charge," noted Mia. "I agreed to the introduction to you and Wong so that my charge would be dropped. I thought if you arranged for Taggart and me to meet Wong, it would look like I had fulfilled my end of the bargain."

Mr. Frank felt like he had been offered a solution to his problem on a silver platter. *Mia and Wong together … plus Taggart.* His mind went over the scenario. *Contact Wong and tell him Taggart might be corrupt and that they should meet him … Wong will be less suspicious if I am there. Suggest we meet in the usual place … a tiny restaurant with a back door where I can come and go unseen. Wong's bodyguards usually sit in the restaurant having tea while Wong meets me … his trusted friend … in the office down the hall.* He smiled to himself at being considered a trusted friend. *I will have plenty of time to shoot the three of them and escape out the back before the bodyguards have time to react. They don't even know who I am.*

"I know you could not risk showing up," added Mia, "but it wouldn't really matter if Wong played along."

Mr. Frank gave an evil grin as the last of his plan came together. *Yes, tell Wong to take all precautions. No guns, phones, or electronic devices for either Mia or Jack ... make them both go through the ropes before meeting with them in case Mia has been turned and it is a ruse by the Canadian Security Intelligence Section or the RCMP to capture me.* He breathed a sigh of contentment. *Only one last detail ... Jia-li ...*

"So what do you think?" asked Mia. "I'm sure you can order Wong to do it."

Mr. Frank tried not to let the annoyance of his thoughts being interrupted show and he threw out a question to stall for time as he put the final garnish on his plan. "This Jack Taggart ... working Intelligence ... he could be of value down the road. Perhaps you could seduce him at some point?"

"I don't think so," replied Mia. "I made certain ... overtures ... during his interview with me. I suspect he is too intelligent to fall for that."

"Have you told your mother?" asked Mr. Frank, staring intently at Mia's reaction.

"Nothing about the interrogation, but there is more."

"More? What possibly more could there be?"

"Of no consequence to you, but the police have a picture of the man who drove over my father twenty-five years ago. They allowed me to see their file. It was a poor-quality photo that back then was unrecognizable, but they enhanced it and you can see the man's profile. They gave me a copy. He is Asian, which shows he wasn't some government —"

"You have the picture? Show me!" said Mr. Frank, abruptly.

"I left it in my car, but I have a copy on my iPhone that I sent Mom," replied Mia. "I didn't think you would be interested or find it relevant," she said, as she fumbled with the buttons on her phone to retrieve the photo, "but then again, he looks to be Chinese …"

"You sent your mother a copy of the photo? I thought you said you didn't tell her?"

"I told her I complained to the police when I received a ticket for my car accident about their investigation into my father. I said they called me in to show me the file as proof they had tried to solve the case. It was Taggart's idea.

"I see. Your father died long before my time, but I am still interested. It is likely a dupe made up to convince you to co-operate with them."

"Maybe, but I don't … here it is," she said, holding the photo up for Mr. Frank to see, while staring at him in the hope that by some remote chance he might know the man.

Mr. Frank grabbed the phone from her hand and held it closer to his face and peered intently at the photo as his eyes registered surprise.

"Do you know him?" asked Mia, excitedly. "You look like you think you —"

Mr. Frank glanced up and shook his head. "No, of course I do not know him," he said, mockingly. "I am, however, impressed with how good the enhancement is." He handed her phone back and said, "Which makes me more convinced that it is a fake. Nevertheless, you are right, it is not relevant. What is relevant is the matter at hand."

Mia nodded in response.

"What did your mother say?"

"She didn't get back to me on it, but I could tell when I first told her that she didn't believe me. She has been angry all these years. Me, too, I guess. I wanted her to know that the police weren't refusing to charge someone. I don't think it is a fake. I think they really don't know who did it."

"I suppose you need to cling to some hope. How about your mother? Did she believe your lie that they showed you the file as a result of your complaint when you had the car accident?"

"Maybe. She could tell I was holding something back. She's in Calgary and won't be home until after midnight tomorrow. She wants to talk to me Thursday morning.

"And the rest? Your drug charge?"

"I didn't think she needed to hear that over the phone. I didn't want her to worry. I was going to wait until she returned. She will need to know sometime. I'm sure we will be getting a new case officer ... that's if the benefactor ever decides to use us. I imagine we'll be left to cool off for years to come."

"Don't be sure of anything," said Mr. Frank, ominously. "And do not say anything to your mother until the benefactor decides what is right. I will be meeting her when she returns. If she is to be told, I will tell her."

"Did I do the right thing by pretending to co-operate with the police?"

"Definitely." Mr. Frank smiled while giving her a reassuring pat on the back. He tried not to frown when he saw that his touch caused her to step back. "I am positive the benefactor will wish to proceed with the scenario that you have set up."

"And you will be able to get Wong to co-operate?"

"I expect it would work better if Wong believes Taggart might be corrupt. His demeanour will reflect that and make it more believable for Taggart to presume that you did your best."

"How long before you know, and, if approved, how long before the meeting would take place?" asked Mia.

Mr. Frank stared at her for a moment. *If your mother wasn't away, I would kill you all tomorrow night* … "I could see it happening in the next forty-eight hours. Go home and relax. You've performed admirably. In the meantime, I will look after things. We'll meet tomorrow and go over the details. If the plan is approved, which I am sure it will be, you can then contact Taggart to pass on the details."

As Mr. Frank trudged back to his car, he went over what he would later tell the benefactor.

Unbeknownst to me, Mia had become involved in drug trafficking. She was caught and panicked. Knowing about Wong, she went to him to kill the witness. It was a foolish venture. The RCMP turned Mia and came up with a ruse to trap Wong. Taggart pretended to be a dirty cop, but Wong became suspicious and called me, requesting I meet him immediately at the restaurant. When I arrived at the back door, he let me in and confessed what had transpired, but was concerned Mia was trying to set him up. Mia then saw me and panicked. A fight broke out and Taggart, who hadn't been properly searched, pulled a gun and killed Wong. I wrestled the gun away from him, but in so doing, it discharged and killed him. Mia grabbed me and screamed out to the bodyguards, accusing me of killing Wong. I was forced to kill her and flee before the bodyguards arrived ... plus I thought it wise that they didn't find out about the benefactor's association with Mia or myself.

Mr. Frank smiled to himself as he thought of ending his account. *I was saddened by how Mia disgraced herself and went to Jia-li to explain what had happened. Unfortunately, she became enraged over her daughter's death and said she was going to go to the authorities. In the end, I had no choice but to kill her as well.*

Chapter Forty-One

On Wednesday morning Jack called Jim Purney and told him Benny Wong may have somehow corrupted the computers at the Asian Organized Crime Task Force office. Jim was skeptical that the system could be compromised, but promised to investigate immediately and would liase with Roger Morris.

At one-thirty that afternoon, Jim was no longer skeptical and called Jack.

"I think we've discovered the leak," said Jim.

"So I was right," said Jack.

"Partially. It isn't any of the Force computers. I'm at the home of Constable Josephine Bagley. She works for AOCTF, but has had a back injury and has been working from home, doing reports and analytical services for them. Her computer has been corrupted, likely when she downloaded something."

"Great work, big guy. I bet Roger Morris will be pleased to hear that," Jack remarked. "He was concerned it was one of his people or perhaps one of the Chinese translators."

"He might be pleased, but some other people aren't," growled Jim.

"What do you mean?"

"This particular spyware is something like I've never seen before and as far as I can tell, neither has anyone else. It's way over my head, so I called in a couple of buddies who work for the CSE to take a look. They're with me now."

"CSE? Who are they?"

"The Communications Security Establishment of Canada. They're our national cryptologic agency. Code-makers and code-breakers, amongst other things. One of the things they do is provide information on technology security and assistance to federal law-enforcement and security agencies. They've only been here half an hour, but I can tell they're concerned."

"Will they be able to trace it back to Wong or perhaps someone working for him?"

"In time, I'm sure they can. They're seizing Bagley's computer and taking it with them. I might learn more later."

It was three-thirty in the afternoon when Mia received a cryptic message, giving her a location to meet Mr. Frank an hour later.

Mr. Frank arrived on time and parked near the Prospect Point Café in Stanley Park, before walking a short distance down Bridle Path. He was pleased to see that the path through the forest was deserted. Once he crossed over Rawlings Trail, he counted his steps, and, upon reaching one hundred, veered off into the bush a few steps to wait.

"I'm already here," whispered Mia, stepping out from behind a tree.

Mr. Frank nodded, but put his finger to his lips for her to be quiet. They both stood for a couple of minutes peering through the bush at the path. When nobody appeared, Mr. Frank turned and said, "I met Wong this morning and he agreed to meet you and Taggart tomorrow night."

"Perfect," replied Mia, feeling relieved that everything was going as she had hoped.

"Wong is understandably paranoid about the meeting and is concerned he is being set up." Mr. Frank paused. "Can't say as I blame him, I feel uncomfortable about it, too."

"Surely you won't be there?" exclaimed Mia. "The benefactor would never risk putting you in a position like that where you could possibly be apprehended, especially when your presence is not necessary to complete the charade."

Mr. Frank eyed Mia for a moment. *She is right of course … Jia-li has taught her well.* "The benefactor has not given me an answer on that yet," replied Mr. Frank.

"But —"

"You are a valuable asset and if my presence there will aid your credibility, I may be instructed to go. Wong will still meet with Taggart, whether I am there or not. Either way, now that the police have me on their radar, I expect I will be leaving Canada soon."

"Did you tell Wong that you think Taggart is corrupt?" asked Mia.

"I told him that you felt that Taggart was genuinely corrupt, but of course he will need to decide for himself," replied Mr. Frank.

"That's okay. Taggart is perceptive. As long as Wong thinks Taggart might be corrupt, his actions and demeanour will lead Taggart to conclude that I have done what he asked of me. There would be no reason for you to risk attending. Wong must realize and respect your position, as well."

"Perhaps, but the decision of whether or not I attend is up to the benefactor. You will go to Chinatown tomorrow night at eight o'clock and park near Main Street and East Hastings. Then you will receive further instructions over your phone, at which time you will leave your car and walk to wherever the instructions tell you."

"Wong wants to make sure the police are not following us," said Mia.

"Of course. He is worried that it is a trap. You must tell Taggart that Wong will have both of you searched prior to meeting him. No phones, guns, or any electronic devices are allowed once you leave the car."

"Taggart is a policeman. I expect he would carry a gun."

"Not if he wants to meet Wong he won't. Wong said he spoke with Taggart before and was warned of a possible contract on his life. Wong is worried that if Taggart is corrupt, that he may try to fulfil the contract himself."

"I see." Mia paused and asked, "What if Taggart does succeed in tricking Wong into confessing about the murder ... or murders, according to Taggart?"

"Wong isn't a fool. If Taggart does manage to trick him, it wouldn't happen for a long time to come. Certainly not on the first meeting when you are there."

"But if Wong is caught, is there not a fear that he might co-operate with the police and expose us to gain leniency?"

"I am sure these are questions the benefactor is already considering," replied Mr. Frank. "There are possible solutions. Perhaps when the charade has gone on long enough, Wong may be tipped off that it is a trap. By then, you will be free of your charge."

It was a quarter to six and Jack and Laura had each parted company in the office parking lot to go home when Jim Purney called Jack on his cellphone.

"Who the hell are you investigating?" asked Jim.

"Hi to you, too," replied Jack. "What are you talking about? I told you, I'm working on Benny Wong. Top bad Chinese guy in the city. Why? What's up?"

"What's up? Man ... a lot of people are asking that question," he muttered. "I heard back from my buddies at CSEC. This spyware has a lot of people panicking, to the point that they are calling everyone in Ottawa who worked the day shift today to get back to the office immediately."

"I take it they are concerned that more than one laptop is being hacked?"

"You've got that right. Whatever it is they are looking at has huge ramifications, both in Canada and in the States. Some of our government computer systems share the same protection."

"I thought your Communication Security buddies would be used to looking at spyware and dealing with hackers on a daily basis. Isn't that a big part of their job?"

"It is, which is why they're upset. They've never encountered something like this before. They're trying to trace it from where it's bouncing from one URL address to the next, which is normal for hackers to do to try and hide themselves. What isn't normal is that my buddy thinks they are bouncing a beam off the side of a mountain to throw us off. That type of sophistication is still in the theoretical stages here. They didn't think anyone had actually developed it yet."

"So we've got some real computer geek involved," noted Jack.

"More likely a team of geeks. I don't know what you're getting into, but Wong may be a lot more than he appears."

Jack paused as he received a text from Mia that read: *UBC same spot — 6pm.* "Have to go Jim," said Jack. "I'm going to meet a source connected to Wong. Is there a problem if the bad guys know we're on to their spyware? It would help me with a UC scenario that I plan to do."

"I'm sure with the steps being taken that whoever

is responsible will already know that we're on to them, or will by tomorrow. That's why everyone is in a scramble to protect what we can before it's compromised further."

"Good. If I learn anything relevant from my source, I'll call you back."

Jack called Laura before she pulled out of the lot and told her he wanted her to return and go with him to meet Mia.

"She does makes you nervous, eh?" snickered Laura.

"You've got that right," replied Jack. "In more ways than one."

It was a quarter to six and Mia was on her way to the university parking lot when Jia-li called her.

"Hi, honey," said Jia-li. "I'm calling to make sure everything is okay and that we're still on for ten o'clock tomorrow morning."

"Yes, everything is going fine," replied Mia. "I'll be there. What's the weather like in Calgary? It's cloudy here and looks like rain."

Jia-li glanced up at the clouds from where she was parked on Gore Avenue in downtown Vancouver and replied, "Sunny, but windy." *At least it was when I left there this morning ...* "What are you up to tonight?" asked Jia-li. "Sounds like you're on the speakerphone in your car?"

"I'm meeting some, uh, people at school in fifteen minutes. Have to work together on a project."

Perfect … "That's good. Study hard. You've only got another year to go."

After Jia-li hung up from speaking to her daughter, she got out of her car and steeled herself for the decision she had made. *I've never murdered anyone before … but I certainly know someone who has …*

Chapter Forty-Two

As Jack drove Laura to the university for their meeting with Mia, he told her about the phone call he had received from Jim Purney.

"So you were right," said Laura. "She was holding out on us."

"I'm positive she knows about the spyware," agreed Jack. "That's why she was worried about us putting in a report."

"Maybe Wong had Mr. Frank tell her about it to ease her nerves," suggested Laura. "To convince her she would never be caught because they would know if the police were on to them."

"Possibly, or it could be deeper than that," brooded Jack. "The way the Communication Security people are reacting, it could be a lot bigger than we realize. I'm wondering if Wong got Mia to corrupt the computers at the Rolstads' PR firm. That would also explain her knowledge about it."

"So much for her crap about listening to dinner or party conversation."

"I'm sure she does that, too," replied Jack. "There is something else to consider. She told me Wong wanted her to try and get a job with the Rolstads' firm when she graduated. Their Ottawa office provides spin doctors for our politicians. Try and imagine what Wong would gain if he could corrupt the computers there."

"Oh, man ... we're lucky to be finding out now. I told you I didn't trust her. The little bitch is in a lot deeper than she's letting on."

"I agree."

Laura shook her head. "So how do you want to play it when we meet her? Come down hard on her or what?"

"Let's see what she has to say first. I don't want to do anything that would jeopardize my chance of meeting Wong. It would be nice to know what the Communication Security people find out before disclosing what we know."

"Good point. There she is," said Laura, pointing to Mia's car.

Mia quickly got out of her car and into the back seat behind Jack and Laura. She immediately admitted she met Mr. Frank yesterday right after they had left her at the university. She said she told him what Jack told her to say, then met him again this afternoon and learned that the meeting with Wong had been arranged for tomorrow night.

Jack and Laura listened silently as Mia talked about the security measures that Wong demanded for the meeting.

Laura raised one eyebrow at Jack when Mia said that Wong would not allow any weapons or electronic devices at the meeting.

Jack ignored Laura. "What impression did you get from Mr. Frank?" he asked. "Do you think he believes I'm a dirty cop?"

"I went by the scenario you requested," replied Mia. "First I showed him the picture to scare him and then —"

"Showed him the picture?" asked Jack. "I didn't give you a copy of the picture we have of him. You were only to say you saw it."

"You're right," replied Mia. "Sorry, I feel a little flustered talking to you two. That was the picture I told him about. It was the picture you gave me of the man who killed my father that I actually showed him."

"Why? Because he is Chinese and you were hoping he might recognize him?" asked Jack.

"Yes," sighed Mia.

"That was a long time ago," noted Laura. "His appearance will not only have changed, but he may not be living here or even be alive."

Mia nodded silently and her eyes moistened.

"I'm sorry for your disappointment," said Jack.

"Yeah, thanks," sighed Mia. "For a moment I thought Mr. Frank did recognize him, but it turned out he was simply impressed with the quality of the photo enhancement."

"So then what happened?" asked Jack.

"I gave him the line you told me," replied Mia. "I said you told me you were looking for a part-time job to supplement your income and that you wondered if you could perhaps be of value to Wong in ... some special way."

"Did he question you further on that?" asked Jack. "Or comment on what he thought?"

Mia shrugged. "He seemed interested, but made it apparent that Wong would be the one to decide. As Wong has agreed to meet you, I presume everything is okay in that regard."

"And how are you holding up?" asked Jack. "Are you nervous about your role in this?"

"Of course I am," admitted Mia. "Who wouldn't be? You told me that these guys are killers. All I want to do is get it over with and never have anything to do with them again."

By the tone of her voice, Jack believed her. "Did you talk with your mom? How did it go?"

"I called her yesterday as soon as you dropped me off, but she's in Calgary at the moment and won't be back until midnight tonight. I gave her the story you told me, about having an accident and complaining to the police about my dad's case as the reason I saw the file"

"What did she think?" asked Jack.

Mia frowned. "She's pretty dubious. She thinks everything, including the photo, is probably fake. I told her I don't believe it is, but after so many years of her thinking otherwise, it might be hard for her to accept."

"And about your drug charge and assisting us?" asked Laura. "What did she say about that?"

"I didn't talk about that," replied Mia. "I'm meeting her tomorrow morning, but because this is happening tomorrow night, I think I'll wait until it's over. I don't want her to worry."

Mr. Frank arrived at his apartment building and sat in his car for a moment as he went over his plans for the following night, before reaching under his dash and removing a revolver.

Wong had provided him with the five-shot snub-nosed Smith & Wesson that morning and it caused him to smile. *It is like a man providing the hangman with the rope to hang him with.*

Chapter Forty-Three

At six o'clock in the evening, while Mia was still meeting with Jack and Laura, the owner of a florist shop in another part of Vancouver was closing for the day.

Lok Cheng shuffled over and locked the door to his shop. He appeared older than his sixty-six years of age. His bald head tended to make his ears look too large and his round face had taken on a more haggard appearance since his wife had died of cancer the year before. They had never been able to have children and the store had been her love. After her death, Lok found some comfort in maintaining its existence as a means to keep him busy and to fight the loneliness.

He went back behind the counter and picked up a small leather bag containing the cash deposits for the day. He was about to set the alarm and head out the back door to his car when a knock at the front door caused him to stop.

He peered at the face looking at him through the glass and beamed with delight when he recognized Jia-li. He put the bag down and seconds later, welcomed her inside and locked the door behind her, before giving her an affectionate hug.

"You caught me just as I was leaving," he said. "It is so good to see you. I have been hoping that someday you would return to my shop. It's been a year since I saw you."

"I know," replied Jia-li. "I came then to offer my condolences. You had been married … what? Forty years?"

"Forty-one," replied Lok, sounding flippant as though it was nothing.

"That's a long time," noted Jia-li. "You must miss her?"

"Time passes." Lok shrugged. "Can you join me for supper? We could take my car or walk. Whatever you would like. I do need to drop off my cash deposits at the bank first."

"Either way is fine," replied Jia-li.

"So how have you been?" asked Lok.

"I'm okay," replied Jia-li, but her voice revealed her sadness.

"What's wrong?" asked Lok. "I can see that something is troubling you."

"I was thinking about how long you were married. I was wondering … your wife … do you think she ever knew about us?"

Lok frowned as he went behind the counter and picked up his leather bag, before turning to face her.

"She may have suspected we were lovers, but she never said anything. That was so long ago. I thought my heart would never recover when you told me we could not be lovers anymore. I never stopped loving you."

"Deep down I was embarrassed," said Jia-li. "I knew you were married, but I was so lonely after my husband was killed ... and you were there to comfort me. You are thirteen years older than me. At the time, you seemed so mature and I felt protected and safe with you, but eventually I came to realize that your promises to leave your wife were not genuine."

"I couldn't bring myself to hurt her," admitted Lok. "But now she has left me. I am available," he said, with a certain amount of optimism in his voice.

Jia-li nodded politely and continued, "Being your lover was not the biggest mistake I made."

Lok misread Jia-li's thoughts and smiled. "Yes, there are worse mistakes than what you and I did. It was fun, what we had together."

"Fun?" said Jia-li, sharply.

"I'm sorry. That is not what I meant," he hastened to say. "I meant it was good ... you and I ... the feelings we had for each other. It was not a bad thing. It just happened."

"It ... just ... happened," repeated Jia-li, sounding robotic.

"We are human," Lok said, shrugging again. "My wife and I were not getting along ... you needed comfort. We were there for each other."

Jia-li eyed Lok for a moment. "You have no idea of the grief and anger I felt over my husband's death.

I devoted my life to raising my daughter to follow in my footsteps."

"How is Mia?" asked Lok, feeling uncomfortable with Jia-li's demeanour.

"I am as proud of her as I am ashamed of myself," replied Jia-li.

"I don't understand?" replied Lok.

"I received this picture from her," said Jia-li, holding out her iPhone for Lok to see. "It was provided to her by the police yesterday. It is a picture of the man who killed my husband."

Lok stared at the photograph and his hand subconsciously touched the three moles on his lower jaw as he gawked at Jia-li.

Lok's attempt to scream only came out as a choking, wheezing sound as Jia-li thrust a steak knife into the base of his throat below his Adam's apple, before sawing upwards. She released her grip as Lok stumbled back, gasping and clutching at the knife protruding from his throat. A gurgling cough sprayed blood onto Jia-li, but she stood, transfixed, with her eyes wide open in shock.

In her mind, Jia-li had envisioned Lok clutching his throat and falling to the floor. She thought she would stand above him and curse him for what he had done, perhaps as he looked up at her in fear as he died.

There was no fear in Lok's eyes. It was rage she saw glaring back at her as he grabbed at the counter for support with one hand while the other bloody hand slid down the wall and hit the panic button on his alarm system.

Instantly, the deafening sound of a siren pierced the air.

Chapter Forty-Four

It was eight-thirty Thursday morning when Jack and Laura sat across from their boss's desk while Jack gave an update on the investigation. Staff Sergeant Rose Wood listened carefully, then said, "Benny Wong didn't get where he is without being cunning and suspicious. How do you intend to convince him that you're dirty? You will have to give him something if he is ever going to open up to you."

"I have some ideas," replied Jack. "I know it will take time, perhaps even months, to gain his trust. Tonight I'll lay the groundwork with a two-pronged attack to put him off balance psychologically. I already paved the way for the first step the night he caught us following him."

"That being that you received information that someone tendered his name for assassination?" replied Rose.

"Exactly." Jack handed Rose an envelope containing a picture. "My idea is to show him this picture and tell him it is the person who may be receiving the contract to kill him."

"Whose picture is it?" asked Rose, abruptly, as she stared at the photo.

"Don't worry," replied Jack. "It's a surveillance picture of an undercover Chinese member out of Toronto. I didn't want to use anyone local. My idea is to say we have a source close to the killer, but that his assignment has been put on hold."

"You hope to scare him so he will be relying on you to protect him," noted Rose.

"Exactly. I'll tell him that because of my position in Intelligence, it would not draw suspicion from my bosses to be in contact with him, as I would ostensibly be looking to find out who wants to kill him. The more chance I get to mingle with him, the more chance I have to gain his trust."

"And your other prong of attack?" asked Rose.

"I'll tell him that AOCTF discovered their member's home computer was being hacked several months ago. I've spoken to Roger Morris about it and he has no problem with me telling him because he will soon figure it out anyway, if he hasn't already."

Rose studied Jack's face and said, "So you won't be putting in any more reports to AOCTF resulting in more bad guys being sent to Hong Kong?"

"Hey, we didn't give that report to AOCTF," replied Jack. "I-HIT did that blunder."

"I agree that it was a blunder for I-HIT," replied Rose, sourly, "but for you two, I think you both look at it as a triumph."

"We did discover that the Chinese were behind it, which saved us a lot of time focusing on the Vietnamese, so I suppose some good came out of it," said Jack, glancing at Laura.

"Some good," Laura replied innocently.

Rose shook her head. "So for this first meeting with Wong, is that all you're going to tell him?"

"No," replied Jack. "The part about the hacked computer is incidental. I plan to tell him that a group in our office, of which I am not officially a part of, is helping AOCTF and that the investigation has acquired a high-level source who works for him. I'll say this person is thinking of going into Witness Protection and giving evidence against him for murder."

"That ought to get his attention," noted Rose.

Jack nodded. "My idea is to follow that up by finding out who in his organization knows about different murders, ostensibly to help him pinpoint who it is. I'll tell him I'll gain access to AOCTF wiretap and perhaps some of the reports that were purposely never put on the corrupted computer. I'll say that with his help, I'll be able to figure out who their source is."

"And what about Mia Parker or Mr. Frank?" asked Rose. "Where do you envision they fit into all this?"

Jack shrugged. "If Mia makes the introduction tonight like she says she will, she'll be out of the picture as far as I'm concerned. As far as Mr. Frank goes, his role might only be Mia's contact person and not worthy of attention, either. I've spoken to Connie and she agrees that Wong is our primary objective."

Rose nervously drummed the fingers of both hands on her desk for a moment as she stared at Jack.

"I'll be okay," said Jack, hoping to reassure her.

"No guns, no phones, and no backup," stated Rose. She stopped drumming her fingers and grimaced instead.

"I'm not worried about tonight," said Jack, assuredly. "It will only be after Wong says something to incriminate himself that things could get dicey."

"And tonight's scenario?" asked Rose. "Any thoughts on where it will be?"

"I'm to meet Mia at UBC and go in her car. She said we will go and park in Chinatown near Main Street and East Hastings at eight o'clock. She will get a call or a text on her cell, directing us to go someplace on foot. We are to leave all phones or electronic devices in her car before we get out. Perhaps one of Wong's bodyguards ... maybe Zhang or Shen will be there to lead us, but I'm only guessing."

"And you are to be unarmed," noted Rose.

"I'll leave my gun at the office before I go," said Jack. "I don't want to risk someone breaking into the car and stealing it. I'll have my phone, but will also leave it under the seat of her car once we get the call."

"You won't have cover and you won't be armed," said Rose, sounding angry.

Jack shrugged. "What's the worst that could happen?" He saw Rose about to state the obvious and hastened to add, "If they decide not to trust me, they simply won't talk to me and tell me to get lost. If that happens, they're going to figure that the police will know that I am meeting with them. It would be stupid for Wong to try and harm me, plus he would have no reason to do so. He knows he would be caught."

"And if this works and he does start to confide in you, what then?" asked Rose. "Don't you think he would try to kill you if he becomes suspicious for any reason?"

"Yes, but let's cross that bridge when we come to it. There is no way I would question him about who he has murdered at the first meeting. It will take time to gain his trust."

"And Mia Parker ... do you trust her not to tip him off?"

"No," replied Jack.

"No?" repeated Rose, looking startled.

"There is a possibility that she might have clued Wong in, but I trust my instincts enough that I think I would know. From a safety aspect, it wouldn't change anything. Wong simply wouldn't tell me anything."

"We do think she is holding something back from us," said Laura. "It might simply be we need more time to gain her trust."

"Like knowing that Wong somehow got spyware on an AOTCF member's computer?" noted Rose.

Jack nodded. "That and there is something else I can't put my finger on at the moment. I get the feeling she has done more than she is letting on ... or perhaps it involves some other crime she is connected to. I'm not sure, but if it doesn't interfere with us catching Wong, then I'm happy enough to leave it alone. Let's get through tonight first and see how that goes."

Laura watched Rose nod in agreement and felt her stomach churn. *No gun, no phone, no backup ... and an informant you don't trust ... right, what's the worst that could happen? Oh, man ...*

On Thursday morning, Connie entered her office as the phone rang. It was from Detective Wilson of the Vancouver City Police Homicide unit. After the initial pleasantries were exchanged, Wilson said, "I have a memo that you wrote a couple of weeks ago asking to be notified of any homicides involving Asians. You still interested?"

"Definitely," replied Connie. "I'm working on a case with our Intelligence Unit. A month ago I started off with one murder and the case has increased to four."

"Let me guess. You working with Jack Taggart again?" chuckled Wilson.

"Yes ... and it's not funny! Why are you laughing?"

"I was involved in a case with him where two guys running a meth lab for the bikers were killed shortly after he started to investigate. Involved a guy by the name of Cocktail. You remember?"

"I remember."

"It turned out good. Messy, but good."

"By messy ... you mean someone getting blasted with a shotgun?"

"Yeah, that's the case."

"A case typical of Taggart," replied Connie.

"You sound like you blame him for it. As I recall, he wasn't even in the city when that happened. Also,

are you forgetting he solved that murder for us with
the Mexicans? When they kidnapped that Canadian
girl in El Paso?"

"Who could forget. So what?"

"We were stumped until he came along. Sure,
he likely did some things that were unorthodox, but
he sure as hell got results. I also heard what he went
through down in Mexico. Don't know why you're
bitching about him. I'd be honoured to buy him a beer
sometime."

"Yeah, well, you may call what he does unorthodox, but some people might call it something else.
Something against the statutes in the Criminal Code."

Wilson paused, then said, "Yeah, okay, maybe you
have a point. I've heard a bit of scuttlebutt about other
cases he was involved in. Rumours that ... well, on one
hand makes me want to shake his hand ... and on the
other hand, makes me think I want to cuff him. He is
a bit of an enigma."

"I know exactly what you mean. Anyway, please
don't tell me I have another body connected to my case?"

"On the surface, I don't think so," replied Wilson.
"The victim's name is Lok Cheng. Sixty-six years old
and was knifed when he was closing up his flower shop
in Chinatown last night. He managed to hit a panic
button and set off a siren, giving us a time of death at
six-o-seven."

"I don't know the name," replied Connie. "Any
history?"

"Not that I can find as far as police contact goes.
He used to be an airline pilot but retired several years

ago and took over his wife's flower shop when she died of cancer last year."

"Robbery?" asked Connie.

"Looks like it. His day's cash deposits are missing. We found his empty bank bag tossed in a garbage bin in the back alley. The attacker left the knife sticking out of the guy's throat. Despite the siren going off, whoever did it either wore gloves or was cool enough to wipe off any prints."

"Witnesses?"

"No. A few people heard the alarm and because it was closing time, they thought he had accidentally hit the button by mistake when he was setting the alarm. The front door was locked and the perp went out the back."

"Do you figure the perp locked the front door after entering or was it someone the victim knew?" mused Connie.

"I've been asking myself the same thing," replied Wilson.

"It doesn't sound like anything I would be interested in," replied Connie, "but send me the basic particulars and a photo of the vic anyway. I'll run it past our Intelligence Unit and AOCTF in case it's a match for any surveillance photos they have. I'll also ask them to mention it to their sources in the event anyone knows or hears anything."

It was two hours later when Connie opened the envelope that had been dropped off for her. She stared at the picture of Lok Cheng's bald head in disbelief, then ransacked the old file box in the corner of her office to compare the photo of the hit-and-run driver from twenty-five years ago. The moles were a perfect match.

Goddamn you, Jack Taggart!

Chapter Forty-Five

Mia arrived at her mother's apartment on schedule and rang the intercom.

"Stay there, I'll be right down," said Jia-li tersely.

Mia paced nervously as she waited. She knew by her mother's harsh words that something was wrong. *Mr. Frank has spoken with her ... she knows I was charged with drugs and am pretending to work for the police ...*

"We need to walk," ordered Jia-li, as soon as she came through the doors.

Mia saw the dark bags under her mother's eyes and could tell that she had been crying. "Mom, it's going to be okay," she whispered softly, reaching out and giving her arm a squeeze. "My drug charge ... this thing with the police ... it will all go away."

Jia-li jerked her arm back and stared open-mouthed at Mia. "What are you talking about?" she demanded.

"You ... you didn't know?" said Mia.

"No, I don't know! What is going on?"

"Then what … I thought Mr. Frank told you?"

Jia-li grabbed her by the wrist, jerking her toward a path that meandered amongst a cluster of apartment buildings. "I have not spoken to Mr. Frank in three months," she said flatly. Once they reached a deserted area near a flowerbed she let go of Mia's wrist and turned to face her. "So you tell me what is going on. What is this talk of drugs and police? Does it involve the photo you sent me?"

"Sort of," admitted Mia.

Jia-li's mouth drooped open in shock, then her face darkened with rage. "Was that all lies?" she shouted.

"No, Mom," Mia hastened to say. "Don't shout," she added, looking around nervously. She had never seen her mother lose control in a public setting, especially about anything related to the benefactor. "It was only the circumstance surrounding how I viewed the file about Dad's hit and run that was, uh, not entirely accurate."

Jia-li gave Mia a hard look, then lowered her voice. "Start at the beginning. Tell me everything."

Mia told her mother about her meeting with Mr. Frank in the hotel room and how he spilled wine on her while attempting to have sex with her. She saw her mother clench her jaw and knew she was becoming more enraged. "I was able to handle him," Mia said quickly. "Nothing happened."

"Nothing happened?" repeated Jia-li. "You know you cannot lie to me. Tell me the truth!"

"What I told you is the truth," replied Mia. "It's just …"

"Just what?" demanded Jia-li.

"I felt funny when I left. A tingly feeling. He had poured me a glass of wine from a bottle he had on ice in the bathroom. I didn't watch ..."

"He drugged you?"

"I don't know. I hadn't had lunch that day. An empty stomach ... a glass of wine. I don't know. Then I got in the car accident."

Jia-li listened carefully as Mia told her everything that had transpired, going into great detail of Taggart's interrogation, including how he spurned her sexual nuances.

"He sounds like a better man than Mr. Frank," noted Jia-li.

"Perhaps," admitted Mia, before continuing on with all that had transpired up until the intended meeting with Benny Wong tonight. When she finished, she expected her mother to be angry, but instead, saw a calmness come over her.

Jia-li stroked a lock of hair away from Mia's face and said, "It is over. After you finish what you must do tonight, neither of us will ever work for the benefactor again."

"Perhaps the benefactor will only have us go through a cooling-down period," said Mia, frowning.

"No," said Jia-li, adamantly. "We are finished working for the benefactor. Never again."

Mia saw the hatred in her mother's face. "Mom ... what's going on? You looked like you had been crying before I came by. Now you're angry. I've never heard you talk about the benefactor like this before."

Jia-li stared quietly at Mia, then forced a smile.

"I finished a … long-term assignment. As a result, I know that the benefactor will agree to never contact either of us again."

"In Calgary? I thought you were doing a simple assignment."

"Things were not what they appeared."

Mia nodded. "I understand … something you can't talk about."

"Yes. It was like an awakening," replied Jia-li, looking thoughtful.

"An awakening?" Mia was puzzled, but knew better than to ask. *One thing is for certain, she doesn't want to work for the benefactor again.*

"How do you feel about that?" asked Jia-li. "To never work for the benefactor again?"

Mia smiled warmly. "Well, to tell you the truth, I am happy that it is going to be over. I know it is childish and perhaps selfish of me, but I really didn't ever want to see Wolfenden again."

"You won't have to," assured Jia-li.

"And the business with that woman being driven over … I never thought the benefactor would resort to such measures in Canada. The risk of discovery would far outweigh the gain."

"Until recently, I never thought they would, either," replied Jia-li, coldly.

Until recently? Something did happen in Calgary … She reached for her mother's hand and said, "After tonight, I will be happy never to see Mr. Frank again, as well. I will even be happier if he doesn't show up tonight. It's not like he is really needed."

"He will not show up," said Jia-li. "I have been around long enough to know that the benefactor would never risk his safety under these circumstances. Do what you must with the police to get those parasites off your back. Appease Taggart and then we will start our life anew."

"Taggart will not be a problem," replied Mia, giving her mother's hand a reassuring squeeze. "Compared to Mr. Frank, he is weak and naive. It is easy to see that he has a soft heart." She snickered.

"You think it is funny that he has that quality?" asked Jia-li, pulling her hand away.

"I'm laughing at how naive he is. He looks at me like I am a child caught up in something I don't understand. He told me that if I am straight with him that he will protect me until the day he dies, even if it means letting Wong go."

"Do you believe him?"

"Yes, I can see it in his face. He means what he says, that is what is so funny."

Jia-li frowned. It had seemed like a nightmare for her since Mia sent her Lok Cheng's picture. Listening to her daughter caused her to reflect on how brainwashed she had made her. It was like an added slap in the face, alerting her to the tragic way she had brought her up.

"Mom? What is it? Don't you see how funny that is? He is the one who is like a child."

Jia-li swallowed and fought to gain her composure. "No, my love. It sounds like he is an honourable man. You shouldn't laugh at that."

"Perhaps, but he's not thinking of what is good for

his country. That he would value my life over taking down a top gangster like Wong? Ridiculous. It is people like Taggart, apathetic to the common good, who are endemic of the thoughtless and unsophisticated ways of Canadians. People who lack proper vision and loyalty to their country. No wonder their institutions are so corrupted."

"You have values and are taking political science. Perhaps someday you will enter politics and make a difference. Free from the benefactor, you can do what your heart desires."

"Mom, you are really talking strangely. You don't sound like yourself."

Jia-li took a deep breath and slowly exhaled. She placed her hand on Mia's shoulder and looked her straight in the eyes. "I have allowed my own bias over the years to blind me and influence you in a direction that is not right."

"What? Oh, you mean you agree that Dad's case was not covered up by the police?"

Jia-li nodded, uncertain as to what to say next.

"So what," said Mia. "We may have been wrong about that, but there is no doubt as to the lack of scruples and corruption in this country's government. There is no denying that!"

"No, you are right about that," sighed Jia-li. "Still … there are some things …"

"Things?" asked Mia, stepping back.

"We have lived a life of deception. Has it ever occurred to you that we might have been deceived ourselves?"

"You mean, by the benefactor?"

"Yes."

Mia shrugged. "If we have, I am sure it was for the common good. Regardless, after tonight it will be over."

Jia-li thought about Mia's role in introducing Taggart to Wong tonight. *She needs to have her wits about her ... there will be time to tell her the truth later.*

"What are you thinking?" asked Mia. "Are you worrying about tonight?"

"A little, but I feel comfort with what Taggart has told you. I value your life over that of anyone, let alone a criminal like Wong."

Mia smiled. "That is because you are my mom. Of course you would think that, but Taggart is a fool. Don't worry, once I make the introduction to Wong, my part is finished. I'm sure Wong won't say anything to incriminate himself tonight."

"You shouldn't care if the police succeed in trapping Benny Wong. He is a common criminal."

"Yes, but obviously of use to the benefactor."

"Let the benefactor worry about that. It is time for you to do what is right for you."

"You have never spoken to me like this before," replied Mia, eyeing her mother curiously.

Jia-li forced a smile, but her lips quivered and she knew that Mia could see that it was not genuine. "The time has come for us to look after each other."

"Haven't we always done that, mom?" replied Mia, wrapping her arm around Jia-li's waist.

Tears welled in Jia-li's eyes.

"Mom? What is it? What aren't you telling me?" pleaded Mia.

"That I feel so much shame that I wasn't a good mother," cried Jia-li. "I should never have allowed the benefactor to use you."

"Oh, mom," said Mia, hugging her fiercely. "I should never have complained to you. I can handle Wolfenden. Like you said, it is only a game."

Jia-li squeezed her eyes tight. *It is not a game when a mother is filled with enough hate to turn her daughter into a prostitute ...*

Chapter Forty-Six

After lunch, Jack and Laura returned to their office and Jack checked his desk phone and discovered he had a message to call Detective Wilson at VPD Homicide. He was in the process of dialling when Rose and Connie walked in and stood staring at him.

Jack eyed the large manila envelope that Connie was carrying and could tell by the way she scowled that something was wrong. Rose also looked concerned. He hung up the phone before Wilson answered. "What's up?" he asked.

"What's up?" repeated Connie, as she reached inside the envelope. "I'll tell you what's up!" she seethed, before tossing two photos onto Jack's desk. "What do you have to say about these?"

Jack gazed at a picture of an older Chinese man with the handle of a steak knife protruding from his throat. He glanced at Laura who was looking over his shoulder and they both shrugged at each other.

"Take a look at the second picture," snarled Connie.

Jack looked at the second picture. It was a profile of the victim's head. He stared briefly at the knife handle and the blood that had run down the side of the victim's neck, before his eyes focused on three moles along the victim's lower jaw. *Guess I know what Wilson was calling about …*

Seconds later, Laura muttered, "Oh, man …"

"Yeah! 'Oh, man' is right," stated Connie. Her eyes burned into Jack's. "Well?"

"I'm not a homicide investigator," said Jack, "so I'm not sure, but is there any possibility this guy suffers from muscle spasms and accidentally knifed himself while having a steak?"

Laura's snicker was cut short by Rose. "This is no joking matter, you two. Your intended undercover operation has been blown out of the water."

"I'm meeting with Wilson from VPD Homicide in an hour," said Connie. "We're bringing Mia Parker in for questioning."

"What makes you think it was her?" asked Jack.

"Get off it," said Connie. "He's the same guy who drove over her father twenty-five years ago. Two days ago you gave her a copy of his picture and now he's dead."

"You agreed with my interview and went along with me giving her the picture," said Jack, defensively.

"Yeah, I did, but I sure as hell didn't know she was going to go out and knife him! I didn't think she knew the guy!"

"I don't think she did," replied Jack. "Before you

rush off, why not pull up a chair and fill me in on the details?"

"I don't need to sit for that," replied Connie. "The details are pretty simple and brief."

Jack listened as Connie told him everything she had been told about the murder. When she finished, Jack said, "The murder happened at six-o-seven. I can tell you that it wasn't Mia Parker who did it. She has an excellent alibi for that time."

"Yeah? And what's that?"

"She was with us," said Laura, retrieving her notebook and showing it to Connie. "We were at UBC meeting her in our car. That's when she told us Wong had agreed to meet her and Jack tonight."

"Oh, Christ," said Connie. She looked at Rose and shook her head, then added, "Well something stinks."

"You're right, it does," agreed Jack. "Sit down and let's talk about it."

Once Connie and Rose sat down, Rose turned to Jack. "You said it yourself, Mia Parker had an excellent alibi at the time. Was that a … coincidence?" she added, with a look that Jack knew referred to past cases where he had used the word himself to hide his actions.

"Exactly what I was thinking," said Connie. "Did she get someone from Wong's organization to knock Cheng off and used you two as patsies for an alibi?"

"She told us she had shown Cheng's photo to Mr. Frank," noted Laura. "If we are right in our assumption that she didn't know they were going to kill Betty Donahue, maybe they didn't tell her they were going to kill Cheng as well."

"But what would be the point of killing Cheng if it wasn't a favour for her?" asked Connie.

"Until two days ago, we didn't know Mr. Frank was connected to Wong," said Jack. "Maybe Cheng was, too. They may have murdered him to hide some other crime or the possibility we would connect something with their organization. I didn't get the feeling from Mia last night that she knew who had driven over her father."

"I agree with Jack on that," said Laura. "In fact, she thought Mr. Frank did recognize him, but when she asked, he said he was simply impressed with the quality of the photo enhancement."

"There is another thing to consider," said Jack. "If Mia is behind Cheng's murder, she would have tipped Wong off about me. Why would Wong jeopardize everything by killing Cheng? Why wouldn't they wait until later when presumably we would let Mia off the hook?"

"What about Mia's mother?" asked Connie. "Could she be a suspect?"

"Her mother was in Calgary," noted Laura. "Not due back until late last night. Mia wasn't even going to meet her until this morning."

"You would also have to wonder how Jia-li would have known Cheng," added Jack, "let alone to track him down so fast, even if she did return earlier in the day."

Connie rubbed her eyes with the palms of her hands, then sighed and let her arms drop to her lap, while staring at Jack.

"What are you thinking?" asked Jack.

Connie grimaced. "That I better call Wilson and clue him in that Mia Parker has an alibi. I think your undercover scenario is the only chance we have to get Wong."

"Good," replied Jack. He glanced at Rose and asked, "So everything is okay with you? We're back on track then?"

"For now," replied Rose, "but we'll take it one day at a time and re-evaluate after every step. As far as tonight goes, Laura and I will park someplace in Chinatown and wait, so call us as soon as you're done." She glanced at Connie and added, "And if you have any more problems or concerns, I want you to call me direct immediately."

Connie nodded submissively.

"Chinatown is a busy area," said Jack. "If I need help, I suspect it will be a 911 call to VPD."

"Except your phone will be back in Mia's car," grumbled Laura.

Jack grinned. "If it comes to that, I'll make sure it's a bad guy calling for help and not me."

The attempt at humour did not go over well with Rose. "Are you going to question Mia tonight about Cheng's murder?" she asked, bluntly.

"I don't think that would be wise," replied Jack. "If she had nothing to do with it, all it would do is cause her to lose focus when she takes me to meet Wong. If she did have something to do with it, I don't think it would be prudent for me to stick my nose into a case that belongs to VPD unless they want me to."

"I agree with you on that issue," said Connie. "I'll talk to Wilson, but I'm sure he will want to hold off until we see how far you get with Wong."

Everyone nodded in agreement, but Jack saw that Connie was frowning.

"So why the long face, Connie?" asked Jack. "If you're still thinking about Cheng, in reality, he isn't even your case."

"Yeah, but I feel that his murder is the result of my case," retorted Connie. She scowled at Jack and muttered, "Two minutes ago I was really pissed off at you. Now I have to suck up to you and ask you to continue with the undercover operation."

"Sucking up to me isn't necessary," replied Jack. "You already did a number on me the day you had me deliver Nancy Brighton her mail. She's a spunky lady and deserves justice for what happened to her sister. I'm more than glad to be assisting."

Connie nodded politely to hide what she was thinking. *The thing is, Jack, I know all too well what you consider justice to be ...*

Chapter Forty-Seven

At seven o'clock, Jack met Mia at the university parking lot and got into her car. He saw that she was wearing a snug-fitting sweater and tight blue jeans.

"No, I'm not trying to seduce you," she said, aware that his eyes had scanned her body. "I was told these jerks will search us tonight. I thought it would save them the trouble. Obviously I'm not hiding anything."

"That's for sure," agreed Jack emphatically, before smiling. The situation they were entering was stressful and he hoped that a little humour would alleviate it. He was relieved to see her smile back.

Mia found a place to park her car in the heart of Chinatown and at precisely eight o'clock she received a call on her cellphone. Jack leaned over in the seat to hear the conversation. It didn't do him any good. The caller was a man who spoke Chinese and it was apparent that Mia was fluent.

After hanging up, she said, "We're to leave the car and walk to the southwest corner of Main and East Hastings. There is a moving company on the corner and we are to go to the alley behind it. We will find instructions inside a discarded take-out food container stuck under a Dumpster."

"Was that Mr. Frank?" asked Jack.

She shook her head. "I don't know who it was."

"In the future, I would prefer you speak English," said Jack.

"Don't trust me?" smiled Mia, feigning mock innocence as she touched her chest with her hand.

"Probably about as much as you trust me," replied Jack.

Mia stared blankly at him for a moment. "Actually, I do trust you," she said.

Her comment made him feel uneasy. It gave him the feeling that she was more in control than he was.

They each tucked their phones under the seat and walked in silence. Minutes later they arrived at the Dumpster and Jack retrieved a discarded Styrofoam food container from underneath. Inside was a note telling them to cross East Hastings and go north in the alley to East Cordova Street, then dogleg down to another alley to another Dumpster. They did as instructed, only to find a note directing them to a third Dumpster.

After the third Dumpster, the note gave them an address to go to. They had entered a less desirable part of the city and Jack was conscious of Mia slipping her arm through his as they passed a cluster of drug addicts making a transaction on the sidewalk.

Eventually they came to the address on the note. It was a small hole-in-the wall restaurant and Jack grabbed hold of the doorknob, but paused to look around. The restaurant was a two-storey building with living quarters on the second floor. The building itself was wedged between a pawnshop and a dry cleaners.

He casually glanced up and down the sidewalk. He didn't see anyone who might have been following them, but remembered that the last time Wong's men had cornered him in an alley he hadn't seen anyone either, until it was too late.

He took a deep breath, nodded to Mia and was about to open the door when he heard the impatient muttering of a heavyset Chinese woman who had stopped behind him and was waiting to enter, along with her husband. He guessed the couple to be in their early-sixties. The husband was tall and thin and his wife was short and overweight.

Jack opened the door and gestured for them to enter ahead of him. As he did, the woman nodded politely, while giving him a smile that showed she was missing most of her teeth. She said something to him in Chinese, so Jack smiled and nodded in return as they entered.

The restaurant had less than a dozen seating areas, comprised of mismatched kitchen tables and equally mismatched chairs. A strong odour of garlic and other spices permeated throughout the steamy room. *I'm in the real Chinatown …*

The only patrons already in the restaurant were a young Chinese couple who were giggling over some fortune cookies and two Chinese men who were sitting together in the rear. Jack recognized them as Dai and Rong, the two Dongfang brothers who had previously accosted him in the alley with Laura. At that time they each held newspapers over their arms to hide their weapons. This time they had no newspapers. A sign that Jack took to mean they felt safe in their current environment. It gave him the feeling that he was in the lair of a predator.

Jack made eye contact with them and Dai stared back, then nodded for them to take a seat near the middle of the restaurant.

As soon as they sat down, a young waiter appeared through a set of swinging bar-style doors in a narrow hallway behind Dai and Rong. Dai barked at the waiter in Chinese as he went past. The waiter glanced at Jack and Mia and quickly disappeared behind the doors again.

"You know those two guys at the back?" asked Mia. "They're really checking us out."

"Yes. The guy on the left is Dai and the other one is Rong. I've run into them before. Wong uses them as protection."

"Then where is Wong?"

"Likely close by." Jack eyed her and said, "You're doing good. You look relaxed."

"Thanks, but I'll be happy to get it over with."

Seconds later, the waiter returned with a teapot and hustled over to where Jack and Mia were sitting.

The waiter's hands trembled as he poured them some green tea while casting a quick peek back at Dai and Rong.

Mia looked at Jack and raised an eyebrow. "You want any food?" she asked. "I'm not hungry myself."

"Only green tea for me as well," replied Jack, glancing at the waiter. "Perhaps later."

The waiter nodded, then hustled over to give the older couple each a menu before meeting the young couple who were waiting at the till and munching on their fortune cookies.

Would be interesting to see what my fortune would be, thought Jack. A few minutes went by and Jack saw Dai answer his cellphone. When he hung up, he looked at Jack and gave him a nod and gestured for them to follow him down the hallway.

Mia glanced at Jack and whispered, "Guess it's showtime. Hope it all works out for you."

Jack and Mia followed Dai down the hall and Rong tagged along behind. The first set of swinging doors they passed on the left opened in to the kitchen, where Jack caught a glimpse of an older Chinese couple cleaning dishes.

In the hall past the kitchen was a door leading to the woman's washroom. Directly across from that was the men's washroom. They continued past and Jack sidestepped as another door on his left opened in front of him, blocking his view of the hallway momentarily. Once the door opened wider, he saw it was the same waiter carrying a box of food items up from a dingy basement.

The next door on the right past the basement led to a small office. At the end of the hallway was the fire-escape door leading to an alley. Dai gestured for Jack and Laura to enter the office.

The windowless office was comprised of an old wooden desk with an oak swivel chair behind it. In front of the desk were three kitchen chairs that were made of chrome and had seat pads covered in red plastic, which had split open in several places. The desk itself had a pile of Chinese magazines on one corner, a spike receipt holder containing a skewered bundle of restaurant receipts on the opposite corner and a bookkeeping ledger in the middle.

Dai told Jack and Mia to remain standing as Rong entered and closed the door. Moments later, Dai thoroughly patted Jack down as he looked for a weapon. His search of Mia was slightly less thorough, opting instead to use his fingertips to probe around her chest. When he was finished, he stepped back and Rong used an electrical wand to scan their bodies. Satisfied that they were both free from weapons or communication devices, Dai told them to return to the restaurant and have their tea while they waited.

On their way back to their table, Jack noticed that Dai went into the kitchen while Rong returned to his table to watch them. He heard Dai's footsteps on the floor above his head and a minute later, Dai returned and sat with Rong.

A few minutes later, Jack heard more footsteps from above, where they descended stairs into the kitchen, before entering the hallway. It was Wong and his two other bodyguards, Zhang and Shen. Wong walked down the hallway to the office while Zhang and Shen joined Dai and Rong at their table.

"The top boss has arrived," said Mia. "Are you going to go talk to him?"

"Not until I'm told to. The two guys that joined our friends at the table are Zhang and Shen. I think the big guy, Zhang, is in charge of Wong's security. Sit tight until we're told otherwise. Wong is probably waiting for Mr. Frank to arrive."

Mia shrugged in response. "Who cares about him? Wong is who you want. How long do you plan to wait?"

"Patience. Give them time." Jack glanced sideways at Mia. *Interesting that she would call the top guy by his surname … but show respect for Frank by addressing him as Mister…* It caused Jack to reflect upon his past dealings with Mia as he sipped his tea. *She told me her mother was an "entrepreneur" … exact word I trained my sons to say.*

Mia had thoughts of her own and was anxious to get it over with. *There is no way the benefactor will risk letting Mr. Frank show up. Mom even said so …* She smiled to herself. *After tonight, my part will be over.*

Jack's subconscious was alerting him to the danger he was in and his senses became more alive. He heard the older woman with the missing teeth speaking in Chinese to her husband behind him … bits of Chinese conversation from the bodyguards came to him from the opposite direction. He glanced at Mia. *I don't feel like I'm in Canada. I feel like … I'm in your country … this sophisticated spyware that —*

Wong stepped out of the office and Jack's thoughts were interrupted as he watched him go down the hall and open the fire escape door, allowing Mr. Frank to step inside.

Jack felt relieved. *Okay, everything is going according to plan. So far, so good.*

Mia stared down the hall, unaware that her mouth was agape. *Something is really wrong ... why is he here?* She saw Zhang give a wave of his hand, directing her and Jack to go down the hall. *Mom's talk of an awakening ... of being deceived ourselves ...* Her hand trembled as she put her teacup down while her brain tumbled thoughts around like clothes in a dryer.

Chapter Forty-Eight

Jack nodded curtly to Zhang as he walked past the table where the bodyguards remained seated. He heard Mia stop behind him and speak in Chinese to Zhang. The tone of her voice sounded harsh and condescending.

Zhang glowered at Mia who had asked him if he was a rice farmer, adding that proper guards would post someone at the rear fire-escape door as well as at the office door. He answered back abruptly in Chinese, "The guest Mr. Wong has allowed in is a trusted friend. We have been told to keep our distance from him. As far as you and the police officer go, we know that you are unarmed."

Mia gave a nod of her head to indicate Jack and said, "That man may be far more dangerous than you know." She saw Jack glaring at her, so she abruptly left to join him, but felt comfort when she heard the chairs scrape as the men got up from the table.

"What was that all about?" whispered Jack, tersely. "I told you to speak English."

"Sorry. Zhang really leered at me and was being intentionally rude. I put him in his place."

Jack eyed the bodyguards who had risen and were approaching. He knew Mia had lied to him. Zhang was too professional to act that way and whatever she said had caused them to glance suspiciously at him. *Too late to back out now ...*

They entered the office and Jack saw Wong seated behind the desk while Mr. Frank stood and gestured for them to take a seat in front. Mr. Frank was dressed in black slacks and a black windbreaker open at the front to reveal a dark blue shirt. He appeared to be of an athletic build and matched Jack's height.

Jack focused his attention on Wong, who was small in stature. At sixty-seven years of age, his muscles had deteriorated, leaving a drooping waddle of skin hanging below his chin. His face was fat and round, making his balding head look too big for his body. His skin was mottled with age spots and he was wearing a faded checked shirt buttoned to the top. Jack mused that for those who didn't know him, his appearance made him look decrepit, hiding his true nature. Jack speculated as to how Wong had climbed his way to the top of his organization. *Smart ... cunning ... ruthless ... violent? Likely all of that ...* Jack observed a work of art hanging on the wall behind Wong. It was made of wood and depicted a vicious-looking golden dragon over a background of fire. *Symbolic of the man I face ...*

Mr. Frank's focus was on the details of his plan and he felt his adrenaline surge. *The next few seconds and they will all be dead* ... He eyed Taggart closely. *Wait until they are seated ... step in behind ... shoot Taggart in the head first, followed by two more rapid shots ... Mia, then Wong. I'll be out the back door before the bodyguards have time to enter the hallway.*

Taggart sat in the chair farthest from the door and Mia sat in the middle, leaving the chair by the door for Mr. Frank. He remained standing, ostensibly to close the door while reaching for the five-shot snub-nosed revolver tucked in the back of his waistband under his jacket.

Mr. Frank felt his body twitch in surprise when Zhang walked past the doorway. He looked into the hallway and saw Zhang taking up a position near the rear door and the other three bodyguards loitering close by.

As a trained Intelligence case officer, Mr. Frank had received training in firearms and hand-to-hand combat, but he knew his current plan would not end well with the close proximity of the bodyguards. *Remain calm ... trust my training ... revamp the plan ...* He glanced around the room and pursed his lips to hide a smile before closing the door and taking a seat. *A gun will not be necessary ...*

Wong glanced at the three people seated in front of him and his eyes settled on Taggart. "So I am told that you have some information that may be of interest to me?"

Jack nodded. "I work for an Intelligence Unit dealing

with organized crime. About six months ago AOCTF felt they had a leak in their office, so a group in my office started their own project ... on you, specifically."

Jack caught Wong's surprised glance at Mr. Frank, who remained stoic. Wong turned his attention back to Jack and said, "That sounds preposterous. Why on earth would —"

"Yes, I know," interrupted Jack. "You are a legitimate businessman. You told me that the night your men cornered me in the alley."

"Six months ago?" questioned Mr. Frank.

"Yes ... and I know what you're thinking," replied Jack. "The report naming the Vietnamese who killed Betty Donahue was a plant provided to AOCTF."

"You're saying the report was false?" said Wong, looking at Mr. Frank who frowned.

"Yes, I actually helped draft that report myself to help the team who are working on you," said Jack, looking at Wong. "They wanted to verify what someone close to you was telling them in regard to your relationship with the Vietnamese. They all had a good chuckle when the Viets were killed. Not to mention, the team in my office were thrilled to discover that their source was reliable."

"How do we know that you are not trying to cover up for some leak by saying you meant it to happen?" said Mr. Frank, contemptuously.

"If that were true, would we know that Bien Duc and Tom Nguyen were murdered in Hong Kong and the driver of the car, Anh Dang, was killed here?" He turned to Wong and said, "We were watching Duc and Nguyen and waiting to see who would kill them. The team did not wish to save them because it might alert you that there is an informant close to you. I can even tell you that Duc wasn't at a meeting with the other Vietnamese bosses the week before, because they were planning to kill him."

Wong glowered back at Jack. "Who is their source?" he hissed.

"I do not know yet, but I suspect in time I could find out," replied Jack. "I have been assigned to work mostly on Satans Wrath. It is another team that is working on you, but sometimes we assist each other."

Wong sat back in his chair and folded his arms across his chest a moment, giving himself a moment to calm down and think. Eventually he looked at Jack and said, "What you said sounds interesting and naturally has aroused my curiosity, but you have told me nothing. Even if what you say is true, it is not anything I could act upon. Do you have anything else to throw on the table to make me think you would be worthy of my, uh, friendship to you?"

"Certainly," replied Jack. "I know that this young woman beside me is of particular value to your organization." Jack saw Wong glance at Mr. Frank, who nodded. *Something isn't right ...* "I am in a position to make her charges disappear," he added.

"And why do you think that whatever she is charged with is of concern to me?" asked Wong.

"If, as people in my office have said, you did contract out a certain venture to the Vietnamese to protect Mia from being charged ... a venture that failed ...

I would think you would value my assistance in that matter, as well," replied Jack.

Wong clasped his hands together and rested his chin on his fingertips as he stared silently at Jack. "You are in a position to make her charges disappear?" he said, coldly.

Jack nodded.

Wong stared hard into Jack's eyes and said, "Perhaps you could be of value ... but I don't see her being of use to anyone," he said, with a flicker of his eyes toward Mia, "except the police."

Wong's voice had taken on a deadly tone and Jack heard Mia inhale sharply.

"So as far as that matter goes," said Wong, looking toward the door, "Zhang!"

Jack heard the bodyguards running down the hall and caught the evil grin on Wong's face as he looked at him and said, "There is no need to put yourself in jeopardy when I can make her disappear immediately."

"Jack!" cried Mia, leaping to her feet as Zhang burst into the room with pistol in hand.

Chapter Forty-Nine

Laura adjusted the defrost switch to clear the fog off the windows as she and Rose sat waiting. They were parked in an SUV on East Hastings, two blocks east of where Mia had parked her car. They did not want to risk getting any closer, even though they knew that Jack and Mia would have to walk to some other unknown location.

"I hate the waiting part," said Laura, momentarily drumming on the bottom of the steering wheel with her fingers.

Rose nodded in agreement. "Sometimes I think providing cover is the worst part. Especially when you have no idea where they are."

Laura leaned back in her seat and stretched her arms behind her head. "The thing is, knowing Jack, he's probably sitting in a lounge having a martini and telling jokes. Likely has the bad guys wrapped around his little finger."

"I hope so. It's the not knowing that drives you nuts," replied Rose. "Hang on, got a call ... it's from Connie."

"Is Jack doing the UC?" asked Connie immediately. "I've tried to reach him and can't."

"Yes, we haven't heard back from him yet," replied Rose. "He's been out of the car about forty-five minutes."

"I heard from Wilson at VPD Homicide. He discovered something interesting about the guy who was knifed in his flower shop."

"Lok Cheng?" replied Rose.

"Yeah, him. He died twice."

"You mean he was resuscitated and —"

"No. He died of SIDS when he was three months old. Whoever was murdered in the flower shop had assumed his identity. Whoever it is has been living under that false name for at least thirty years."

"Illegal immigrant?"

"Maybe," replied Connie. "But I thought I would pass it on. Let me know when Jack is done, will you?"

"Worried about him?" mused Rose.

"I always worry about that guy," replied Connie seriously, before hanging up.

Rose passed the information on to Laura and they sat silently mulling it over for a moment. Laura glanced at her watch and said, "Come on Jack, phone! Give me that 'a few drinks, a few laughs, nobody got hurt' call."

As if on cue, her phone buzzed and she smiled and grabbed it. Disappointment registered on her face when she saw that it was from Jim Purney.

"I tried to call Jack, but he isn't picking up," said Jim. "It's about the computer that was hacked that belonged to the member from AOCTF. Do you know where he is?"

"Yes," replied Laura. "Rose and I are covering him ... well, in the vicinity. He's doing a UC. What's up?"

"On Benny Wong?" asked Jim, tersely.

Oh, man ... "Yes on Benny Wong," replied Laura, seeing the concern on Rose's face that matched how she felt herself. "Hang on, I'm going to lean over so Rose can listen in."

Laura explained the circumstance to Rose and then told Jim to continue.

"I received a call from a friend who works for the Communications Security Establishment. He got a call from Ottawa ... and it's midnight there, so you know it's serious. I suspect it is something they'll want to keep hushed up."

"We're listening," said Rose.

"Someone has clued in that we are looking at the spyware we discovered and are making a preemptive strike."

"What kind of pre-emptive strike?" asked Laura.

"Stealing information before we can counter the threat. CSE expected the hackers would know they were on to them, but hadn't realized the full scope of the problem and are trying to stop the hemorrhaging, which is gushing out all over. A ton of information is being hacked out of government and military computer systems, both in Canada and in the U.S. as we speak. It is the biggest threat to national security that we have ever had next to an all-out war."

"Oh, shit," said Rose. "The Chinese!"

"Number-one suspect, but we don't know for sure. Tell Jack he better be damned careful. These aren't your run-of-the-mill street criminals."

After hanging up, Rose and Laura looked silently at each other. They both thought the same thing.

We would tell him ... if we knew where he was ...

"I'm calling Connie back," said Rose, trying hard to keep the panic from her voice. "I'll have her contact Wilson at VPD and give him my number. If there are any calls regarding situations in Chinatown tonight, I want to be notified immediately."

Probably should contact the coroner as well, thought Laura.

Chapter Fifty

Jack heard Wong say something in Chinese and saw Zhang take aim with his pistol at Mia as the other bodyguards appeared from behind. He instinctively leapt from his chair, grabbing Mia by the wrist, and yanking her to one side while putting himself between her and Zhang. "Kill her and you will have to kill me, too," he yelled.

Good, thought Mr. Frank. *Kill them both …*

Wong barked out an order in Chinese and all the bodyguards put their weapons away. He looked at Jack and said, "Did you really think you could trap me that easily? Willing to throw your life away for this young woman? Tsk, tsk," he sneered. "Obviously you are not the corrupt police officer you pretend to be."

"There is a reason she needs to be kept alive," replied Jack, calmly. "Tell your goons to leave and I will explain it to you."

Wong ran his tongue around the insides of his chubby cheeks, puffing them out like a chipmunk playing with a walnut as he stared briefly at Jack. Then he gave another order and the bodyguards left, closing the door behind them. "Have a seat, Officer," said Wong, "and tell me why she is so precious to you." He then gave an impish smile and said, "Are you lovers?"

"Yes," blurted Mia.

"No, we're not," said Jack, taking his seat again while nodding for Mia to do likewise. "She is only saying that because you scared her." He turned to Mia and said, "Isn't that right, Mia? Tell the truth. There is no need to lie."

Mia stared at Jack. *Is he insane? Jumping up and putting himself in front of Zhang's gun to protect me ... does he have a death wish?* Her eyes drifted over to Mr. Frank. *You sat there and did nothing ... strange, somehow I knew you wouldn't. It was Jack's name I cried out for help.*

Wong looked at Mia and asked, "Were you lying about being his lover? If you were his lover, it would help convince me that he is who he says he is."

Mia glanced at Jack. *Hope to hell you know what you are doing ...* She then glared at Wong and said, "Yes, I lied. I thought you were going to kill me. I would have said anything."

"I see," replied Wong. He looked at Jack. "So why is she so important to you?"

"Because if something happens to her, I would be blamed for it," replied Jack. "I told my people that I was meeting with you on the pretext of being a dirty cop and that Mia would help me. As a result of her introducing me to you, it has been left up to my discretion as to whether or not her charges will be dropped."

"Your people know you are meeting with me tonight," repeated Wong. "I suspected as much."

"Yes, they think I am *pretending* to be a dirty cop," he replied, before smiling. "I told them that to protect myself. This way if AOCTF or the task force in my office gets wind of my meeting with you from whoever their source is, it will not arouse suspicion."

Wong looked momentarily taken back as he studied Jack. *His smile and easygoing conversation ... it does not sound like a man who is lying or has something to fear...* "So you're saying you're a double agent."

Wong glanced at Mr. Frank and spoke in Chinese, asking him if that was the correct term. Mr. Frank gave a barely perceptible nod. Jack didn't speak Chinese, but he guessed correctly the question Wong had asked. Jack glanced at Mr. Frank. *There is something very interesting about this guy ...*

"As Mr. Wong noted earlier," said Mr. Frank. "You have not offered anything of value. Tantalizing pieces perhaps ... like bait on a hook ... but nothing of actual benefit."

Jack leaned forward in his chair to see past Mia and said in a friendly tone, "Sorry, we haven't been introduced yet." He stuck out his hand and said, "You are?"

"Who I am isn't important," replied Mr. Frank, ignoring the handshake. "Is there nothing else you have to say?"

"Well, besides knowing that the task force in my office plans to arrest Wong in the near future for a couple of murders, there is something —"

"They plan to arrest me for a couple of murders?" blurted Wong. He looked at Mr. Frank who shrugged in response, indicating he knew nothing about it.

Again, Wong turns to Mr. Frank to see if he knew anything about it. These guys don't act like they work together. "Yes, although I do not know which ones," replied Jack. "I suspect it will involve putting someone on the Witness Protection Program and having them testify against you. Perhaps even wiretap."

Mia was also astute at studying body language, only she was watching Jack. *He is clueing in that Mr. Frank is not some underling … there is no way the benefactor should have sent him … or does the benefactor know?* Her brain started to put the pieces together.

"Again," said Mr. Frank. "All you are saying are words. Nothing concrete." He stood up, looked at Wong, and said, "There is something I would like to caution you about that I need to tell you in private." He glanced at Jack and Mia and said, "There is no need to go, I will simply whisper what I have to say in his ear."

Jack was concerned that his credibility would be further challenged before he was finished, so he stood up and said, "There is something concrete that I can give you." He took a photo out of his inside jacket pocket and tossed it on the desk in front of Wong.

"He looks Chinese, but I do not know him," said Wong, looking up at Jack.

"Remember when your men stopped me in the alley? I told you then that someone was contemplating having you killed. This picture is of the hit man who will be taking out that contract. I got a copy of it from the task force. Are you sure you wish to dismiss me like a wayward beggar?" he added, sarcastically.

Mr. Frank moved in front of Jack and bent over the table to study the picture with Wong. Jack saw Mr. Frank's elbow jerk forward and briefly thought he had slammed Wong in the head with the heal of his hand. *What the hell?*

"What have you done!" shrieked Mr. Frank, stepping back.

Jack saw Wong, slumped forward in his chair. The curled metal bottom of the receipt spike protruded from his eye socket. The spike itself had penetrated his brain, killing him instantly and the blood was turning the receipts jammed to the bottom into a sodden mass.

Jack looked at Mr. Frank in shock, who was now shouting in Chinese.

"He said we did it!" screamed Mia. "They're going to kill us!" she cried, leaping to her feet in a desperate bid to flee the office.

Chapter Fifty-One

Mr. Frank stepped back and watched Mia rip open the door and rush into the hall, with Jack close behind her. As he expected, panic had taken over everyone in the restaurant. People were yelling and the pounding of feet approaching from both directions in the hall told him the bodyguards would make Jack and Mia's escape impossible. Their attempt to escape added further credence to his assertion that they had murdered Wong.

If there was even a remote chance that Jack and Mia would not be immediately killed, he had a backup plan and felt for the grip on his revolver. If he had to kill the four bodyguards plus Jack and Mia, it was still possible, despite only having five bullets. He was an expert marksman and coupled with a surprise attack, he would save Mia for last and simply snap her neck.

The first bodyguard Jack saw was Zhang, who had come barrelling down the hall from the rear exit and was upon him. Zhang's pistol was clearing its holster when Jack grabbed his wrist, forcing Zhang to point the gun at the ceiling.

Behind Jack was the partially open door leading to the basement and he caught a glimpse of the other three bodyguards on the opposite side pulling their weapons as they raced toward him. He knew he couldn't make it to the rear exit in time ... but perhaps Mia could.

"Run to the fire escape!" he screamed. "I'll hold them off! Run!" He used his other hand to grab Zhang and spin him around while forcing him backward down the hall toward the basement door. He hoped to use Zhang as a shield to protect him and once Mia escaped out the back, perhaps shove Zhang down the basement stairs and try to wrestle his weapon away.

Mr. Frank partially pulled his own gun out. He had not entered the hallway out of an expectation of a barrage of gunfire in the hall from the bodyguards as they killed the two hapless victims. That didn't happen. *There is no way I can let her escape ...*

"They'll kill you!" cried Mia, unaware that her decision to reverse direction in the hall caused Mr. Frank to change his mind about putting a bullet through her brain.

Before Jack could respond, Mia grabbed Jack by his shoulders and used her feet to kick off the side of the wall, sending the three of them crashing down the rickety basement stairs with Zhang taking the brunt of their weight as his head bounced and twisted off the steps.

Mr. Frank stood in the office doorway and watched them disappear from sight into the basement. There was no escape for them down there. He had checked it out in an earlier meeting. It was a windowless room filled with rows of wooden racks containing mostly canned goods and food for the restaurant, illuminated by a few dirty light bulbs hanging on cords from the ceiling.

He shook his head at the ineptitude of the three bodyguards who ran toward him. A fat and toothless Chinese woman had burst out of the washroom, first running one way and then another in her own panic before the bodyguards floundered to get past her. The delay was only temporary as they shoved her aside and scrambled toward the office to check on their boss.

"One of you! Guard the basement door!" ordered, Mr. Frank in Chinese.

Rong, with pistol drawn, stopped at the entrance to the basement and saw his targets on the landing below him and quickly took aim.

Chapter Fifty-Two

In the fall down the stairs, Jack landed on top of Zhang, who was momentarily dazed. They had fallen down half a dozen steps to a landing, where the stairs then continued at a right angle down another half dozen steps to the basement floor. Jack heard the thump of Zhang's gun bounce down the remaining steps and the metallic sound as it hit the cement floor.

Mia got to her feet first and he saw her hesitate as she stood behind him, illuminated by a hazy light bulb above her head. "Find his gun," he yelled, before being distracted by Zhang who grabbed his shirt, wrenching him downward.

Jack responded by delivering a solid punch to Zhang's solar plexus, knocking the wind out of him and leaving him gasping for air. He looked up to see why Mia was still there and saw Rong appear at the top of the stairs and take aim, as Mia simultaneously smashed the overhead light with her fist.

Jack scrambled to race down the remaining stairs behind Mia, but Zhang lunged, tackling him from behind and sending him crashing down the remaining steps with Zhang on top.

Zhang was still winded, gasping for air, but he used his weight to his advantage to pin Jack to the floor as he wrapped his fingers around Jack's throat.

Jack used his hands to hit Zhang as hard as he could in the elbows. It loosened his grip, but he was still pinned to the floor and saw Zhang bring back his fist to deliver a blow intended to break Jack's nose and leave him momentarily blinded.

Oh, fuck … Jack squirmed, turning his head, while briefly wondering if a punch to his nose might be better than being nailed in the temple. The punch never came. Zhang loosened his grip and in darkened shadows he saw Mia pointing a pistol at the back of Zhang's head.

At the top of the stairs, Rong had hesitated to shoot in case he hit Zhang. He had heard the gun clatter on the cement floor and Jack's yell for Mia to get it. When Zhang lunged after Jack, Rong took a couple of steps down, then paused. He decided that continuing down the stairs with the light from the hall illuminating his body from behind was not a good idea. He quickly retreated back into the hall and cautiously peeked from around the doorframe before calling out, "Zhang?"

Jack got up while clutching Zhang by the shoulder. "Face down on the floor," he whispered, before adding, "and be quiet." When Zhang quietly obeyed, Jack looked at Mia and saw that she was pointing the gun at him.

"You take it," she whispered. "I've never used one before."

Jack felt relief and said, "I can tell. First thing you learn is don't point it at people you don't want to kill."

"Zhang?" came Rong's voice from above again.

Jack took the gun and stuck the muzzle in Zhang's ear and said, "Listen carefully if you want to live. Say exactly what I tell you to. Nothing else. You will answer in Chinese. I may not understand it, but my friend here does. "

Zhang nodded in compliance.

"Tell them to stay up there and be quiet for a moment."

Zhang yelled out in Chinese and Jack looked at Mia who nodded that he had done as instructed.

Jack whispered in Mia's ear so Zhang could not hear and said, "I don't want the guys upstairs to know we have a hostage. If they come trooping down the stairs it may be to our advantage if they think Zhang has captured us."

"I understand," Mia whispered in response.

Jack looked at the narrow passageways leading between eight wooden shelving units. Another passageway at the rear of the units allowed entry to each aisle from both ends. Four dingy lights hung from the ceiling to illuminate the rows.

He tapped Mia on the shoulder and pointed. "I want you to sneak over there and break those three light bulbs. They're far enough down the rows that you won't be seen from above if you enter the rows from the back."

"There's a fourth bulb back amongst the rows behind you," noted Mia.

"I know. Meet me and Zhang there once you're done."

Rong heard the sound of a bulb being broken and then another as the shadows below turned into darkness. "Zhang?" he yelled again. "You okay?"

Seconds later, Zhang cursed in Chinese. "Yes, I'm okay, you idiot ... except for a sprained ankle. I dropped my gun but found it. They are playing cat and mouse with me. I don't want all of us bumbling around in the dark. We're liable to shoot each other. There are glass bottles and things they could use to bash someone on the head. Stay there and cover the stairs. I'll either flush them out toward you or shoot them myself."

Moments later, Mia broke the third light bulb and felt her way back amongst the rows until she came to the last passageway. Under the remaining light she saw Jack, who had Zhang lying face down on the floor with his hands tied behind his back with his own belt. "What now?" she asked. "It will only be a matter of time before they come down here after us. I also doubt that anyone would call the police."

Jack thought the same thing. He knew the owners of the restaurant would be too afraid to do anything. The only two customers left were an older couple who appeared to be new to the country and he had a sinking feeling that they would not want to get involved.

"Do you think there is any chance we could convince him that it really wasn't us who shot his boss?" asked Jack, indicating Zhang with the pistol.

"He might lie and say he believes us," replied Mia, "but you are Caucasian and I am only half-Chinese. I have my doubts he will trust us on that." She looked at Zhang and said, "Isn't that right?"

Zhang turned his head and glared back in response.

"What I figured, too," replied Jack.

"Are we going to shoot our way out?" asked Mia.

"I hope not."

"We're just going to wait?" whispered Mia.

Jack put his fingers to his lips when he heard Shen talking to Rong at the top of the stairs in Chinese.

When the conversation ended, Mia translated and said, "Basically Shen told Rong to go out to the trunk and grab the autos. Rong said he was expecting Zhang to flush us out soon and didn't think they would need them."

"Oh, great," said Jack, bitterly. "Just what we need. They'll likely have Uzis, Mac-10s, or knowing these guys, maybe AK-47s. Whatever they have won't matter when all we have is a pistol."

Mia realized she was starting to shake and knew she was going into shock. Jack saw her and gently squeezed her arm for reassurance. "So what do we do?" she said in a shaky voice, trying not to cry.

"I'll get you out," he said, sounding confident. "But I need to know what's going on."

"I don't understand," replied Mia. "The gangsters upstairs are trying to kill us."

"That's part of it," he replied, taking her by the arm and leading her farther away from Zhang so they could talk privately. "I need to hear the other part."

"The other part?"

"Yes, if we're going to get out alive, you need to be straight with me. You can start by telling me who Mr. Frank really is. And don't give me that crap that he works for Wong. What he did was a desperate act to try and kill us, as well. If he only wanted Wong out of the way, he could have come up with an easier plan than to shish kebab his eyeball with us in the room."

Mia stared back at him as a lifetime of training told her to lie.

"Come on, Mia. Level with me!" whispered Jack, tersely. "There is a hell of a lot more to that guy than you've told me … and I'm not just talking about hacking computers."

"You know about the computers?" asked Mia.

"Yes. Quit screwing around. Who is Mr. Frank?"

"He's my case officer," she blurted. Her voice trembled as did her body. Exposing a secret she had kept all her life seemed more frightening than the men she faced upstairs.

"Your case officer?" In the dim light Jack could see and hear her fear. He felt stupid that he had not clued in earlier. "You're a Chinese spy! You don't work for Wong at all, do you? He works for you."

"Not me. Mr. Frank … or well, our benefactor, as we say."

"Your benefactor? You mean Chinese Intelligence."

"Yes."

"Why did Mr. Frank try to have us killed?"

"I think he screwed up. He slipped a drug into my wine the day I had the accident in front of Nancy's house and tried to force himself upon me. He also gave me the bags of drugs I was caught with. I was concerned it was too much, but he wouldn't listen. After I was charged, he knew that if I received a criminal record that the benefactor would learn of his actions. I'm sure he went to Wong to have him kill the witness without approval."

"So Mr. Frank is responsible for having Betty Donahue killed?"

"Yes, but you know how that went. Everything got screwed up and then you appeared on the scene. I think Mr. Frank felt like he was being backed into a corner. His hope was to kill Wong and me to keep us from talking. I don't know about you. Maybe you were in the wrong place at the wrong time ... or perhaps it fit into his cover story for later."

Jack glanced around at the darkened basement and heard the murmurs from the men upstairs. He shook his head at the predicament they were in and looked at Mia, asking, "Why didn't you run out the back door like I told you? Why did you save me?"

"I don't know. At first I thought you were a schmuck and that I could play you. Then in the meeting when I thought Wong was going to kill me ... it was you I turned to for help. I don't know why I did it. It was probably a mistake."

"Not for me, it wasn't."

"Maybe I was starting to clue in about Mister ... fuck the mister part ... that asshole, Frank. He deceived me ... probably about a lot of things." She saw Jack staring at her intently, so she shrugged and added, "Maybe I decided it was time to be a real Canadian."

Jack sighed. "Well, thanks for saving my life." *At least for the moment.* "You said that Mr. ... asshole Frank probably deceived you about a lot of things. Are you referring to your father's hit and run?"

"Of course not," said Mia abruptly. "I was a child then. Frank recruited me last year in university. I had nothing to do with him before then. I was referring to him telling me that it was the benefactor who ordered the witness killed."

Jack knew she was lying about being recruited last year and understood why. It was something he would talk to her — and her entrepreneurial mother — about later.

"What are we going to do?" asked Mia. "What's going to happen?"

"What's going to happen is that Frank is going to go down," replied Jack, determinedly, as he looked toward the basement stairs.

"Forget about him. The guy is a trained agent. If he succeeds in killing us, he'll have figured out some way to bullshit the benefactor. He'll also have a Plan B. If by some miracle we survive, I'm sure he's plotted a secure escape route along with a new identity to disappear. He won't be caught. All we can do is try to stay alive and hope someone comes to save us."

"Yeah, well maybe you don't know about my Plan B," said Jack.

"What's your Plan B?"

"It's kind of complicated," whispered Jack in response.

"Fuck, you don't have a Plan B, do you?"

Jack put his finger to his lip to silence her when he heard all the bodyguards gathering at the top of the stairs.

Chapter Fifty-Three

Mr. Frank saw the horrified look on Dai and Shen's faces as they examined Wong slumped in his chair with his head to one side. His one eye remained open while blood and fluid from his brain dripped onto the desk from his other eye.

Mr. Frank did his best to look hopeful as Dai checked for Wong's pulse. Dai shook his head a moment later. Mr. Frank let out a big sigh, closing his eyes briefly to fake his grief. Then he spoke to them in Chinese, knowing that it would subconsciously make them feel united. "I tried to stop them, but I was too late," he lamented. "The woman distracted us. I didn't realize what was going on until Taggart stabbed him. He tried to punch me in the throat after, but I blocked his blow and then they ran."

Excited voices from the front of restaurant interrupted their thoughts. "Shen … the staff and the customers," cautioned Dai. "We may not have much time."

"We will make time," replied Shen harshly. "The people who work here would not dare to call the police on us. There were two customers, but they are old and I suspect not familiar with Western culture. Go back out front. Tell the staff to go upstairs and wait. If the customers have not already fled, say that the police have been called. Tell them they must leave if they do not wish to get into trouble and be taken in for questioning. Then lock the door and come back."

When Dai hurried back down the hall, Mr. Frank turned to Shen and said, "Taggart is a police officer. I am sure someone paid him big money to do this. He will have a plan. Maybe he will say that it was us who murdered Mr. Wong. We are Chinese. The authorities will not believe whatever we say. You need to kill them both immediately!"

Shen's face looked pale, but he nodded in agreement. Mr. Frank knew then that his importance as a trusted friend of Wong gave him the power to influence the bodyguards and he used it to take control of the situation. "Quickly, let's go get them and get out of here," he said, gesturing with his hand toward the hallway.

In the darkness below, Mia listened to bits and pieces of what she heard and whispered in Jack's ear. "Frank is near the top of the stairs and is taking control. Rong told them that Zhang sprained his ankle, but is okay and said to wait while he flushed us out. Frank said they've wasted enough time ... talk of checking to see if the restaurant has a flashlight. More talk of the autos ...

"Zhang!" yelled out Mr. Frank. "In about two minutes we'll be sending some backup down. Do you hear me? Zhang?"

The sound of a shot echoed loudly in the basement and Mr. Frank and the four bodyguards instinctively leaped back. The noise was followed by the sound of a body falling against some shelves and knocking items to the floor. Before anyone could respond, the remaining light was smashed as a second shot rang out.

Jack cried out in pain as Zhang yelled, "Got them! The woman through the head and Taggart through the knee when he broke the last light."

"Finish him off!" yelled Mr. Frank.

Jack's tearful voice drifted up the stairs. "Please don't kill me," he begged. "I have a wife ... children ... no! Please don't! You'll never get away with —"

A third shot rang out. "He tried to grab my gun," yelled Zhang. "I put one through his other kneecap."

"Good," whispered Jack into Zhang's ear. "If you don't want us to kill you or any of the others, you're going to get them down here so we can escape. The only one I am really after is Frank. I know you don't believe me, but he killed your boss, not to mention some other people."

"Finish him off!" yelled Mr. Frank, from the top of the stairs.

"No," replied Zhang. "Taggart killed my boss. His death will be more painful. Come and help me drag him to the bottom of the stairs. I want to see him beg before I kill him."

Mr. Frank knew it was time for him to go. "It is possible someone may have heard your shots," he yelled. "I would suggest you make it quick and get out of here!"

"I will!" replied Zhang. "Help me drag him out!"

Mr. Frank watched Shen, Dai, and Rong run down the steps, before he headed down the hall to the fire escape. He shoved the door open and stepped outside as he heard yelling from the basement. He turned in time to catch a glimpse of Mia and Jack enter the hallway behind him. He was about to stop the door from swinging shut when he saw that Jack was holding a pistol.

Their eyes momentarily locked and Mr. Frank leapt to one side in the alley as the door closed.

Jack quickly shut the basement door, then fired a warning shot through it, before handing Mia the gun.

"What are you doing?" she asked. "I can't —"

"Yes you can. Lie on the floor off to the side and point it at the door," he commanded. You'll hear the stairs creaking if anyone tries to come up. If they do, fire a shot through the door. They're not going to risk getting themselves killed for a boss who is already dead. I'm going after Frank!"

Seconds later, Jack stepped into the dimly lit alley. To his right, he saw a figure moving in the shadows and took a step in that direction, before realizing the figure was too short and not trying to escape, but coming toward him. He turned around and saw Mr. Frank ... barely out of arm's reach, taking aim at his face with a revolver. *Shit, now I find out he has a gun ...*

"We know who you are!" said Jack quickly. "We have your photo. We know you're with Chinese Intelligence ... the benefactor."

"We know?" sneered Mr. Frank. "Don't you mean ... you know?"

"It's *we*," replied Jack. "We've been on to you for some time now, trying to identify your contacts. We know you fucked up. Given the opportunity, your so-called benefactor will probably kill you for what you've done. Put the gun down. Your only hope is to co-operate with us."

"Yeah, right," muttered Mr. Frank.

"Think about it," continued Jack. "You really have no choice. Kill me and both East and West will be looking for you. How long do you think you would last?"

"I'm willing to take my chances."

"Your value could preclude that. As far as killing the witness and that guy in the flower shop ... I'm sure something could be arranged. You undoubtedly have priceless information you could exchange for leniency."

"The guy in the flower shop? Lok Cheng is dead? She got him already?"

She got him? thought Jack.

"Thanks for the info. I'll figure out a way to use it," said Mr. Frank, sounding matter of fact. "Killing her former case officer ... well, that makes it all too easy," he added, straightening out his arm as he squeezed down on the trigger.

A shot reverberated in the alley and Jack instinctively blinked and cringed at the same time. His jaw went slack when he saw Mr. Frank collapse like a rag doll to the ground, with blood draining out the back of his head where the bullet had exited.

Jack spun around. The heavyset, toothless Chinese woman stepped out of the shadows while pointing a pistol at him. *Christ, I hate days like this ...*

Chapter Fifty-Four

"You are not in danger if you obey my instructions," said the woman, in perfect English.

"Then why are you pointing the pistol at me?" asked Jack. He glanced at Mr. Frank's body and added, "Thank you, by the way. You're a hell of a good shot."

"Not really. You were lucky ... more ways than one. A moment ago I heard you refer to the benefactor ... that is who you owe your life to," she said, moving closer before stopping out of reach.

"Not like the other people you or the benefactor have killed in this country," Jack remarked.

The woman frowned. "He is the first person I have ever killed," she replied, gesturing at Mr. Frank with the muzzle of her pistol. "In fact, I believe he is the first person ever killed in Canada that the benefactor has ... would ... approve of. And, of course, that was done to save the life of a Canadian national."

"The first person?" queried Jack. "I am familiar with a hit-and-run murder about twenty-five years ago done by one of your Intelligence people. A murder that killed Mia Parker's father to gain control and manipulate his wife. In fact, that same Intelligence officer was murdered in his flower shop last night. I take it the benefactor was afraid he had become a loose end?"

A siren pierced the air a few blocks away, startling the woman. "If the benefactor had approved such an operation twenty-five years ago," she replied hastily, "do you really think the person who did the murder would remain in Canada afterward? Let alone Vancouver? I was told you are on an Intelligence Unit. Use your head."

"Perhaps you thought he was safe until recently when —"

The siren was coming closer and the Chinese woman interrupted. "No more talk! Take Mia and leave immediately."

"What? Have me call her outside so you can shoot her, too?"

The woman frowned, then yelled something in Chinese.

Jack saw Mia open the back door and he yelled, "Don't come out! Run! Escape out the front!"

Mia looked apologetic, then was shoved out the door by the tall, thin Chinese man who stopped and stood in the doorway, pointing a gun at her. Jack saw that he had Mia's gun tucked in his waistband.

"For your information," said the woman, still pointing her pistol at Jack, "my colleague picked the lock and went back in the restaurant several minutes ago. If we had wanted to kill her, she would already be dead. No more talk. Get the hell away from here now!"

With Mia present, Jack couldn't resist one last remark. "So you're saying that the Chinese Intelligence officer who murdered Mia's father twenty-five years ago did it without the approval of the benefactor?"

"What?" exclaimed Mia.

"Start running!" snarled the Chinese woman, as she stepped back inside the rear exit to join her colleague. "I am sending Wong's bodyguards after you!" she said, as she closed the door.

"What were you saying about my dad?" cried Mia, grabbing Jack by the front of his shirt.

"Not now! Run!" yelled Jack, grabbing her by the hand.

Chapter Fifty-Five

Rose and Laura heard the sound of a siren several blocks away and looked at each other.

"Who knows?" said Rose. "We're in a busy area. I think we should sit tight unless we hear from Wilson."

Seconds later, sirens echoed off the buildings from several different locations, including two marked VPD cars that went racing past them. "Forget Wilson, this has got to be Jack," said Laura, putting the car in gear and screeching out on the street to follow.

They had only driven about four blocks when they saw Jack and Mia appear from around a side street, running at full tilt. Jack held up his badge and flagged down one patrol car that pulled over to the curb.

Laura parked in the street behind the patrol car and ran to check on Mia who stood on the sidewalk, covering her face with her hands, and sobbing. "You okay?" whispered Laura.

"They killed my dad," she cried.

"You guys on your way to a shooting in an alley?" asked Jack, through the open window of the patrol car, as Rose came up beside him.

"You got it," replied the officer. "Was it her father?" he asked, indicating Mia.

"No, forget her, she had nothing to do with it. She's having a reaction because her dad died years ago when he was run over by a Chinese guy. This is different. In a nutshell, I was in the alley working undercover and witnessed the shooting you're on your way to. The guy is dead. There are two suspects."

The officer quickly jotted down the description of the Chinese woman and her tall companion. He then glanced at Rose and asked, "Anyone else see it?"

"No," interjected Jack.

"I'm his boss," explained Rose. "Myself and the other member on the sidewalk were parked a few blocks away."

The officer turned his attention back to Jack. "Is the shooting connected to the UC you were doing?"

"Yes, and there is something you should know. Both suspects work for a Chinese Intelligence service. So did the victim in the alley."

"You're saying they're spies?" asked the officer, looking at his partner in disbelief.

"Yes ... and the woman doesn't fit the James Bond image. Short, fat, and toothless ... but I can tell you she is a crack shot."

"And you're saying you saw her shoot the guy?" the officer confirmed.

"I was talking to the victim when I heard the shot come from behind me. The bullet went past my head. I turned and she was holding the gun and was the only person there. She also admitted it to me. I know the victim only by the name of Mr. Frank. He had a gun and was going to kill me when this Chinese woman intervened and saved my life."

"She saved your life?"

"Yes, but don't rely on any sense of compassion from her. If she's cornered, I'm sure she'll try to shoot you, too."

"Tactical has been called already," replied the officer. He glanced at Mia, who was being comforted by Laura and asked, "What about her? Did she witness it?"

"No, she came along after," replied Jack.

The officer nodded, thinking he understood. "Memories. They can come back to haunt you unexpectedly," he said, softly. "Sorry about your dad."

"You only get a call about the shooting in the alley?" asked Jack.

Oh, man, thought Laura.

"Yeah, switchboard says three calls. All with Chinese accents. Two were anonymous."

"A restaurant backs on to the alley where the body is," continued Jack. "Inside an office in the restaurant is another body. That victim is Benny Wong."

"The triad leader?" asked the officer.

"The one and only. He's got a receipt spike rammed through his eye, shish-kebabing his brain."

"Oh, Christ, Jack," muttered Rose.

The officer glanced at Rose, then looked at Jack. "You do it?" he asked.

"No. The dead guy in the alley did it shortly before he was killed. I was going after him to arrest him when he got the drop on me. One more thing: last I saw, Wong had four bodyguards in the restaurant. They are also armed, but will probably ditch their weapons when they see you guys arrive."

"Alright, hop in with us," the officer ordered. "We'll head over."

"Can't right now," replied Jack.

"If you think I'm going to let you walk away, you better think again."

"Time is of the essence. I have a source I need to meet who might tell me where the suspects went." It was a lie, but one Jack felt he had to tell to get away and do what he planned to do.

Rose heard her phone ring and saw that it was Wilson. She answered immediately. "We're on it! We're with Jack and a couple of your guys now."

The officer in the car shook his head at Jack. "You're not going anywhere until I get some more answers. To start with, I want to see your complete identification. You, too, ma'am."

Rose handed her phone to the officer and said, "Talk to this guy."

Seconds later the officer handed the phone to Jack and said, "Okay, I've been told to let you go, but Wilson wants to talk to you."

"Hey, Jack," said Wilson. "Sounds like you had a little excitement tonight?"

"More than a little," replied Jack.

"Understood, but I'll need to meet the both of you in my office right away to get full statements. Is that okay with you? Or, uh, do you need time to, uh, calm the young woman down so she can give a statement? I know how finicky your people can be over little details sometimes. Connie in particular."

Jack smiled to himself and breathed a sigh of relief. Wilson gave him more trust and understanding than most of his own people would. "I hear what you're saying ... and don't think I don't appreciate it, but what happened is straight up. I'll send Mia over with Laura immediately. As far as I go, there is someone I need to meet with first. Someone who might point us in a direction to look for the suspects. I can meet you immediately after. Shouldn't be more than an hour or two."

"Man ... that's great to hear. Do what you have to do. Tell Laura that I'll be at my office in twenty minutes."

Jack hung up and gave Rose her phone back. As the patrol car drove away, she eyed him curiously. "I got the feeling that you and Wilson are close?"

"I've had a couple of cases with him in the past," said Jack, shrugging. "I really respect the guy. Sounds like the feeling is mutual."

"Can't say I like the idea of a VPD Homicide cop buddying up to you."

"If he thought I was dirty, I would be in cuffs right now. Besides, you heard what I told him. There's nothing to hide."

"Good," replied Rose, sounding like she meant it. She eyed Jack briefly, then abruptly asked, "Where were you when Benny Wong was skewered through the eye?"

"Sitting across from him at his desk," he answered, promptly.

"Damn it, Jack!"

"Honest, I didn't kill anyone," he said, defensively.

"Well, that would be a pleasant change," she said dryly. "If it's true."

"Rose is my boss," Jack said to Mia. "Please tell her who killed Wong."

Mia looked puzzled. "It happened like he said. I was there. Why are you doubting him? You do work together, right?"

Rose stared at Mia, but didn't answer.

"Thanks, Mia," said Jack. He looked at Rose. "My trust in Mia has grown considerably tonight."

"I bet it has if she is vouching for you," said Rose.

"It's not that," replied Jack. He glanced at Mia and gave her an affectionate pat on her back. "Tonight she saved me from being killed. Probably twice. First by shoving me out of the line of fire down a set of stairs and then again right after when she scooped up a bad guy's gun."

"Really?" said Rose in surprise.

"Yes, I'll tell you all the details later," replied Jack, "along with a bunch of other things." He looked at Mia out of the corner of his eye to indicate he did not want to talk in front of her, but at the same time, did not want to destroy the level of trust that had been built by excluding her himself.

"Laura, take Mia back to the car. I need to talk to Jack," said Rose, picking up on the cue.

Once Laura and Mia were out of earshot, Rose said, "So you found out that we're dealing with Chinese spies."

"Mia told me. Mr. Frank was her case officer."

Rose glared back at Mia. "So the little bitch was playing us. She isn't some hapless kid who didn't know what she had got herself into."

"It started out that way, but she did save my life tonight. I think that is worth something."

"Was it her who tipped off the others about the meeting tonight? The ones who showed up to kill Mr. Frank?"

"I don't think so. I'm kind of curious about that myself."

"I wonder how long she has been doing it," said Rose, nodding toward Mia.

"She told me she was recruited last year, but she is lying to protect someone."

"Do you know who?"

"Her mother. Mia has been trained all her life."

Rose looked at Jack as she put it together. "A moment ago Mia said it was them who killed her father. Is she talking about Chinese Intelligence?"

"Yes."

"My God! They did that to recruit Mia's mother … who then turned her own daughter into one!"

"I'm positive, although it may have been done by a rogue officer. Earlier, Mia didn't think I knew her mother was involved, but she must realize I've clued in. I want to confront Jia-li without Mia being around or getting hold of her. I think I can turn Jia-li and my chances of success are better in a one-on-one situation. The Chinese will know we'll be on to her, but she could still be a wealth of information."

"Maybe they've already killed her," said Rose.

"I doubt it. They let Mia and I live. If they killed Jia-li, we would know. They wouldn't want the economic and political fallout that would come from that. Also opening up the public's eyes would ultimately generate more funding for counter-intelligence services."

"Then go for it, but there is something else going on tonight that you need to know."

"More? After what Mia and I have been through ... you're telling me there's more?" said Jack, feeling exasperated as his brain told him he had enough to deal with.

"Not involving us directly. There is some major computer hacking taking place tonight, all over North America. Government and military computers are being hit. Little doubt that it's the Chinese who are behind it. The techs on our side are throwing everything they have at the problem to try and stop it. If Jia-li co-operates, ask her about it. I don't know much about that stuff, but I bet she uses computers to relay info to her people. Maybe she knows something that will help."

"I'll do my best."

"You seem confident that you can get her to turn," noted Rose.

Jack nodded grimly as he glanced at Mia sitting in the car. He knew who killed Lok Cheng. He also realized that the killer had not told her daughter about the murder. "Sometimes I can be quite charming," he said.

Rose knew by his tone of voice that charm would have nothing to do with it.

Jack stared at Rose and added, "Especially when I'm holding a trump card."

Rose's thoughts went to Lok Cheng's murder in the flower shop. She saw Jack reading her mind. "Your trump card is last night's murder, isn't it?"

Chapter Fifty-Six

Jack nodded grimly at Mia as he got in the back seat and sat beside her, while Rose got in the front with Laura. Mia stared at Jack, tears running down her face, as she waited for an explanation.

He held her hand between his and said, "I found out from Frank right before he was shot that it was a Chinese Intelligence officer who murdered your father." He purposely didn't tell her it was a case officer. *Her mom's case officer, no doubt ...*

More tears welled up in Mia's eyes and he squeezed her hand, hoping to absorb her pain. "I think it was done as a ruse to befriend your mother and have her become indebted to ... the benefactor," he added.

"You know," replied Mia, lamely.

"Yes, I know."

"Mom was a spy to start with, but wanted out," she said, pulling her hand away. "They must have done it to bring her back into the fold."

Jack paused as Mia used her fingertips to wipe the tears from her cheeks. Her body was shivering from shock. "You going to be okay?" he asked.

Mia shrugged. "I'm okay. What my body is experiencing is a normal reaction following a tragic or shocking event."

Jack was taken back at her clinical response, but realized she had her master's in psychology. *Then again, her training started long before university ...* "I'm having Laura go with you to give a statement to a Detective Wilson," he said. "When you're done there, you and I will talk some more."

"Is my mom going to be arrested?"

"As soon as you're dropped off, I'll go over to meet with her. If she co-operates, I think everything will work out okay."

"Tell her it was a Chinese Intelligence officer who killed Dad. She'll co-operate. If you like, give me a phone and I'll tell her myself."

"Perhaps later, but not until I am with her."

"Of course. That was stupid of me. You think she might have evidence she'll dispose of or something."

"Possibly," admitted Jack.

"What should I tell the police in the meantime?" asked Mia.

"The truth. What else?" replied Jack.

"No, but how far back do I go? What do I tell him about things not related to tonight?"

"Laura will tell Wilson that you are our informant. I have worked with him before. He is trustworthy and his interest is only in tonight's homicides. Start by saying you were introducing me, through Frank, to Benny Wong. Give all the details and everything you can remember from the time we left your car. I see no reason for you to discuss anything else with him at this time. If you feel uncomfortable, ask to speak with Laura."

Mia nodded.

"There is one thing I need to know," continued Jack, "and we can talk as Laura drives," he said, with a nod at Laura to get going. "How is spying carried out here?"

Mia took a deep breath and slowly exhaled. "Well, basically, much of the spying in Canada used to rely on information gathered by selected students who were only in Canada for a short time. Some was done by others who were working toward their doctorates and offered to work for free for certain companies for a year or two on the pretext of gaining experience."

"And I gather many Canadian companies are naive enough to jump at the opportunity for free labour," mused Jack.

"That, and it makes them feel good to think they are helping a foreign student."

"Who is helping themselves to the technology," noted Jack.

"Of course, or corrupting their computers for future purposes," said Mia. "In China, of course, spying on Westerners is different. Hotel rooms are bugged and have hidden video cameras. Blackmail or even false allegations of rape are made to compromise people, but to my knowledge that generally wasn't tried in foreign countries."

"Wasn't?" asked Jack.

"I have no personal knowledge that what I just described is taking place in Canada, but things are expanding rapidly. I wouldn't count it out. Industrial espionage is huge and there's new technology."

"Like computer hacking?" asked Jack.

"Definitely. That takes place on a daily basis," Mia replied.

"How about police computers?" asked Jack. "I know you expressed concern before about us mentioning you in reports."

"I don't know if the police computers are safe. I worried about it when you first interviewed me. I panicked a little, wondering whether or not to tell Frank the truth."

"And did you?" asked Jack.

"Yes. The plan was not to tell Wong, but Frank knew." She glanced at Jack's face to see if he was angry. "I also told my mom everything."

"It's okay," he said. "Your actions tonight saved my life. I owe you. At the moment, is there anything else you know about computer hacking?"

"No, but in China new technology is a priority, especially if it can be stolen and save the country millions in research. I think it is common knowledge, at least with all Intelligence agencies, that there is technology to surreptitiously switch on the camera in your mobile phone, as well as audio."

"Do you have any special gadgets?"

"Not really. All I have ever been given is a spy pen that is sold commercially to anyone these days."

She paused, glancing at Jack and said, "I also lied to you before about getting ahold of Mr. Frank through a computer chat room. If I want to send a secret message, all I do is prepare it and put it in the draft folder of my computer. A short time later it disappears."

"You were afraid that if you had told me that, I would clue in that I was dealing with spies."

Mia nodded. "I don't know who retrieves it out of my computer or how that works."

"Thanks for telling me now," said Jack. "I'd like to know what your specific assignments were?"

"My job was to befriend fellow students, particularly any whom were going into technological or political fields. It was anticipated that I would get a job, perhaps in Ottawa with a public relations firm catering to politicians. What is commonly called a spin doctor."

"Have you supplied any information or come up with something of value for the Chinese to date?" asked Jack.

"Yes," sighed Mia. "About two weeks ago for the first time. I met a Member of Parliament ... Sterling Wolfenden."

Jack saw Rose and Laura exchange a glance, then Laura shook her head and muttered something about her cat as she continued to drive.

"It was during a house party at the Rolstads' place," continued Mia. "I seduced him and recorded it all and passed it on to Frank. Wolfenden told me he has been meeting with military people and going to the Boeing plant in Seattle. He is flying in from Ottawa on Sunday and wants to meet me."

"Imagine his disappointment when I show up," said Jack, dryly.

Chapter Fifty-Seven

Jack stood outside Jia-li's apartment and rang the buzzer. When she answered, he said, "It's Jack Taggart. I was with Mia tonight and something happened. I need to talk to you." He heard her panicked response as she quickly allowed him access.

Jia-li hurried to Jack in the hallway. "Is she okay?" she asked, fearfully.

"Mia will be okay," replied Jack. "Things got a little out of hand tonight, but she didn't get hurt. Let's go inside. The two of us need to talk in private."

Jia-li looked at Jack sharply. It was obvious from what Jack said that he knew Mia had confided in her about meeting Wong. She nodded and gestured for him to follow her back inside her apartment. Once there, Jack sat on the sofa and Jia-li sat across from him.

"Okay, first of all," said Jack, "listen to what I have to say. I know your instincts and training will urge you to interrupt and lie, but please don't say anything until you hear what I have to say first."

My instincts? My training? Jia-li was about to deny she knew what he was talking about, but saw that he was reading her mind and opted to stare at him in stony silence instead.

"Mia said she has told you everything leading up to the meeting tonight with Wong and her case officer, Mr. Frank."

Jia-li cringed inwardly at Mr. Frank being identified as a case officer, but remained stoic.

"So, with that in mind, I'll start from where she and I were directed to a small restaurant where the meeting was to take place," continued Jack.

Jia-li listened intently and sat rigidly in her chair as Jack told her everything that had happened, up until he ended up in the basement with Mia and Zhang.

"That was when she admitted to me she was a spy," he said, "but at the same time she denied you were involved. I knew, but didn't say anything then."

Jia-li's face looked as if it were carved from stone, but she kept quiet until Jack told how they escaped the basement and that he went out the back door after Mr. Frank.

"You left my daughter with the gun and went after Mr. Frank without a weapon?" she asked.

"Yes, I wanted her to have protection, but it was a mistake. It turned out that Frank had a gun."

Jia-li was quiet as Jack told her about Mr. Frank pointing the gun at him and the conversation they had. "He told me then that Lok Cheng was your case officer," said Jack. It wasn't exactly true, but Jack did not want to give Jia-li an opening to lie and say that

Mr. Frank was referring to someone else.

Jia-li's mouth opened and she started to shake her head in denial, but Jack said, "Please, there is more." He then told her about the Chinese woman who saved his life and had Mia brought outside. He said his conversation with the woman confirmed his suspicion of who Lok Cheng really was.

"That was when Mia was there," blurted Jia-li. "Does she know Cheng was my case officer?"

"Not yet. I purposely referred to him in front of the woman as a Chinese Intelligence officer to hide the fact from Mia that it was your case officer."

"Why?"

"To give you the opportunity to tell her yourself," said Jack. He saw Jia-li momentarily close her eyes to try and shut out the stress she felt. "However," he continued, "Mia is not stupid. She will soon figure it out ... but as she is your daughter, I think it best she hear it from you first."

Jia-li's only response was to massage her temples with her fingertips.

"After that we ran like we were told to do and flagged down a police car." Jack was silent for a moment, then let out a sigh, leaned forward, and said, "On her way to the police station, Mia told me she seduced one of our Members of Parliament two weeks ago. She also realized I knew about you and wanted to call you in the belief that you would confess once you found out who murdered your husband." Jack paused, then added, "Of course, she doesn't yet realize that you murdered that person."

Jia-li stared sadly back at him. "I don't want a lawyer. Arrest me and take me in. I will tell you everything."

"There are some things I would like to know first."

"About what?"

"How long have you been spying in Canada?" asked Jack.

"For over thirty years," admitted Jia-li. "I was a spy long before I came to Canada."

"Long before?" asked Jack.

"Both my parents worked for an Intelligence Unit in the People's Liberation Army. As a child, I was taught to report anyone with views contrary to what the benefactor said was appropriate."

"And your spying continued when you moved to Canada," said Jack, matter-of-factly.

"I didn't want it to. I was in love and wanted a family. I wasn't interested in politics … but life isn't always what you want it to be," she added, bitterly.

"Sometimes bad things happen to good people," said Jack. "Tell me about who you targeted."

Jack listened as the words poured out of her. She told him she had spied on seven men, counting her husband. Jack was sombre as he wrote down the names. One was a Supreme Court judge, two were politicians, one of which worked for the Minister of Justice. Three, including her current target, were involved in scientific or commercial research projects, including a company that contracted out to the military.

Jia-li continued to talk and gave Jack a brief overview of spying and espionage. He heard how the benefactor hoped to influence the licensing of foreign powers to be able to control Internet providers and phone companies. She explained how journalists were corrupted or used without their knowledge to collect sensitive information.

By the time she warned Jack about the potential for the benefactor to utilize the services of the triads in Canada to bug and video massage parlours, he felt overwhelmed with the information he had collected, but knew he had more to learn.

"What can you tell me about computer hacking?" he asked.

"That it goes on every day. Company secrets are stolen. Major companies in Canada have actually gone bankrupt as a result of the secrets we have stolen from them. The last three names I gave you ... I can tell you that every one of their personal laptops has been compromised."

"Do you know anything about the actual technology of the spyware? How it works?"

"Not really, other than sometimes it is like a Catch-22. Using it to hack computers that have high protection could alert people to its existence. Like a fisherman casting his net, one must decide when the net is full before taking action."

"Such as a time of war?"

"Perhaps, or if the spyware is discovered or if new technology can be developed ... then they may not have to worry about the discovery of the old. I am only talking about ultra-secure computer firewalls. Many computer systems are not a problem and the information can be gathered easily. But as far as my knowledge of the technical side of it, I simply know how to install it by using a memory stick. I have one I can give you."

"In a moment. First I am wondering how the benefactor found out about tonight? Mia said she only told you and Frank about it. Frank wouldn't have said anything and Wong only knows the benefactor through Frank. I have also been careful not to put anything on a computer. That leaves you. Did you tell the benefactor about tonight's meeting?"

"Yes, I did," admitted Jia-li. "Come with me into the den," she said, getting up, "and I'll show you an email I sent to the benefactor this afternoon."

Jack followed Jia-li into the den, saw a computer, and grabbed her by the arm. "No way, you're not touching it," he said. "We'll be getting a warrant and seizing it."

"I don't intend to touch it," she replied. "As far as a warrant goes, I'll give you full permission to take whatever you like. What I want to show you is a hard copy of an email I sent. It's under the blotter on top of the desk."

Jack let go of her arm and retrieved the email himself. "What's this?" he asked. "I can't read it."

"It's simplified Chinese," replied Jia-li. "Keep it and get it translated."

"Isn't it coded?" asked Jack.

"Not by me. I simply prepare it and put it in the draft folder of my email and it disappears. I don't know who retrieves it. What you are holding is a copy I printed for myself."

"Why did you print a copy? I'm sure that isn't allowed."

"I will give you the gist of the main points; then you will understand."

Jack took out his notebook as they stood in the doorway to the den. "Give them to me one at a time."

"Point number one," said Jia-li, bitterly. "I know my daughter is facing a drug charge because of Mr. Frank's stupidity in trying to drug and seduce her, leading to her arrest by the police."

"She told me," replied Jack.

"Which leads to point number two," said Jia-li, pointing to some text on the email. "I said I know Mr. Frank went to Benny Wong to have him murder a Canadian national who was a witness to the drug charge. It resulted in the wrong person being murdered by mistake."

"A seventy-four-year-old woman by the name of Betty Donahue," said Jack.

Jia-li swallowed to try and maintain her composure before pointing to another indentation on the email. "Point number three. The police implicated my daughter in the botched murder and she is pretending to allow the police to use her. Tonight my daughter will complete the ruse Mr. Frank has arranged for her by taking an undercover RCMP Intelligence officer by the name of Corporal Jack Taggart to meet Wong in exchange for having her charges dropped."

Jack wrote her comment in his notebook, then looked at Jia-li. "It looks like there is more," he said, indicating another indentation in the email.

"Yes, there is more." She did not need to read from the email to continue. "I wrote that I know who killed my husband ... all so that I could be manipulated because I had expressed a desire to quit. I also said that if anything ever happens to Mia ... or myself, that I have a detailed account of every asset I know who was turned or compromised and that a lawyer will turn that information over to both the news media and the police upon my death."

"But you've told me," said Jack, "which means your life — and Mia's — could be in danger."

Jia-li shook her head. "With what happened tonight, they know you will have figured it out ... leading to a detailed investigation of my past, along with everyone I have ever associated with. I'm sure the benefactor is taking immediate steps to get as much information from anyone I have told you about, or if not them, at least their computers, before countermeasures are taken."

"Large-scale computer hacking on an unprecedented scale started a few hours ago," said Jack. "Government and military systems both in Canada and the U.S. are being hit."

Jia-li nodded knowingly. "I'm sure other countries as well. The technology used to hack won't be limited to North America. Knowing that it is about to be discovered would cause them to grab as much information as they can."

"Time to pull in the net," said Jack.

"Exactly."

"Front-page headlines tomorrow," noted Jack.

"Possibly, but I doubt it," replied Jia-li. "Perhaps in time it will make the news, but Intelligence agencies are not anxious to cause embarrassment to the officials who govern them, particularly in cases of sexpionage."

"Sexpionage?"

"The old term is 'honey-pot operations.' Regardless, informing the public is also a double-edged sword. If the public were informed, it would alert them to their own naïveté and potentially pave the way for other things."

"Such as?"

"Like allowing for easier monitoring of email, electronic devices, or the need to protect commercial enterprises ... particularly in the communications sector. However, not informing the public prevents a political backlash. In these tough economic times, money and jobs are a huge political factor. China has the money ... and can dangle it like a carrot in front of the politician's faces."

"There is another factor to consider before laying accusations out to the media," said Jack. "You're a journalist. You must know that to make accusations against anyone ... let alone a member of the government ... could result in an expensive lawsuit unless there is strong evidence. Knowing what is going on and proving it are two different things."

"Spoken like a policeman," replied Jia-li, with a hint of contempt in her voice.

"Yes, I am a policeman ... and getting back to that, how did you feel when Mia told you she seduced Wolfenden? A man who is much older ... and married with children."

Jia-li swallowed and turned her head to look away.

"As a matter of interest," said Jack, intentionally sounding casual, "were you really proud of her for doing that? I've known other mothers who have turned their daughters into prostitutes, but they were usually drug addicts or —"

"No!" shouted Jia-li. Tears welled in her eyes. "I am anything but proud," she said quietly, then glared at Jack and added, "You do not shock me or make me feel worse with those words. I know what I have done. I will never forgive myself and your attempt to humiliate me is like sprinkling water on a garden during a monsoon."

"I can see that you are angry with yourself," said Jack. "I'm sure you were angry at the man who started you down this path as well. The man who killed your husband."

Jia-li stared blankly at Jack in response.

"At the moment, a very talented detective is interviewing Mia," continued Jack. "He is also investigating Lok Cheng's murder. I have not told him anything yet, but it won't take him long to discover your connection. He will suspect that Mia was an accessory because she had to have shown you his photo in the first place. Did the two of you conspire together to kill him?"

"Leave Mia out of it," said Jia-li angrily. "You do not have to threaten me with her. She has been through enough!" She gave Jack a hard look, then her face mellowed. "Can't you see I am willing to confess to everything? It is the one decent thing I can do for her."

"You're doing the right thing," said Jack, softly.

"A lifetime of prison will never be enough punishment for how I raised my daughter," added Jia-li, as tears clouded her vision.

"Well, the thing is, I don't completely agree with you," said Jack. "Your daughter saved my life tonight. You must have done or taught her something that was good."

"It was always within her spirit to try to be good," said Jia-li, letting out a sob. "To do what she thought was right and to please me … despite the terrible path I forced her to travel."

"And pleasing you didn't include killing Lok Cheng?" asked Jack.

Jia-li looked sharply at Jack. "I murdered Lok Cheng by myself," she said, abruptly. "I stabbed him in the throat and stole his cash receipts to try and make it look like a robbery."

Jack stared silently at her, hiding his thoughts.

Jia-li misread Jack's moment of silence as a sign he did not believe her and said, "Okay, Mia did send me a photo of him when I was in Calgary, but she did not know that I knew him. I flew back on Wednesday afternoon, but had told Mia I wouldn't be arriving until midnight. Unless she found out tonight, she doesn't even know the man is dead."

Jack swallowed as his conscience played havoc with his brain.

"Write down what I told you!" Jia-li snapped at him. "I will sign it. You should have given me the police warning, informing me of my right to counsel, but no matter. Give me the warning now and I will repeat what I said."

"Your email saved my life tonight," said Jack.

"I guess you were lucky," she replied. "I didn't know that when I sent it." She frowned. "We are wasting time. I know you will want to take my statement immediately out of fear that I will change my mind. Let's return to the living room and I will give it to you. Then put me in jail without seeing Mia."

"I don't mind you talking to her."

Jia-li shook her head. "I cannot bear to face her. She must feel utter contempt toward me for what a fool I have been." Tears flowed from her eyes and she covered her face with her hands as she stood, slowly rocking her upper body back and forth to try and alleviate the pain. "I even slept with Cheng after my husband died," she uttered, before lowering her hands and looking at Jack. "It sickens me," she said in a half-whisper, letting her words trail off.

"Mia's decision to save my life tonight was intentional," said Jack.

Jia-li shrugged.

"I think we each owe her something," said Jack, softly. "You could start by telling her the truth about what you did. You murdered the man who killed her father and your email to the benefactor effectively removed her from the spy game. She needs to hear that from you … and she needs to hear it now."

Chapter Fifty-Eight

Detective Wilson placed Jia-li in an interview room separate from Mia's, then headed for his office to talk to Jack. On the way, he was joined by Laura and Connie, who had been at a nearby coffee shop.

"Anything new in the search for the Chinese couple from the restaurant?" asked Laura.

"No, I checked a moment ago. They've disappeared," replied Wilson. "We're also having trouble identifying the body in the alley. There is no identification, wallet, or keys on him."

"We only know him as Mr. Frank," said Laura.

"Yeah, that's what Mia told me, too," replied Wilson, "as well as her mother, Jia-li."

"You've spoken to Jia-li?" asked Laura, in surprise.

"Jack brought her in a couple of minutes ago. She's in an interview room," explained Wilson.

"So she's not co-operating," Laura said, frowning.

"No, I think she is. She suggested that one possible way to help us find the Chinese couple would be to watch the port to see if they try to board any Chinese-based ships that are docked. Not a bad idea."

"Unless it is a ruse to use up manpower and have us looking in the wrong place," said Connie.

"Jack believes she is being honest," replied Wilson.

"Why did he bring her in?" asked Laura.

"He didn't say yet. He's waiting for me in my office, let's go find out."

"Did Mia give you a complete statement?" asked Connie, as they walked toward Wilson's office.

"Yes ... and I think it was an honest one," replied Wilson.

"Be interesting to compare it with Jack's, once you get his," mused Connie. She caught Laura's glare and added, "Don't give me that. You know him better than anyone."

Seconds later, they joined Jack in the office. He was sitting and reviewing his notebook, but glanced at Connie and said, "I thought you might show up."

"I heard about the excitement," replied Connie, while sitting down. "I thought maybe Wilson and I should collaborate on some things."

"Yeah, she has a real interest in comparing the statement you'll give with that of Mia's," replied Laura.

Jack frowned at Laura. "Statements should be compared."

Laura felt irritated. *Is he chastising me for warning him ... or for not trusting his judgment to*

*have known the statements would be compared ...
Probably the latter ...*

"First of all, why did you bring Jia-li in?" asked Wilson, as he sat down behind his desk. "Does she have a role in what happened?"

"You might say that," replied Jack. "She murdered Lok Cheng in his flower shop last night. She admitted it to me and is anxious to give you a statement and confess."

Wilson, Laura, and Connie all looked at each other in surprise. Connie was the first to respond. "My God, Jack! You brought in a live one. This is a real turning point for you!"

Jack ignored Connie and turned his attention to Wilson. "Jia-li was spying for the Chinese," he said, gravely. "Lok Cheng was her former case officer. She did not want to spy when she moved to Canada, so Cheng murdered her husband without her knowledge as an inducement to keep her on the hook. She clued in when Mia sent her the enhanced photo."

"I'll take a statement from her immediately," said Wilson, getting to his feet. "Has she been warned?"

"Not yet, but sit down. There is more to discuss." Jack waited until Wilson sat down again and said, "Murdering a man who murdered your husband ... how much time do you think she will actually serve?"

Wilson glanced at Connie, then shrugged. "I don't know ... maybe seven years."

"Providing the statement you take is admitted and she's convicted," added Jack.

"Of course," replied Wilson.

"She sent an email this afternoon to the Chinese, outlining the meeting I was having tonight with Frank and Wong. She made it clear that she and Mia were no longer going to act as spies. Ultimately, her email saved my life. I think the benefactor, as they call their agency, ordered a hit on Frank."

"That's nice, but it doesn't detract from the fact that she knifed some old guy in the throat," replied Wilson, "even if he was a spy."

"Mia also saved my life tonight. Twice. She had a chance to flee, but opted to come back and shove me down a basement stairwell out of the way of gunfire and a second time in the basement when she grabbed a bad guy's gun and got the drop on him."

"Makes the daughter look good, but it has nothing to do with the mother," replied Wilson. "I'm sorry, you must feel like you owe them, but if you think those are mitigating factors, that is something for a judge to decide upon sentencing."

"You've done well, Jack," said Connie. "Don't screw it up by talking like this."

"So you think we should trust the justice system?" replied Jack, looking at Wilson.

Laura rolled her eyes. *Oh, man … here it comes …*

Wilson shrugged. "We have to do the best with what we have."

"What if I told you that Jia-li has given me the names of six people she recruited who are spying against Canada and are in positions to do dramatic damage to our economic stability and military operations? Albeit, some don't realize they are being used."

"You want to cut a deal with her?" asked Wilson. "I think I would need the names to pass on to the Crown and let them decide."

"That could be a problem," replied Jack. "This is too big for the local prosecutors to decide on their own. They will need to go to Ottawa. The names I have been given are big enough that the people doing the deciding could be some of the same people who are working for the Chinese. Jia-li gave me six names. I am sure others have been corrupted whom Jia-li knows nothing about. Actually, I even have a seventh name. Mia admitted to me that she recorded a sexual encounter two weeks ago with Sterling Wolfenden."

"The Member of Parliament?" asked Wilson.

"The one and only."

"Can you give me the other six names?" asked Wilson, reaching for a pen.

"I'll give you three of them," replied Jack. "They alone are enough for anyone of pragmatic intelligence to guarantee she will not be charged. The other three I will hold in abeyance."

"Why?" asked Wilson.

"Because I don't trust our justice system. Once there is signed documentation saying she will not be charged, only then I will release the other names. In the meantime, they can know that I am dangling three more names over their heads. Something I'm sure the media would be most interested in if they ever found out."

"I understand," said Wilson, nodding.

"Of course, having a decision made not to charge her would take months," replied Jack, "and the spies would no doubt be putting in overtime until then, perhaps corrupting others as well."

"What are you getting at?" asked Wilson.

Jack looked at Connie. "Any suggestions? One of the names I have been given is a Supreme Court judge and another is a politician who works for the Minister of Justice."

"What do you mean, do I have any suggestions?" replied Connie, defensively. "These aren't our decisions to make. You should spill the beans on everyone. Not just three."

"We have all cut deals with criminals in the past," noted Jack, "either to work our way up the ladder or to make a deal to save time in court. Should we risk jeopardizing Canada's future by going through channels? We know that in time, the outcome should favour Jia-li by giving her complete immunity from prosecution. Unless, of course, the decision is made by someone who does not understand the big picture and says she should be charged."

"A charge that could still be tossed out in court," noted Wilson. "I see what you're getting at."

"I don't," said Connie.

"Do you think she should be charged?" asked Jack.

"She likely won't be, but that's not our decision to make," said Connie. "It's up to Ottawa."

"Do you trust the people in Ottawa more than you trust the people in this room?" asked Jack.

"Well …" Connie paused as she looked around the room, before swallowing and continuing, "no, but …"

"Do all of us agree that ultimately Jia-li shouldn't be — and likely won't be — charged in consideration of her co-operation?" asked Jack.

Wilson and Laura both nodded and everyone turned to stare at Connie. Her face took on an ashen hue and her voice was a whisper. "How can we not go through channels?" She looked at Wilson. "You're investigating a guy being murdered in his flower shop. If you don't solve it, someone else will come along."

"Not if I were to say that when I was in the alley with Frank that he confessed to murdering Cheng," said Jack. "Kind of a dying confession, in a way."

"Oh, fuck," muttered Connie.

After a moment of silence, Wilson cleared his throat and said, "Given what you have told me, I could live with that." He looked at Connie. "Providing the four of us agree and everyone keeps their mouth shut."

Connie felt the pressure mount as all eyes stared at her. Her mind replayed what she had been told. *It makes sense, but it isn't right …*

"It isn't technically right," said Jack quietly, "but I feel it is morally just."

"I'll never be able to sleep at night," replied Connie.

"I bet you'll find that you'll sleep really well … once you make the right decision," said Jack.

Connie remained silent a moment longer. "Okay, I'm in," she said, with her voice cracking as her mind told her she was going against everything she believed in.

Everyone else in the room took a deep breath and slowly exhaled.

"Jack, I've got one question," said Wilson. "You obviously felt Jia-li shouldn't be charged. Why didn't you simply say that Frank told you he did it? Why did you involve us?"

"Connie told me she respects you," replied Jack. "I figured if you suspected I lied to you that it would be too easy for you to put the pieces together. Airport video of Jia-li flying back from Calgary early. Perhaps DNA or some other evidence. Not to mention that she would blurt the truth out to you if you interviewed her."

"Yeah, well why did you have to let me in on it?" grumbled Connie.

Jack looked at Laura and said, "You tell her."

"He wanted you to see the big picture," Laura said with a smile.

Moments later, Jack met Jia-li in the interview room and took a seat facing her.

"Well?" she said. "Let's get on with it. Are you going to take my statement?"

"No," replied Jack. "There is no need. You won't be charged with Cheng's murder in exchange for your co-operation."

"You … you can't know that yet," replied Jia-li, looking inquisitively at Jack. "You could never receive authority for such a request this fast."

"I was never one to trust authority to start with," replied Jack. "After talking with you and Mia tonight, I am even less inclined."

"But —"

"It's okay. The investigating officer has agreed that your co-operation is more valuable than putting you in jail."

"But I have already told you everything," said Jia-li.

"I know, but I only told them half of what you told me," replied Jack. "They agreed that was enough."

"Half?" asked Jia-li.

"Once I am positive that you are in the clear, I will provide everything you have told me to the Integrated National Security Enforcement Team for follow-up. INSET includes agents from the Canadian Security Intelligence —"

Jia-li burst out crying so Jack moved his chair beside her and put an arm around her shoulder and hugged her. "Everything will be okay," he whispered. "Mia will be joining us in a moment. Think about how you will tell her."

"I can't," she cried. "It's too awful."

"You must," replied Jack. "You have raised her to be an operative. It will not take her long to figure it out. It is best she hears it from you."

"But —"

Wilson knocked lightly on the door before opening it. He ushered Mia into the room and left again, closing the door behind him.

Mia saw the grief on her mother's face and rushed to her side. "Mom, everything will be okay. Please tell them what they want to know."

"She already has," said Jack. "It's you she needs to talk to."

"I don't know where to start," said Jia-li, looking at Jack.

"Tell her everything you told me tonight," he said. "Start with your own loss of innocence when you were a child … when your parents worked for Intelligence. If you prefer to speak in Chinese, go ahead. I'll wait outside. Open the door when you are finished."

"I am done speaking Chinese," said Jia-li. "From here on in, it will be English."

Jack nodded, then left the room and closed the door behind him before taking a seat at a nearby desk. Over the next half hour, he heard Mia's anguished cry when she learned her mother had committed murder, then overheard Jia-li's reassurance that all would be okay.

When the room became silent, Jack opened the door. When he saw Jia-li holding Mia's head to her chest while stroking her hair, he knew that things would work out for the two of them.

Three weeks passed before Connie walked into Jack and Laura's office and tossed a newspaper down on his desk. "Did you read it?" she asked. "About Wolfenden?"

Jack nodded. "It was on the news last night. He is stepping down and retiring for personal reasons."

"Yeah, real personal … and intimate," she said, pulling up a chair. "I wonder if his wife knows?"

"She does," replied Jack. "Less chance of him being blackmailed if the truth is already out."

"You certain?" asked Connie.

"I'm certain," replied Jack. "Rose used to work for INSET. We have our sources."

"And the others who were corrupted?" asked Connie.

"I don't know," replied Jack. "Some will have their security clearances lifted, others may be allowed to continue, depending upon their co-operation. Some don't even realize they were set up. It's all political and dirty."

"Wilson and his guys did come up with Mr. Frank's address three days later," said Connie. "He worked as a consultant for a communications security firm. They reported him missing, but by the time Wilson got to his address, it had been cleaned out. Or at least his computer had been taken."

"Yes, we heard," replied Jack. "He had also assumed the identity of a child who died forty years ago from a heart disorder. They still don't know who he really is, other than he lived alone."

"I doubt they ever will," said Connie.

"So much for any loved ones in China bringing the body home," added Laura.

"Also no sign of the Chinese couple," added Jack. "I'm betting they're back in Bejing." He gave a lopsided grin. "Maybe I should send them a thank-you card through the Chinese Embassy."

Connie eyed Jack silently for a moment as she brooded. "This big picture you talk about is a dirty one," she said.

"Sometimes," admitted Jack. "It never seems easy, that's for sure."

"What if I had refused to go along with your big picture?" asked Connie. "Knowing our past history, I'm surprised you let me in on the decision."

"Perhaps he knows you better than you think," noted Laura.

Connie pointed her finger at Jack and hissed, "Yeah, well, don't think for a moment that I would ever let it happen again!"

Jack looked at her and smiled politely.

Epilogue

Former Chinese spies have reported that China has more than one thousand spies in Canada, more than in any other country outside China. The Canadian government fears that the Chinese have stolen considerable business and industrial secrets from the country. Richard Fadden, the head of the Canadian Security Intelligence Service, implied in a television interview that various Canadian politicians at provincial and municipal levels had ties to Chinese Intelligence. In another interview, he claimed that some politicians were under the influence of a foreign government, but he withdrew the statement a few days later. It was assumed that he was referring to China because in the same interview he stressed the high level of Chinese spying in Canada, although he did not specify which country's government. His statement was withdrawn a few days later.

In 2009, Canadian researchers found evidence that Chinese hackers had gained access to computers possessed by government and private organizations in 103 countries, although researchers say there is no conclusive evidence that China's government was behind it. Beijing also denied involvement. The researchers said the computers penetrated include those of the Dalai Lama and Tibetan exiles.

In 2011, Canada suffered a major systems breach when hackers cracked computer security systems at the Department of Finance and Treasury Board. The departments were hit hard by the attack, as computer systems were shut down while security loopholes were closed. Communications Security Establishment Canada insiders say they know who the culprit was. The information was never made public, but the perpetrator is broadly thought to be China.

A Canadian Broadcasting Corporation news release dated May 15, 2012, in part notes:

- *The former head of U.S. counter-espionage says the Harper government is putting North American security at risk by allowing a giant Chinese technology company to participate in major Canadian telecommunications projects.*

- *The Canadian government itself was hit with its worst-ever hacking attack from China, penetrating the highly classified computer systems in at least three federal departments: Finance, Treasury Board, and Defence Research.*

- *Documents obtained by the CBC show the hackers managed to steal large amounts of classified data before the computer systems could be shut down.*

- *Eighteen months later, those computer systems remain corrupted and unable to connect directly to most of the Internet without losing more data to the as-yet-unidentified Chinese spies.*

- *More recently, a former executive of the now bankrupt Nortel has blamed Chinese technology theft for hastening the demise of the former Canadian telecom giant.*

A link to the full article is available at: http://www.cbc.ca/news/politics/story/2012/05/15/pol-weston-huawei-china-telecom-security-canada.html.

Links to a website provided by the Canadian Security Intelligence Service to inform the public about methods used in economic espionage are available at: https://www.csis.gc.ca/prrts/spng/mthds-eng.asp.

A detailed account of electronic spying is available in a cyber-security newsletter from the National Security Group at: http://www.ciu-local16.ca/Documents/CSN49.pdf.

* * *

Statistics collected in 2006 show that Canadians of Chinese descent, including mixed Chinese and other ethnic origins, make up about four percent of the Canadian population, or about 1.3 million people as of that time.

Canadians of Chinese descent have greatly enriched Canada's development and heritage and continue to do so. The ramping up of political tension and spying by the People's Republic of China is an unfortunate situation, but one that Canadians need to be aware of and respond appropriately to, including those who have made Canada their new home.

As of the writing of this novel, the government tabled legislation to give the police and Canadian authorities the power to conduct online surveillance. It was met with a public backlash and politicians, ever attempting to be politically correct, tried to pass the legislation off as a tool to use to catch child molesters. It is far more than that. Perhaps, if the public were aware of the outside political influences unfolding in Canada, it would assist them in making a more informed decision. We are a democracy and Canadians of all creeds need to take part when it comes to protecting our sovereignty and thwarting the unwanted advances of foreign powers.

More Jack Taggart Mysteries by Don Easton

Angel in the Full Moon
A Jack Taggart Mystery
978-1550028133
$11.99

In this sequel to *Loose Ends* and *Above Ground*, Jack Taggart continues as an undercover Mountie whose quest for justice takes him from the sunny, tourist-laden beaches of Cuba to the ghettos of Hanoi. His targets deal in human flesh, smuggling unwitting victims for the sex trade. Jack's personal vendetta for justice is questioned by his partner, until he reveals the secret behind his motivation, exposing the very essence of his soul. This is the world of the undercover operative: a world of lies, treachery, and deception. A world where violence erupts without warning, like a ticking time bomb on a crowded bus. It isn't a matter of if that bomb will go off — it is a matter of how close you are to it when it does.

Samurai Code
A Jack Taggart Mystery
978-1554886975
$11.99

In the fourth Jack Taggart Mystery, the implacable Mountie goes under-cover to follow the trail of a cheap Saturday-night special found at the scene of a murder. He traces the gun until the trail leads him to a suspected heroin importer. Taggart poses as an Irish gangster and penetrates the criminal organization, only to discover that the real crime boss is a mysterious figure out of Asia. When Taggart and his partner find themselves alone and without backup in the lair of one of the largest yakuza organized crime families in Japan, the clash of culture explodes into violence when their real identities are discovered.

Dead Ends
A Jack Taggart Mystery
978-1554888931
$11.99

Intrepid Mountie Jack Taggart is hurled into a world where moral-ity, justice, and the legal system are pitted against one another. Taggart investigates the murder of someone who was in the wrong place at the wrong time. Wiretap information identifies a shadowy gang member known only as Cocktail as being responsible. Taggart and